Unknown Family Connections

A Pride & Prejudice Variation

By Shana Granderson, A Lady

CONTENTS

DEDICATION

This book, like all that I write, is dedicated to the love of life, the holder of my heart. You are my one and only and you complete me. You make it all worthwhile and my world revolves around you. Until we reconnected I had stopped believing in miracles, now I do, you are my miracle.

ACKNOWLEDGEMENT

First and foremost, thank you E.C.S. for standing by me while I dedicate many hours to my craft. You are my shining light and my one and only.

I want to thank my Alpha, Will Jamison and my Betas Caroline Piediscalzi Lippert and Kimbelle Pease. A special thanks to Kimbelle for her forthright and on point editing. To both Gayle Serrette and Carol M. for taking on the roles of proof-readers and additional editing, a huge thank you to both of you. All of you who have assisted me please know that your assistance is most appreciated.

My undying love and appreciation to Jane Austen for her incredible literary masterpieces is more than can be expressed adequately here. I also thank all of the JAFF readers who make writing these stories a pleasure.

Thank you to Veronica Martinez Medellin who was commissioned to create the artwork used for the cover.

INTRODUCTION

** This is a book of two volumes, but all in one book. It is a one off, standalone story. **

Over 150 years in the past an Evil Duke plotted to separate his first and second sons. He was a man who had two interests: money and status. Lord Sedgewick Rhys-Davies, the 3rd Duke of Bedford sets off a chain of events that ultimately ends up doing the exact opposite of what his original evil intent was in the far future.

Mr. Thomas Bennet lives with his second wife and family on his estate Longbourn in Hertfordshire. As far as he knows, he is an indirect descendant of the last Earl of Meryton whose line died out with him over 150 years ago. The family has owned Longbourn and Netherfield Park for as long as anyone remembers. There is an entail on Longbourn, but not the one we are used to. As in the canon, this Bennet dislikes London, and the *Ton* and he and his family keep away from London society. His second wife is the daughter of an Earl but just goes as Mrs. Bennet.

The Bennet's new tenants at Netherfield Park are the Bingleys. One of the major deviations from canon in this tale, Jane Bennet has more than a little backbone while Bingley has little or none. How will Darcy behave, will he make assumptions and act on them? Will Elizabeth allow her prejudices to rule? When Wickham slithers onto the scene will he cause havoc?

The 7th Duke of Bedford is ill, and he will be the end of the line as there are no living relatives to inherit the dukedom and vast Bedford holdings. He removes an old letter from a safe in his study written by the 4th Duke. Witten on the outside of the letter is: 'Open **_ONLY_** if there are no more Rhys-Davies heirs.'

The Duke opens the letter and learns of the 3rd Duke's evil and there is in fact an heir, although a direct descendant, he is not a Rhys-Davies.

This is the story of different families and what happens when their lives intersect and are changed for ever. There is quite a bit about Lizzy & Darcy, but there are not always the main focus of the story as the title infers.

PROLOGUE –
THE HISTORY

1655, Longfield Meadows.

His Grace, Sedgwick Rhys-Davies III, was enormously proud to be the powerful Duke of Bedford. As did many peers of the realm, he would keep a low profile until 1660 when Charles II was restored to the throne after the failure of Cromwell's attempt to create a republic. At that point he would return to the prominence that he held before the civil war. To him, connections and wealth were important above all things, even family. Part of his hubris was to hide the fact that the first Duke of Bedford had been a lowly knight who had managed to save Mary Tudor's life when she was put upon by brigands in 1554. When she became Queen Mary I, to express her gratitude she elevated Sir Sedgwick Rhys-Davies to Duke, the highest rank a peer could attain, and awarded him estates, town homes in London, and money.

The current Duke was the third of his line and hated above all else the fact that the first Duke had been but a lowly squire before being knighted for heroism in battle. Rather than celebrate his grandfather's heroic deeds, the third Duke ran away from it.

Everything the current Duke did was to distance himself from his grandfather's history prior to his elevation and try to erase his low past, but there were too many alive who knew the history of the Dukedom of Bedford. This gave Lord Sedgewick a boulder sized chip on his shoulder. If any mentioned his grandfather's position prior to being elevated, unless the person could be useful to him, the Duke dropped the connection.

His disdain was not only about his grandfather's position before his knighthood. Far worse than that, he had been nearly destitute. To the current Duke, money and the power and influence that was attained from having it, were everything. That knowledge was one of the drivers that kept the current Duke grasping for as much money as he could get his hands on, regardless of how much he had. Sedgwick III ignored the fact that his grandfather had been awarded seven estates. He resided at Longfield Meadows in Yorkshire, the largest of them. It provided close to ten thousand pounds a year and was among the largest incomes in the realm even before one counted the income of the satellite estates.

The other six estates added close to twenty thousand pounds a year to his annual profits. Included in the Queen's award was the money from the defunct Dukedom of Bedford, which, at the time, was three hundred and fifty thousand pounds. The three large townhouses in London and their accounts were remitted to his control, all at addresses others coveted. The Duke could not see what his grandfather had become; his concern was only about from *where* he had come.

The third Duke was also extremely short-sighted in his business dealings and estate management. He was loath to spend money on repairs for his tenants or improvements on his estates, even if his stewards could prove to him that an initial outlay of capital would earn him a good return. Lord Sedgwick balked at any outlay of funds.

With the exception of the Duke, the Rhys-Davies were a close-knit family. The oldest son, Lord Birchington, Sedgwick IV, was twelve and was called Sed by the rest of the family. Sed was two years older than Thomas. Next was Amelia, born three years after Thomas, and who was in turn followed by the youngest, Elizabeth, who was but three.

The Duchess, Esther Rhys-Davies, was the only child of Thomas and Horatia Bennet, the Earl and Countess of Meryton in Hertfordshire. Esther's parents had both died during an influenza outbreak in 1651. With their deaths, so too had the line ended. The Bennet name died, as there had been no special remainder from the King, for the title had been purely male primogeniture. As the properties were not gifts from the crown, none of them reverted to the Crown so Esther inherited the family estates in Hertfordshire, Netherfield and Longbourn, a few acres of land in London that the Earl had won on the Grosvenor Estate in Mayfair, London, and a little over fifty thousand pounds.

With no heir, the late earl had written the marriage articles in such a way that the property and funds would remain his daughter's and would never be controlled by the Duke. Esther's father had long regretted permitting his daughter to marry the proud, arrogant, and disagreeable man, which was his impetus to make sure that the property could only be inherited by one of his blood. Esther herself could bequeath the money and property to any of her children; even after her demise it would not fall into the hands of the Duke.

As her first son would one day be the fourth Duke of Bedford and inherit all of the ducal properties and wealth, and her daughters had handsome dowries, Esther settled her late father's property and wealth on her second son so he would never need to seek a profession. What his mother gifted Thomas was irrevocable, and no matter how much her husband blustered or tried to claim that the estates and money should be his to control, he had no power to change the disposition of his late father-in-law's will.

1656

Sed and Thomas were the best of friends, remaining close regardless of their father's efforts to drive them apart, or so it was until Sed was sent to school. When he was thirteen, ignoring his wife Esther's pleas, the Duke sent Sed to Eton a year earlier than the norm to separate his heir from Thomas.

Thomas was a kind, compassionate, gentle, and generous

young man—all traits that his father did not want to influence his heir—traits that the father derided and believed would weaken a man. When Sed had breaks from school, the Duke made sure his second son was not at home or saw to it that his heir was elsewhere—anywhere his second son was not.

The father would take Sed on trips ostensibly to inspect their satellite estates, keep him in Town, or send his wife, second son, and daughters to friends or a smaller estate for the summer.

1659

At fourteen, Thomas, who loved to study and learn, was sent to Harrow. The Duke had seen his goal come to fruition, for the relationship between the boys was effectively destroyed as they had not seen one another in three years. Their father also continued to poison Sed's mind against his younger brother.

Where Sed had mostly been an average student at Eton, his brother excelled in his classes at Harrow. Only those who thought having a marquess as a friend was beneficial to them would claim Sed as such, while Thomas made genuine friends who sought out his company and conversation and he theirs—friendships which would last a lifetime.

In his first year at Harrow Thomas met and became the best of friends with Hastings Jamison, the son of a minor country squire with a small estate, Ashford Dale, in Bedfordshire. Even though the Jamisons were not much better than tradesmen in the Duke's arrogant opinion, when Thomas requested to spend holidays and term breaks with them, the Duke readily granted his request. It suited his purpose to ensure his sons remained apart.

The Duchess was distraught at the way her husband was corrupting her older son while treating her younger son as though he had no worth. Seeing the way her husband treated her kind and considerate Thomas, and how he was effectively driven away from his childhood home, reinforced her opinion that she had been right to ensure Thomas had his own means to live independently. In further support of her son, and without her husband's knowledge, she changed the bequest regarding the age that Thomas would receive all from five and twenty to one and twenty.

Christmastide of 1659 was the first time that Thomas visited Ashford Dale with his friend and met the rest of Jamisons. In addition to meeting his friend's parents, he also met his younger sister, Karen, who was but eleven. When the Jamisons addressed him with his title, he asked them just to call him Thomas, or Tom. He knew his father hated the shortened version of his name, intoning that Tom was *common sounding*, so Thomas invited everyone he came to be acquainted with to call him thus. Tom was extremely comfortable with the Jamisons that first Christmas—though he privately considered Karen to be a rather annoying little girl.

During his years at school, his mother would often write to him and lament the situation with her husband, but Thomas knew she had no power to change anything. Eventually the letters from his mother ceased arriving. Knowing his father, Thomas saw his hand in the cessation of that correspondence and hoped his mother was aware he was regretful but would not reach out and cause her further hardship with the Duke.

1662

In his continuing campaign to keep his sons apart, the Duke sent Lord Thomas Rhys-Davies to Oxford, ignoring the tradition of all Rhys-Davies men studying at Cambridge. As long as his second son was kept away from the older, he cared not where he attended as long as it was not Cambridge.

Unfortunately, his efforts bore fruit. Over the years of separation from his younger brother, his heir had been remade in his father's image. Lord Sed had been told that his brother had not cared to write to him nor respond to any of his letters, severing even this avenue between them. What neither knew, though Thomas suspected, was that the Duke had intercepted letters between his sons from the very day that Sed had been sent to school.

In his machinations, never did the short-sighted Duke consider what would happen if something occurred to Sed and Thomas became the heir. All Sedgwick III cared about was that he had, in his mind, succeeded in his design.

Thomas, exclusively called Tom by those who knew him, was most pleased that Hastings also attended Oxford. In the absence of his brother and family by blood, Hastings had become a brother of the heart and the Jamisons his surrogate family. Karen, now fourteen, was more tolerable, but they had to exert extreme patience around her when they spent more than a few hours with her as she was uninterested in the things they were interested in. She felt the same about their preferences.

A practice that would carry over for many years had been started Eastertide a year earlier. Tom and the Jamisons travelled to neighbouring Hertfordshire to visit one of the two estates that would be Tom's on his gaining his majority. Tom worked closely with his stewards to learn how to manage his estates—lessons his father had denied him—fully intending to be a hands-on master rather than leave the work to them and be an absentee landlord.

Tom excelled at Oxford just as he had at Harrow, and was a well-rounded student, a top-level opponent in fencing, and a boon on the cricket field. Though forced apart from his family, Tom was content with his lot, almost appreciating that he was never invited to Town by the Duke and was an unknown in society.

November 1665

With two estates that together had a clear five thousand per annum plus five acres of land in Mayfair, Tom Rhys-Davies was a wealthy man in his own right. From the day he gained his majority on the nineth day of October 1665, he was independent. This ensured he had no need to request any support from his father. The Duke had once again tried to challenge his son's right to inherit, and like all previous attempts, this one had been futile, costing the bitter man money with no return. As soon as he lost that case, the Duke revoked his second son's legacy and stopped paying him any further allowance. If that was not bad enough, he sowed further discord over the years telling Sed that his younger brother had stolen part of his inheritance.

Tom, by his own admission, was a man violently in love. The once-annoying Karen Jamison had grown into a wonderful young woman of eighteen. She was kind and intelligent, and shared Tom's love of the written word. While they had other things in common, that was one of the things he believed would sustain them over many years. He knew that at one and twenty he was too young to marry, but he also knew that he would never marry any other, and from their conversations he was certain that Karen was just as much in love with him.

It had been six long years since Tom had visited his ancestral home, and both he and Hastings were in their final year at Oxford. He had thought it would be many years before he saw Longfield Meadows again when a black-edged notice was delivered to him in early November at the apartments he shared with Hastings in Oxford. It was with trepidation that Tom opened the missive. He was devastated to find it contained the news his mother had passed due to a tragic accident. Tom privately believed that it was his father's callous treatment of the late Duchess which driven her into an early grave, and his anger simmered.

Tom expected his brother's cold shoulder given that Lord Birchington had not replied to even one of his letters over the years. He strongly suspected that his father intercepted the post at Longfield Meadows, but he did not know that the Duke had charged Sed's valet to intercept and forward any post to or from his second son to himself. Sed barely acknowledge Tom, but his sisters greeted him warmly.

Tom was disgusted at his father's granting a betrothal of Amelia to an aging earl and was currently planning to barter Elizabeth to the highest bidder as soon as she was out, if he even waited those four years. The Duchess had begged the Duke not to consign her daughter to a life of misery with the Earl, but, as he always had done, the Duke turned a deaf ear to his wife's entreaties. Amelia believed that their mother had lost the will to live. She had started to take long walks, and one morning after the Duchess left the house it had started to snow.

When Lady Esther had not returned after four hours, a search was conducted. They found her body but a few hundred yards away. She had evidently slipped and hit her head hard, and the cold had taken her. During their talk, both sisters relayed to Tom how callous Sed had become thanks to their father's corruptive influence.

It was too late to help Amelia, but Tom swore to Elizabeth that he would find a way to save her. He would mourn his beloved mother for a year, and then he would propose to Karen Jamison. As he was getting ready to leave, his mother's former lady's maid surreptitiously slipped a letter from her mistress into one of Tom's jacket pockets, which his valet discovered while unpacking for him after he had returned to Oxford. Tom sat down with a glass of port and opened the unexpected missive.

9 October 1665
Longfield Meadows

My darling son Thomas,
I know that you have written letters to me as I have to you, but for his own selfish reasons your father has decided that the more he isolates you from the family the better. If I could explain your father's callous behaviour, I would, my sweet son, but I cannot.

If you are reading this, then I am with my parents in heaven.

I used to have four of the sweetest children, until your father decided to corrupt Sed and turn him against you. I have never understood the avarice that drives your father, and that is why I made sure that you and you alone will inherit Papa's property and wealth. No matter what your father attempts, he will never be able to take what is yours by law.

This cruel separation has all but broken my heart, my darling son. I know not why we have had to endure such torture. With all that I am, I believe that there is some part of the sweet boy that was your brother left deep within Sed. My hope is that he will rediscover that part of himself one day before it is too late.

Tom scoffed at what his mother wrote about his brother. Not for her hope, but that there was any redeemable part of Sed's character. If there was, Tom had seen none of it during his short stay at the estate in Yorkshire.

If I know you, my son, you think that I err, and you could be correct. But a mother has to have hope that all of her children can be good people. You, Thomas, are the best of people. You are loyal, and I know that you will care for all of those dependant on your estates in Hertfordshire.

Always remember that although you were born with the name Rhys-Davies, you are also a Bennet. Our line ended with the death of my father, but it was an honourable name with a rich history. The earldom became defunct with my Papa's passing. It is a great pity that you are not allowed to inherit the title. I see so many characteristics of my father in you that in my mind the name Bennet lives on, regardless of what your last name is.

Marry for love, my son, and do not allow your father to try to dictate your choice of bride. His pride is such that regardless of how estranged you are from him he will feel that he has the right to approve of or deny your choice of wife and force his will on you.

I charge you to pay him no heed, and although it seems that Amelia is lost in a terrible arranged marriage, I beseech you to protect your baby sister.

With all my love,

Your Mother,
ER-D

December 1666

Tom Rhys-Davies had recently completed the year of mourning for his mother. Then, as he had promised himself, he made the journey from Longbourn to Ashford Dale to propose to Miss Karen Jamison, the woman who possessed his heart. The fact that Hastings, who was as close as any brother of the blood could be to Tom, would be his brother in fact, was an added bonus.

On his arrival at the Jamison's estate, he requested to see the master. The manservant who doubled as a butler showed him to the master's study. Tom, who did not believe in platitudes, got directly to the point. "Mr. Jamison, I request your permission to have a private audience with Miss Jamison," Tom words were more statement than request, which made Karen's father smile.

"Let me summon her for you, Tom. And, if she accepts you, I will be proud to call you son," Mr. Jamison said as he rang for his man.

Karen arrived, and Mr. Jamison kissed his daughter on the forehead on the way out of his study, partially closing the door. "Hello Tom," Karen welcomed him warmly, but Tom, more focused on her eyes than her words, was relieved to see the look of love directed at him.

Tom dropped to one knee and took Karen's hands. "As I promised, I came here as soon as I was able. I am but two and twenty but waiting the whole of a second lifetime would not change the fact that you are the only one that I would ever desire as my partner in life, Karen. I have declared my love for you before, and I reiterate it now. You are the only one that I will ever love as a wife, and I ask for your hand in marriage as I hope to give you mine. Karen Jane Jamison, will you fulfil my heart's desire and agree to be my wife?"

"Yes, Tom, yes. Yes. I will marry you. You are the only man

that I would ever agree to marry," Karen averred.

A minute later, Mr. Jamison returned and did not have to ask her response, just as he had not needed to ask what Tom would say to his daughter. He gave his consent and blessing as he shook Tom's hand. Tom had brought a draft settlement with him, and Karen's father was shocked when he saw Tom's true wealth enumerated. Tom was settling five and twenty thousand on his daughter who only had a dowry of two thousand pounds! The settlements were signed as Mr. Jamison could see nothing that needed amending, and he shared the good news with his wife and son, who were waiting for his pronouncement in the parlour of the small manor house. Hastings gave his best friend a bear hug, administering a friendly warning to never make his sister unhappy.

Tom made the three-hour journey back to Longbourn knowing that although he did not need his father's permission, he was a gentleman, and this news was something that his father should hear from him, not from an announcement in *The Times*. He would go alone; he would not subject his beloved to the vitriol that his father tended to spew.

~~~~~~~/~~~~~~~

Knowing that his father was at Longfield Meadows for the Christmas season, Tom made the four-day journey, experiencing the freezing temperatures of the north that he did not miss in Hertfordshire. His last stop was the little market town of Lambton in Derbyshire. He intended to depart early in the morning for the last leg of his journey, into the southern part of Yorkshire to the Duke of Bedford's primary estate.

As he was enjoying an ale in the public dining area, he saw a gentleman and his two sons enter. They seemed to be well known and respected by all. He overheard a man refer to the gentleman as Mr. Darcy. Tom smiled to himself as he knew the Darcys owned much of Derbyshire in the form of their estate, Pemberley. His father disdained the connection because no matter how wealthy they were, the Darcys were not titled.

The following morning, Tom was on the road just after he

had broken his fast. Six hours later, he arrived at his childhood home, which he had visited only once in the last seven or eight years. First, he sent one of his men though the servants' hall to have Elizabeth and her governess prepare to leave. Amelia's marriage had been pushed forward and occurred but a month after their mother had died. From the letters he received, he knew that his sister was bitterly unhappy, which made him even more determined to honour his mother's wishes and save Elizabeth from the same fate.

After he knocked on the front door, Tom was shown into his father's study, to find the Duke seated behind his enormous desk. "What do you want here, Thomas? I will not change my mind about your legacy or an allowance," the Duke stated con-descendingly.

"I am not here to ask you for anything, your Grace. As you well know from the court cases you lost, I am well able to sup-port myself," Tom returned, the steel in his voice making his father's frown deepen. Tom felt no filial affection for the man who had caused so much pain and strife in the family, so he used his father's title and no other form of address.

"Yes, you stole..." the Duke started and was cut off by his son for the first time.

"How could I possibly steal that which was lawfully willed to me, your Grace? Have the laws in the Kingdom changed so very much in the year since I completed my studies?" Tom challenged.

"State your business and leave!" the Duke spat out, unwill-ing to further cross swords with his son when he was losing at every turn.

"I am informing you in person, before you see the an-nouncement in the papers, that I am marrying Miss Karen Jamison of Ashford Dale in Bedfordshire. We will marry after Twelfth Night," Tom stated, the factual retelling hiding his pleasure of finally being able to say it.

"You will **NOT** marry a country nobody!" the Duke thun-dered.

"I neither need your consent nor your blessing, your Grace," Tom replied, altogether ignoring the petulant outburst.

"I will refuse to sign the settlement!" the Duke rebutted.

"That is already done, your Grace. You must have just forgotten that I reached my majority over a year ago." Tom replied calmly, enjoying the sight of his father getting angrier with each failed point of argument.

"Then I will disown you! You do not deserve the Rhys-Davies name!" The Duke thought he had just played his trump card, and his anger intensifying when his son remained maddeningly calm.

"That would make little difference for me, your Grace, given the way you have treated me, my late mother, and my sisters these many years. It will be my pleasure to cast off the name Rhys-Davies." Tom was certain that by now his footmen and outriders would have loaded Elizabeth and Miss Kingston's trunks, and that his sister and her governess should have had enough time to enter his carriage which was waiting at the servants' exit. "I take no leave of you, your Grace. You will never see me again!" Tom turned and marched out of his father's study, leaving the man shocked, sputtering.

The Duke could not understand what had just happened! He was normally able to browbeat his opponents into submission, but nothing had worked with his second son. Regardless of his threat, he knew he could never publicly disown his son, certain that, without true cause, polite society would condemn him roundly.

At least he no longer had to worry about his younger son influencing his heir, and he need never acknowledge the boy again. Not want the Rhys-Davies name indeed! The Duke was convinced that his son would come back with his tail between his legs, and when he did, he would beg for his father's forgiveness.

By the time Tom entered the carriage, he had made an irrevocable decision. He would adopt his mother's maiden name. He wondered if she had compared him to her father for just this purpose. His father had just proven again that there was no connection to save. As soon as he could gain an appointment with his solicitor, he would become Mr. Tom Bennet. Elizabeth and the governess remained covered by a blanket until they had exited the estate's grounds, and when she emerged Tom explained that she would be known as Beth Bennet from that day forward.

"I like that name, Tom," Beth said. "Now, what about Amy? She is desperately unhappy, and her husband is a brute despite the fact that he is old!" Beth pleaded.

"We will go and see her, for Staffordshire is on our way south. I cannot promise anything as a marriage is a contract, but I will see if the Earl of Lindenbury can be reasoned with," Tom promised gently, and at the first stop, they relayed the change of destination to his coachman.

~~~~~~~/~~~~~~~

At Longfield Meadows, a maid had been paid to report that Lady Elizabeth and her governess had gone for a walk. When there was no sign of his youngest daughter by dinner, the Duke thought nothing of it, as he cared little for his inconsequential daughter until there might be gained in selling her for as much as he could receive, which would not be for some years.

The next day when it was reported that her bed had not been slept in, and her governess' as well, the Duke authorised a half-hearted search. When no trace of the two was found and with the maid reporting that the young lady's things were all in her chambers, the Duke assumed that she had been taken by brigands. As money was his true god, he determined to pay no ransom should a demand be received and actually considered himself lucky, as he would keep her dowry of five and twenty thousand.

Seeing his father's lack of care for his sister's welfare, Sed questioned his father's character for the first time, as Elizabeth had never done any harm to anyone. After hearing that he would gain her dowry in his coffers, the feeling passed as he considered the sum of all that he would inherit one day. On his father's orders, he was not informed that his brother had been at the estate. The Duke instead stated that his brother had chosen to break with the family, and that they were all better off because of it.

~~~~~~~/~~~~~~~

Two days later, Tom Bennet's carriage arrived at Lindenbury. The occupants of the carriage could not miss the black cloth wrapped around the gate posts. When they approached the manor house, it was a smoking hulk. The steward informed them that a fire had started in the master suite at some point the previous evening and neither the Earl nor the Countess had survived. The servants had all made it out alive, but for some unfathomable reason, the doors to the master suite had been locked from within.

Their hearts heavy with sadness, brother and sister departed the estate. They surmised that Amelia had decided to end her suffering and had chosen to join their beloved mother in heaven rather than be tied to such a man.

~~~~~~~/~~~~~~~

April 1667

Tom and Karen Bennet were married after the Bennets observed a three-month mourning period for Amelia. They determined that they would not let anyone know of their true wealth. They lived in a quiet community and were determined not to stand out in the shire. As they had children—Tom Junior, then Esther, Jane, and Elizabeth--their son's inheritances and their daughters' true dowries were kept secret. Most of their fortune was invested, and Netherfield Park was leased out through an agent, a solicitor named Henry Gardiner, with clear instructions that the name of its owner must never be revealed to tenants. Beth Bennet decided, after her sister's experience, that she would not marry. Her governess became her companion and she settled into a quiet, happy life as a spinster aunt to her nephew and nieces.

By mutual agreement, the connection to the Duke of

Bedford was *never* discussed among Tom, Karen, and Beth, or any of the Jamisons who were aware of it. The Bennet children grew up never knowing of the connection. With Karen's whole-hearted endorsement, Tom placed an entail on all of his properties so that they could never be broken up or sold off and could only be inherited by direct descendants of himself and Karen Bennet.

The old Duke died of an apoplexy in 1669 and Sed became the fourth Duke of Bedford. He never attempted to contact Tom, in part ashamed of his behaviour toward his brother, as he had come to see the ill-will in his father's teachings over the years. He also felt that he needed to respect Tom's decision to break with the family, as he believed his father's assertions that it had been his brother's choice. Years later, when his own son was an adult, Sed found an old trunk buried deep within the attic. Upon opening it, he discovered all of the letters that he, Thomas, and his mother had written to one another which his father had intercepted.

He knew Tom had taken on their late grandfather's name, so a night after its discovery, Sed sat and wrote a long and detailed letter about the truth of his family and what his father had done to destroy it. On the outside he wrote '*Only to be opened if there is no Rhys-Davies heir to the Dukedom.*' The Duke informed his son of the letter and charged him to inform his wife and son of its existence and that each heir and his spouse should be told the letter existed, but that it should not be opened unless the worst happened and there was no Rhys-Davies heir. Once the current generation of Bennets and Jamisons passed away, there would be no one left that knew of the connection to the Rhys-Davies.

In 1724, the late Tom's son, Tom Junior, was approached by the Grosvenors about the five acres that had been won by the late Earl of Meryton, as they wanted to develop some land and build townhouses. Rather than sell, Tom Bennet stated that in return for two townhouses, he would give the land over to the project. After the contracts were signed, the building of what would become known as Grosvenor Square began.

For almost one hundred and fifty years, generations of Bennets and Rhys-Davies lived their separate lives never knowing of the connection between them.

FAMILY TREE

The Bennets and Rhys-Davies families from 1655 - 1810

Bennets	**Rhys-Davies**
Thomas and Horatia	Sedgewick III - D 1669
Last Earl & Countess of Merton both D 1651	3rd Duke of Bedford, Married Lady Esther Bennet
Esther (Duchess of Bedford D 1665)	
Bennet & Earl of Meryton Line ends	Sedgwick IV, Thomas, Amelia, Elizabeth
	D1666 D1708
1666 Thomas & Elizabeth Rhys-Davies become:	
Tom & Beth Bennet	
Tom - Karen Jamison 1666	Sedgwick IV - Lady Emily Smythe 1668
D 1709 D1711	D 1701 D1689
Tom Esther Jane Elizabeth	Sedgwick V Prudence James
D1728 D1730 D1733	D1701 D1689
Tom - Kate Wainwright 1689	Sedgwick V - Lady Chastity Browning 1681
D1753 D1762	D1748 D1751
Thomas, Elizabeth, Esther	Sedgwick VI
Elizabeth compromised by Ned Collins	
Thomas - Lydia Granger 1746	Sedgwick VI – Lady Clarissa Browning 1730
D1779 D1751	D1769 D1738
Thomas, Esther, Mark	Sedgwick VII, Harrison
D1751	D1738
Thomas – Fanny Gardiner 1785	Sedgwick VII – Lady Rosamund Barrington 1768
D1787	
Jane	No children
Thomas – Lady Priscilla De Melville 1789	
Elizabeth, Tom, Esther, Mark	

18

VOL 1, CHAPTER 1

T he current Thomas Bennet was the great-great grandson of the former Thomas Rhys-Davies who became Tom Bennet. Like the three masters of Longbourn and Netherfield after the split in the family occurred, he did not know he was a direct descendant of Lord Sedgewick VII, the seventh Duke of Bedford. The first Tom Bennet had made it seem, in the family bible, they were cousins of the last Earl of Meryton this obscuring the truth of his heritage. Like his predecessors, Thomas Bennet eschewed Town, even though with the wealth that the Bennets had accumulated over four generations, they would have been welcomed by the *Ton*. Bennet hated the hypocrisy and debauchery indulged in by many of its members.

Following the tradition set by the original Tom Bennet, Netherfield's agent was the current master of Longbourn's former brother-in-law, Frank Phillips, who had taken over the Gardiner solicitor's practice when old Mr. Gardiner retired. The agency for the two townhouses on Grosvenor Square was in the hands of barristers and solicitors of the Norman and James company, led by Sir Randolph Norman. The aforementioned barrister personally took care of any of Thomas Bennet's legal issues.

As far as his neighbours knew, Longbourn earned less than three thousand a year. Few knew that Netherfield belonged to the Bennets, not even close friends like Sir William and Lady Sarah Lucas. The Bennets preferred to live frugally, so close to five and seventy percent of the fifteen-thousand-pound profit from the two estates and the rents from the townhouses was invested. Most of this was with Bennet's other former brother-in-law, Edward Gardiner, who ran Gardiner and Associates. This firm included an import/export company and other ventures, so that should one market falter the company had diversified enough to be fully sustained and able to weather any economic storm. The current master of Longbourn and Netherfield continued the practice of vastly understating his daughters' dowries. The amount reported to the general public was that each had but a meagre two thousand five hundred pounds.

The only blemish for the Bennet family was when a Mr. Ned Collins compromised Thomas Bennet's Aunt Elizabeth after he had heard some gossip that her dowry was larger than what was publicly reported. Bennet's father had given only a two-thousand-pound dowry to the disgusting man who had forced his daughter into a marriage she did not desire.

Ned Collins felt cheated, so he started the myth that the Bennet estate was entailed away to the male line and that if the Bennets bore no male heir the estate would devolve to the Collins' family line. Although a falsehood, his illiterate son believed him, and passed that erroneous belief onto his only son, William. William, by all accounts, was just as much of a dimwit as his father.

Not only did the entail not support his claim, but the day after his Aunt Elizabeth's forced marriage Bennet's grandfather added a clause to the entail expressly forbidding anyone of the Collins line from inheriting! Further, should someone from the Collins line, or any other, compromise another Bennet daughter who was heir to the estate, not only was the estate automatically willed to the next daughter in line, but the reprehensible man would receive only the same two-thousand-pound dowry as was given when Bennet's Aunt Elizabeth had been compromised, and no more. There was a codicil which also suggested that if a compromise occurred, the Miss Bennet who was compromised could take charge of her dowry and leave without shame so she would not be tied to such a man. No other Bennet daughter would be forced into an unwanted marriage again.

Thomas Bennet had married the woman that he loved, Fanny Gardiner, the daughter of his local solicitor. Though not as intelligent as he, it had not affected their relationship as there had been enough love to overcome that particular difference. In 1787, Fanny Bennet had given birth to Jane Amelia Bennet, but, to Thomas's great despair, she had become violently ill with childbed fever. Before Fanny Bennet drew her final breath, she had extracted a promise from Thomas to find a woman that he could esteem and respect so their daughter would know the love of a mother.

In 1789 Thomas fulfilled that promise when, by pure chance, he met Lady Priscilla De Melville. In mid-1788, Lord Jersey and his family were on their way from their estate in Essex to visit friends in Buckinghamshire when their coach's wheel cracked close to Longbourn. One of the grooms sought assistance at Longbourn; Thomas Bennet agreed to help and brought some of his men with him.

Bennet had invited the De Melvilles to stay at his estate while the wheel was sent to the nearest wheelwright in Stevenage. When Bennet's men returned, they informed him that it would take up to a sennight as the wheel could not be repaired and a new one would be fabricated. The Earl of Jersey had been willing to take rooms at the inn in Meryton for himself and his family, but Bennet would not hear of it. Lord Cyril and Lady Sarah De Melville were travelling with their younger daughter, Lady Priscilla, who was twenty.

Lady Priscilla had participated in three London seasons and had found no one that excited her interest. That was, until she met Thomas Bennet who was seven and twenty at the time. She quickly fell in love with him and his adorable two-year-old daughter, Jane. The Earl and Countess could see that Bennet was a good man and accepted an invitation to return a fortnight later when they would be returning to Town after visiting friends.

The apparent lack of wealth and connections of Thomas

Bennet did not worry Lord Cyril and Lady Sarah; their main concern was their daughter's felicity, and they could see that Priscilla had finally found a man to whom she was attracted and who she respected.

Within a week of their return, Bennet requested and was granted a courtship. Once he saw that the Earl and Countess did not have any concern when they believed him a poor country squire and that their daughter's wellbeing was their only priority, Bennet sat the three down and explained the truth of his wealth to them and that he was related to the last Earl of Meryton. To say that the De Melvilles were shocked when they discovered that Bennet was almost as wealthy as themselves was an understatement.

A month later, the couple married in a small and private ceremony. By then Bennet had begun to address his bride with the endearment Cilla on occasion. Lady Priscilla's older sister Lady Marie and her husband the Marquess of Holder, her brother Lord Wes and his wife Lady Isabelle, the Viscount and Viscountess of Westmore, attended the wedding along with the Phillips and Gardiner families.

Their first daughter, Elizabeth, was born in 1790 and her Aunt Marie and Uncle Percy were named her primary godparents. Elizabeth was followed in January 1792 by Thomas Junior, who would be called Tom and became the godchild of Lord and Lady Westmore. Then in October 1793, Esther Mary was born and finally, in 1799, the unexpected gift of the baby of the family, Mark. The final two children had a mixture of both sets of aunts and uncles as their godparents.

In keeping with their desire to not flaunt their wealth and connections in the environs of Meryton, Lady Priscilla was introduced as Mrs. Bennet and only used the honorific when in Town visiting her parents. Very few in Meryton outside of the Phillips and Lucas families knew the truth of the Bennets' connections and who Mrs. Bennet had been prior to her marriage. For at least six weeks each summer, and alternating Christmastides, the Bennets would travel to the Jersey main estate,

Broadhurst in Essex, so the children could be spoilt by their doting grandparents. Whenever the De Melvilles could, they would stop in at Longbourn to visit their family.

September 1810

"Father, who will the new tenants at Netherfield be?" Mark Bennet, who was eleven, asked. He was always interested in knowing who was leasing Netherfield, for at the age of five and twenty, the estate would become his.

"A Mr. Charles Bingley from Yorkshire. He is a tradesman's son who is trying to elevate himself. He is renting the estate for a year to learn how to manage one before he purchases his own," Bennet shared what he knew. The question pleased him, as it always did, because it proved his son's interest in his future home.

Bennet and his wife were fully involved in their children's education and upbringing. There were governesses, tutors, and masters who all helped educate the Bennet offspring. Having seen the results often, they did not hold with the *Ton's* opinion that children should be seen and not heard. Tom was in his second year at Oxford, for the Bennets followed the family tradition of sending their sons to Harrow and Oxford.

"I assume that, as usual, Sir Randolph's investigators have done their due diligence?" Jane asked. To no one's surprise, Priscilla had accepted and treated Jane as if she were born of her body, as had the rest of the De Melville family. Jane showed a serene façade to people who did not know her, but she was not one that would allow people to mistreat herself nor those she loved.

"Please Papa, what did the investigators discover about this family?" Elizabeth requested, her eyes alight with the expectation of scandal, or, at the least, some unexpected occurrence as was the case for many hoping to escape the scrutiny of Town when they leased close to London. Where Jane was the image of her late mother, blond and tall with cerulean blue eyes, Elizabeth was like her mother in both looks and character. She had wavy chestnut curls, was shorter of stature, and had bright green eyes that missed little.

Bennet felt that knowledge was power, so, unlike so many of the day, he did not hide uncomfortable facts from his children, male or female. He summed up the report for his expectant family, "Charles Bingley is five and twenty. His father made his fortune in trade, and the younger Bingley inherited when his father and mother were killed in an accident some three years ago.

"According to the investigators, he is an affable and ebullient man, but a feckless one with little resolve of his own. Please be aware of that, girls," Bennet looked at his three daughters. The youngest, Esther, a name traditionally used by all Bennets, was sixteen and would turn seventeen next month, at which time she would be out in local society. The assembly at the end of October would be her first official event in Meryton society.

"Yes, Papa," all three chorused.

"You are all good girls. To continue, he has a good friend, Fitzwilliam Darcy, who advises him. In fact, however, it is more that he seems to lead his younger friend into decisions as if he were the parent and Bingley his child. The friend is the nephew of Lord Reginald Fitzwilliam, the Earl of Matlock, and, from what it says here, he can be rather rude and arrogant. Mr. Darcy owns an extremely large estate, Pemberley in Derbyshire. There was something that happened with his sister, who is not yet sixteen, this past summer; but they could not determine what it was.

"Bingley has two sisters. The older is Mrs. Louisa Hurst, married to a gentleman, Harold, from the second circles. He is the heir to a small estate in Yorkshire, the same county from which the Bingleys hail. It is reported that he is extremely indolent, only exerting himself for sport. The rest of the time he sponges off his brother-in-law and eats, drinks, and sleeps the days away.

"The youngest, Miss Caroline Bingley, is two and twenty and according to this report, is reputed to be an avid social climber. She has set her cap at Mr. Darcy, but he is not at all interested in her. She over dresses and is reportedly quite vulgar, always going on about her dowry of twenty thousand and trying what she may to hide the fact that she is but a tradesman's daughter. Unfortunately, the older sister follows the younger's lead, and the brother does not have enough force of character to check her.

"She is the type of person behind our reason for hiding our true wealth and connections. She is only interested in that which will advance her in society, and is extremely pretentious," Bennet related to his three daughters and youngest son.

"Be aware of her, my children," Priscilla Bennet cautioned her brood. She too had remained silent while they had listened to what the investigation had turned up. "She will not be a true friend and thus you must look for ulterior motives if she tries to befriend any of you."

Bennet gave a cryptic smile, "I left the best for last. Mr. Darcy's aunt is none other than Lady Catherine de Bourgh, the patroness of that half-witted cousin of ours who is still, after all these years, writes to remonstrate with me about how I dared remarry and steal his inheritance by siring sons."

"Thomas," his wife scolded her husband, "why do you not consign the drivel that the man writes to the fire?"

"I know not why you insist on my destroying that which amuses me, wife. I married you, is that not hardship enough?" Bennet exercised his sardonic wit and gave his wife a teasing wink. "I love to laugh at the depths of his ridiculousness," Bennet explained. "You know we have men watching him at all times in case he tries to harm one of our sons in an attempt to *reclaim* his *rightful* inheritance."

"Those are facts of which I am well aware, Thomas. I just wish you would have him served with papers which would kill this illusion once and for all," Priscilla averred.

"Yes, dear. I can see I have tolerated his idiocy enough, so I will write to Sir Randolph in the morning." In fact, Bennet too had decided to act in the near future based on the darker-toned drivel and the advice of Collins ridiculous patroness for the parson to seek legal redress. His wife's concern had but moved up the timetable.

~~~~~~~/~~~~~~~

At the estate of Longfield Meadows in Yorkshire, the seventh Duke of Bedford sat at his desk with a letter in his hand, a letter written by the fourth Duke about one hundred and fifty years ago—one that he and every Duke since the fourth had hope they would never have to open.

Lord Sedgwick Rhys-Davies VII had been happily married to his duchess, Lady Rosamund, called Rose, for close to forty years. The one big regret he had was that he and his wife had never been able to birth a live child. If it were not for the letter in his hand, the Dukedom of Bedford and the Rhys-Davies line would die with him and everything revert to the crown. He knew he did not have unlimited time, as the doctor had warned him not to exert himself overmuch due to his weak heart.

He rang for his butler and asked the man to request that his wife join him. He stood slowly and joined Rose on the settee. "Rose, I cannot put this off any longer. I must open this letter; we both know that I cannot allow the line and the name to die with me." His wife nodded, acknowledging the truth of his words. The Duke broke the seal very carefully, not wanting to damage the extremely old missive.

The two read the three-page letter written by the fourth Duke. They read it twice to ensure that they did not misunderstand the words on the pages. "What motivated such cruelty of a father with regards to his own family?" Lady Rose asked as she cried softly for the pain their long-dead family members must have endured.

"From what my great grandfather says, it was avarice and misplaced pride. A great wrong was done, and it will be up to us, more accurately to you, to correct it if I pass before I have a chance to do so." Seeing his wife was about to protest, the Duke, close to seventy, rested a finger on her lips. "We all die, my love; it is just that we know that my death will be sooner rather than later. I believe, or hope, that I will have a year. I have much to do and will be busy with our holdings, especially Dennington Lines, until close to Easter. If it were not for the restrictions that I have from my doctor and you to enforce them," the Duke kissed his wife's cheek lovingly as she tried to hold back her tears, "I would have been able to complete everything in less than half of the time.

"When I am done with all that I must do, I will have Sir Randolph contact the next Duke and apprise him of what happened to cause the schism in our family. I have to thank goodness for the third Duke's pride which prevented him from disowning Tom Bennet, as he then became known. That would have caused this line to die in truth," the Duke soothed his wife.

"You will send our courier to Sir Randolph with the proof and the trunk of letters the third Duke preserved?" the Duchess asked.

"Yes, my dearest, everything will be on its way come the morrow," the Duke confirmed.

~~~~~~~/~~~~~~~

The clerk at Norman and James who received the papers from Longfield Meadows three days later knew this was something that needed to be brought to Sir Randolph's attention immediately.

The man waited patiently until Sir Randolph had read the current Duke's letter, then the letter from the fourth Duke. "Have this all stored in the delicate document storage location until we hear from his Grace," Sir Randolph instructed the clerk.

"B-but Sir, the heir is a client of ours," the clerk stammered.

"He is, but this is a matter that we are executing for another client, so until his Grace instructs us otherwise, we will do nothing other than his written instructions request. Do you understand, Cartwright? Without my *expressed* permission, you may not mention this to *anyone* on pain of instant dismissal!"

The clerk swore on his honour that he would not breathe a word to anyone then carefully removed the documents to the preservation storage.

~~~~~~~/~~~~~~~

Reverend William Collins had been awarded a living by the only person in the land that would have awarded him a curacy, never mind a living. He was exactly what Lady Catherine de Bourgh wanted in a parson, a sycophant who took her word as gospel. Collins was standing before her shaking with equal parts fury and fear.

A bailiff from the court in London had just handed him a wad of paperwork that proclaimed what his own grandfather, Ned Collins, had claimed was a complete fabrication. He did not believe it, so to make sure that he was correct in his disregarding of the papers, he went to seek the opinion of his great and beneficent patroness.

He bowed and scraped before the *great* lady in her throne-like chair which sat on a raised platform to ensure she was able to look down on all in her domain, the room surrounding it showing off her wealth and taste. To any with a modicum of taste and class, it was stuffed with items both gaudy and garish. "If you would kindly condescend..." Collins started and was immediately cut off.

"Yes, yes, Mr. Collins, why are you here? This visit was not scheduled, and you know how I value obedience and punctuality!" Lady Catherine chastised.

"These papers came for me from Town, and I beg your beneficence in reading them and giving me your all-knowing opinion, your Ladyship," Collins bowed low again.

Lady Catherine was about to dismiss the papers out of hand as based on what her parson said, they contradicted her pronouncements on the matter when she spied the name of the most powerful barrister affixed to the action. The name was enough for her to actually peruse the documents. She frowned when she read the first paragraph, as it was not at all as she expected per his claims, so she continued on carefully, including the copy of the articles of entailment. "You have no claim, Mr. Collins," Lady Catherine stated curtly, ignoring that his pallor had turned decidedly white.

"B-b-b-but you said…" Collins tried to regain her support of his purpose.

"You lied to me and would have made me look the fool had I supported you! The entail was never to the male line, and not only that, but the Collins line can *never* inherit, even were you to be so disreputable as to compromise one of your Bennet cousins. It states here that there are *two* sons! You never told me that!" Lady Catherine thundered. "Now leave me, I will have advice for you another day."

Collins bowed and scraped his way out of the drawing room, looking more like a crab than a man.

~~~~~~~~/~~~~~~~~

The Bingleys moved into Netherfield in mid-October. "Charles, how could you drag me to this backwater place?" Miss Bingley whined.

"You may leave if you wish, Caroline; I am sure that Darcy will be happy with Louisa as hostess." Bingley knew that his friend would *never* offer for his younger sister, but his name was an effective tool to garner her cooperation. His friend had more than once requested that Bingley talk to his sister and warn her away from her relentless campaign to become mistress of Pemberley. As was his wont with anything that might lead to a confrontation, Bingley had put off the difficult conversation with his sister, as he valued peace above all else.

"What stuff and nonsense, Charles," Miss Bingley said, reversing her position as her brother knew she would once he announced his friend's coming. "When will Mr. Darcy arrive?" Miss Bingley fairly cooed.

"He will be here in a fortnight, in late October," Bingley informed his sister.

"Then I will have to make sure that everything is perfect

for his arrival." Miss Bingley left her brother's study with purpose, telling herself that once Mr. Darcy saw her skills as a hostess he would finally do what he should have already done and offer for her. As she breezed out of the study, the butler, Nichols, informed the new master that Mr. Thomas Bennet had arrived to call on him. Content with his sister leaving, Bingley did not notice the reverence with which the butler spoke his visitor's name.

VOL 1, CHAPTER 2

November 1810

Fitzwilliam Darcy, called William by those close to him, master of the great estate of Pemberley in Derbyshire and scion of earls, would have begged off if not for his promise to his best friend, Charles Bingley. He had saved his sister, Georgiana, who everyone called Gigi, from ruin when purely by chance, he had arrived in Ramsgate two days earlier that his original plan.

When Mrs. Younge, his sister's companion, opened the door she had lost all colour in her face, which had immediately raised Darcy's suspicions. Then, he heard his sister's voice from behind the closed drawing room door, followed by that of the worst libertine he had the unfortunate experience to know, George Wickham.

Darcy had burst into the room, and in two strides reached the man holding his baby sister's hand. He had grabbed the blackguard by his lapels and lifted him clear of the floor. As the man spluttered and fought for breath, he heard his sister crying from the shock of seeing her brother's unbridled fury.

He had lowered Wickham back to the floor only to see one of the man's trademark smirks. Without thinking, Darcy landed a facer with all of his might. The sound of the miscreant's nose breaking had given him some measure of satisfaction. Darcy had instructed his sister to stay where she was after summoning her maid to sit with her.

Before dragging Wickham into his study, he asked the maid why his sister was unchaperoned. What he had heard was of the utmost concern; the maid reported that Mrs.

Younge had encouraged her young mistress to spend time with Mr. Wickham and had facilitated their time alone. He dismissed Mrs. Younge on the spot. When she asked about back pay, he had told her she was lucky that he had not summoned the magistrate. The woman left without further complaint. Darcy could remember the conversation with Wickham as if it were yesterday.

"What is the meaning of this behaviour towards my sister, Wickham?" Darcy demanded.

He surmised that the libertine thought he had a bargaining chip from his speech, "We are to be brothers, Darcy; I am engaged to your sister. Will you not congratulate me?" Wickham again sported his trademark smirk, or as much of one as he could manage with his nose bleeding and one front tooth missing.

"How will you live, Wickham? Do you have a profession to support my sister?" Darcy took a measure of comfort in seeing the miscreant looking unsure of himself. "I know you did not study the law as you claimed when you signed away all claim to the living at Kympton. From what I hear, you lost your four thousand pounds at the tables, which led you to try and renege on the signed document that I have. So tell me, how will you live?"

"She has thirty thousand pounds. That should keep us for a little while," Wickham tried to bluster.

"You will not see one penny of her dowry, Wickham!" Darcy relayed with pleasure, and he watched the avaricious man blanch.

"You would never deny your sister her dowry!" Wickham was starting to panic, his eyes flaring.

"No, I would not, but you would. Did you think my father, who must be turning in his grave at the thought that you would attempt this with his daughter, did not protect Miss Darcy against those of your ilk? ONLY if both Richard and I approve beforehand will her dowry be released. As you have not sought either of her guardians' permission, you will get not one farthing!" Darcy watched while his erstwhile friend tried to come up with a way out.

"If you do not pay me the value of her dowry, I will tell one and all that she is ruined!" Darcy could see that he believed those *words would be a trump card.*

"First, who do you think will believe the word of a steward's son over mine?" Darcy growled. "You had better let your accomplice know that if either of you breathe a word of this, or approach ANY that I care for again, you will have Richard to deal with." Darcy enjoyed the abject fear that Wickham displayed. Darcy's cousin, more like a brother, was a Colonel in the Royal Dragoons, and he knew that Wickham was well aware Richard disliked him, would take true pleasure in gutting him, and would make sure that none would ever find the body. "Adding to that, if I hear you blackening my name again, I will call in your debts! I own well over two thousand in vowels you signed and then ran with your tail between your legs like the cur that you are, leaving your debts unpaid. That will be more than enough to make sure you will not leave Marshalsea for the rest of your life! So what will it be, Wickham?"

"I will do as you say." The coward resigned himself to the knowledge that another in his long line of 'get rich off another's money' schemes had failed.

"There is one more thing; you will tell my sister the truth. I will not have her believing you cared for her when we both know you care for none but yourself! It is non-negotiable!" Darcy had demanded.

Darcy frogmarched Wickham back into the drawing room to stand before his sister. He first laid out Wickham true history, acknowledging his failure to inform her of these truths in a mistaken attempt to protect her delicate sensibilities. He then gave Wickham a curt nod, and the rake told Miss Darcy the truth—that he was only interested in her dowry and on revenging himself on her brother. To Darcy's relief, his sister stood and followed his example by slapping Wickham with all of her might. Once Wickham left, she had burst into tears, begging Darcy's forgiveness.

As Darcy returned to the present from his vivid memories of Ramsgate, he thought of his beloved sister Gigi at Matlock House with their aunt and uncle, Lady Elaine and Lord Reginald Fitzwilliam, the Earl of Matlock and his Countess. When they returned from Ramsgate, Darcy had been open with the four Fitzwilliams, telling them all that happened. But no matter how many times he had told his sister that he had forgiven her, her spirits were still exceptionally low.

His older cousin by about one year, Lord Andrew Fitzwilliam, Viscount Hilldale, and his brother Richard, the Colonel, who was a year younger than Darcy, had wanted to hunt Wickham down. The combined influence of their parents and Darcy had calmed the Fitzwilliam brothers somewhat, although Richard vowed to himself that if Wickham ever crossed his path, he would deal with him with the intent of it being the final time anyone would have to do so.

Gigi had been inconsolable for the first few weeks after their return from Ramsgate. She understood that a practiced deceiver and seducer had plied his trade with her, but she was not so sanguine about the fact that she had agreed to an elopement knowing that it would hurt her family and cause a scandal.

A month after the near disaster and after serious and exhaustive vetting, Mrs. Helena Annesley was hired as Miss Darcy's new companion. Darcy had wanted to cancel his promised visit to his friend's leased estate as almost three months after the fact his sister was still upset, but his aunt and the companion had told him that the slow improvement in his sister would be aided by less of his constant hovering.

All of these events had left Darcy much more unsociable and taciturn than normal, and he did not like social situations even in the best of situations. He constantly berated himself that at the age of six and twenty he had failed his parents, his father especially, in protecting his sister from a libertine.

~~~~~~~/~~~~~~~

Priscilla and Thomas Bennet smiled indulgently as their three daughters spoke excitedly about the assembly that would be held in Meryton that night. Jane and Elizabeth had both come out in Meryton at the age of seventeen and made their curtsies before the Queen at eighteen, sponsored by their grandmother. Given the Bennets' distaste for London society, neither had had a coming out ball nor a London season—by their own choice. If they had desired such, their parents would not have denied them.

Normally, they were blasé about the monthly assembly, but Esther turned seventeen last month, and it was her first public dance. Her sisters were excited for her. The two older Bennet girls never lacked for partners but would not dance every dance due to the abundance of young ladies and dearth of men locally. The sisters would sit out at least two dances, sometimes more, to allow others a chance at being asked to dance.

Charlotte Lucas, who was a good friend to both of the older Bennet sisters, and one of the few outside of the inner circle who knew the truth of the Bennets' wealth and connections, respected her friends more than they would ever know for being so considerate of others at the assemblies. As the three girls were discussing their dresses, Charlotte Lucas was announced by Mr. Hill.

"Welcome Charlotte! We were just discussing our dresses for tonight," Elizabeth rose to welcome her friend.

"Esther, please tell me you do not intend to take a book with you tonight," Charlotte teased, knowing that the youngest Bennet sister preferred reading Shakespeare to dancing.

"My sisters have already admonished me, Charlotte," Esther harrumphed. "I will leave my book of sonnets at home!"

"Have you met the tenants at Netherfield yet, Charlotte?" Priscilla Bennet asked.

"I have not, Mrs. Bennet, but my father has. His assessment of Mr. Bingley closely aligns with Mr. Bennet's. My father, who likes everyone he meets and, as you are well aware, has nothing negative to say about anyone, has done otherwise with regards to Mr. Bingley's *supercilious* sisters, as he had dubbed them." Charlotte smiled at remembrance of her father's descriptions about the airs and graces of the sisters.

"Papa did not meet the sisters when he called on Mr. Bingley." Mark grinned at his father who had mentioned his disappointment of not doing so on his return home. Having just completed his lessons with his tutor, he had entered the drawing room at the tail end of Miss Lucas's comments.

"No, Mark, I did not have the *pleasure,* but I understand that the whole of the Bingley party will be present at the assembly tonight," Bennet replied, mussing his son's hair when the youngest Bennet came to a stop next to his father.

"Thomas, have you seen Mrs. Nichol's reports of that pretentious woman's treatment of the Netherfield servants?" Priscilla Bennet asked and Bennet nodded ruefully. "We need to have Frank point out the clause in the lease that states that they can be evicted with no notice and no refund of rent if they mistreat the staff. I suggest that Mr. Bingley be given one warning. If he does not have the backbone to deal with his sister, then we will exercise that clause!" She would not abide anyone treating her servants disrespectfully, and until Mark inherited the estate one day, she was the true mistress of Netherfield Park.

"I will ride to see Phillips now." Bennet rose, kissed his wife on her cheek, and called for his stallion Orion to be made ready.

~~~~~~~/~~~~~~~

"Mr. Phillips to see you, Mr. Bingley," Netherfield's butler announced.

"Good morning, Mr. Phillips. Would you like to retire to the study with me?" Bingley asked.

"No, Mr. Bingley, for what I have to say needs to be heard by all the residents." Phillips nodded as Mr. and Mrs. Nichols entered. The couple had been the butler and housekeeper at the estate for well over fifteen years.

"Why have you summoned my servants," Miss Bingley's piercing voice was heavy with disdain.

"It is odd that you should ask that, Miss Bingley, though they are not *your* servants as they are employed by the landlord, who pays their salaries." Seeing that Miss Bingley was about to interject, Phillips proceeded without hesitation. "Mr.

Bingley, I assume that you read the lease before you signed it?"

"Well, err, mostly," Bingley owned.

"It was your responsibility to do so prior to signing it! Do you remember clause 10.4?" Phillips asked, sure that the man had hardly read more than two words of the entire four-page document.

"I cannot say that I remember that clause," Bingley admitted.

"You do remember initialling each clause and signing the bottom of each page, do you not?" Phillips prodded, and Bingley allowed that it was so. "Please read clause 10.4 aloud, Mr. Bingley, noting that section ten deals with reasons that your lease may be terminated and you, evicted."

Miss Bingley looked at the scene as if scandalised at such a demand being made by a mere solicitor. Her brother took out the documents in question and read:

"*10.4: The tenant acknowledges that the hiring and firing of any staff employed at Netherfield Park other than their personal servants is only at the discretion of the landlord. If the tenant has an issue with an employee's performance, that is to be reported to the landlord's agent, the butler, or the housekeeper. If, for whatever reason, any member of the tenant's household is disrespectful, or is verbally or physically abusive to ANY staff member, it is grounds for the immediate voiding of the lease and the forfeit of any money prepaid for the term of said lease.*"

"I assume that is self-explanatory. There will be no further warning," Phillips informed the four family members, directly staring at Miss Bingley when he made his pointed statement. "Good day Mr. Bingley, Miss Bingley, Mr. Hurst, Mrs. Hurst." He gave a curt bow and exited the drawing room with the Nicholses.

"This is not to be borne, Charles. Let them keep your money, we will return to Town and leave this backwater," Miss Bingley asserted.

"If we are evicted, then any money that is forfeit will come from your allowance and dowry!" Bingley stated firmly, standing up to his sister for the first time in his life.

"You would not dare!" Miss Bingley screeched.

"Try me, sister, for if you cause us to be evicted you will pay in full!" Bingley stormed out of the room before his sister could attempt to manipulate him and weaken his resolve.

After Bingley's exit, Miss Bingley turned to her sister. "Louisa, you do not think that Charles was serious, do you?"

"I do, Caro, and if I were you, I would watch how I treat the servants from now on, otherwise it will cost you some years' worth of allowance," Mrs. Hurst opined.

"All because of servants! They are nothing; it is my right to treat them as I wish!" Miss Bingley insisted.

"As they are not our servants, no, you cannot," Mrs. Hurst corrected her angry sister, then she said the one thing that she knew would gain her sister's compliance. "Caro, you have seen how Mr. Darcy treats his servants have you not?"

"Yes, he is far too liberal with them. They do not know their place. When I am mistress…" She twisted her neck, so she was looking down on her sister despite the fact that she was sitting next to her.

"Your intention to induce Mr. Darcy to offer for you will never work if you treat servants the way you normally do." Louisa manipulated the situation to be able to appease both her siblings.

"That is a good point, Louisa. I will have to amend the way I interact with the servants while Mr. Darcy is in residence," Miss Bingley schemed.

~~~~~~~/~~~~~~~

Darcy was impressed with what he could see of the estate as his carriage moved the up the drive from the gates. The sight of the manor house did nothing to change his opinion. From what he could see it was a large and very well-kept building. He was greeted by Bingley, and, to his chagrin, Miss Bingley was there and applied a death grip to his arm as soon as she found an opportunity. Thankfully, Bingley asked Darcy to join him in the study.

"Bingley, before you start, why does your sister still behave as if I am her property? Did you not tell her that, even were she to compromise me, I would *never* offer for her?" Darcy asked pointedly.

"I...er...I meant to, I just have not found the right time Darce, I am sorry." Bingley flushed red from embarrassment.

"I would suggest that you talk to her sooner rather than later. If her behaviour continues, I will bar her from all of my houses and will give her the cut direct in public. I like you, Bingley, and have tolerated Miss Bingley's overt hints and actions only because of our friendship. There is a limit to my patience with her, and I am fast reaching that point," Darcy stated unequivocally. "Now, what is it you needed to discuss with me, Bingley?"

Bingley related the facts of the solicitor's visit earlier in the day, and Darcy asked to see a copy of the lease. Darcy sat with a cup of coffee and read the pages of the document. When he was done, he was impressed for the lease was both iron-clad and extremely thorough. It was the type of lease he would employ if he ever leased any of his properties out.

"What this Mr. Phillips told you is completely accurate, Bingley. I have been telling you for a long time that you need to take the trouble to check your sister. If the landlord..." Darcy scanned the front page. "By-the-by, who is the landlord? I do not see his name anywhere." Darcy asked as he scanned the document again to see if it was perhaps on another page.

"The landlord does not want his name known; I only deal with the agent," Bingley confirmed.

"Understood. Ah yes, *if* the landlord choses to do so, he could have evicted you and kept all of the funds you paid. As soon as your sister mistreated the staff, you were in violation of your lease. A warning shows that you have a little respite, but I would bet that if the behaviour is repeated, you will not be so lucky next time," Darcy explained. As he often did when Darcy expressed his opinion, Bingley accepted it.

Darcy went up to his chambers where Carstens was waiting for him. He soaked in the tub and then his valet assisted him in dressing. When he arrived in the drawing room, Bingley informed him of their social obligation that night. Darcy was none too happy when his friend revealed that an invitation to the local assembly had been accepted on behalf of the whole party. At first Darcy claimed he was too tired, but as soon as Miss Bingley heard that Darcy would not be attending the assembly, she offered to stay at Netherfield with him. Bingley was not surprised when Darcy suddenly found the assembly attractive enough to want to attend.

As was her wont, Miss Bingley descended the stairs almost an hour late, and in the most hideous, burnt orange gown with unseemly ostrich feathers included in her headdress, the pungent, and repugnant, scent that she had applied liberally preceding her. It took all of Darcy's self-control not to cover his nose.

~~~~~~~/~~~~~~~

At Longbourn, the five Bennets were ready a little more than ten minutes before the scheduled departure time, and Mark was on hand to see his parents and sisters off, understanding that the ripe old age of eleven was *slightly* too young to join them for such an event. The Hills and his governess, Miss Jones, would look after young Master Bennet while the family was away.

The Bennets arrived early and were happy to speak to their friends until the assembly commenced. Priscilla Bennet sat with Lady Lucas, Mrs. Phillips, Mrs. Goulding, and Mrs. Long, discussing their fundraising efforts. Lady Sarah Lucas and Hattie Phillips were the only ones outside of the Bennet family who knew that most of the anonymous donations to the committee came from the Bennets.

As much as Lady Lucas and Mrs. Phillips both enjoyed gossiping, with regards to the Bennets nothing would induce them to break their silence or reveal their true situation. Over the years the Bennets had confided in the Lucas parents, who were close friends. Each lady could not help but smile inwardly when they heard the number of two thousand five hundred spoken about the Bennet girls' dowries when they knew the true number was around fifty thousand pounds each.

Bennet was in a discussion about the war against the little tyrant with Sir William Lucas and Mr. Phillips, which had commenced after Phillips had confirmed that the message to the Bingleys had been delivered in a way that left no room for misunderstanding.

The three Bennet sisters were talking to Charlotte and Maria Lucas, Mandy and Cara Long, and Annette Goulding. Most of the talk centred around the party from Netherfield and the numbers of men and women that would be in the party. The number varied greatly depending on who was telling what they had heard from which particular *reliable source*.

~~~~~~~/~~~~~~~

George Wickham was in a gambling hell in a rather seedy part of London. He was down to his last five pounds, as the cards had not been in his favour. Just when he was about to despair, he noticed a man in the scarlet coat of the militia and recognised him from the Lambton area. Tim Denny would still have positive memories of him as he had not ruined Denny's sister and did not owe the man money. Wickham made his way across the smoke-filled hall and was pleased with the reaction he saw the moment Denny recognised him.

"Denny, when did you join the militia?" Wickham asked as they shook hands.

"That is *Lieutenant* Denny to you, Wickham," Denny ribbed.

"How is life with—which unit are you with?" Wickham pressed. A plan was forming. It could be worse; militia officers did not go to war, and he would get three square meals a day and be paid on top of it. Besides, he was sure that there would be many suckers like Denny who he could relieve of their property and purses.

"The Derbyshire Militia is my unit. I am actually here on a recruiting trip. You were born in Derbyshire, so you would qualify if you were interested," Denny informed Wickham.

"What is the cheapest commission?" Wickham asked.

"An ensign, seven and a half pounds. Do you have it?" Denny enquired.

"Sadly no, my friend. It is a long story, but I was cheated out of a clerical living, so I have but five pounds to my name." Fearing the retribution that Darcy promised, Wickham omitted his name from his litany of woes.

"This is what I will do. I will put your name down and purchase the commission for you. We will be in the Town of Meryton in Hertfordshire in three weeks, so meet us there." Denny shook Wickham's hand again and was off. Wickham would have to forego most of his usual activities until he left for Hertfordshire in order to make the last of his funds stretch. At least he was staying at Mrs. Younge's boarding house on Edward Street for free, for the stupid woman still fancied herself in love with him.

VOL 1, CHAPTER 3

T he two oldest Lucas boys danced the first set with Jane and Elizabeth Bennet, Franklin Lucas with the former and his younger brother John with the latter. Esther opened the assembly with Julian Goulding, while her parents danced a few couples down the line from their youngest daughter and watched her with obvious pride.

The Netherfield party had not arrived by the time the first set finished in fact, they only arrived as the second set was ending. Darcy would not have been unhappy about being so late but for the reason, which, of course, was the cloying Miss Bingley. He was hoping that she would not be fishing for compliments about her outfit, he did not know if he had it in him to prevaricate as much as would be needed to find a compliment.

As he entered, Bingley saw a blond angel being led back to Mr Bennet, who had thankfully called on him at Netherfield, so he led his party over. He greeted Mr. Bennet first, then turned his attention to the blond goddess in an obvious bid for an introduction.

Darcy stalked off before he could be introduced, believing that the whispers throughout the room as they entered were from people discussing Bingley's wealth, and his own, which happened at practically every ball they attended. Had Darcy listened and not assumed, he would have heard comments on a visage, the pleasure of being able to meet new friends, and planning of invitations so that they would feel welcome in the neighbourhood, for none were vulgar enough to talk about money. In his preoccupied state, he did not see the looks of disdain that he was receiving from the locals for his rude and arrogant behaviour in being unwilling to stay for an introduction to one of their most prominent members.

"Good evening, Mr. Bennet," Bingley bowed.

"Welcome, Mr. Bingley," Bennet returned. "Would you introduce me to your party, please?"

"Well I never!" Miss Bingley fairly screeched. "How can it be that this man asks you to introduce us? Does he think he is above us and our wealth?"

"Caroline! Please forgive my sister, Mr. Bennet," Bingley asked contritely, not missing the looks of scorn directed at himself and his party from those nearby.

"That, I assume, is your younger sister, Miss Bingley," Bennet glanced at her then proceeded without allowing Bingley time to respond. "Given that you and your sisters are the children of a tradesman, I will forgive Miss Bingley's rudeness this one time." Miss Bingley's pallor was changing colours, soon almost matching the colour of her hideous ensemble. "As I am a landed gentleman, as are a good number of those here, you are the lowest ranked in the room. Therefore, it is *my* prerogative to request the introduction."

"Caroline, hold your tongue! Not another word!" Mrs. Hurst hissed at her sister quietly, and Miss Bingley's surprise ensured her silence, as she was not used to her sister censuring her.

"May I introduce the rest of my party?" Bingley asked nervously and Bennet nodded. "Mr. and Mrs. Harold Hurst, my brother-in-law and sister, my younger sister you already identified. This is …" Bingley trailed off, for the first time noticing that Darcy was no longer with his party.

"My wife Mrs. Bennet, my oldest daughter, Miss Jane Bennet, and my two younger daughters, Miss Elizabeth and Miss Esther Bennet." Each lady curtsied as they were introduced.

"Miss Bennet, may I have the honour of your next set?" Bingley requested hopefully.

"I am sitting out the next, Mr. Bingley," Jane replied. Seeing the question in his look she explained that all the young ladies would sit out at least two sets to allow others to dance.

"But I have the one after that free, if you would like it."

"Thank you, Miss Bennet." Bingley then turned to her sisters. "Are either of you free for the next set?"

"I have a partner, Mr. Bingley," Elizabeth informed him.

"My card has a space on it," Esther replied shyly.

"Then shall we, Miss Esther?" Bingley offered the youngest Bennet sister his arm and she laid her dainty hand on it lightly.

Darcy had begun to notice a chill in the air as he walked around the room, but it was not the weather. He danced a set each with Mrs. Hurst and Miss Bingley, and having discharged his duty to his hosts, he stalked around the room with his mask of hauteur and disdain firmly in place. He had developed the mask soon after coming out into society. It was bad enough when he was merely the heir, but when he returned to society after mourning his father, he felt like a fox trying to escape a pack of rabid hounds. He found the mask effective at keeping any but the most determined from him, and for those he would make a curt comment and excuse himself. Most got the message; Miss Bingley was an unfortunate exception.

The time dragged on. He again walked around, and this time he began to notice that not only did no one seem interested in him, they also seemed disdainful of *him*! How could it possibly be that these inconsequential nobodies with no class, wealth, or connections were disdainful of him? He was Fitzwilliam Darcy!

Bingley approached his friend and got his attention. "Come, Darcy," said he. "I must have you dance. I hate to see you standing about by yourself in this stupid manner. The next set will begin in under three minutes. You had better dance."

"I certainly shall not. You know how I detest it unless I am particularly acquainted with my partner. At such an assembly as this, it would be insupportable. Your sisters are engaged, and there is not another woman in the room with whom it would not be a punishment to me to stand up with," Darcy returned with disdain.

"I would not be so fastidious as you are for a kingdom!" cried Bingley. "Upon my honour, I never met with so many pleasant girls in my life as I have this evening; and there are several of them who are uncommonly pretty. Did you not meet the Bennet sisters? They are all handsome women, Darcy."

"You danced with the only handsome girl in the room," Darcy averred, looking at the eldest Miss Bennet who was talking to a friend across the hall.

"Oh! She is the most beautiful creature I ever beheld!" Bingley followed his friend's eyes to see who he was referring to. "In fact, she is an angel. But there is one of her sisters, sitting down just behind you, who is very pretty and, I dare say, very agreeable. Do let me ask Miss Bennet to introduce you."

"Which do you mean?" Darcy asked and, turning around looked for a moment at Elizabeth until he caught her eye. He withdrew his own and coldly said: "She is tolerable, but not handsome enough to tempt *me*. I am in no humour at present to give consequence to young ladies who are slighted by other men. You had better return to your current partner, for you are wasting your time with me." Bingley was ashamed of his friend's rude words, and it did not help that he was receiving frosty looks from those around him.

Elizabeth, who had been sitting out one of her two planned non-dance sets, heard every word. She had enough self-confidence to know the rude man's words were not true, as her mother praised her and her sisters' inner and outer beauty consistently. Her first inclination was to give the arrogant and proud man a set-down, but her manners won out and she refrained.

Darcy heard a tinkling laugh as the young lady who had been sitting nearby walked past him. He was aware he had been overheard, which was part of his aim so he could destroy any hopes of those present, so far below him, who might think he would lower his standards to dance with them. As the Bennet daughter with the chestnut curls walked past him, she turned and gave him such a look that, if he had been made of water, would have frozen him instantly.

She had the greenest eyes he had ever seen, and they were blazing with anger directed at him. It was then he looked at her, truly looked at her for the first time, and discovered his words a lie. While it was true that she looked different from her blond sister, more petite though full figured, she was the opposite of his assertion to Bingley. He had never before seen a woman as beautiful as she.

He watched her join her sisters, some friends, and an older couple he assumed were her parents. It was then he noted that their gowns were much finer than he would expect to see in a market town. He cringed when all of those around her turned and looked at him as if he were the lowest in the room. Darcy suddenly wanted to find a rock beneath which to crawl and hide.

"Lizzy, what that man said about you was beyond the pale," her mother agreed when Elizabeth had relayed what had transpired. "However, we will not be the cause of gossip; you know how your father and I feel about that subject."

"I know, Mama. I will not repeat what happened to any outside of this circle," Elizabeth promised.

"You are a good girl, Lizzy," her father added. "Miss Lucas and Miss Maria, I ask the same of you, not to repeat what that man said, despite his lack of manners. I will inform your father so you will not be withholding information from him." He smiled gently at them when both Lucas girls promised Mr. Bennet that they too would remain silent on the subject.

"Bingley, what say you that we leave?" Darcy approached his friend.

"I think that is best, Darce," Bingley replied and went to collect his sisters and brother-in- law. "Sir William, my friend is fatigued from his travels today, so we are departing early. Thank you for inviting us to the assembly." Bingley said to their host before they departed.

The remaining participants at the assembly enjoyed the

rest of the dance, and the Netherfield Party was missed by no one.

~~~~~~~/~~~~~~~

The carriage had hardly begun to move when Miss Bingley, still smarting from Mr. Bennet's set down, railed against the country bumpkin. "Miss Bingley, I am afraid what Mr. Bennet said to you was completely factually correct. It is birth, not wealth, that sets the social order," Darcy informed the outraged woman.

"Did you notice those pretentious Bennet women? Their gowns looked like Madame Chambourg creations! They must be cheap imitations; she has not even accepted Louisa and me as clients," Miss Bingley attempted another avenue for which to vent her scorn.

Darcy ignored her prattle as he looked out of the window into the darkness of the night. He too was still smarting from being laughed at and disdained by those he felt were far below him.

"They call the Miss Bennets the jewels of the county. Oh, they are prettyish, I suppose, but I have heard they have dowries of only two thousand five hundred pounds, which makes them nothing to my twenty thousand pounds," Miss Bingley cooed, hoping that Mr. Darcy would take note.

He did, but not in the way she hoped. *'Prettyish indeed. They make you look homely, Miss Bingley, and they know how to dress! If only Miss Elizabeth was not so far below me! For Gigi's sake, I have to make a brilliant match,'* Darcy told himself. As he ruminated, he came to the realisation that other than Miss Bingley and Mrs. Hurst, no one had mentioned his wealth, Bingley's, or that of anyone at the assembly. It puzzled Darcy exceedingly, for it was most singular. Then it hit him; the only vulgar ones at the assembly were with him in the carriage, Miss Bingley and Mrs. Hurst. The sisters had taken every opportunity to slip in mentions of their dowries in an attempt to highlight their wealth and superiority!

~~~~~~~/~~~~~~~

It was widely known that the Dukedom of Bedford was one of the wealthiest in the Kingdom, but very few knew that the true income from the estates, investments, and the commercial interests was around two hundred thousand per annum.

In the current Duke's mind, it was karmic justice that all of this accumulated wealth would go to the descendants of Thomas Rhys-Davies. Lord Sedgwick gave a wry smile as he corrected himself, to Tom Bennet. The third Duke had cared for nothing but status, wealth, and his name, so how ironic was it that his actions had set in motion a chain of events that would erase the Rhys-Davies name from the Dukedom of Bedford. In his letter to Norman and James, he had stated that the heir would not be required to change his name. He laughed ruefully to himself by imagining the third Duke turning over in his grave as all of the discord that he had sown came back to roost.

The Duke of Bedford was currently in Liverpool visiting the main offices of his shipping company, the Dennington Lines. It was the largest private shipping concern in the realm, and his shipyards held the contracts to build close to sixty percent of all Royal Navy ships. His tour of all the Dukedom's holdings was taking longer than he had expected. He had hoped to be done in Liverpool before the end of November, but it seemed that he was growing weaker and was only able to work for a few hours during the day, less than he had planned.

Lord Sedgwick still had to reach the shipyards in the south, and the six satellite estates, including one in Ireland, two in Wales, and one in Scotland. At this rate, he would be lucky to be done by May or June of the coming year, and that was if his health did not decline further.

His Duchess had insisted she accompany him on his travels. At her suggestion, he had sent an express to Norman and James, vesting Power of Attorney with his wife in the matter of the Bedford heir should he become incapacitated, or die.

"My love, can we not suspend this trip and return to Longfield Meadows?" Lady Rose begged her husband one evening.

"Once I have completed my work here, we will return home for Christmastide, and I will not try to travel again until late March, when the temperatures start to rise in spring. It will set my timetable back significantly, but you know I can deny you nothing that you ask me, Rose my love," the Duke promised.

The Duchess was happy with the concession and sent letters off that afternoon to have the house prepared for them to spend close to four months in residence.

~~~~~~~/~~~~~~~

As was the norm, the day following the assembly, Charlotte Lucas visited Longbourn to discuss the previous night's dance with her friends. Charlotte was six and twenty and feared that she was well and truly on the shelf. She had a paltry dowry of five hundred pounds and hated the fact that she would be a burden on her parents and her brother Franklin once he inherited.

Unlike her friends, Jane and Eliza, Charlotte had no romantic notions of marrying for the deepest of true love. She would be happy with any respectable man that could provide her a modest home of her own. As she often told her friends, she believed that felicity in marriage was a matter of chance. Jane and Eliza had roundly rejected her notion that it was better not to know too much about one's spouse before the marriage.

"Welcome, Charlotte," Jane smiled at their friend, "I trust that you enjoyed the assembly last night."

"I did. What about you? Aside from that arrogant man slighting you, that is?" Charlotte enquired as Elizabeth pulled a face indicating her distaste at the mention of the haughty man from Derbyshire.

"As I gave my word last night, I will not spread the story of his rudeness to me, but nothing will induce me to like the man. Charlotte, you danced just as many dances last night as I, but I missed Tom exceedingly, for we always need more men who do not think themselves above their company," Elizabeth responded wryly.

"Speaking of Tom, how is he doing in his second year at Oxford? I am happy that he and Nick are sharing accommodations," Charlotte stated. With only two months in age between them, the third oldest Lucas brother, Nicholas, or Nick as everyone called him, and Tom Bennet, had been the closest of friends since they were able to walk.

Sir William, a former tradesman who never had the benefit of a gentleman's education, had despaired that he did not have the funds to send his three sons to school. A year before Franklin was of age to attend, Bennet told Sir William that he had convinced his alma maters of Harrow and Oxford to offer scholarships to all three Lucas sons. What the Lucas family would never know was the Bennets had provided all of the necessary funds for the three boys to gain their educations. And not only the tuition fees, but everything, including board and lodging.

Rather than question his good fortune, Sir William had accepted the gift on behalf of his sons. Franklin had graduated Oxford two years previously, John a year later, and now Nick was in the second year with his best friend Tom Bennet. Also with them in the same year was a distant cousin of the Bennets, Robert Jamison.

"You know Tom, he always finds the best in any situation, and like most of us Bennets, he loves to read and learn," Jane smiled at Charlotte.

"May I tell Charlotte, Jane?" Elizabeth asked conspiratorially.

"Go ahead, Lizzy," Jane shook her head in amusement at Lizzy's excitement to share.

"Tell me what?" Charlotte asked, her curiosity piqued.

"You know we often spend Christmastide at Broadhurst with our grandparents and aunts and uncles?" Elizabeth asked cryptically.

"Yes, it has been so since your father married the current Mrs. Bennet," Charlotte quirked a brow in question.

"Grandmama has agreed to invite you to accompany us to Broadhurst for the Christmas season," Elizabeth revealed.

"As long as my parents agree, I would love to accompany you to Lord and Lady Jersey's estate," Charlotte replied joyfully. She was sure that her parents would not object, but she would still ask out of respect before she could accept.

The conversation then shifted to the Netherfield party. "What did you think of Mr. Bingley, Jane?" Charlotte asked.

"He is a pleasant man, I suppose," Jane replied, "but in some ways he reminded me of a puppy dog always seeking his master's approbation."

"I believe he was planning to ask you for a second dance, Jane," Charlotte opined.

"Then it is well that they departed early. It saved him the embarrassment of my refusing a second set," Jane revealed.

"I am not surprised that you are careful, Jane. You have the luxury to have already refused an Earl and a Marquess. Unlike me, you can afford to be particular in your choice. Even if you never marry, with your fortune you will never be a burden on your family as will be the case for me." Charlotte turned maudlin as she considered her future prospects, or lack thereof.

"Never give up hope, Charlotte; you never know," Elizabeth tried to console her friend.

~~~~~~~/~~~~~~~

"We have received an invitation to Broadhurst for Christmas, Reggie," Lady Elaine, the Countess of Matlock, shared with her husband. "Sarah writes that her children and grandchildren will be present."

"I wonder if that includes their youngest, Priscilla," the Earl asked. "Did she not marry some country squire or something?"

"Yes, it was Benetton, or Benham, or something like that," the Countess replied.

"What are we discussing?" Andrew, Viscount Hilldale, asked.

His parents shared the news of the invitation to Broadhurst with their oldest son and heir. "Are you still pining for that young lady who you met at the Gardiners' house those few times we met with Gardiner on Portman Square?" the Countess asked. "If I do not err, she volunteered at Haven house while in Town. Such a nice young lady."

"Ah, the delectable Miss Jane Bennet. I will meet her again, mother. Before you say it, as far as I know her family has no great wealth or connections, but I have more than enough of both. She was delightful, not only in her outward appearance, but she seemed to be a genuinely good person, none of the fawning, primping, and preening that we see among the Ton," Andrew informed his parents.

"As long as she is at least a gentleman's daughter, son, we would support you if you were able to find her and convince her to give you a chance," the Earl chuckled.

"If all else fails, after Twelfth Night I will ask Mr. Gardiner where she lives and seek her out." Andrew, Lord Hilldale, was resolved to see if he would be able to win the heart of the only lady who had ever captured his interest. "What about William and Gigi?"

"William is staying in Hertfordshire and will collect Gigi by the end of the month for a quiet Christmas at Pemberley. He needs to build his strength to face the dragon in her lair at Easter," the Countess said laughingly. No one realised that Miss Georgiana Darcy had been about to enter the drawing room when she heard part of the conversation and decided to redirect herself to the music room rather than disturb those within.

"It is pleasing that my sister stays in her *fiefdom* of Rosings and does not sally forth to command the rest of us to bend to her will," the Earl stated irreverently. His sister, Lady Catherine de Bourgh, was somewhat of a joke to the rest of the family. Unfortunately for his nephew, William had committed to take on his later father's duty and keep an eye on Rosings Park. That meant that he had the misfortune of spending Easter with her and her sickly daughter, Anne.

His sister was still pushing the myth of a cradle betrothal, trying to guilt William into marrying Anne de Bourgh. William knew from his father's own mouth that no agreement had ever been forged, so he ignored his officious aunt as much as much as he was able. The Earl watched the situation from afar but would only step in if his intervention was needed.

It was also common knowledge among the family that what was driving Lady Catherine's insistence that William marry Anne was her belief that with Anne ensconced at Pemberley, she would be left alone to run Rosings, which in a few months would become Anne's on her five and twentieth birthday in May.

"As William and Gigi have plans to go to Pemberley, I will respond to Sarah in the affirmative. Now, if my sons would settle down and give me some grandchildren, I would be set for life." The Countess looked at her older son. He was only eight and twenty, not that old for a man still to be in the unmarried state, but that did not stop his mother from dreaming of the future for both of her sons.

The Earl and Countess were working on a plan for their second son, Richard. At six and twenty, he was one of the youngest colonels in the Royal Dragoons. When Richard was shipped to the peninsula, he was a full Lieutenant. He had distinguished himself greatly, first at Roliça in August of 1808, where he had saved a general's life and was promoted to Captain. Richard next saw action in December of the same year at Sahagún, where he led his men in a key victory that impressed General Wellesley, who gave him a field promotion to Lieutenant-Colonel, skipping over the rank of Major.

His last battle, before returning home with a serious shoulder injury, was in January 1809, the Battle of Corunna in Spain, commonly known as the Battle of Elviña. Once again, Richard Fitzwilliam had distinguished himself with both bravery and tactical ability that led to him being promoted to full colonel.

He was currently on assignment training new Dragoon officers and men, so he was safe—for now. His parents, however, were fully aware that when he was medically cleared, he would return to the Continent. Hence the impetus to find an option that would give their son an occupation that did not involve placing his life in danger.

To that end, the Earl was negotiating to purchase the estate of Brookfield in Nottinghamshire. The final living member of the Brookfield family was extremely ill, and the heir had his own large estate in Devon. Not wanting to be like a vulture waiting to pick the meat of a carcass, the Earl had sent word to the heir that *when* he inherited, *if* he was interested in selling, he might consider contacting Lord Matlock. The heir had responded, affirmatively, saying that at the appropriate time he would give Lord Matlock the right of first refusal.

~~~~~~~/~~~~~~~

Bingley was infatuated with the blond angel he had danced with at the assembly. She fit all of his criteria for beauty, so he was ready to fall in love with her. He put out of his mind that she was the fifth in a long line of angels he had *fallen in love* with, certain that this was the only one who had ever truly mattered.

"Darcy, I am to ride to Longbourn to pay a visit on the Bennet family; will you not accompany me?" Bingley asked.

Darcy hesitated. He did want to see the beauty from the assembly that he had insulted with an untrue statement, but knowing how far below him the family was, he did not want to raise any expectations by calling on them. "Sorry, my friend, but I have matters of business to which I must attend. Are you sure it is wise to call on them so soon?" Darcy asked, trying to steer his younger friend in a direction of his choosing as he normally did.

"Yes, Charles, why would you call on those country mushrooms who insulted me so infamously?" Miss Bingley asked, agreeing with Darcy as always. He could say that the sky was green, and she would agree.

"She is the most beautiful angel I have ever beheld and, as her father called on me, it is entirely prudent that I return the call." Bingley sprang out of his chair and called for his horse. Darcy, not wanting to be trapped in a drawing room with Mrs. Hurst and Miss Bingley, followed Bingley out and locked himself in his friend's study.

VOL 1, CHAPTER 4

"Thomas is that man so insensible that he would write to you after being warned of the penalties that could be imposed on him if he does not give up his maniacal claim?" an exasperated Priscilla Bennet asked.

"Here, my love, read the missive for yourself. He does not repeat that particular claim," Bennet informed his wife, handing her the letter from his cousin as they sat on a settee in the study at Longbourn.

5 November 1810
Hunsford Parsonage near the Great Estate of Rosings Park

Dear Sir,
The disagreement subsisting between your branch of the family and mine always gave me much uneasiness, and since I have had the misfortune to lose my father who forbade contact with the Bennets, I have frequently wished to heal the breach. For some time, however, I was kept back by my own doubts, fearing lest it might seem disrespectful to his memory for me to be on good terms with anyone with whom it had always pleased him to be at variance.

"You see Priscilla, he is on a peace-making mission," Bennet joked.

"Who would write in such a way to one to whom he had never been introduced?" an incredulous Mrs. Bennet asked.

"Read on, my love," Bennet urged.

My mind, however, is now made up on the subject, for having received ordination at Easter, I have been so fortunate as to be distinguished by the patronage of the Right Honourable Lady Catherine de Bourgh, widow of Sir Lewis de Bourgh, whose bounty, infinite wisdom, and beneficence has preferred me to the valuable rectory of this parish, where it shall be my earnest endeavour to demean myself with grateful respect towards her ladyship, and be ever ready to perform those rites and ceremonies which are insti-tuted by the Church of England.

Moreover, as a clergyman I feel it my duty to promote and establish the blessing of peace in all families within the reach of my influence and on these grounds, I flatter myself that my present overtures are highly commendable.

"He is insensible! Is he the only one in the realm who does not know how uneducated and ridiculous Lady Catherine de Bourgh is? Infinite wisdom indeed! The accurate statement would be infinite ignorance and arrogance!" Pricilla Bennet marvelled at the sycophant's stupidity. The nonsense and his obsequiousness mixed with a level of pomposity jumped off the pages at her. Priscilla Bennet read on.

I now understand that one of my antecedents was in error about the nature of the entail placed on the Longbourn estate, and hope that the misunderstanding will be kindly overlooked on your side, and not lead you to reject this olive branch.

"At least he has accepted reality, although the more I read, the more ridiculous this man looks to me." Mrs. Bennet shook her head in wonder that such a man had ever been ordained, then continued with her perusal.

I cannot be otherwise than be prepared to offer your amiable daughters my olive branch. I beg leave to apologise for the past mis-understandings, as well as to assure you of my readiness to make them every possible amends—but of this hereafter. If you should have no objection to receive me into your house, I propose myself the satisfaction of waiting on you and your family, Monday, No-vember the eighteenth, by four o'clock, and shall probably trespass on your hospitality until the Saturday sennight following, which I can do without any inconvenience, as Lady Catherine is far from objecting to my occasional absence on a Sunday, provided that some other clergyman is engaged to do the duty of the day.

I remain, dear sir, with respectful compliments to your lady and daughters, your well-wisher and friend,

Reverend William Collins

"What is the *olive branch* that the man keeps on about, Thomas?" Priscilla asked with true trepidation, fearing it was what she dreaded. "Does the man not realise that the eighteenth is the Sabbath, not a Monday?"

"The *olive branch* is what you think, my Cilla," Bennet leaned over and kissed his wife. "As far as the day goes, he must, like his patroness, believe reality will bend to his will."

"Does this idiotic man think that one of my girls would be interested in him?" Mrs. Bennet exclaimed with disgust, "Or that we would *ever* allow any of our girls to be married to an obsequious sycophant, who at the same time thinks that his office as a man of the cloth elevates him above society? The man does not even have the manners to wait for an invitation; he *invited* himself!" Mrs. Bennet fumed.

"Did you notice the lack of any mention of either Tom or Mark?" Bennet observed.

"Are you going to allow him to visit us, Thomas?" his wife asked as she calmed herself down.

"It seems we must, if for no reason than that he is to be disabused in person of his ever being accepted as a match for one of our daughters," Bennet suggested.

"So be it, but I want him in a chamber on the top floor, the farthest from our precious girls' chambers, and he is to be watched at all times!" Mrs. Bennet demanded to which her imminently sensible husband agreed without argument.

~~~~~~~/~~~~~~~

The same afternoon that the Bennet parents read the ridiculous letter from the sycophantic parson, the three Bennet daughters were shopping in Meryton with Charlotte and Maria Lucas when the Derbyshire Militia marched through the town on their way to the encampment just south of the town.

"Ooooh, I do so think a man in a scarlet coat looks very well. I would not complain if I were to marry an officer," Maria Lucas exclaimed.

"And how would you live, Maria? Do you forget that you and I have only five hundred pounds which would generate a whole *twenty pounds a year*? What do you think that will buy you? You will have no new clothes, no balls, no entertainment, and if that is not bad enough, you would live in cramped quarters and have no servants," Charlotte said, giving her younger sister a lesson in reality.

"B-b-but surely an officer earns a good salary," Maria stammered, much less sure of her assertions when seconds ago she had begun to imagine a life of constant entertainment and balls for herself.

"Officers in the militia are usually poor; most of them are not even gentlemen. Most *gentlemen* who become officers join the Regulars," Elizabeth explained firmly. "Unless you marry the colonel of a regiment, you would be lucky if the junior officers bring in one or two pounds a month. Charlotte is correct, Maria; you would not live at a standard close to what you are used to."

"I would rather stay single for the rest of my life than marry a man just because he wears a certain colour jacket," Esther opined.

Seeing how distressed her sister was, Charlotte pulled her into her arms. "Maria, we did not mean to upset you, but you cannot live on a scarlet coat, or even a handsome man, alone. Please promise me that you will stay within the bounds of propriety around these men. Trust me when I tell you that they will take a small amount of flirtation as a sign that you are willing to give much more than you actually are."

"A woman's reputation and virtue are extremely brittle, Maria. It is the most valuable thing that we have and once it is lost, it is lost forever," Esther told her friend, gently taking Maria's hand and gave it a light squeeze after Charlotte hugged her younger sister.

"It seems that I have a lot to learn from all of you," Maria sniffed.

While the Bennet daughters were in Meryton, Mr. Bingley came to call. He was shown into the master's study, and when Mr. Bennet suggested that they greet his family in the drawing room, he smiled to himself when Bingley lit up at the prospect, Bennet suspected, of seeing Jane again.

Bennet almost felt badly for the young pup—almost. Jane had no interest in Bingley, but she would be polite to him. On entering the drawing room, Bennet did not miss the crestfallen look the younger man sported when only his wife was within.

Bingley asked after the Miss Bennets, and after some inconsequential discussion about the weather, made his excuses and departed. He had been so preoccupied with his disappointment that Miss Bennet had not been at home waiting for him to call, he did not notice that although the manor house looked deceptively small with the way the front façade was presented, it was far larger inside than one would think looking at it from without. There was a stand of large trees on either side of the house which obscured its true size from view, which was by design.

~~~~~~~/~~~~~~~

Wickham was restless to leave Edward Street for Hertfordshire. He had to make do with Mrs. Younge and was beyond sick of her company already, but he needed to use her hospitality until the nineteenth of the month, the day he had agreed to meet Denny in Meryton.

Usually, Wickham enjoyed his time in London. But with his dwindling money, not to mention a number of debt collectors after him, he had enjoyed none of his normal vices of gambling, women, or drink of late.

As much as he feared Colonel Fitzwilliam, he was not worried about running into him in the militia as he knew from discreet enquiries that the Colonel was in the Regulars. Wickham scoffed when he thought about how Richard Fitzwilliam had willingly put himself in harm's way, for he would never do anything that *ridiculous*. There was only one thing Wickham genuinely cared about, and that was himself. He had heard that the Colonel had been injured, but unfortunately, he was on the mend, meaning that Darcy's threat still remained valid.

He would endure Mrs. Younge for the next few days until he no longer needed her. It suited his purposes for her to believe him in love with her, so even when he left, he would not disabuse her of that nonsense in case he needed her succour in the future.

Each time he looked at his reflection in a mirror, Wickham felt anger at his nemesis's build. His perfect nose was at an angle, and one of his front teeth was missing! What Darcy had done to him would make it much harder to charm what he wanted out of the residents of the town to which he would travel.

It was just one more thing to be added to the ever-growing list of offences for which Wickham held Darcy responsible. He was sure, as sure as he was alive, that one day he would make Darcy pay for all of the offences that the master of Pemberley had perpetrated against him.

~~~~~~~/~~~~~~~

Miss Bingley could not but notice her brother's interest in Miss Bennet. There had been a dinner at Lucas Lodge a few evenings previously and her brother had not moved from Miss Bennet's side, although, strangely, Miss Bennet seemed quite indifferent to her brother. It was at that dinner at the home of that 'nobody knight' that Miss Bingley had been grievously wounded. As she sat at her dressing table contemplating which of her superior gowns she should wear that day, she could hear the conversation in her head word for word.

Someone had prevailed on the middle Bennet daughter to play the pianoforte, and Miss Bingley was sure that the country hoyden would soon demonstrate her inferiority. That, to her irritation, was not the case. As much as she did not want to admit it,

Miss Bingley had never heard better. She gave up her idea to show Miss Eliza up by exhibiting after her since she quickly understood that her own playing would have been nothing in comparison to what she was hearing.

Then, to make matters worse, the chit sang like an angel. She had the best contralto that Miss Bingley could remember hearing. Miss Bingley could not understand how a country miss from an inconsequential family could be so talented and accomplished.

She walked over to where Mr. Darcy was watching the chit sing to find that he was mesmerised by her performance, so Miss Bingley had decided to say something to break the spell.

"I can guess the subject of your reverie," Miss Bingley asserted as he sidled up to Darcy.

"I should imagine not," he replied dismissively. Miss Bingley had never allowed anything to deter her, and now was no different.

"You are considering how insupportable it would be to pass many evenings in this manner—in such society; and indeed I am quite of your opinion. I was never more annoyed! The insipidity, and yet the noise—the nothingness, and yet the self-importance of all those people! What would I give to hear your strictures on them!" Miss Bingley stated spitefully.

"Your conjecture is totally wrong, I assure you. My mind was more agreeably engaged. I have been meditating on the very great pleasure which a pair of fine eyes in the face of a pretty woman can bestow." He corrected her dismissively, though Miss Bingley preened in supposing her meant her.

Miss Bingley immediately fixed her eyes on his face and expressed her desire of his sharing what lady had the credit of inspiring such reflections, believing it to be herself, which meant that at last she was to gain his offer of her becoming the Mistress of Pemberley!

Mr. Darcy replied with great intrepidity, "Miss Elizabeth Bennet."

"Miss Elizabeth Bennet!" repeated Miss Bingley. "I am all astonishment. How long has she been such a favourite? Pray, when am I to wish you joy?" As she spoke the words, her insides were in

turmoil. *This was not the answer she wanted to hear.*

"That is exactly the question which I expected you to ask. A lady's imagination is very rapid; it jumps from admiration to love and from love to matrimony, in a moment. I knew you would be wishing me joy." Darcy knew he had made a mistake by mentioning the lady's name, but it had been a reflex response, and he had not, as was his wont, considered the impact of his words.

"Nay, if you are serious about it, I shall consider the matter is absolutely settled. You will have a charming mother-in-law. I will allow that she seems to be very genteel, but I am sure she will always be at Pemberley with you."

Miss Bingley remembered that she had heard the Bennet estate was entailed, and assumed, as many did, that it was entailed away from the female line. She was not aware that she had made two errors: one, she never ascertained what kind of entailment it was, and two, as she had never visited Longbourn, she had no idea that there were Bennet sons, so she believed that the Bennets would lose their estate on the death of the family patriarch who had so insulted her.

She had tried to intimate that Mr. Darcy would have to support the widow, but he seemed to ignore her inferences. Even if it meant a compromise, she would have Pemberley and Darcy House as her own!

~~~~~~~/~~~~~~~

Darcy was well and truly confounded. He had developed feelings for a country miss, feelings, he lectured himself, that he could never act on and still fulfil his duty to his name and family. However, during the gathering at the knight's house when he had discovered she was a woman of such musical talents, for which her lack of connections may be overlooked by some, she had refused to dance with him.

After the best playing and singing performance he could remember hearing, her younger sister, Edith, no Esther, began to play. She was good. Not quite at her sister's level, but certainly not inferior. In fact she was on par with Gigi. Someone had requested lively airs to dance to, and the youngest Miss

Bennet had obliged.

Sir William had stopped Darcy to make some inane comment about dancing when Miss Elizabeth walked nearby, and her neighbour had put her forward as a dance partner. She had demurred, telling Sir William that it was not her purpose in walking across the room to be asked to dance.

Darcy had then immediately requested a dance, and she had refused him without any consideration, in words he would never forget: '*I find that I am not in the mood to* tolerate *dancing, and I am in no humour to give* consequence *to the activity this evening.*' She had turned and walked away without looking back once, which he knew because he had watched her every step as she separated herself from him.

She was magnificent; she had just given him a very public set down, one which no one would be able to identify as a set down. Damn her lack of wealth and connections!

~~~~~~~/~~~~~~~

A note arrived from Netherfield addressed to Jane Bennet. Jane's mother handed her daughter the note. "Beware of Greeks bearing gifts, Jane," Mrs. Bennet cautioned her daughter.

Jane opened the note and prepared to read it to her mother and sisters, for Mark had decided that he would rather visit his horse than listen to his sister read her missive.

10 November 1810
Netherfield Park

My dear Miss Bennet,

"I did not realise that you were friends with one of the supercilious sisters, Jane," Elizabeth teased.

"That is not kind, Lizzy—even if it is true," Jane teased in return and continued to read.

The gentlemen are to dine with the officers this day, so we, my sister Louisa and I, will be quite on our own.

We invite you to join us for dinner so we will not be bored with just the two of us here. It will be a good opportunity to get to know you.

Please say you will attend,
Caroline Bingley

"They want to make themselves feel superior and will be trying to find out about our wealth and connections," Jane guessed. It took her no time at all to see the true motives behind the invitation.

"Feel free to decline, Jane," her mother told her.

"Lizzy is not the only one who likes to sketch characters, Mama. I will join them and see just how ridiculous their questions are." Jane smiled playfully at her sister.

"You will not tell them about our connections, will you Jane?" Esther asked.

"No, little sister, I will not cast pearls before the swine. Even without Papa's report of their social climbing ways, a few minutes of their airs and graces was enough to see what they are. I will tell them about my *birth* mother and her family. They have met Uncle Frank, and I am sure they will ask about Uncle Edward and Aunt Maddie. If they ask where they live in London, I will mention the old house that they still own, so I will not be telling a lie, just bending the truth somewhat." As Jane smiled, she was looking forward to a most amusing conversation at Mrs. Hurst's and Miss Bingley's expense.

"Which carriage will you take, Jane?" Elizabeth asked. "I suggest the older, small one, it will not raise any questions like our other coaches would."

"I agree with Lizzy," Mrs. Bennet added, the amusement in her eyes brightening at the true pleasure of having such intelligent and good-humoured daughters.

"Then, that is the carriage I will use," Jane decided. Her mother summoned the butler to instruct him to have the vehicle prepared for her daughter to depart at five.

~~~~~~~/~~~~~~~

When Mark Bennet escaped the drawing room, he

knocked on his father's study door. "Papa, will you come riding with me, please?" he beseeched his father.

"I do have time, son, but were you not with your mother and sister in the drawing room?" Bennet grinned, knowing that his eleven-year-old was not one to sit still in the drawing room for long, and he had no lessons on Saturdays, so a ride would be a good way to burn some of his youthful energy. "Have Hill tell the stable master to prepare Orion and Calista, and I will meet you in the stables in a half hour once we have both changed."

To keep up the illusion that Longbourn was not as profitable as it was, there was a small stable where callers' horses would be kept, but behind the large barn was an extensive set of stables, for all of the current Bennets loved all things equestrian.

Bennet and Mark mounted their horses and trotted out, past the home farm toward an open field. Until six months ago, Mark had ridden a cob. As he approached his eleventh birthday, Bennet had taken him to see Mr. Bennington at Bennington Fields, who bred some of the finest horseflesh in Hertfordshire and the surrounding five counties. Bennet would not allow a stallion yet, but when Mark chose a three-year-old light chestnut mare reported to be very gentle and fully trained, he purchased her for his son, who named her Calista.

Once they reached the open field, father and son gave their horses their head, and within seconds both were at full gallop. Darcy and Bingley had been riding the fence line between Netherfield and Longbourn when Darcy sighted the two riders. He could not help but notice the quality of the two horses, and the horsemanship of their riders thundering toward the low fence. Both horses jumped and landed not far from the two friends. Up close, Darcy's estimation that they were quality horses was confirmed.

"You have my apologies, Mr. Bingley, if we startled you. This lad," Bennet pointed to his son, "is my younger son Mark, and I have been teaching him to jump his birthday present,"

Bennet explained.

"No harm done, Mr. Bennet. Darcy, you have not been introduced, have you?" Bingley asked and Darcy shook his head. Darcy felt somewhat chagrined that he had eschewed the introduction at the assembly. "Mr. Bennet, my friend Fitzwilliam Darcy of Pemberley in Derbyshire, Darcy, Mr. Thomas Bennet of Longbourn."

"And Neth..." Mark almost blurted out.

"And we help keep an eye on Netherfield for the owner," Bennet gave his youngest a side-long look. Mark realised he almost let the cat out of the bag.

Darcy saw the look and did not know what to make of it. Miss Bingley claimed that Longbourn was entailed away from the female line and the Bennets had no heir. Yet before him was a Bennet son, and the father had said a younger son.

"Mr. Bennet, did you say that this is your younger son?" Darcy asked pointedly for clarification.

"Yes, that is what I said," Bennet responded, not adding more than he was asked.

"My older brother, Tom, is at Oxford," Mark reported proudly.

"We are Cambridge men," Bingley informed the Bennets.

"It is a long-standing Bennet tradition to attend Harrow and Oxford," Bennet told the two friends nonchalantly.

"Your horses are of very high quality," Darcy stated, his tone almost accusatory.

"Yes, they are, Mr. Darcy, they are most *tolerable* mounts. I see clouds moving in, we will head for home. Mr. Bingley. Mr. Darcy." The two Bennets wheeled their horses, rode a hundred yards in the opposite direction, and then turned and rode at a gallop to jump the fence, sailing over it easily.

Darcy was not happy. This was not the first time one of the Bennet family flung his words back at him, and how dare they? Did they not know who he was? As he had the thought, Darcy was horrified, for he realised he sounded just like his Aunt Catherine de Bourgh!

"Are you determined to be rude to the Bennets at every turn?" Bingley asked.

"Well, even if they assist the landlord, they should not be trespassing on land that is not theirs," came Darcy's petulant reply. He knew that it was a nonsensical thing to say, but that is all he could think of in defence of himself, though he knew he was without any.

VOL 1, CHAPTER 5

As the three male residents of Netherfield rode down the drive in Darcy's carriage, they passed a carriage heading toward the house. Bingley did not miss seeing that Miss Bennet was within. He did not realise his sisters had been circumspect and not told him they were entertaining Miss Bennet for dinner. As they suspected, had Bingley known ahead of time, he would have forgone the dinner with the officers as he had tried again and again to be in her company, failing more often than he succeeded.

"I think I should remain at home," Bingley looked longingly toward the house where the carriage had halted.

"That is within your discretion, Bingley, but you will be slighting our hosts for this evening, and do not forget it was you who beseeched me to join you," Darcy chided his friend. The truth was, he would have rather been anywhere but left in the house alone with Bingley's sisters.

"I will keep our prior engagement," Bingley returned petulantly.

Jane Bennet exited the carriage and had just managed to gain the protection of the portico when the heavens opened with the rain that had been threatening all afternoon; it was more a deluge than rain. "Welcome Miss Bennet; what a quaint carriage," Miss Bingley said, pointing out again, not subtly, that Miss Bennet and her family were poor, the proof being in front of them.

"It does the job; thank you for the compliment," Jane returned with a serene smile, and Miss Bingley was irritated that her barb seemed to miss its mark. "I passed a carriage departing; luckily, the men were able to leave before the heavens opened. The bridge at the end of the drive floods easily."

"How would you know that Miss Bennet?" Mrs. Hurst asked.

"My father knows the landlord and keeps an eye on the estate for him," Jane prevaricated to cover her fluff.

"I am sure that it is good to be able to earn a little more money, my dear Miss Bennet," Miss Bingley offered with false affection.

"Some, like my father, help others as it is the right thing to do, not to earn money or praise," Jane replied in a soft tone, which almost took the sting from the rebuke. It was sweetly said, but both sisters felt the implied criticism in her words.

Just then Nichols announced that dinner was served. The three ladies sat, Miss Bingley at the head, her sister to her right, and Miss Bennet to her left. Just after the soup was served, Miss Bingley began her interrogation. "Where is your mother from, Miss Bennet?" she asked innocuously.

"The lady who gifted me life was from Meryton, Miss Bingley," Jane averred truthfully.

"And her family?" Mrs. Hurst followed up.

"Her father was the late Mr. Gardiner, who was the town solicitor before my Uncle Frank, who I believe you met, took over the practice." Jane gently wiped the corner of her mouth with her napkin as the footman cleared the dishes and another two paced the first course on the table.

"A solicitor, so a tradesman, then," Miss Bingley smirked as she served herself.

"That is correct, Miss Bingley. Was your father not in trade as well?" Jane asked innocently, maintaining her smiling façade despite wanting to put the pretentious women in their places.

Miss Bingley, who had just demonstrated her decided lack of manners as she served herself before her guest, and her sister's pallor darkened as their roots in trade were mentioned. The rest of the course passed in relative silence as the sisters fought to regain their equanimity. Neither understood their plan to discompose Miss Bennet and show her how unsuitable she was for their brother was rebounding on themselves to show how ill-mannered they were despite all their refined schooling.

~~~~~~~/~~~~~~~

Darcy was stuffed between a Lieutenant Denny and Captain Carter during the raucous meal. He was debating whether it would not have been better to stay locked in his room at Netherfield rather than among such low-class company when he heard someone address him from across the table. "I apologise, Mr. Bennet, I was deep in thought." Darcy could not think what the man had to say to him after the snide comment earlier that day.

"No need to apologise, Mr. Darcy. I was saying that one who will claim an acquaintance with you, no matter how tenacious, will be arriving the day after the morrow," Bennet said with a smirk.

"I know no one in this part of the country," was the haughty reply.

"A distant cousin of mine who has taken orders will be arriving, a Mr. Collins," Bennet explained.

"There is none of my acquaintance with that name," Darcy reiterated intimating that Bennet's claims were a falsehood.

"He is the new clergyman at Hunsford. Your aunt from Rosings Park is his patroness," Bennet clarified.

"How would you know that Lady Catherine is my aunt?" Darcy asked curtly, his suspicions raised.

Bennet knew he had erred, and as much as he disliked prevarication, he knew it was called for in this instance. "My very distant relation wrote a rambling letter where he mentioned that his patroness' nephew, with the name of Darcy, was in the area that he is visiting. Evidently your aunt informed him of the fact when he requested time away from Hunsford."

Darcy remembered he had made mention of his travel plans to his aunt. It was when she had demanded he attend her at Rosings Park for some contrived reason in her quest to force a match neither he nor his cousin Anne desired. "Based on past history, your cousin must be a most peculiar man," Darcy replied letting his mask slip for an instant, and it was not missed by Bennet.

"If his letter inviting himself here was anything to go by, I would have to say that you have the right of it," Bennet allowed.

While he was talking to Mr. Bennet, who Darcy had to admit seemed to be a highly intelligent man even if he were not consequential enough to form a friendship with, he had missed Denny telling Carter that his old friend Wickham would be one of the new recruits coming from London.

Darcy did not see the hypocrisy of forming a friendship with Bingley, a tradesman's son, while at the same disdaining the connection with a landed gentleman. If he were honest with himself, he would have admitted there was a specific reason he did not want to get close to Mr. Bennet—Elizabeth Bennet. The country miss with the fine eyes and beautiful looks invaded his dreams, and, when he did not regulate himself, his waking thoughts as well. He would also have been surprised to realise that in two of his letters to his sister he had mentioned the lady's name more than once.

~~~~~~~/~~~~~~~

The rain had not let up, it had intensified. The sisters' questioning resumed and, as she delivered tea to the ladies, Mrs. Nichols winked at her mistress's oldest daughter, which Miss Bingley and Mrs. Hurst overlooked, as they both ignored servants as a matter of course.

"Do you ever spend time in Town, Miss Bennet?" Miss Bingley began. "We are often in London with our friends in the *Ton.*" Jane knew from the report her father had that this was a lie. The only member of the *Ton* they were associated with was Mr. Darcy, who had been seen with the brother, not the sisters, at events in Town.

"Yes, I have an uncle in London," Jane allowed.

"Where is his house?" Mrs. Hurst asked.

Inwardly Jane was most pleased with the way the question had been phrased, for there was no need to tell an untruth. "My uncle Gardiner has a house near Cheapside close to his warehouses."

Miss Bingley was about to make a snide remark about another uncle in trade when she remembered her mortification at Miss Bennet highlighting the Bingleys' closer ties to trade. Not wanting to revisit that mortification, she said, "Well I suppose that not all of us have connections in the highest circles of society." This particular barb was said with a such smugness Jane almost lost her ability to hide her own amusement.

"You are correct, Miss Bingley, not everyone is so fortunate," Jane replied ambiguously. *'If they knew that we are closely related to the De Melvilles, they would be fawning all over me. Both have tried to gain access to Almack's and have been repeatedly denied. Grandmama is one of the patronesses, and I shall write to her and amuse her with tales from this evening!'* Jane smiled with an effort, trying not to burst into giggles at the ridiculousness of the women. Thankfully, their questions had so far been driven by their assumptions, which allowed Jane to answer truthfully.

"It is so sad that your little estate is entailed away," Miss Bingley said, sure that the prospect of losing her home would be the one thing sure to discompose Miss Bennet.

"And what estate did you grow up on, Miss Bingley?" Jane deflected the question neatly.

Both sisters' pallor darkened once again while Jane's amusement increased. Having lost at every turn, Miss Bingley decided another avenue of attack was in order. "I have heard tell that you and your sisters have dowries of a mere two thousand five hundred pounds." Both sisters tittered as they amused themselves with the vulgar subject the younger one had raised.

"You are correct that it is the sum which is known, Miss Bingley," Jane averred honestly.

"My sister and I each have twenty thousand pounds," Miss Bingley crowed triumphantly, until she noticed that Miss Bennet looked singularly unimpressed. "With the small amount reported, you and your sisters will be even poorer than you are now!" Miss Bingley spat out spitefully, becoming increasing upset at being unable to crack Miss Bennet's serene façade.

"While I appreciate the consideration, I urge you not to worry about my siblings and me. We have more than we need, and we do have family who loves us," Jane said. As her statement could be interpreted in multiple ways, she was pleased that they chose the one that best fit their preconceived notions.

"As *entertaining* as this had been, I must return home." Jane stood. Before she could express her thanks, she heard Mr. Bingley's voice. She sighed inwardly, for she had been hoping to miss this particular scene.

"That is not an option," Bingley reported. It was then that the women noticed the three men were dripping wet. "The bridge is flooded, and the water is flowing over the top. We left Darcy's carriage on the other side and braved the elements to arrive home, and are quite soaked, as you see."

"Mr. Darcy, you will catch your death. Allow me to accompany you upstairs so I may be of service to you." Miss Bingley jumped out of her seat, stopping short as the object of her avarice held up his hand.

"*That* will not be necessary, Miss Bingley; Carstens will be the *only* one to assist me." Darcy turned on his heel and stalked out of the room, stomping up the stairs in anger. He could not believe that the harpy would suggest such a thing, and in company! It was time to talk to Bingley again.

Reluctantly, Bingley was about to follow his brother-in-law upstairs to bathe and change into dry clothes. He wanted to be with his angel, but unfortunately, he was not fit for company. "If you would like to inform your family, a groom will ride over the fields to deliver a note," Bingley offered before he left.

Jane sat at the escritoire in the corner of the drawing room to write her missive then handed it to the butler, asking him to thank the groom who would brave the weather to deliver her message to Longbourn.

~~~~~~~/~~~~~~~

The five Bennets were in the family sitting room when Hill delivered the note from Netherfield. Bennet read it aloud for his wife and children.

Papa and Mama,

The bridge is flooded, I am stuck with these people for the night. If the bridge is not passable in the morning, please bring Mars for me to ride back. I do not want to spend time with Mr. Bingley for he will make the wrong assumption, though I worry that he already has.

I will be well tonight, but please rescue me on the morrow. I have much to tell you,

Jane

"May I lead Mars to Netherfield in the morning if the bridge us unpassable, Papa?" Elizabeth asked.

"You may, Lizzy, as long as you have a groom ride with you," Bennet allowed.

"Yes, Papa." As much as Elizbeth liked to have her independence, she honoured her father's wishes that none of them ever leave the house unaccompanied. The girl's companion, Mrs. Cecilia Ponsonby, was not happy on a horse, so it was usually a groom or a footman that rode with them if their father was engaged with estate business. The best was when both their father and mother accompanied them. Mrs. Bennet was an excellent horsewoman and had brought her beloved Neptune to Longbourn with her.

~~~~~~~/~~~~~~~

Once the three men had bathed and changed, they returned to the drawing room to join the women. If any of the men noticed the frosty silence, they did not comment on it. Upon entering, Bingley made a beeline for Miss Bennet. To his chagrin, she was not seated on a settee but in an armchair that was not near any other place to sit.

"You are welcome to stay as our guest as long as is needed, Miss Bennet," Bingley said as he bowed before his angel gallantly.

Darcy was observing their interaction and was surprised when Miss Bennet hardly reacted to Bingley's assertions. She did not fawn over him as Darcy would have expected, given their disparate financial positions.

"Thank you, Mr. Bingley, that is most generous of you. I believe, however, that I shall be returning home on the morrow," Jane replied evenly.

'If Miss Bingley were stranded at one of my homes, wild horses would not succeed in dragging her away!' Darcy's confusion deepened. He did not like the fact that the Bennets, and Miss Bennet especially, were not fitting into the roles he had assigned them in his mind. 'Ah, she is trying to increase Bingley's ardour by playing hard to get. I am sure that she is just another fortune hunter!' Darcy relaxed at finding an answer, if only to convince himself of the rectitude of his feelings towards the Bennets, most especially the enticing Miss Elizabeth.

Bingley would not be deterred. "Do you like to dance, Miss Bennet?" he asked.

"As do most, Mr. Bingley," Jane replied, hoping he was not planning an impromptu dance and about to ask for her to partner him here and now.

"In that case, we will have a ball," Bingley decided on the spur of the moment.

"Charles, you cannot be serious," Miss Bingley sounded horrified, and turned to Mr. Darcy, "You know how some of our party disdain dancing!"

"If you mean Darcy, he may remain in his chambers if he

does not want to dance," Bingley replied flippantly. "It shall be in a sennight," Bingley plucked a date out of the air with nary a care for all the work that would be needed to prepare for such an event in a short time.

"Mr. Bingley, there is no need to hold a ball because I said I like to dance," Jane hinted.

"That is not it," Bingley prevaricated, thinking that Miss Bennet was too modest to accept such an honour. "I-it is to introduce us to all of our neighbours in the area," Bingley found a reason that sounded almost plausible. "We will also invite the officers so that they too have a chance to become known to those of the neighbourhood."

"If only there was not so much dancing at a ball," lamented Miss Bingley. Jane had to put her hand over her mouth to stop herself from bursting into laughter at the patently ridiculous statement. Darcy saw her reaction, and his confusion deepened.

"It would not really be a ball then, would it Miss Bingley?" Jane asked as she stood. "Ladies and gentlemen, I wish you a goodnight and thank you once again for your *warm* hospitality. I am sure that my chambers will be *tolerable*." With that Jane swept out of the room before anyone could respond. She smiled to herself, shaking her head to the housekeeper who offered to guide her as she knew exactly where her bedchamber was. She was sure that as soon as she was gone the sisters would start to relay the intelligence that they thought that they had gleaned during the earlier part of the evening.

Jane's estimation was accurate. "The pretensions of that woman! She is the daughter of a country solicitor's daughter. That awful tradesman, Mr. Phillips, the one that thought he could threaten us, is one uncle, and there is another one, also a tradesman who lives in *Cheapside!*" Miss Bingley sneered.

"Do not forget, Caroline, that they will be without a home after their father passes, and also their pathetically small dowries," Mrs. Hurst added spitefully.

"Why would they lose their home after Mr. Bennet

dies?" Bingley asked in confusion.

"Did you not know that their pitiful little *farm* is entailed away from the female line and there are only three poor daughters?" Miss Bingley related triumphantly.

"You have been misinformed, Miss Bingley," Darcy spoke up.

"About what, Mr. Darcy?" Miss Bingley was aghast that her Mr. Darcy had told her the intelligence she had taken pains to gather was not correct.

"The estate. First, your brother and I have ridden along the fence line, and from what I can see, Longbourn is as large, possibly larger, than Netherfield. Secondly, we met Mark Bennet this morning, Mr. Bennet's *second* son. The older son is at Oxford. There is an heir and a spare, so why would you think that the Bennets will lose their estate, even if it is entailed away from the female line?" Darcy asked.

For a minute both Miss Bingley and Mrs. Hurst looked like perch pulled from the water and gasping for air. "Why would Jane Bennet mislead us so?" Miss Bingley was indignant at having been made to look the fool in front of Mr. Darcy.

"Did you ask the chit if she had brothers, or did you assume you knew all as you always do?" Hurst asked, surprising everyone as they all assumed he was asleep on the chaise.

"Well, I, for one, do not care if the angelic Miss Bennet has enough uncles to fill up all of Cheapside," Bingley stated as firmly as he was able.

"I think your sisters are inferring that their lack of connections will materially reduce the chance of any of the Miss Bennets making a good match," Darcy explained, almost to himself.

"Remind me again where the money for your and my wife's dowry came from, *sister*?" Hurst asked pointedly.

Miss Bingley and her sister chose to retire rather than respond. If nothing else, Mr. Darcy had received the message the Bennets were far below them. "How can you allow your husband to remind Mr. Darcy of our roots?" Miss Bingley hissed as she and her sister walked up the stairs.

"You know I do not control what he says and does, Caro. Do not worry; Mr. Darcy will not focus on that when you bring twenty thousand pounds with you," Mrs. Hurst said to placate her.

"It is time I give that man a nudge," Miss Bingley said as she swept into her suite.

~~~~~~~/~~~~~~~~

Darcy asked Bingley if they could talk in the study. Once the door was firmly closed, Bingley poured a snifter of brandy for both. "You needed to talk to me, Darce?" he asked.

"It is about your sister," Darcy informed his friend.

"Are you finally going to grant her heart's desire and offer for her?" Bingley ribbed. No matter how much he hated confrontation with his sister, he knew that was one thing his friend would *never* do.

"Hell would have to freeze over first!" Darcy retorted.

"I know that you have been most magnanimous in putting up with Caroline, and Louisa as well. I have not had the heart to tell Caroline that you will never offer for her," Bingley owned.

"Your heart is not the problem, Bingley; you just do not want to have to deal with the tantrum that will ensue." Bingley had the decency to look chagrined. "There is nothing I can do that will force you to take her in hand, my friend, but I will say this for the last time.

"I will not offer for her, even if she engineers a compromise. She will be compromised, but I will not rescue her from her own machinations. I am tired of her intimating she has an intimacy between myself and my family that does not exist. She claims to be my sister's *dear* friend, when in truth Georgiana cannot endure being in her company. She talks as if she is known by my aunt and uncle. The truth is they, and my cousin Andrew, the Viscount, refuse to be introduced to her. If you do not check her soon, and she keeps behaving in the vulgar fashion she does, as both of your sisters do, my family and

I will have no choice but to give them the cut direct." When Darcy completed what he wanted to say, there was silence.

Bingley was shocked to his core. He had always thought his friend had only been half serious with a mild aversion to his sisters, but this was far more. If his sisters received the cut direct from some of the leading members of the *Ton* they, and he along with them, would be ruined in society. He knew he needed to have an uncomfortable conversation with his brother-in-law, and then a most unpleasant one with his younger sister.

Bingley decided to procrastinate. "Darce, I will talk to her after the ball, I promise."

Darcy had his doubts, but he was not about to call his friend a liar. They soon wished one another a goodnight and made for their suites.

VOL 1, CHAPTER 6

When Georgiana Darcy arrived in the breakfast parlour at Matlock House, her aunt, Andrew, and Richard were all seated and enjoying that morning's fare. Seeing her niece's questioning look at the Earl's empty chair, the Countess explained, "Uncle Reggie had an early meeting with Lord Jersey this morning." Then she noticed the letter in her niece's hand. "Is that from William, Gigi?"

"Yes, it is, Aunt," Georgiana replied as she sat.

"What did that reprobate of a cousin of mine have to say?" Colonel Fitzwilliam teased.

"Richard, William is nothing of the kind," his ward replied indignantly. "He is having a good time with Mr. Bingley, except for *those* sisters. There is something that I do not quite understand, though."

"What is that Gigi?" Andrew asked, truly intrigued as there is little their Gigi did not understand.

"He had mentioned the same lady three times over the last two letters that I have received from him. William never mentions any particular lady but once in effort to share his day, except when he complains about Miss You-Know-Who!" Georgiana frowned as she scanned a sheet to make sure she had stated her concerns accurately.

"And what is the name of this mystery lady that seems to have caught your brother's attention?" the Countess enquired.

"A Miss Elizabeth Bennet," came the answer. Georgiana thought she had said the wrong thing when all three of her relatives froze, Andrew with a loaded fork halfway between his plate and his waiting mouth.

"Could it be?" the Countess asked.

"Of what are we talking?" a thoroughly confused Georgiana asked.

"The lady that Andrew met is a Miss Jane Bennet," the Countess informed her niece.

"I wonder if they are related," Andrew asked no one in particular.

"Would you like me to ask William if his Miss Bennet has a sister Jane?" Georgiana volunteered.

"No Gigi, please refrain. I do not know if the lady has any interest in me, and I would rather not have mine broadcast to anyone else yet, even if my younger cousin is normally the soul of discretion," Andrew averred.

"Would that not be a coincidence if she is the same Jane Bennet as Edward Gardiner's niece?" the Colonel opined.

"Andrew, dear, I almost forgot. I was at a committee meeting with Mrs. Gardiner. She let it slip that her niece Jane will be in residence from early December until they all leave to spend Christmas together with some of their family, so mayhap you may gain answers to a few of your questions at last," his mother smiled as she gave him the news she knew he longed for.

As suspected, the information brightened Lord Andrew Fitzwilliam immediately; the object of his attention would be at Portman Square in but a fortnight! "If it is the same family, let us hope that William is not being his normal self," Andrew stated.

"My brother is always a gentleman," Georgiana defended. Not wanting to disillusion their Gigi, none of the three Fitzwilliams responded, and the subject was deftly changed by the Countess.

~~~~~~~/~~~~~~~

Thankfully, the rain ceased during the night; but unfortunately, the bridge that led to Netherfield remained uncrossable by a vehicle. After breaking her fast, Elizabeth changed into a hunter green riding habit and made for the stables where a groom was holding Mercury and Mars, as well as his own mount, all of them already saddled.

Elizabeth gave her horse a carrot and a piece of apple, and Mercury rubbed his muzzle against his owner's shoulder in appreciation. After rubbing his neck, Elizabeth led her stallion to the mounting block. Once she was seated, she nodded to the groom, who followed her into the field that led to Netherfield Park.

Once in the field, Elizabeth allowed Mercury to run, and oh how her horse could run! Darcy himself was enjoying his morning ride when he saw the black and white horse flying across the field toward the boundary fence. About a hundred yards behind her, he spied a groom leading another fine horse. The rider of the first horse was a lady, and it took some seconds to identify her—but it was Miss Elizabeth! 'How do the Bennets keep so many fine horses?' Darcy ruminated angrily. 'Resisting my feelings for Miss Elizabeth is becoming harder, but I must remind myself of the unacceptable connections the Bennets have.' He again forgot, most conveniently, that a significant portion of his wealth was invested with Mr. Edward Gardiner, and the same tradesman he disdained in the Bennets' connections was helping pay for his lifestyle. He also seemed to have forgotten that Bingley's roots also were in trade.

Unlike her father and brother, Miss Elizabeth did not jump over the fence, but waited at a gate until the groom arrived and opened it. Once the groom had remounted, they headed towards the manor house.

"Good morning, Miss Elizabeth," Darcy lifted his top hat as she drew near him.

"Mr. Darcy," Elizabeth inclined her head, saying as little as she could and still remain polite to the rude, proud, and arrogant man.

"I assume you have brought that horse," he pointed at Mars, "for Miss Bennet as the drive is not open yet."

"You are correct, sir. Very astute," she replied. While she

inwardly chastised herself for being so sarcastic, Darcy's mind was whirling with the excitement of her being so playful with him. For the rest of the short ride to the manor house, Elizabeth pushed Mercury ahead and did not look toward the insufferable man again.

At the stables, one groom held Darcy's black stallion as he dismounted while another brought a mounting block to Miss Elizabeth's side. "Thank you, Greg," Darcy heard her say.

'That is most singular; how does she know a servant's name here at this estate? Of course, her father keeps an eye on the estate, or mayhap he used to be employed at their estate,' Darcy rationalised to himself. "May I show you to the breakfast parlour, Miss Elizabeth? I believe your sister is breaking her fast," Darcy asked aloud.

Elizabeth very nearly told the man, who she very much disdained, that she knew the way, cutting herself off just in time. "Yes, please do, Mr. Darcy." She replied politely. As she looked down, Elizabeth noticed that she had a little mud on her hem from her gallop across the fields. It did not bother her; she accepted it as a consequence of the pleasure she had indulged in without care, as she would be returning home soon. She turned to the Longbourn groom and asked, "Jack, do you have the valise with my sister's clothing?"

"'Ere, Miss Lizzy," the groom said, handing a valise to the young miss.

When the two entered the breakfast parlour, Bingley and Hurst stood and bowed, while the supercilious sisters scowled. Miss Bingley got a decidedly pinched look on her face when she saw Miss Elizabeth walk in with Mr. Darcy. Darcy stood slightly closer to Miss Elizabeth in hopes Caroline would get his message.

"Miss Eliza, how did you get here when the bridge is still not ready for use?" Miss Bingley asked, ignoring the expectation that as her brother's hostess it was her task to welcome a guest. "I see from your muddy hems that you must have gone tramping in the mud to get here."

SHANA GRANDERSON A LADY

"Actually, Miss Bingley, Miss Elizabeth rode here and has Miss Bennet's horse for her to return home," Darcy interjected before Elizabeth could respond. Rather than appreciate his help, Elizabeth found his answering a question put to her patronising.

"Jane, are you ready to change?" Elizabeth asked, ignoring Miss Bingley and Darcy as they obviously needed no input from her.

"I am, Lizzy. Will you accompany me?" Jane responded as she stood and pushed her chair back, relieved that she could soon leave.

"Are you sure you both need to leave so early?" Bingley's voice was filled with obvious disappointment.

"Our mother requires us at home, Mr. Bingley," Jane replied, and before the man could object again, the sisters made their way up to Jane's bedchamber. Not a quarter hour later the Bennet sisters returned to the breakfast parlour.

"I thank you all for the hospitality that I was shown," Jane addressed the room and Elizabeth covered her mouth to hide her smile. The others may have been ignorant, but Elizabeth easily detected the sarcasm in her sister's tone. The two sisters curtsied and left before any of the seated party could respond.

"How uncouth, to come calling at such an hour!" Miss Bingley started. "I assume you would not allow dear Georgiana to go riding across the countryside unaccompanied. It shows an unseemly independence. I would dare say you do not find her eyes so fine any longer, do you Mr. Darcy?" Miss Bingley tittered at her own perceived wit.

"You are correct, Miss Bingley. I would not allow my sister, *Miss Darcy*, to ride unaccompanied," he allowed, intending to continue to explain the truth of the matter, but before he could continue the shrew cut him off.

"You see, Louisa, Mr. Darcy would never allow dear Georgiana..." Darcy returned the favour and cut Miss Bingley off.

"As your brother seems to have omitted telling you, I will do so now." Bingley lost the colour in his face, thinking his friend was going to repeat all he had said in the study the previous night. "Neither my sister nor I have given you leave to address her so familiarly. She is *Miss Darcy* to you; do you understand, Miss Bingley?" Her mouth gaped open, as she realized her actions had angered the last person in the world she would wish angered. Miss Bingley nodded.

"Now, if you had given me leave to finish what I was about to say, then you would have heard that Miss Elizabeth was *not* unaccompanied. There is a groom with her. As she is not here for a visit, but to assist her sister, she has not broken any rules of propriety. As to her eyes, they shined particularly prettily after her exercise. Excuse me, Bingley. I have business to attend."

Darcy stood and bowed to the room and left Miss Bingley still frozen in place after his set down. '*Damn that harridan for making me defend Miss Elizabeth in front of all of them, and myself for my unguarded words at Lucas Lodge!*'

~~~~~~~/~~~~~~~

Mr. William Collins was determined to fulfil his all-knowing, wise patroness' charge. He could still hear her wise words as he packed for his trip to Longbourn, which would commence on the morrow.

"*Go forth to Hertfordshire, Mr. Collins; marry one of your unfortunate cousins, bring her back to Hunsford, and I will wait on her. Make sure she is modest and demure for I will not countenance impertinence. You need to set the example of matrimony to my, I mean, your parishioners. Do not return in the single state. If not married, you must at least return betrothed.*

"*Once you are married, I will advise your bride and make sure she knows how to fulfil her duties.*"

Collins could not believe that all-mighty Lady Catherine de Bourg would condescend to teach his wife how to run her house. Per her Ladyship's suggestion, he had already placed shelves into the closets. While he was praising her brilliance,

Collins entirely forgot that he then had nowhere to hang his clothing, which explained why his patroness had complained his clothing was always creased.

A hired gig would collect him at sunup, and he would make sure to arrive at the time he had said he would, even if it meant waiting out of sight of the house until he was sure he would attend his cousins at the stated time, for his patroness did not like it when one was not punctual.

~~~~~~~/~~~~~~~

George Wickham had had enough of Mrs. Younge and of not being able to enjoy his preferred pastimes, so he took the post coach one day early. It was just before midday when he arrived in the little market town of Meryton. Seeing a myriad of scarlet coats, he knew he was in the correct place.

"Wickham!" Denny called as he saw his acquaintance step off the post coach, "You are a day early. Well, never mind. Come on old chap, let us make for the camp and get you in uniform." Denny clapped his friend on the back.

As they walked, Wickham noted that the town was like many others where he had been able to attain credit easily and to leave those debts behind him. He also saw a fair number of young girls walking around. He preferred younger girls as they were far easier to manipulate and would fall for his charms almost before they even realised he was using them. His anger at Darcy grew when he saw the girls' looks when they noticed his nose and missing tooth. He would have to come up with a good story to explain his injuries, one that would paint him as the hero, of course.

Denny led Wickham to the Colonel's hut. "One of our new recruits arrived a day early, sir," Denny saluted smartly. "Wickham, this is our commander, Colonel Forster. Colonel, Mr. George Wickham of Derbyshire."

"What makes you want to join the militia, Mr. Wickham?" the Colonel perfunctorily asked as he glanced up at the man.

"It is a good and honest profession and allows me to

serve this great country that we live in," Wickham lied.

"How did you come by your injuries?" the Colonel wanted to know.

"I came upon a young maiden beset by two brigands. I fought them off her; my injuries are insignificant to theirs, Colonel. It was worth it to preserve the virtue of a young girl." Wickham was impressed that he had come up with such a story on the spur of the moment. It was far better than the truth, which was the opposite.

"What rank are you purchasing, Mr. Wickham?" the Colonel got down to business. His gut was telling him something about the man did not ring true; he would bear watching. No man who would help another in that manner would be wanting only now to join a militia, if he truly had wanted to serve. Many a young man had run away from problems by joining the militia, and they, all of them, were watched until he was certain they had good intentions.

"I owe Wickham some money from a debt of honour, Sir, so I am funding his purchase of an ensign's rank as repayment," Denny said.

It did not sit well with the Colonel that the man could not afford his own commission, and even though he doubted Denny's version of why he was paying, he was not going to call the Lieutenant a liar without being sure.

He had been sorely tempted to tell his tale of how Darcy had cheated him out of the living at Kympton. Before he did, however, Wickham heard the threats echoing in his head and regulated himself. He was well pleased with the story Denny had just told the Colonel. He could use that it was a lie as it gave him some leverage if he needed the odd *loan* here and there from the man. As he did with all of his 'friends,' Wickham was already thinking about how best to use Denny for his advantage. In the end, Denny would be just another burned bridge.

~~~~~~~/~~~~~~~

Jane and Elizabeth first changed before joining the family in the drawing room. "I have *never* been so happy to be home," Jane exclaimed as she gave her mother a hug.

"How bad was it, Jane?" Mrs Bennet asked.

"Mama, those two *ladies* are far worse than even Papa's report said," Jane reported. "You know I do not like to cast such aspersions, but they are horrible! Let me tell you..." Jane reported all from the time that she arrived until the men returned home dripping wet.

"I am so sorry you had to endure their presence; we will certainly not be issuing any invitations to the Netherfield party," Mrs. Bennet said as she hugged her daughter.

"Bingley insisted on returning last night even though I told him they would not be able to get past the bridge with the carriage. I suggested the Red Lion, but the puppy would hear none of it. Why do you suppose he was so keen to return to Netherfield, Jane?" Bennet asked sardonically.

"Do not tease me, Papa; that man did not get the message! I thank my lucky stars I will be with Aunt Maddie and Uncle Edward in a fortnight. Do you know he is throwing a ball next week, believing that will somehow flatter me? Why could he not be like the man that I met at the Gardiners' a few times?" Jane asked wistfully. In the silence that followed her statement, Jane realised that she had just shared information that she had held close to her chest, for she was not sure when, or even if, she would see Lord Andrew Fitzwilliam again. Also, she was not sure he would attach himself to one as low as people believed the Bennets to be.

"Jane, do you have something else to share?" Elizabeth asked with arched eyebrow.

"No, Lizzy, I do not!" Jane gave her sister the look, the very one all who knew her understood—she would not say more on the subject. "What will I do if he asks me for one of the important sets?" Jane frowned. "I do not want him to think that I have any interest in him. From what I have seen and heard, he is enamoured with my looks and knows nothing of who I truly am."

"We will go see Charlotte this afternoon, and then we

can visit the Gouldings," Elizabeth suggested. "Frederick and John will help with two of the three sets, and Julian the other. That way when he asks, you will not have to refuse him, but he will have to be satisfied with one of the other sets."

"That is a good solution, Lizzy. You three will join me, and Mark may too if he has completed his lessons. I owe Lady Lucas and Mrs. Goulding a visit each," Mrs. Bennet winked at her daughters. All three girls smiled back at their mother. Jane relaxed now that she had a solution to the Bingley problem. Her mother and sisters wondered who it was Jane had almost mentioned.

Later that afternoon, Mrs. Bennet, her three daughters, and her youngest son made the two calls. By the time they left the Gouldings, all three Bennet daughters had the three important sets covered.

~~~~~~~/~~~~~~~

"Charles! Are you bound and determined to hold a ball for a bunch of country mushrooms?" Miss Bingley whined.

"I am. It will be on Friday, the three and twentieth day of this month. Just think, Caroline, you will be able to display all of your formidable hosting skills." Bingley knew he was implying that his sister could impress his friend, but what was the harm if it spurred her to action.

"You know what, Charles; you have a good point. Yes, it will be a good thing to highlight my skills as a hostess. It will be a true ball, one worthy of the *Ton!*" Miss Bingley left with a spring in her step. She, who was expert at manipulating her brother, was unaware that he was manipulating *her*. It was not long before Miss Bingley was ensconced with her sister planning an extravaganza, and truly pleased as her brother had given her *carte blanche* and a large budget.

~~~~~~~/~~~~~~~

Lord Andrew Fitzwilliam jumped at the chance when his father asked him to convey some documents to Mr. Edward Gardiner at the Gardiners' townhouse. The Viscount was shown into the study where Mr. Gardiner was examining a ledger. "Welcome, Lord Hilldale, though I admit I was expecting the Earl." Gardiner indicated a chair for his guest.

"My father asked me to bring these to you," the Viscount said as he handed the papers to Mr. Gardiner.

"You need not have bothered, my Lord, a messenger would have been able to bring these to me," Gardiner stated.

"I must admit that I have an ulterior motive, Mr. Gardiner." The Viscount chuckled at his thin excuse being called out, for Gardiner was a businessman of rare acumen.

"Does it have anything to do with a certain niece of mine?" Gardiner asked bluntly.

"It does, sir. My cousin Darcy is visiting his friend who is leasing an estate—Netherfield Park—in Hertfordshire." Hilldale nodded once at Gardiner's obvious familiarity with the name.

"I know it as my family grew up in the area," Gardiner answered evenly.

"He has written to his sister of a Miss Elizabeth Bennet. I was wondering if she is your niece as well, and perhaps sister to the Miss Bennet I have met on occasion at your house," the Viscount asked hopefully.

"Yes, that is indeed correct. May I ask you a direct question, my Lord?" Gardiner probed, and the younger man nodded. "What are your intentions towards my niece?"

"They are completely honourable! I am intrigued by her. Yes, she is beautiful on the outside, but she had an inner beauty and strength of character that shines through. And I know that she is very charitable with all the hours she gives to my mother's committee at Haven House when she is in Town. My aim is hopefully to get to know her and see if we have something to build on, if there could possibly be mutual affection." Andrew would not normally have been so open with a man who was not more than a business associate, but he felt he had to be as there was no mistaking the true familial ties and affections. It was almost as if he was being interviewed by the father of the young lady.

"I can tell you that her dowry is reported to be a mere two thousand five hundred pounds and she is reported to have no notable connections, besides me, for her other uncle on her mother's side is the local solicitor in Meryton, the town near the estate. The estate is entailed and said to bring in around two thousand a year." Gardiner watched carefully as he laid out as many negatives as he could, impressed when the Viscount never flinched or showed any distaste regarding said information.

"She is a gentleman's daughter, is she not?" Hilldale asked and Gardiner allowed that it was so. "I have no need for a large dowry; I have more money than I know what to do with and that is not taking into consideration that one day, far in the future I hope, I will be the next Earl of Matlock. As to connections, I have more than enough. None of that is truly important, for the mutual connection between a husband and wife is a gift too few recognise. Unlike the women here in Town, she has never fawned over me or treated me like a god among men. She was not intimidated by me when we met; in fact, she challenged my point of view and we had more than one discussion which proved she was my equal or better, all of which were characteristics that attracted me to her." Gardiner had no doubt that in his recounting of Jane's attributes the Viscount was completely sincere.

"In that case, Lord Hilldale, my niece Jane will be arriving here in late November or early December and will be staying with us until we all go visit family for Christmas," Gardiner revealed.

"That means that I will have some weeks before we are to Essex for Christmastide," the Viscount replied, wondering how soon he could be in her company.

"Essex?" Gardiner questioned. He knew that the Fitzwilliams normally spent that time of the year at the primary Matlock estate, Snowhaven, in Derbyshire.

"Yes, my mother accepted an invitation to Broadhurst, the De Melville's estate." Mr. Gardiner had a look like he was about to break out in laughter, but he schooled his features.

"Yes, my Lord, I know of Broadhurst in Essex," Gardiner responded, amazed at the coincidence. It seemed the Viscount would be spending more than just a few weeks with his niece but was not aware of the fact—yet.

VOL 1, CHAPTER 7

M r. William Collins arrived promptly at four in the afternoon on the day that he had said he would, which happened to be a Sunday. He was a corpulent man, to put it gently, of medium height. From his odour, he obviously did not consider personal hygiene a priority.

Trying hard to keep a straight face, Bennet stated, "Welcome Mr. Collins. I am surprised that as a member of the clergy you travel on the Sabbath." He had not noted anything about the day in his return letter to the now spluttering man to see if he would realise his error on his own; it was apparent he had not.

"A-as I am a clergyman and my patroness gave me leave to travel, I have done nothing wrong," Collins blustered.

"Besides travelling on the Sabbath," observed Esther, who was the most pious member of the family.

"Young girls should be silent until their betters address them," Collins glared in an attempt to be intimidating, but only looked all the more ridiculous.

"Mr. Collins!" Bennet fired out angrily. "How dare you address one of my daughters so? If you ever show *any* disrespect to a member of my family or household while you are a guest under my roof, you will be thrown out and *never* be permitted to return. *Do I make myself clear!*"

"Y-yes, C-c-cousin," the now frightened and profusely sweating man replied.

"In that case, this is my family, all except my son and *heir* Tom who is at Oxford. Mrs. Bennet, Miss Jane Bennet, Miss Elizabeth, Miss Esther, and Master Mark," Bennet made the introductions curtly. "I suggest that you retire to your chambers and enjoy the bath that will be ready for you. When you have changed, have someone direct you to my study."

With some of the lowest bows any of the Bennets had ever beheld, the sweating man followed Hill inside, much to relief of the Bennets' noses. "Thomas, that is most definitely the most ridiculous man I have ever had the misfortune to meet," Mrs. Bennet verbalised what they were all thinking.

"Mama, was that stink emanating from our cousin?" Mark asked, pulling a face.

"It was, my son, but it is not polite to mention such to him," his amused mother responded.

"Well, it is not polite to assault our noses in that fashion," Elizabeth pointed out and no one argued with her.

As Collins followed the butler to his chambers, he could not comprehend the inside of the house that he was seeing. To Collins, the front of the manor house looked much smaller than Rosings Park, quite insignificant, but that was not the case on the inside. He could not reconcile what he was seeing with the façade that he had noted on his arrival.

'I have to marry the oldest so all of this will be mine,' he told himself. 'I do not care what any piece of paper says, a Collins will be master here!'

After climbing up three flights, he was shown to a large bedchamber, more than double the size of his in the parsonage at Hunsford. "Is this the family wing?" Collins asked, hoping that he would be close to the three prettiest young ladies he had ever beheld, most specifically the oldest.

"No, Mr. Collins, this is a guest floor," Mr. Hill replied evenly. "Is there anything else before I leave you?"

"I am family, I demand to be moved to the family wing!" Collins blustered, most put out.

"After your bath, you are free to take that up with the master when you meet with him." Hill bowed and left before the indignant parson could utter another word.

~~~~~~~/~~~~~~~

"It is so good to be on the way back to our estate my love," Lady Rose told her husband as the two sat in the most well-sprung and comfortable of the Bedford coaches.

The Duke had managed to complete his review of his holdings in Liverpool the previous day and had agreed to leave at dawn. He was happy to be on his way to Longfield Meadows. The Duke loved his home estate and took pleasure in its management. He had not owned such to his wife, but he was experiencing more tiredness and shortness of breath. He knew if he informed her, she would want to nurse him, but he wanted what he suspected would be his final Christmastide at the estate to be a happy one.

"You know Rose, I have been thinking much on the third Duke and how terrible he was. Could you imagine us, or any other we know, sowing discord and division among his own sons as the fourth Duke related in his letter?" the Duke asked.

"It is hard to conceive of one such as he," the Duchess responded thoughtfully. "It just shows that there is justice in the world, Sed, even if we are not here to see it."

"What do you mean, love?"

"After all of that man's efforts, it is his pride which will defy his intentions. With all the conflict he caused within his own family, if he were alive today, he would see the direct descendant of the son he cast out assume the title knowing it is the Bennet line that will be the saviour of the Dukedom in the end. I am certain his heart would explode," the Duchess explained.

"How did his pride save the Dukedom?" He asked, chuckling as the question spawned the answer. "Oh, he did not formally disown Thomas, which makes his line eligible to inherit the Bedford title and all that goes with it! You are correct, love; his improper pride did have one positive result."

"Did you say that you will not insist Thomas Bennet change his name to be the eighth Sedgwick Rhys-Davies?" the Duchess confirmed.

"That is correct, Rose. I will instead insist that he keep his name as it is. You talk of justice across the years; I can think of no more righteous thing than for the original Tom Bennet's name to be the one that carries the Dukedom forward!" the Duke stated with no equivocation, his grin proving his pleasure of defying his ancestor and redressing the unnecessary cruelty.

"I do not know how I will carry on without you, Sed," the Duchess allowed her fear of losing the love of her life to come to the fore, and tears began to run down her face. They, like all of the Dukes before her husband, had an arranged match. Unlike many of the others, the two had fallen in love over the years, and except for the inability to bring a live child into the world, they were the happiest and most loving of couples.

"Please promise me something, Rose." The Duke wiped the tears away and then took his wife's hands in his, gazing lovingly into her eyes.

"If it is within my ability to do so, you know I would do anything that you ask of me," the maudlin Duchess replied.

"Do not sit and pine for me after I am gone." The Duke placed his finger on his wife's lips when he saw she was about to interject. "From birth, I have been prepared to take over the House of Bedford. I was trained and prepared for any eventuality as a duke. Thomas Bennet will only learn of this on the day that we meet with him. We have no idea who his wife is and if she will be able to take on the weight of the duties required of a duchess. The *only* thing that will give them a chance to succeed is if you, my dearest wife who I love more than anyone, are there to assist and guide them."

The Duchess was silent for some minutes as she cogitated over what her husband was asking of her and soon realised that there was no choice. She would accept her husband's charge and carry on without him the best she could, all the while trying to make sure the new Duke and Duchess were successful, for it was possible they had no connections of note.

Rather than giving up, Lady Rose would have a purpose and a whole set of tasks many would consider overwhelming.

"You have my most solemn promise that I will help them as much and for as long as they desire it, Sed," the Duchess agreed. Her husband relaxed, feeling as if a great weight had been lifted from his shoulders. He regretted not opening the letter years before, but there was nothing he could do to change the past.

<center>~~~~~~~/~~~~~~~</center>

Collins knocked on the study door. His determination to secure the delectable Miss Bennet had only increased on his way down to the study as he saw more of the house, for even he could see that the Bennets were obviously far wealthier than was reported.

Once he was seated, Bennet did not wait for any pleasantries. "From your letter, did I understand that your *olive branch* will be to marry one of my daughters?" Bennet asked pointedly.

As he so often did, Collins completely missed the tone his cousin was using and expected that his task to secure his bride would be much easier now, as everyone was of the same mind. "Once I marry Miss Bennet, when the sad time comes that you leave to your eternal reward, I will be the next master of the estate and will even allow your wife and unmarried daughters to remain here, as long as they are willing to take on some of the chores, of course," Collins offered munificently, oblivious to the growing anger in his cousin opposite him.

"Are you completely insensible? Mayhap your brain is addled. You will *never* be granted the hand of *any* of my daughters!" Bennet angrily held up a hand to silence before the indignant man could protest. "If you think that even with a compromise, I will give you one of my daughters, then you are more stupid that even I believed you to be. Any attempt at such will result in my calling you out! I warn you now, I am a champion with both the sword and the pistol, and no matter how small of a target is it, I will not miss your heart!"

Collins was quaking with fear. Even with his selective hearing, he could not misconstrue what his cousin was telling him. "B-b-but I-I a-am a-a cl-cl-clergyman with the p-patronage of the g-great and w-wise L-Lady C-C-Catherine d-de B-B-Bourgh," the petrified parson managed to squeak out.

"Before I address that nonsense, did you or did you not meet my son Mark when you arrived?" Bennet demanded and Collins nodded weakly. "Did you hear me say that my *heir* was away at university?" Bennet waited and received another weak nod. "Then how in that tiny brain of yours would you think that even if I were to fail in my duty as her father and allow my Jane to marry you, that you would ever be master here?" Bennet thundered.

"B-because L-Lady C-Catherine said it w-w-would be s-so," Collins replied, regaining some measure of assurance as she had told him it would be so.

"You revere your patroness?" Bennet interrogated Collins further and received the expected nod, this one emphatic. "It seems you revere her more than you do God as you travelled on the Sabbath. Do you know that your *wise* patroness is considered a joke among polite society? She was never educated but thinks she is all wise and all knowing, when in fact she is an officious busybody who is more ignorant than you are!" Collins looked scandalised on behalf of his patroness, but wisely held his tongue. "These are the terms of your completing your stay here, Mr. Collins. You will not approach my daughters nor are you to attempt to engage them in conversation unless they first approach you. Under no circumstances will you try and offer for or compromise any of them. You already know what will happen if you do," Bennet pointed to the foils that were in the corner of his study to make his point. "You *will* bathe every day while you are here, and lastly, you will not mention your patroness. If you cannot abide by these rules, I will be happy to have your trunk and you moved to the Red Lion Inn in Meryton. Will you follow my rules?"

"Yes, Cousin Bennet. I will not break any of your rules."

Was Collins' sullen answer.

"As far as your being a clergyman, you know your rank is just above a tradesman, do you not?" Bennet asked, and almost grinned when he saw the look of horror Collins sported. "Did they not teach you at the seminary that a clergyman is meant to serve his parishioners, not the other way around? You were taught, were you not, that God is the ultimate authority, and not some puffed up self-important lady?"

"If it is all the same to you, I will take a tray in my chambers this evening. I have a lot on which to think," Collins stood and exited the study, his world spinning about his head.

~~~~~~~/~~~~~~~

The next day, Wickham strutted down the main street thinking about how well he looked in his scarlet coat. He entered the tailor's store knowing that he needed some new clothing for when he would need to escape angry fathers and creditors, as it inevitably *would* be required.

The tailor, Mr. Gibbs, was happy to measure the officer. Once all of the decisions had been made and styles selected, the order was very substantial given the number of items included. "That will be forty-three pounds sixpence please, Mr. Wickham," the tailor asked politely.

"Put it on my account," Wickham stated with his usual bravado.

"You do not have an account here, Sir."

"Open one for me, then it will not be an issue!" Wickham attempted to gain what he desired using the same commanding tone he believed all men of wealth used.

"Not knowing your experience in other locales, I will inform you, Mr. Wickham, that no merchant offers accounts in Meryton unless the person is a long-time resident of the area with a solid history of financial stability. We know of far too many fellow merchants who have lost their livelihood over unpaid debts," Gibbs informed the man.

"In that case, I will take my custom elsewhere!" Wickham stormed out of the store in a petulant huff.

After a further two hours, Wickham was truly frustrated. Not one of the merchants would open an account for him, all telling him a version of the reason the tailor had stated when he had been denied. How would he live in this town where he would have to pay for everything with blunt? What if merchants in other towns started to do the same thing? It would make his life infinitely harder. *'This is all that prig Darcy's fault! If he had given me my due, I would not have to beg like a pauper!'* Wickham told himself.

He ignored inconvenient truths like how he had wasted four thousand pounds, did nothing with his university education, and neither took orders nor read the law. He had it in his power to change his stars, but that was too much effort for him. He was determined to make his fortune without working for it.

~~~~~~~/~~~~~~~

"Darcy, will you ride with me to Longbourn? I am to deliver the invitation to the ball in person," Bingley beseeched his friend.

Darcy's mind was split. On the one hand, he would see Miss Elizabeth, and he was interested in seeing the Bennet's house as he had picked up on some contradictory signals regarding their wealth. The problem was raising expectations. Even were they a little wealthier than he thought, they still had no connections of note.

Just then Miss Bingley piped up and decided the issue for Darcy. "Do not make poor Mr. Darcy visit such nobodies at their hovel. Louisa and I are here, we will be *happy* to entertain our friend."

"Wait, Bingley, I will ride with you. Allow me to go and change, and I will meet you at the stables in half an hour," Darcy told his friend as he stood and left the drawing room before the shrew had a chance to react.

Miss Bingley's eyes narrowed as she watched him leave, most unhappy that her Mr. Darcy would be in the company of that chit Eliza Bennet once more.

~~~~~~~/~~~~~~~

Charlotte Lucas arrived at Longbourn at the agreed upon time to meet her friends before they walked into Meryton. When she entered the drawing room, there was a man dressed in all dark clothing present with whom she was not acquainted.

"Welcome, Charlotte. This is our cousin Mr. Collins of Hunsford in Kent. Mr. Collins, Miss Charlotte Lucas of Lucas Lodge, our closest neighbour," Mrs. Bennet made the introduction.

"I am pleased to meet you, Miss Lucas," Collins stood and bowed low. As he appraised her, Collins noted that she was not a beauty like his off-limit cousins, but she did seem like a modest lady—one of his patroness's criteria for his wife.

"And you, Mr. Collins," Charlotte responded with a curtsy.

"We are off to Meryton with Charlotte, Mama," Jane reminded her mother. "Mark will be with us as he has completed his lessons." Seeing the forlorn look on their cousin's face, who assumed that he would be excluded, Jane took a modicum of pity on him. "We will have a footman with us as an escort, but if you would like, you are welcome to walk into the Town as well, Mr. Collins."

"I thank you, Miss Bennet, I would enjoy that," Collins gave his cousin one of his low bows.

Once everyone had their outerwear, Jane and Elizabeth took the lead followed by Esther and Mark. The footman was between the former pair and Charlotte and Mr. Collins at the rear.

"Jane! Why did you invite that foolish man along?" Elizabeth whispered.

"I took pity on him, Lizzy. You have naught to concern yourself with. He knows Papa's rules, and besides, now we are an even number of walkers!" Jane rationalised. Elizabeth huffed but made no further comment.

"My friend mentioned that you were granted a living

soon after taking orders, Mr. Collins. It is a credit to you as most new clergymen start out in a curacy," Charlotte noted as they walked side by side.

"It was good fortune, Miss Lucas. By happenstance, my patroness, the wise and beneficent Lady Catherine de Bourgh, asked the bishop at my seminary to send her some candidates who had taken orders, and I was the one that the great lady selected." Collins looked to make sure that his cousins were out of earshot, for he did not want his cousin to make good on his threat and evict him from Longbourn.

Knowing the Bennets as well as she did, Charlotte Lucas knew all about Lady Catherine de Bourgh. However, following her own philosophy on marriage, she was willing to put up with much to secure a husband and a home of her own. Her bigger fear by far was that she was rapidly becoming a burden to her family.

"It sounds like you have a truly excellent situation there, Mr. Collins. I am sure that Mrs. Collins is proud to be your wife," Charlotte prodded.

"There is no Mrs. Collins, to my chagrin. I am in a bind. My patroness instructed me to return a betrothed man, if not actually married, and my cousins are not available to me. I am adrift as I do not desire to lose my patroness's condescension by disobeying her. She does not like to have her orders countermanded, not at all." The man looked genuinely distressed.

Charlotte decided that it was time to take the horse, lead him to the water, and make sure that he drank. "There is a solution before you, Mr. Collins. I am looking to marry a respectable man who has a home for me to keep, and you need to be betrothed when you return to your patroness. I have never been romantic like your cousins, so I propose a situation that will solve both of our dilemmas." Charlotte surprised herself at her forwardness, but she made the calculation that at her age and with no prospects, it was what she had to do.

"You are agreeing to marry me, Miss Lucas?" Collins asked. He was so surprised that a solution his problem with his patroness had fallen into his lap in such a fashion that he missed that he never actually proposed to the lady.

"May I ask how old you are, Mr. Collins?"

"I am five and twenty, and yourself, Miss Lucas?"

"Add one to your age. I must inform you that my dowry is small, only five hundred pounds." Charlotte did not want to hide her situation from her betrothed. *Her betrothed*! Hardly knowing him at all, Charlotte recognised the deficiencies in the man she had agreed to marry, but she felt that she would, in time, soften the edges on the man. Also she calculated that she would be able to direct him. "When would you like to marry, Mr. Collins?"

"In December before the Christmas season," Collins stated.

"Would you be willing to wait util after Twelfth Night? I have accepted an invitation to go to a friend's family for the holiday and I am loath to renege after our hosts are expecting me." Charlotte was vague without telling a lie, but she would give up her holiday if the man stood firm.

"As I will return betrothed, that is not a problem. Should we go see your father now, Miss Lucas?" Collins wanted to make it official before the lady changed her mind.

"We will walk to Lucas Lodge on our return. Also remember, Sir, that I am of age and do not need my father's consent or blessing, although I would prefer to receive both," Charlotte stated reassuringly.

"Then it will be as you say, Miss Lucas," Collins acquiesced as he offered his betrothed his arm. Charlotte rested her hand on his arm lightly as they walked on, both happy with the resolution.

~~~~~~~/~~~~~~~

After his disappointment trying to establish credit, Wickham was walking down Meryton's main street with Denny when he spied a group of women, a man, a boy, and a footman trailing behind them. Three of the young ladies were among the most beautiful he had ever seen. There were a tall

105

blonde and two shorter ladies, one with chestnut curls and the other one in with sandy blond hair.

"Denny, who are those ladies?" Wickham asked, pointing at the group across the way.

"The three pretty ones are the Misses Bennet, and the plain one is Miss Lucas. Would you like to meet them? I was introduced to them one night at the Lucas estate," Denny offered.

The two officers crossed the street and bowed to the party. "Good morning, Mr. Denny," Jane spoke for the group.

"May I introduce a new officer to the unit, Ensign Wickham?" Denny requested. Miss Bennet inclined her head. "Miss Bennet, Miss Lucas, Miss Elizabeth, Miss Esther, Master Bennet, this is Mr. George Wickham of Derbyshire. Wickham, the Bennets and Miss Lucas. I apologise sir, but I am not acquainted with you." Denny told Collins.

Before anyone could perform the office, Mr. Collins did so himself. "Well met, Mr. Denny and Mr. Wickham, William Collins at your service." As was his wont, Collins made one of his exaggerated bows. As the group was talking, Mr. Bingley and Mr. Darcy rode towards the Bennet sisters and their party.

Darcy did not miss how pretty Miss Elizabeth looked as she and her party spoke to two officers who had their backs to him. By the time Darcy was level with the group, Bingley had vaulted off his horse and was making a beeline for Miss Bennet, but she did not seem happy to see him. Darcy started to question why a poor country miss did not show any affection for his friend when he noticed who one of the officers was. "Wickham!" Darcy exclaimed.

Having been engrossed in telling his tale of how he became to be injured to the delectable Miss Elizabeth, Wickham had not paid attention to who was on the horses. His head whipped around when he heard his name. When he spied his nemesis on his big black stallion, all the colour drained from Wickham's damaged face and his charming look was replaced by one of abject fear.

Elizabeth noted both men. One was deathly afraid, the other angry. She watched as Mr. Darcy wheeled his horse without another word and began riding back the way he had come. Elizabeth watched as Mr. Wickham attempted to regain his equanimity as soon as Mr. Darcy withdrew.

Bingley had not noticed his friend was no longer with them. "Miss Bennet, good morning, he bubbled. "I was on my way to Longbourn to deliver your invitation to the ball. It seems that I have been saved the rest of the ride." Bingley proffered the invitation, which Jane accepted, making sure their hands did not touch.

"On behalf of my family, I thank you for the honour," Jane said coolly.

"May I have the honour of securing the first and supper sets, Miss Bennet?" Bingley asked assured of a positive response.

"I am afraid not, Mr. Bingley. Those two sets are already reserved. Once word of your ball circulated, my sisters and I were asked for a number of sets, including the two you mentioned and the final set," Jane informed the crestfallen man. "I do have the set after supper still open, Mr. Bingley." She would not refuse to dance with the puppy, but she would not allow him any set other than a meaningless one. "Did you know that Mr. Darcy seems to be returning to Netherfield?" Jane pointed out.

"Then I must follow him." Before he departed, Bingley turned to Mr. Denny. "Mr. Denny, please inform the Colonel that all of his officers, and their wives for those who are in the married state, are invited. It is this Friday coming." Bingley bowed, and the extremely disappointed man mounted his horse and turned to follow his friend.

Jane reminded herself to thank Lizzy for her suggestion to lock up the important sets so she would not have to refuse Mr. Bingley. Luckily, he did not ask for a second set, as she would have refused a second with the man.

Once Mr. Wickham had plastered his charming smile

back on his face, he turned once more to Miss Elizabeth. "I am sure you noticed the strained way Darcy and I were just now." Elizabeth allowed it was so. "How long has he been in the neighbourhood?" Wickham fished for intelligence.

Elizabeth decided to play along to see what she would learn, as she did not find Mr. Wickham trustworthy at all, though the normally observant Elizabeth missed the fact that Charlotte and her cousin had not ceased talking one to the other. "He has been here above a month. His friend who you saw now, Mr. Bingley, is leasing the estate of Netherfield Park. He is such a rude, proud, and disagreeable man," Elizabeth shared her sentiments of Mr. Darcy.

Wickham thought that he had found fertile ground for his tale of woe and was about to take a chance at blackening Darcy's name as he believed that with the antipathy that Miss Elizabeth had for his nemesis, she would never reveal what he said to Darcy. Before he could say any more, the Bennets were hailed by a lady.

"Hello nieces, nephew, Charlotte," Mrs. Phillips said. Charlotte then introduced Mr. Collins before he could do it himself, and Denny performed the honours for Wickham. "It is fortuitous that I saw you. Please remind your parents that they are invited to my card party this evening, and you as well, Charlotte. Mr. Denny, Mr. Wickham, you are both welcome too."

Both officers indicated their gratitude as they accepted. For Wickham, it meant free food and drink, and the opportunity to spin his yarn for Miss Elizabeth.

VOL 1, CHAPTER 8

"Welcome to Lucas Lodge, Mr. Collins," Sir William welcomed the pastor in his normal ebullient way after Charlotte had introduced the corpulent man.

"Papa, may Mr. Collins and I meet with you in your study?" Charlotte asked.

Collins was about to make the request that he and Sir William meet, but he supposed that having his betrothed with him would help smooth the way, if it were needed.

Once the three were comfortable in the small study, Sir William spoke first. "You asked for this interview, Charlotte, though I am at a loss to why you requested it. Why is Mr. Collins here?"

"It is not every day that your oldest becomes betrothed, Papa, so I felt that I should attend you and my betrothed as I am sure you will have questions that only I will be able to answer," Charlotte replied without emotion.

"*BETROTHED!*" the normally jovial Sir William fairly yelled. "Did you compromise my daughter, sir?"

"I most certainly did not!" Collins replied, truly aggrieved at the intimation.

"Charlotte, tell me how this came about? Did you not meet this man at Longbourn this very day?" a befuddled Sir William wanted to know.

"Yes, Papa, we met today. You know I am not a romantic, that all I always wanted was a respectable man who could give me a stable home of my own. As a clergyman, Mr. Collins has a respectable profession, and I understand that he has a nice sized parsonage and attached glebe lands. He has stability, Papa. You know that such appointments are for life unless there is some serious wrongdoing," Charlotte stepped around the desk and took her father's hand as she looked him directly in eyes so he could see the truth in hers. "This is *my* choice; it is what I *want*."

"It seems, Sir, that I must welcome you as a son-in-law and you have both my consent and blessing. Have you set a date yet?" Sir William asked having accepted that it was, in fact, his daughter's choice.

"Miss Lucas suggested a date after Twelfth Night, and I concur," Collins spoke for the first time since he had taken his seat.

"I assume that you are able to support a wife, Mr. Collins?" Sir William asked as the shock started to wear off.

"Yes, I am well able to do so between the glebe lands and tithing, I have an income of close to five hundred per annum. Even without Longbourn, which I had been led to believe would be mine one day, we will be quite comfortable. As the parsonage is a gift of the living, my only costs are food and servants, and my beneficent patroness, the Honourable Lady Catherine de Bourgh, will advise us on the best way to spend our money. She is, after all, most wise and always has good advice such as placing shelves in my closets," Collins preened.

'I will say naught now, but after we marry, I will have a thing or two to say about Lady Catherine and her vast wisdom. I will run my house. His recounting of having put shelves in the closets is above ridiculous. Where would I hang my gowns?' Charlotte thought to herself, but wisely remained silent as her betrothed prattled on about the great lady.

If Sir William thought he had been surprised, that was nothing to the reaction of his wife, two sons, and younger daughter. After the shock wore off, the rest of her family wished Charlotte and her betrothed happy, and Lady Lucas breathed a sigh of relief. She knew how Charlotte felt about being a burden, and they both felt the same about marriage, which Charlotte had learnt at her mother's feet.

"You will be able to manage him, I think," Lady Lucas said quietly to Charlotte as they sat to one side while Mr. Collins sat with her father and brothers going on about his patroness. Both mother and daughter thought Nick was lucky he was at Oxford and missing the parson's loquacious praise for his patroness.

"I believe you are correct, Mama. He does seem easily led, does he not?" Charlotte asked cryptically, then proceeded to tell her mother the truth of the suggestion from her rather than a proposal from the loquacious clergyman.

"Well done, my girl," Lady Lucas smiled.

~~~~~~~/~~~~~~~

When Elizabeth reported her observation of Mr. Darcy and Mr. Wickham to her parents prior to their departure for the Phillips' house, she found Mr. Bennet had already received some information from the town. "That one will bear watching; he had the temerity to try and place a large order with Mr. Gibbs on credit. He was told the town policy and yet he went to a half dozen other merchants to try to gain credit from them. He was also seen leering at some of the younger girls in a most unbecoming way."

"Even though it seems that there is something between him and that disagreeably haughty Mr. Darcy, I pegged him as a liar, Father," Elizabeth stated.

Before her husband could respond, Mrs. Bennet spoke. "Lizzy, I love you as much as any mother could love a daughter or a son, but it worries me that you seem to have a blind spot when it comes to Mr. Darcy, as you do anyone who has crossed you in some way."

"But Mama…" Elizabeth started to say.

"Yes, Lizzy, he slighted you. That is what I mean; you are terribly slow to forgive, and once your prejudices take hold you are reticent to let them go. Yes, the man is haughty, but he wears a mask. I know from my mother, Marie, and Wes, that he has been hunted like prey since he was eighteen, some nine years ago! After his father was lost, it only became worse.

In addition, his ridiculous aunt claims a non-existent engagement to her sickly daughter.

"His aunt's claims exist only in her own mind, which is driven by her desire to control her daughter's inheritance. So, she is another fortune hunter, not unlike Miss Bingley, but in this case, it is a member of his family trying to manipulate him. Where our wealth is hidden and not fodder for the *Ton*, Mr. Darcy's is well known and is the object of many. Imagine how you would feel if everywhere you went all people talked about was your wealth.

"On top of that, remember the report said that there had been something with his sister not long before he came here. He and his cousin, Colonel Fitzwilliam share guardianship of Miss Darcy, and have for these past five years. She is now fifteen or sixteen years old, younger than Esther," Mrs. Bennet pointed out. "I am not excusing his rudeness to you; I am just saying that is it not possible he was upset? That the tirade was a release of tension and not truly aimed at you? Do not forget that he had shown no inclination to dance, and Mr. Bingley was hounding him to do so. All I am asking is that you consider your motives for holding onto anger for these weeks now." Priscilla Bennet kissed the oldest child of her body and then herded her family toward the door after kissing Mark and admonishing him to go to bed when Miss Jones sent him.

"I promise to think on what you have said, Mama," Elizabeth told her mother just before they entered the carriage for the one-mile ride into Meryton.

"Is Mr. Collins not joining us, Papa?" Esther asked.

"He will be there, my sweet daughter, he is at Lucas Lodge," Bennet replied. Jane and Elizabeth looked at each other in question. They would certainly need to have a conversation with Charlotte at Aunt Hattie's.

~~~~~~~/~~~~~~~

On arrival at the Phillips' home, which was attached to the solicitor's office in Meryton, Jane and Elizabeth saw Charlotte sitting on her own and started to make for her when they were waylaid by their aunt. "How are you, nieces? Were you enjoying yourselves when I saw you earlier today?" Mrs. Phillips asked. The Phillipses had never had any children of their own, so they doted on their Bennet and Gardiner nieces and nephews, even if only Jane was the only Bennet related to them by blood. The other four Bennets treated them and the Gardiners as much like aunt and uncle as they did their mother's brother and sister.

"We are well, Aunt Hattie. It was much more pleasant when the unwanted company left us," Elizabeth responded. Before Mrs. Phillips could enquire about what her niece meant, she moved to welcome the Longs and Gouldings. Hattie Phillips was nothing if not a skilled hostess.

Jane and Elizabeth sat on either side of Charlotte Lucas on a settee. "Has our cousin been with your family all afternoon, Charlotte?" Elizabeth opened.

"He has, Eliza, why do you ask?" Charlotte asked in return.

"We thank you for removing the burden of him sitting and sulking at Longbourn. Let me guess as there is no embargo on his going on about his patroness at Lucas Lodge, he did just that?" Jane smiled.

"He did. Before you say more, I need to inform you both of something before my father makes an announcement this evening," Charlotte looked down, getting the idea that her betrothed was not a favourite among his cousins.

"Please do not tell me that he proposed to you after Papa told him in no uncertain terms that he was not allowed to offer for any of us," Elizabeth stated, her eyebrows raised in alarm as she saw Charlotte's reaction. "No, Charlotte, how can this be?"

"Not all of us have the security that you and your sisters have, Eliza," Charlotte gave a wobbly smile of reassurance. "You know that I am not romantic, and you also know what my opinions on marriage are." Both Bennet sisters nodded mutely. "Do not look at me like that, either of you. I am much relieved that I will no longer be a burden on my parents or my brother

113

in the future. He seems to be a good sort of man, and—I think I will be able to steer him in a better direction. You know me, I will not allow his patroness to rule my roost."

Jane and Elizabeth recovered their composure. "You have the right of it, Charlotte. It is unfair of us to judge your decision through the prism of our eyes and situation," Elizabeth owned. "If you are happy, then I wish you well." Elizabeth hugged her friend in contrition.

"That applies to me as well, Charlotte. We should not have judged your choice. It is, after all, yours to make, not ours," Jane added as she too hugged her friend.

As the three were sitting and talking Elizabeth noticed that Mr. Denny had arrived with Mr. Wickham in tow. Before the men could make their way to where the two oldest Bennet daughters sat, Sir William stood and clinked his glass to get the attention of all present and cleared his throat. "It is my distinct pleasure to inform all of our friends here assembled, with our hostess's permission," he raised his glass to Mrs. Phillips who inclined her head, "that my Charlotte and Mr. Collins are betrothed and will marry in January."

Many wished the newly betrothed couple well. Jane leaned over to Charlotte and asked quietly so only Charlotte could hear her, "Does that mean you will still come to Broadhurst with us?"

"Why do you think we are marrying after Twelfth Night?" Charlotte smiled conspiratorially.

After the well wishes had subsided, the two officers made their way across the room to where the three ladies were seated. "Good evening, ladies," Wickham bowed with a flourish. "Congratulations on your betrothal, Miss Lucas," Wickham gave his wishes. "Miss Elizabeth, if you are not going to play cards, may we talk?" he asked hopefully.

"I do not enjoy cards overly much, Mr. Wickham; yes, we may talk," Elizabeth allowed. She caught Jane's hand before her sister stood and followed Charlotte, "Advise Mama and Papa to stay near me," Elizabeth whispered to Jane who nodded her understanding.

Wickham sat on the chair closest to the end of the settee where Elizabeth sat. She wanted to escape his unappealing presence, but her curiosity had won out so she would listen to what the slimy man had to say. Elizabeth was relieved to see her parents standing silently behind Mr. Wickham. They were close enough to hear the conversation, and with the man trying his best to work his charms on her, he was not aware of their presence.

Mr. Wickham assumed that he had enthralled Miss Elizabeth so he could talk to her at his leisure, and that she would be willing to hear anything from him. After her comments about his nemesis earlier, he was sure that she was ripe for his version of the history of his acquaintance with Mr. Darcy.

Mr. Wickham quickly began his chosen subject. He inquired how far Netherfield was from Meryton after Miss Elizabeth had mentioned that was where the gentleman was residing in the area; and, after receiving her answer, he again asked in a hesitating manner how long Mr. Darcy had been staying there.

'*Did you forget you asked the same question earlier today?*' Elizabeth asked herself. Then aloud replied, "A few weeks," and then, in an attempt to spur him on, added, "He is a man of exceptionally large property in Derbyshire, I understand."

"Yes," replied Mr. Wickham; "his estate there is a noble one. A clear ten thousand per annum. You could not have met with a person more capable of giving you certain information on that subject than myself, for I have been connected with his family in a particular manner from my infancy." He nodded when Elizabeth looked suitably surprised. "You may well be surprised, Miss Bennet, at such an assertion after seeing the very cold manner of our meeting earlier today. Are you much acquainted with Mr. Darcy?"

'*Do you think me a simpleton? Only a dullard would have seen the two of you today and not known that!*' "As much as I ever wish to be," Elizabeth offered with as much warmth as she could muster. "I have not spent much time in his company, but I think him very disagreeable."

"I have no right to give *my* opinion," said Wickham, "as to his being agreeable or otherwise. I am not qualified to form one. I have known him too long and too well to be a fair judge. It is impossible for *me* to be impartial. But I believe your opinion of him would in general astonish—and perhaps you would not express it quite so strongly anywhere else. Here, you are in your own family."

'*You must really think me unintelligent; you were itching to tell me your tale. Do you now know how inappropriate such a conversation is with one you just met?*' Elizabeth glanced at her father, and with a quick nod of approval, allowed the man think that he was taking her in. "Upon my word, I say no more *here* than I might say in any house in the neighbourhood, except Netherfield Park. He is not at all liked in Hertfordshire. Everybody is disgusted with his pride. You will not find him more favourably spoken of by anyone." Elizabeth told the man who she judged was itching to hear **negativity** about Mr. Darcy.

"I cannot pretend to be sorry," said Wickham, after a short pause, "that he or that any man should not be estimated beyond their desserts; but with *him* I believe it does not often happen. The world is blinded by his fortune and consequence, or frightened by his high and imposing manners, and sees him only as he chooses to be seen."

'*What drivel, aside from the part about his manners, nothing you say is true!*' Elizabeth was growing exasperated with the lying man but wanted to hear the rest of what he had to say. "I should take him, even on *my* slight acquaintance, to be an ill-tempered man." Elizabeth stated.

Wickham only shook his head. "I wonder," said he, "whether he is likely to be in this country much longer." Wickham knew he was walking a tightrope, and if Darcy were to leave soon, he would be a lot safer going against what he had been warned not to do.

"I do not at all know; but I *heard* nothing of his going away. Will your plans in favour of the Derbyshire Militia be affected by his being in the neighbourhood?" *'I could be on Drury Lane with this level of acting,'* Elizabeth smiled at the thought, and Wickham, seeing the smile, believed that it was meant for him.

"Oh! no—it is not for *me* to be driven away by Mr. Darcy. If *he* wishes to avoid seeing *me*, he must go. We are not on friendly terms, and it always gives me pain to meet him, but I have no reason for avoiding *him* but what I might proclaim before all the world, a sense of very great ill-usage, and most painful regrets at his being what he is. His father, Miss Bennet, the late Mr. Darcy, was one of the best men that ever breathed, and the truest friend I ever had; and I can never be in company with this Mr. Darcy without being grieved to the soul by a thousand tender recollections. His behaviour to myself has been scandalous; but I believe I could forgive him anything and everything, rather than his disappointing the hopes and disgracing the memory of his father."

'There you go again contradicting yourself, you are obviously a practiced, but not a very good, liar! What do you imagine this disclosure would be to the memory of the man you claim to love so dearly?' Elizabeth had to concentrate to feign interest of the subject but noticed that her mother was growing angrier by the moment. She listened, sure that if one word in fifty were true, it would be a surprise.

Mr. Wickham began to speak on more general topics —Meryton, the neighbourhood, the society—appearing highly pleased with all that he had yet seen and speaking of the lattermost with gentle but very intelligible gallantry.

"It was the prospect of constant society, and good society," he added, "which was my chief inducement to enter the Derbyshire Militia."

'Yes, and to try and fleece honest, hardworking merchants, evidently! Ogling young maidens too, that is the society you crave?' Elizabeth was disgusted by the man. Not aware of her distaste,

he ploughed ahead.

"I knew it to be a most respectable and agreeable corps, and my friend Denny tempted me further by his account of their present quarters and the very great attentions and excellent acquaintances Meryton had poured upon them. Society, I own, is necessary to me. I have been a disappointed man, and my spirits will not bear solitude. I *must* have employment and society. A military life is not what I was intended for, but circumstances have now made it eligible. The church *ought* to have been my profession—I was brought up for the church, and I should at this time have been in possession of a most valuable living, had it pleased the gentleman we were speaking of just now."

"Indeed!" Elizabeth forced herself to react in the way she assumed that he wanted her to.

"Yes—the late Mr. Darcy bequeathed me the next presentation of the best living in his gift. He was my godfather, and excessively attached to me. I cannot do justice to his kindness. He meant to provide for me amply and thought he had done it; but when the living became vacant, it was given elsewhere."

"Good heavens!" cried Elizabeth; "but how could *that* be? How could his will be disregarded? Why did you not seek legal redress?" '*Now we get to the centre of his lies. I will bet there is a kernel of truth here wrapped in layers of untruths!*'

"There was just such an informality in the terms of the bequest as to give me no hope for legal redress. A man of honour could not have doubted the intention, but Mr. Darcy chose to doubt it—or to treat it as a merely conditional recommendation, and to assert that I had forfeited all claim to it by extravagance, imprudence—in short, anything or nothing. Certain it is, that the living was available two years ago, exactly as I was of an age to hold it, and that it was given to another man; it is no less certain that I cannot accuse myself of having really done anything to deserve to lose it. I have a warm, unguarded temper, and I may have spoken my opinion *of* him, and *to* him, too freely. I can recall nothing worse. But the fact is that we are hugely different sort of men, and that he hates me."

"This is quite shocking! He deserves to be publicly disgraced." Elizabeth egged the clueless man on, a glance at her father telling her she was closing on the edge of his forbearance.

"Some time or other he *will* be—but it shall not be by *me*. Till I can forget his father, I can never defy or expose *him*."

'*That is your biggest lie yet! What do you think you are doing at this very moment? It is obvious to me you never took orders, for if you had you would not be earning a pittance in the militia!*' Elizabeth concluded.

"But what," said she, after a pause, "can have been his motive? What can have induced him to behave so cruelly?" She wanted to hear whatever nonsense the man came up with.

"A thorough, determined dislike of me—a dislike which I cannot but attribute in some measure to jealousy. Had the late Mr. Darcy liked me less, his son might have borne with me better. I believe his father's uncommon attachment to me irritated him exceedingly early in life. He had not a temper to bear the sort of competition in which we stood—the sort of preference which was often given me."

'*I understand that Pemberley is not entailed. If your godfather loved you so well, why did he not take care of you in other ways?*' She aloud made another inquiry just to discover what else the man would say. "I had not thought Mr. Darcy so bad as this—though I have never liked him. I had not thought so terribly ill of him. I had supposed him to be despising his fellow-creatures in general but did not suspect him of descending to such malicious revenge, such injustice, such inhumanity as this. He must hold implacable resentments and have the most unforgiving of tempers. His disposition must be dreadful."

"I will not trust myself on the subject," replied Wickham; "I can hardly be just to him."

'*That is good, for I do not trust you on this or any subject either!*' Elizabeth appeared to be deep in thought, and after a time exclaimed, "To treat in such a manner the godson, the friend, the favourite of his father! A young man, too, like *you*, who *seems* to be amiable." She then added, "And one, too, who had probably been his companion from childhood, connected together, as I think you said, in the closest manner!"

"We were born in the same parish, within the same park; the greatest part of our youth was passed together. We were inmates of the same house, sharing the same amusements, objects of the same parental care. *My* father began life in the profession which your uncle, Mr. Phillips, appears to do so much credit to—but he gave up everything to be of use to the late Mr. Darcy and devoted all his time to the care of the Pemberley property as the steward. He was most highly esteemed by Mr. Darcy, a most intimate, confidential friend. Mr. Darcy often acknowledged himself to be under the greatest of obligations to my father's active superintendence, and when, immediately before my father's death, Mr. Darcy gave him a voluntary promise of providing for me, I am convinced that he felt it to be as much a debt of gratitude to *him*, as to his affection to myself."

"How strange!" cried Elizabeth. *'I can believe his father was an honourable man, but the son is clearly not!'*

"It *is* wonderful how he can fool," replied Wickham, "for almost all his actions may be traced to pride; and pride had often been his best friend. It has connected him nearer with virtue than with any other feeling. But we are none of us consistent, and in his behaviour to me there were stronger impulses even than pride."

"Can such abominable pride as his have ever done him good?" *'He is proud, that is true, haughty and arrogant too, but neither have I seen, nor has the report Papa has ever intimated, anything dishonourable about Mr. Darcy!'*

"Yes. It has often led him to be liberal and generous, to give his money freely, to display hospitality, to assist his tenants, and relieve the poor. Family pride, and *filial* pride—for he is immensely proud of what his father was. Not to appear to disgrace his family, to degenerate from the popular qualities, or lose the influence of the estate, Pemberley, is a powerful motive. He has also *brotherly* pride, which, with *some* brotherly affection, makes him an exceedingly kind and careful guardian of his sister, and you will hear him generally cried up as the most attentive and best of brothers."

'Are you that bad a liar that you do not see all of the contradictions in your speech?' "What sort of girl is Miss Darcy?" Elizabeth asked.

He shook his head dramatically. "I wish I could call her amiable. It gives me pain to speak ill of a Darcy."

'What drivel, for that is what you have been doing this whole time!' Elizabeth was getting frustrated, but she had listened for this long, she would hear him out.

"Yet she is too much like her brother—enormously proud and arrogant. As a child, she was affectionate and pleasing, and extremely fond of me; and I have devoted hours and hours to her amusement. But she is nothing to me now. She is a handsome girl, about fifteen or sixteen, and, I understand, highly accomplished. Since her father's death, her home has been London, where a lady lives with her and superintends her education."

'This is the opposite of how Mama described Miss Darcy. Wait! Could it be that this man was involved in the undefined trouble that was in the report? I wonder if his injuries were of his own making. There is no way that this man exerted himself on anyone else's behalf! It is not hard to see that there is only one that he cares for—himself!' Elizabeth was sure that she had an accurate sketch of the man's character by now, or, more accurately, a measure on his lack of character!

Elizabeth sighed inwardly with relief when her parents intervened to collect her, telling her it was time to depart. As she curtsied to Mr. Wickham, he did not notice the tight smile, believing that he had a staunch ally in his corner.

Once the Bennets' carriage started to move, Bennet held up his hand when he saw Elizabeth was bursting to talk. "At home, Lizzy. We will discuss all at home."

VOL 1, CHAPTER 9

Darcy was fighting a war with himself. What should he do about Wickham? Could he do anything without potential harm to his beloved sister? It was bad enough seeing the libertine, but to see him talking to Miss Elizabeth Bennet made his blood boil.

Why should he care about a woman that could never be anything to him? Why was it that she invaded his dreams nightly? He would never admit it to another living soul, but many of the dreams were decidedly ungentlemanly. If it were only while sleeping and in a dream state that she came to him it would be one thing, but whenever he was not occupied with a task, his mind started to think about her—on its own volition, to be sure, but it happened far too frequently now to ignore. He often found himself wondering where she was, what was she doing, and with whom was she doing it?

If only she were not so far below him there would be a possibility of offering for her, but that was not the case. He could not betray all he believed he had been taught was important in such a way. As he thought about his parents and their love match, a memory he had long suppressed invaded his mind.

He was eleven and his mother was near her confinement with what turned out to be Gigi. "William, I know you are young yet," his mother had said as she patted the bed next to her as she rested. She seemed to be very tired every day and William could not understand why. "You have heard my sister Catherine try to arrange a match between you and your Cousin Anne, have you not?" William had nodded. "Neither your father nor I will countenance an arranged marriage for you, my son. No matter what your aunt tells you, we never agreed to any betrothal between you and Anne. I want you to promise me something."

"Anything Mama," William had promised.

"Follow your heart, William. I want for you what you father and I have, a love match."

Darcy sat up straight as he remembered the promise that he made to his mother. At the same time he remembered his father speaking of duty and upholding the honour of the Darcy name. How was he able to reconcile those two competing messages?

Thankfully for Darcy's equanimity, it rained for four days in a row, and he did not see the libertine Wickham or his tormenter during that time. He knew it was unfair to term Miss Elizabeth his tormentor when she was oblivious of the effect she had on him.

~~~~~~~~/~~~~~~~~

The rain was welcomed by the residents of Longbourn, most especially Jane and Elizabeth. Mr. Bingley had called once prior to the start of the rains but was told that Miss Bennet was not at home. Mr. Wickham, who thought Elizabeth was in his thrall, called twice, and both times he was turned away and not permitted admittance to the house.

Bennet had informed the family that the citizens of the area had been warned, and they had in turn cautioned their daughters, gentlefolk, and tradespeople alike. The three Bennet sisters were gratified that Charlotte had admonished Maria about officers and that she too was being circumspect when in their company.

A letter was received from Tom saying he and his good friend and distant cousin Robert Jamison would go directly from Oxford to Broadhurst where Robert would spend part of the holiday with Tom before returning to his family estate, Ashford Dale, in Bedfordshire. Since the original Tom Bennet had married Karen Jamison all those years past, there had always been a strong family connection between the Bennets and the Jamisons.

The two days before the Netherfield ball were rain-free. Thankfully for Jane Bennet, Bingley was busy supervising the clean-up of his park before his ball, so he did not attempt to call at Longbourn again.

The day before the ball was a warm day for November. The ground was fairly dry, allowing the three Bennet sisters and their younger brother to give their horses some much-needed exercise. A groom and a footman accompanied the four of them, as their father was busy with his steward. Once in the open field that bordered Netherfield, the siblings allowed their mounts to run free as they raced across it.

Darcy had felt very much confined during the interminable days of rain, especially as he had to hide from Miss Bingley's unwanted attention much of the time. He had just slowed Zeus to a walk so he could cool down from a long gallop when he saw four horses racing across the field opposite with two escorts following behind.

He could see that the Miss Bennets had allowed their hair free of restraints. He was about to criticise them when he stopped himself, realising that would be hypocritical, for when he and Gigi rode alone on their estate, his sister rode with her hair down sometimes and he had never censured her for it.

As he watched, he saw them approach the fence line, but they made a wide turn and headed back toward the manor without seeing him, or at least without acknowledging that they saw him. They had slowed to a canter then had given their mounts the chance to walk after their exertion as he turned Zeus back toward Netherfield's stables.

Another thing he could not puzzle out, other than the fact that the behaviour of the Bennets was above reproach, was that he had expected himself and Bingley to be the object of fawning here in society just as they were in Town. At first, he told himself that Miss Bennet was playing 'hard to get' in order to reel in Bingley. He was now in doubt of that judgement. If he did not know better, he would say that Miss Bennet was decidedly not interested in his friend, regardless of his fortune.

On the few occasions he had been in Miss Elizabeth's company, she had never fawned. If he were to be honest with himself, she never sought him out at all. He settled on the answer that she was sensible enough to know she was too low for him to offer for her, so she herself was making sure she did not reach too high. That was an admirable trait so he would not be forced to reject her publicly, which would be uncomfortable.

With this rationalisation accepted as fact by Darcy, he handed Zeus to a groom and asked him to water and then feed his stallion some oats.

~~~~~~~/~~~~~~~

In order not to be crushed together, given their overly portly cousin was one of the party, the Bennets, wishing to maintain the illusion they were not wealthy, took their two oldest carriages when they departed for Netherfield. As much as he did not want to admit it to himself, Darcy was watching the arriving carriages to catch a glimpse of *her*. He would allow himself this one surreptitious look, but he would *not* dance with her.

He had asked her to dance that night at Lucas Lodge and she spurned his offer, so his ego would not allow him to request a set from her again. Darcy was determined he would not dance, not even with the overly perfumed Miss Bingley or her sister. He would be a passive observer this night, nothing more.

Darcy was also aware Bingley had not spoken to his sister as he had requested. Her pursuit of him had not lessened; if anything, it had become more desperate. A night or two before, Carstens had been awoken by the chamber's handle being repeatedly jiggled. As a precaution, Darcy had his man sleeping on a cot blocking the door. Carstens had heard an invective in a female's voice, which he was sure was Miss Bingley's, when the person found the door well and truly locked.

Bingley had informed his friend that he was to go to London for a few days starting on the morrow. He had decided he would follow Bingley to Town and have a hard conversation with his friend away from his sisters. He would give Bingley a choice between making sure that his sister was informed of the repercussions of her pointless pursuit of his person or being given the cut direct. His decision would either maintain their friendship or lose it altogether. His plan was to stay at Darcy House for a few days, and then he and Gigi would make for Pemberley and remain there until his return to Town before his hated annual pilgrimage to Rosings Park for Easter in order to discharge his familial duty to his aunt.

Darcy's attention was pulled back to the window when he saw the carriage he recognised as the Bennet conveyance, which was closely followed by another. As he watched, the parents, an unknown corpulent man, and he assumed the youngest daughter alighted from the first vehicle. To his surprise, he realised the second carriage belonged to the Bennets as well when Miss Bennet and then Miss Elizabeth exited.

She was a vision of loveliness, her hair piled on top of her head with some of her enticing curls cascading down along her neck. She wore a warm coat so Darcy could not see her gown as yet, but it would not be long before he would. She looked up toward the window where he was standing and quickly returned her attention to her sisters, so he was sure she had not seen him.

'How is it that a poor country squire had two carriages? Even if they are older, to be able to maintain the servants needed, and horses—yes, the horses—must be costly. Those are not farm horses, but matched pairs! How is it that the Bennets own so much quality horseflesh?'

Before Darcy could divine an answer, he saw that both Miss Bennet and Miss Elizabeth were looking directly at him. He whirled away with as much dignity as he could muster, irritated that she had spied him when he had been certain she had not.

"What do you think Mr. Darcy means by staring at us so, Lizzy?" Jane asked as they walked up the steps towards Netherfield's doors.

"That proud man only looks upon us to find fault, I am sure!" Elizabeth then remembered her mother's words. "To be honest, Jane, I have no notion of why Mr. Darcy does what he does." Elizabeth replied in a calmer voice and Jane was relieved at the hearing of it.

The Bennets and Mr. Collins traversed the receiving line. Miss Bingley made some snide remarks that none of the Bennets paid heed to and then Jane drew level with Mr. Bingley at the head of the line. "Welcome, Miss Bennet," he said, bowing over her hand.

Jane was about to pull her hand back from his grasp when it seemed he was about to bestow a kiss on it, but she was rescued by Elizabeth's timely intervention. Elizabeth nudged Jane slightly, breaking Bingley's contact with her sister's hand. "My apologies for the interruption, Mr. Bingley, but our family is waiting for us before we go in. Thank you for inviting us to your ball, sir," Elizabeth ran on before Bingley had a chance to react, taking Jane with her.

Mr. Darcy, who had been descending the stairs, saw the whole interaction. '*Miss Bennet cares not a whit for Bingley! Miss Bingley has been going on about Miss Bennet accepting him for his fortune alone. If she did, that would be true, but I get the idea she would not accept him at all! Quite singular!*'

Darcy was then distracted as he noticed Miss Elizabeth in her green velvet gown, which perfectly matched her magnificent eyes. She was a vision, an angel! Bingley always went on about angels, to include the enigmatic Miss Bennet, but here before him was a true angel. Before he could stop himself, Darcy found himself standing before Miss Elizabeth as if his feet had minds of their own.

"Good evening, Miss Elizabeth," Darcy bowed.

"Mr. Darcy," Elizabeth curtsied.

"May I have the pleasure of a set?" Darcy asked before he even realised he was speaking. It was too late now; his honour would not let him retract his offer.

Elizabeth stared at him as if he had grown a second

head. She had no choice as she had no intention of forgoing the pleasure of dancing for the rest of the night. Darcy was beginning to worry that she would again refuse him when she gave her answer. "The only sets I have open are the ones before and after the supper set."

"Then please allow me to pencil myself in for the set prior to the supper set." Darcy took the proffered card and pencil and wrote in his name. He saw for himself that the only open set after he reserved his was indeed the one after supper. He bowed again and walked towards the side of the ball room.

"Eliza, did Mr. Darcy just ask for a set?" A surprised Charlotte asked.

Before Elizabeth could answer, Mr, Collins, who was standing at his betrothed's side, dutifully interjected. "Miss Lucas, did you say Mr. Darcy?" he asked excitedly.

"Yes, that is the name I spoke," Charlotte confirmed.

"Would that be Mr. Fitzwilliam Darcy of Pemberley in Derbyshire? The nephew of my esteemed patroness Lady..." Collins stopped himself, just remembering his cousin's strictures and turned to discover if Mr. Bennet had heard his mistake.

"You can relax, Mr. Collins," Elizabeth assured him. "Yes, that is, in fact, the nephew of your patroness." Elizabeth pointed toward Mr. Darcy, knowing her cousin's penchant for introducing himself. She felt somewhat mischievous as the portly man walked as fast as his plump legs would carry him toward the man.

Darcy watched as Miss Elizabeth spoke to a couple. The corpulent man in black was gesticulating wildly. Then Miss Elizabeth pointed toward him, and the overweight man started in his direction.

~~~~~~~/~~~~~~~

"Wickham, will you not be joining us at the Ball?" Denny asked.

"I...um...will not be attending if that man is in attendance," Wickham indicated. Denny shrugged and joined the rest of the officers, along with Colonel Forster and the latter's young wife, to depart for Netherfield Park.

Wickham had never been in a situation like he found himself in here in this little market town. Not only had he been denied credit everywhere in the town regardless of the type of establishment, when he had had a day of liberty he had gone as far as Stevenage and there too no one would extend credit to him, regardless of how much of his charm he employed. Adding insult to injury, not one girl in Meryton and its environs had fallen for any of his tried-and-true methods of seduction. He could not accept that he was seen for what he was, so he blamed Darcy. He also blamed Darcy for the scars that he bore from when Darcy hit him, the ones that seemed to be inhibiting his ability to make conquests in the area.

Libertine that he was, Wickham took great pleasure in charming what he wanted out of naïve young girls. He had never, nor would he ever, take a girl's virtue by force; it was much sweeter when she surrendered to him. That was a line even Wickham refused to cross.

Normally, he would simply take off in the middle of the night, but even that was problematic. He was a member of the army, albeit the militia, but the same rules for desertion during wartime were enforced—death by hanging! Wickham would not chance being hung, so until he found another solution he was stuck where he was. He had signed a contract that he would not sell his commission for two years. For now, he was secured to his current position in life with a Gordian knot.

~~~~~~~/~~~~~~~

Miss Bingley was fuming. She had seen Mr. Darcy ask the country hoyden for a dance, something he had not yet done with her, his hostess! No matter how many hints she dropped, the man was determined to keep his distance.

And to her frustration, when she had tried to enter Mr. Darcy's suite, the door had been locked and she had been without the key. She would not make that mistake again this night! Her patience was at an end; it was time for her to become the

Mistress of Pemberley and Darcy House!

Louisa would give her some minutes to allow her to accomplish this, and then come to *discover* her sister in an assignation with Mr. Darcy. He would have no choice but to marry her then. Let him dance with *Eliza* tonight, for tomorrow he would be hers!

~~~~~~~/~~~~~~~

"William Collins at your service, Mr. Darcy," Collins blurted out followed by one of his low scraping bows. Although Mr. Darcy did not answer, Collins decided that he should proceed. "I have the distinct pleasure and honour to have been bestowed the living at Hunsford by your astute and beneficent aunt, the great Lady Catherine de Bourgh. Last I saw her and her daughter, the jewel of Kent, or I dare say the Kingdom, some days ago they were in the best of health. Your betrothed…"

"My what?" Darcy growled dangerously. Even Collins picked up the displeasure in his patroness's nephew's tone. "As I would be the one proposing, and as I have not proposed to *anyone*, I am not betrothed! If you do not want to incur my wrath, you will never repeat that falsehood to *anyone*!" Darcy's tone was one that conveyed the message that he brooked no opposition.

"B-b-but I-I-I h-have -i-it fr-fr-from h-her l-ladyship's own m-mouth!" the fear filled man returned.

"It is none of your business, Mr. Collins. Other than in my aunt's imagination, there was *never* an agreement for me to marry my cousin Anne. Return to your party, Mr. Collins." Darcy commanded. With another low bow where he almost kissed the floor, Mr. Collins scurried away.

'*What will Lady Catherine say if she hears that I angered her nephew so?*' As Collins puzzled the conundrum, he remembered that Mr. Darcy was not the first to point out that his patroness may not be as infallible as he believed she was.

~~~~~~~/~~~~~~~

Charles Bingley was despondent. It was very out of

character for a man that normally had an optimistic outlook. One dance! That was all he would have with his angel tonight. He did not blame her. She was a popular figure in the neighbourhood, so it was natural that once word of the ball had gotten out that her dances would have been snapped up.

'Why did I not ask for the first, supper, and final sets the night I had the idea for the ball? That way no one else would have secured any sets before me! She is the most beautiful angel and this time I am sure I am really in love. She is modest and all that is good, so I understand why her behaviour is restrained. I am sure that she feels the same for me that I do for her.' Bingley shared a trait with his younger sister. There were times when he only saw that which he desired to see.

There was the business that he needed to take care of in Town and then he would return to Netherfield. Then, as soon as he refreshed himself, his destination would be Longbourn to request a courtship with most visually stunning woman that he could remember seeing.

~~~~~~~/~~~~~~~

Charlotte found out very quickly that dancing was one of the many accomplishments her betrothed did not possess. It was only halfway through the first dance of the first set and Mr. Collins had trod on her toes twice and gone the wrong direction as many times. She envied Eliza and her sisters, who had been spared her betrothed's requesting them to accompany him for a set. She was racking her brain to find a gracious way to exit the dance floor without humiliating the man more than he was doing to himself.

Not only was there still another dance in this set, but she was to dance with her betrothed for the supper and final sets as well. Charlotte decided that it was time to become lightheaded. She stumbled dramatically but caught herself on Mr. Collins arm.

"My dear Miss Lucas are you ill?" Collins asked with genuine concern.

"I find that I am lightheaded; would you mind if we sit

and talk until supper? I am sure that I will recover after the repast," Charlotte asked with her head down.

"But of course my dear Miss Lucas, your wellbeing is of the utmost importance to me," Collins stated with feeling as he led Charlotte to a chair against the wall. "May I fetch you some refreshment, Miss Lucas?" Collins asked gallantly once his betrothed was seated.

"Thank you. Lemonade would be most appreciated," Charlotte replied. She felt badly that she had used deception, but in this case, it was better than the alternative.

Both Elizabeth and Jane danced with one of Charlotte's brothers. They smiled to one another, knowing what Charlotte had done and why. The dances rolled by and soon it was the set before the supper set. Mr. Darcy came to collect his partner from where she was standing next to her parents.

Darcy led Miss Elizabeth to the line that was forming. Miss Bingley glared, furious to be slighted by Mr. Darcy thusly. The quadrille began and Elizabeth was surprised that he was exceptionally light on his feet given how tall he was. She supposed that he was more than tolerably handsome.

"Come Mr. Darcy, we must have some conversation," Elizabeth asserted. She was sure her partner preferred to dance in silence so she was determined it would not be so. "Is this not a well-organised ball?" she asked.

"It is Miss Bingley outdid herself," he replied, and was again silent.

After a pause of some minutes, Elizabeth addressed him a second time, "It is *your* turn to say something now, Mr. Darcy. I talked about the ball, and *you* ought to make some sort of remark on the size of the room, or the number of couples."

He smiled, "Whatever you wish me to say will be said."

"Very well. That reply will do for the present. Perhaps by and by I may observe that private balls are much more pleasant than public ones. But *now* we may be silent." Elizabeth allowed.

"Do you talk by rule, then, while you are dancing?" Darcy wanted to know.

"Sometimes. One must speak a little, you know. It would look odd to be entirely silent for half an hour together; and yet for the advantage of *some*, conversation ought to be so arranged, as that they may have the trouble of saying as little as possible."

"Are you consulting your own feelings in the present case, or do you imagine that you are gratifying mine?"

"Mine," replied Elizabeth archly; "I have seen you are of an unsocial, taciturn disposition, unwilling to speak. I on the other hand *tolerate* far more than you it seems."

"How near your assertion may be to *mine*, I cannot pretend to say. *You* think it a faithful portrait, undoubtedly." Darcy stated, missing the word that he used at the assembly being used by a Bennet once again.

"I must not decide based on my observations." Elizabeth replied.

He made no answer, and they were again silent until they had gone down the line, when he asked her if she and her siblings often walked to Meryton. She answered in the affirmative, and, unable to resist the temptation, added, "When we met there the other day, we had just been forming a new acquaintance." Elizabeth decided to play ██████ advocate as Mr. Wickham was nought but a cautionary tale to her and gave no clue of her distrust of that man.

The effect was immediate. A deeper shade of hauteur overspread his features, but he said not a word, and Elizabeth, though blaming herself for her own weakness, could not go on. At length Darcy spoke, and in a constrained manner said, "Mr. Wickham is blessed with such happy manners as may ensure his *making* friends—whether he may be equally capable of *retaining* them, is less certain."

"He has been so unlucky as to lose *your* friendship," replied Elizabeth with emphasis, "and in a manner which he is likely to suffer from all his life."

'Why did I say that when I know it is not true? Mama just took me to task over this!' Elizabeth upbraided herself. "Please

accept my apology, Mr. Darcy, that was rude for me to say."

Darcy made no answer but inclined his head in acceptance of her offered apology, and he seemed to be thinking of a response. Darcy decided not to answer directly and changed the subject. "What think you of books?" he asked, hoping she at least occasionally read despite the expectations that she would likely only be able to use the circulating library.

"Books! Not a subject I wish to discuss while dancing," Elizabeth replied with arched eyebrow.

"I am sorry you feel so; but if you would allow the subject, there can at least be no want of topics of discussion. We may compare our different opinions," Darcy offered.

"No—I cannot talk of books in a ballroom; my head is always full of something else." Elizabeth reiterated.

"The *present* always occupies you in such scenes—does it?" said he, with a look of doubt.

'*She is my equal intellectually and does not agree with me blindly. Oh, if only there were not so many social impediments!*' Darcy thought. '*How is it that I have gone and fallen in love with one for whom I can never offer?*' Darcy was shaken at his private admission.

Worried that he would blurt out a declaration on the dance floor, Darcy did not trust himself to talk for the remainder of the set. At the end of the dance, Darcy returned Elizabeth to her parents, bowed, and disappeared into the crowd.

"Well, I never! You danced with Mr. Darcy, Lizzy?" Mrs. Bennet asked with an eyebrow arched in question.

"I did, Mama. May we not speak on it until we are at home, please?" Elizabeth asked, thankful that her partner for the supper set came to collect her as her mother nodded her agreement.

After dinner, Jane endured dancing with Mr. Bingley. He went on the whole time about her being an angel and how pretty she was. Although Mr. Bingley was an accomplished dancer, Jane was never more gratified than when the uncomfortable half hour was over, and she was returned to her parents. She could not wait to depart for London in two days. Charlotte had invited Elizabeth to visit her at her future home for Easter, so Jane suggested that after they returned from Broadhurst they should remain in Town until it was time for Lizzy to depart for Kent. That plan ensured she would not need to see Mr. Bingley and his sisters for several months.

When the ball ended, the Bennets were one of the first families to depart Netherfield.

VOL 1, CHAPTER 10

Bennet requested that his wife join him in his study. "Come in, Cilla. I received an extraordinary letter from Edward Gardiner," he informed his beloved wife.

"What does Edward have to say for himself?" Mrs. Bennet asked as she smoothed her skirts after sitting next to him.

"Here my love, read it for yourself," Bennet handed his wife the missive.

23 November 1810
Gardiner House
Portman Square, London

Thomas and Priscilla,

I almost forgot to write to you on this subject as I had meant to some weeks ago. You have my contrition for the delay. I am not sure if you know, but among others the Fitzwilliams, relations of Mr. Darcy, who I understand you have met, are clients of mine as is the aforementioned gentleman.

I am sure that Priscilla knows exactly who they are as they are good friends of her parents and will be at Broadhurst for Christmas. They have no idea of the connection and will not until we are all in Essex together.

"The Earl and Countess of Matlock—they have been friends of Mama and Papa for many years, but they are nothing like Mr. Darcy. They are open and friendly and have two sons —the heir, Andrew, and Richard, who is in the army, I believe," Mrs. Bennet informed her husband before she read on.

About a fortnight ago, the Viscount, Andrew, was here and was asking after our Jane. He has met her a few times when she has been in London with us and is in her thrall. He sees the real Jane, not just her physical beauty, and has assured me that his intentions are completely honourable. I made sure to stress her reported low dowry and that her known connections of note were to tradesmen.

None of what I said deterred him. He is in earnest and would like to call on Jane when she comes to stay with us. Please advise if I am to allow him that.

Maddie and the children are all well and looking forward to seeing all of you at Broadhurst.
Regards,
EG

"I knew Andrew and Richard when they were younger, and they were always good boys. Everything I have heard of them, and their family speaks well of their characters. Andrew has never been part of the fast set and is not a gambler, nor does he overindulge in drink. My vote, if I have one, is to allow Andrew to call on Jane," Mrs. Bennet stated.

"Cilla, you always have a vote, and you know it." Bennet kissed his wife soundly. "What say you we canvass Jane's opinion on the matter. If she is not interested, he will not be the first titled man she has rejected," Bennet chuckled, proud of his eldest daughter for so many reasons. Though this was lower on the list, in moments like this it was nearer the top.

When Jane sat, her father handed her the letter. Both her parents watched closely as she read its contents. Neither missed the look of pleasure nor the blushes it drew, understanding now what she had not said a few days before. "He does not think me too far below him?" she asked in wonder. Lord Andrew Fitzwilliam *was* the man who had captured her attention, but she always believed that he could not be interested in one as low as the Bennets presented themselves to be. It appeared none of that nonsense mattered to him. The fact she had fortune and connections to spare would be a bonus but were not needed to gain his attention or attract him. He saw her for *who* she was, not *what* she was. For the first time since meeting Lord Hilldale, Jane allowed herself to actually hope she could gain the happiness she had so far believed impossible.

"I take it you have no objection to him calling on you at Uncle Edward's, Jane?" Bennet grinned.

"None, Papa," Jane blushed as she realized her secret was officially no longer hers.

Priscilla Bennet hugged her daughter when they stood. The two ladies exited the study while Bennet composed an express to Gardiner granting his permission for Jane to receive Andrew Fitzwilliam's calls. He did not think it too much to extend his appreciation for the information on behalf of *all* his family so he would know the news had pleased their Jane.

~~~~~~~/~~~~~~~

Later that day, a note arrived from Netherfield addressed to Jane from Miss Bingley. The Bennets were aware that Miss Bingley and Mr. and Mrs. Hurst had departed Netherfield not two hours after Mr. Bingley and Mr. Darcy had departed that morning. Miss Bingley had been abusive to the servants, even striking one, and told them to close up the house.

Jane opened the note and read it to the family:

By the time of your reading, my dear Miss Bennet, we will have departed Netherfield Park, having resolved to follow our brother to Town directly, and of our meaning to dine in Curzon Street, where both my brother and Mr. Hurst have their houses.

I do not pretend to regret anything I shall leave in Hertfordshire except your society, my dearest friend; but we will hope, at some future period, to enjoy many returns of that delightful intercourse we have known, and, in the meanwhile, may lessen the pain of separation by a very frequent and most unreserved correspondence. I depend on you for that.

When my brother and then Mr. Darcy left us earlier, he imagined that the business which took him to London might be concluded in three or four days; but as we are certain it cannot be so, and at the same time convinced that when Charles gets to Town, he will be in no hurry to leave it again, we have determined on following him thither that he may not be obliged to spend his vacant hours alone. Many of my acquaintances are already there for the winter; I wish that I could hear that you, my dearest friend, had any intention of making one of the crowd—but of that I despair. I sincerely hope your Christmas in Hertfordshire may abound in the gaieties which that season generally brings, and that your beaux will be so numerous as to prevent your feeling the loss of the three of whom we shall deprive you.

Mr. Darcy is impatient to see his sister; and, to confess the truth we are scarcely less eager to meet her again. I really do not think Georgiana Darcy has her equal for beauty, elegance, and accomplishments. The affection she inspires in Louisa and me is heightened into something still more interesting from the hope we dare entertain of her being hereafter our sister.

I do not know whether I ever before mentioned to you my feelings on this subject, but I will not leave the country without confiding them, and I trust you will not esteem them unreasonable. My brother admires her greatly already; he will have frequent opportunity now of seeing her on the most intimate footing. Her relations all wish the connection as much as his own, and a sister's partiality is not misleading me, I think, when I call Charles most capable of engaging any woman's heart. With all these circumstances to favour an attachment, and nothing to prevent it, am I wrong, my dearest Jane, in indulging the hope of an event which will secure the happiness of so many?

"What a pretentious, social climbing, and delusional woman!" Jane exclaimed. "Are they all blind? I care no more for her brother now than I ever did. Where did this shrew get the idea I am in any way enamoured with him, or that I should care if she and the rest of them never return?" Jane was angry.

"How dare she call you *my dearest Jane*? You did not give her leave to address you informally did you, sister?" Elizabeth asked, wondering how any halfway intelligent person could be

UNKNOWN FAMILY CONNECTIONS

so blind.

"No, Lizzy, I did not. I will not dignify this with a response. If she or her sister ever try to approach me, I will give them the cut direct!" Jane retorted with anger.

"We will see how happy Mr. Bingley is when he receives a notice from Phillips informing him that he has lost ten months' worth of rent," Bennet frowned as he re-read the note from Mrs. Nichols, shaking his head more than once. She explained how Miss Bingley had verbally abused the servants that morning and that she had struck a maid. A note was immediately dispatched to Mr. Phillips to send a notice of immediate eviction to Mr. Bingley and retention of the funds for breach of contract, and he considered the merits of requesting restitution for those whom Miss Bingley had harmed.

"Not for one instant do I believe that Mr. Darcy would allow his tender aged sister to be betrothed to anyone, least of all the son of a tradesman," Mrs. Bennet opined. "This is part of Miss Bingley's delusion, and what needs to occur to ensure Mr. Darcy will offer for her one day, thinking that one match will lead to another.

"In her mind, because her brother is enamoured with you, she feels that she needs to warn you off, regardless of the fact that you have no interest in him," Bennet surmised. "They will never return to Mark's estate, even should they want to, after Phillips is done with them."

The subject soon changed to Jane's packing for her departure on Monday, of which she anticipated more than she had even two days previously.

~~~~~~~/~~~~~~~

Darcy was halfway to London before he was able to get his temper under control. Miss Bingley had tried to compromise him after the ball! As he thought about the events of the early hours of the morning, his ire rose once again.

Carstens had heard a key in the door an hour after the ball and woke Darcy. The door had opened only inches before being blocked by the cot that the valet slept on. Darcy and his man had listened as the door to the second bedchamber of the suite was unlocked.

Very quickly, Carstens slipped into the master's bed and Darcy hid in the dressing room. A minute later the interconnecting door was unlocked, Darcy watched as Miss Bingley padded to his bed and dropped her flimsy robe, revealing her naked form. She climbed into the bed and sidled up to the man within it.

Not a minute later Mrs. Hurst entered via the same route her sister had with a candle in hand. "Mr. Darcy! Caroline! What is this?" Mrs. Hurst had tried her best to feign surprise.

"Of what are you talking, Mrs. Hurst?" Darcy had asked from behind the woman who almost dropped her candle. "Why are you in bed with my valet, Miss Bingley? The poor man will now be forced to marry you!"

Both Miss Bingley and Mrs. Hurst had begun caterwauling, which had brought Bingley and Hurst bursting into the chambers. "Caroline, what are you doing in a bed, undressed, and with Darcy's valet?" Bingley demanded.

"I thought, that is to say, Mr. Darcy invited me here," the shrew had lied.

"So, I invited you, and you climbed into bed with my valet?" Darcy had turned to Bingley. "Carstens and I will leave these chambers. Get that," he had pointed at Miss Bingley, "out of my bed and out of my chambers. I depart at first light, if not sooner! And Bingley, you and I will talk in Town!" With that, Darcy strode out of the suite with his valet in tow. A half hour later he had returned to find it empty.

Darcy was tired; he had slept less than an hour. There was no getting back to sleep when he returned to his bed, so in the end he departed as soon as dawn began to break. It was time for an ultimatum—either Bingley took Miss Bingley in hand, or there would be a break between them.

~~~~~~~/~~~~~~~

The Fitzwilliam family was sitting in the family sitting room when a note from Mr. Gardiner was delivered.

Lord Hilldale,

I have consulted with my niece's father. He has no objection to you calling on his daughter, so long as propriety is maintained at all times. My niece was informed of your request and has agreed to accept your calls.

Her arrival date is on Monday coming. She will be accepting callers as of Tuesday morning.

Mr. Bennet asked that you not mention this to Mr. Darcy for now; my niece will be able to explain his reasoning should you require an explanation.

EG

"I wonder what my cousin has done this time," the Colonel asked, grinning affably. His cousin was an honourable man, but awkward in social settings. His pride also tended to lead him to make gaffes in uncomfortable situations.

"Andrew will find out when he sees his Miss Bennet," Lord Matlock opined.

"She is not *my* Miss Bennet, Father. It does seem hopeful, though, that she is willing to accept my calls," the Viscount replied, satisfied with the contents of the note as he was truly making strides toward allowing them to get to know one another better.

"I, for one, salute her father for canvassing her opinion on the matter, rather than making a decision and presenting a *fait accompli* to Miss Bennet," the Countess approved.

"Based on the few times that I was in company with the lady, I got the idea that she is not one to accept others making decisions for her without her input. I remember seeing her giving a man a set down at Haven House once when he dismissed her opinion because of her gender. She looks serene, but she has a quiet strength," the Viscount recalled.

"Do not mess it up, big brother," the Colonel ribbed.

"Speak to me when you are courting a lady, *baby* brother!"

"*Touché*, Andrew, *touché*!" The Colonel admitted defeat.

~~~~~~~/~~~~~~~

"Cyril, I received a letter from Cilla," Lady Sarah De Melville, the Countess of Jersey, informed her husband.

"What does our youngest have to say for herself?" Lord Jersey smiled at the pleasant news.

"They are all well. Our grandchildren are looking forward to seeing us. Oh, Catherine de Bourgh's ridiculous parson is betrothed to poor Charlotte Lucas; she will still be one of the party, however. Young Darcy was in the country and slighted Lizzy! Before you ask, Priscilla has promised to tell us more when we see her, but admonishes you not to call him out," the Countess teased. "Mark cannot wait to see Tom again; Priscilla says he is pining for his big brother. This is most *interesting...*" the Countess went silent as she read the next passage.

"Sarah! Do not tell me something is interesting without telling me what it is," the Earl scowled with mock censure.

"There was nothing to tell until I read the rest of the letter complete. You are as impatient as Mark sometimes, Cyril. Young Hilldale is to call on Jane. She arrives at the Gardiners' later today. Evidently, they have met before, and Jane had thought with her *poor connections* and *lack of fortune* a viscount would not consider her.

"Gardiner told Andrew the story that is widely reported about our grandchildren, and Andrew did not care! It seems our Jane has at last found a suitor she is interested in and who is pursuing her for herself. Priscilla asks that we do not reveal the connection to the Matlocks yet. It is up to Jane's discretion if and when to disclose all, unless she wants to surprise him at Broadhurst," the Countess concluded.

"Will we see our granddaughter before we depart Town for Broadhurst?" the Earl asked.

"Yes, the Gardiners are bringing her to the dinner the night before we decamp for Essex. Wes and Marie and their families will be in attendance as well, so we will be a merry party." The Countess thought for a moment and then added, "The Matlocks may have to be included, depending on the status of Jane's connection to Andrew at that time."

"Matlock has always desired a closer connection to me; it seems his wish will be granted," the Earl chuckled.

~~~~~~~/~~~~~~~

Jane was sitting in the drawing room at Gardiner House with her Aunt Maddie the morning after she arrived when the butler announced Lord Andrew Fitzwilliam and showed the Viscount into the drawing room. Lord Hilldale bowed to the ladies who had stood and curtsied.

"Welcome, my Lord," Mrs. Gardiner offered refreshment. After they drank tea, Mrs. Gardiner excused herself to attend to household matters. They were chaperoned, as Mrs. Ponsonby sat in the corner of the room unobtrusively but paying close attention to her charge.

"It is good to see you again, Miss Bennet," the Viscount opened.

"And you, my Lord," Jane responded softly.

"We could make a lot of inconsequential small talk, Miss Bennet, but I will not sport with your intelligence. I know from your Uncle Gardiner that you were apprised of my request to call on you, were you not?"

"Yes, Lord Hilldale, I am aware of the purpose of your call, and I would not have been home to you had it not been my choice to accept it," Jane replied evenly. "Allow me to confirm that you still wish to proceed even after being informed of the *reported* amount of both my dowry and state of my connections."

The Viscount noted that Miss Bennet had stressed the word reported but decided if she had something to tell him, she would in her own time and way. What had been reported was of no matter as it was of little to no consequence to him. "As I told your uncle, I need neither. What I do need is a woman of impeccable character, one who is more interested in *doing* good rather than of giving that impression. I was holding out for a lady who is not a wilting flower, who has an inner strength, who is generous of spirit, caring, and compassionate.

The fact that you are the most beautiful lady that I ever beheld is a true bonus, but it is the rest of these attributes that hold the true attraction for me. The times we have been in company, never have you simpered or fawned over me. When you have an opinion, you defend it. And I saw at Haven House when you know you are right, you are not easily cowed, not even by a large boor of a man."

'This man could not have said more welcome words to me if Lizzy had written directions for him.' Jane's heart started to accelerate with pleasure and her blush revealed it doing so. 'He is a man who knows what he wants, and it appears that he wants me.'

"Miss Bennet, I will not prevaricate and tell you that I am in love with you yet, because I am not. I do, however, already respect many of your qualities and abilities therefore I do you, and you are the first woman who has ever aroused this level of interest and hope for me. I have never taken this step before, and humbly request that you grant me a courtship so we may find out if my belief that we will be truly compatible is correct. Since we last met, I have hoped for nothing as much as this, and if and when you agree the time is right, we will end this courtship in its natural conclusion with us being betrothed to be married." The Viscount's request demonstrated the sincerity of his feelings for the lady.

In hearing his honesty, Jane knew she had to tell him the truth before she accepted his courtship. If they were to move forward, she wanted to make sure there would be no secrets between them so the Viscount could gain the relationship he hoped for.

"My Lord, from the first time I met you, I felt an attraction toward you as I have none other, but I convinced myself that naught would come of it given what you and society believed was the gulf between our ranks, fortune, and connections. You see all of me unlike others before you who only saw my looks." Jane smiled when he shook his head to indicate that she need not tell him that which she did not feel comfortable sharing.

"I feel it important to tell you the fundamental truth of my family's wealth and connections. It is true my *late* mother was the daughter of a solicitor, and two of my natural uncles are in trade. What you, and society at large, do not know is my father remarried two years after my mother's untimely death —to *Lady* Priscilla De Melville."

"We are going to Broadhurst for Christmas!" the viscount exclaimed in his surprise, the information whirling his mind as he attempted to keep up with all she was sharing.

Jane's expression was deeply apologetic. "That, coupled with your request for a courtship, is why I must disclose all to you now. I thought it would be cruel to allow you and your family to arrive at my grandparents' estate and be caught unaware. There is more; my dowry is slightly more than what is reported; it is around fifty thousand pounds." Her smile brightened when she watched the Viscount's mouth drop open.

Jane continued, explaining why her family hid their wealth, her father's antipathy to the *Ton*, and their true position. She left nothing out, not the estates or the town homes. She watched him school his features as she had talked, fearing she had lost his regard because of the deception she and her family had felt the need to employ.

"What of the request not to share our connection with my cousin Darcy? It was hard to comply with as his sister was being hosted at our house, but she moved back to Darcy House yesterday," he shared.

Jane related the tale of his slight and the Viscount's cousin's behaviour in Hertfordshire. "We do not tell people of our wealth and connections as we prefer to be accepted for who we are and not for what we have. Hence our request to keep the connection from your cousin for now. At some point, I am sure it will become public knowledge, but until then..." Jane turned serious as she gathered her courage to make the following statement. "If you choose to withdraw your request because of our decision to hide our true position from society, I will understand."

"Darcy was hosted at an estate that he has no clue belongs to your family!" The Viscount chuckled at the irony. "Miss Bennet, may I call you Jane?" She nodded. "Please call me Andrew, and no more of this lordship nonsense when we are not in society. Your connections and fortune did not have a bearing on my decision to request a courtship, and they still do not. I understand your family's position more than you can guess. How I have wished to be able to do the same! You never lied to me and revealed the facts *before* accepting a courtship and offered me the chance to withdraw without my honour engaged *if* that were my choice," Andrew gave Jane a smile of reassurance. "The salient fact is who you are is unchanged. My request for a courtship is unchanged. It will be my honour to have the opportunity to woo you." He grinned at winning her smile.

"My uncle did tell you falsehoods about me," Jane insisted.

"Not really," Andrew replied. "He *omitted* information, but never stated that your dowry was the lower amount. He said 'reported,' and that is the truth. The question is simple. Will you, Jane Bennet, accept a courtship with me, Andrew Fitzwilliam, regardless of fortune or title?" Andrew asked hopefully, thinking that if she intended to deny his request, she would not have disclosed all to him.

"Absolutely, Andrew. Yes!" Jane replied, the pleasure of saying so lighting up her blue eyes to a shade almost too beautiful to describe. "You have my promise of compete transparency from my side."

"And mine," He vowed. "Do I need to ride to your father's estate to request his consent?"

"No, there is no need, Andrew. My father wrote and gave Uncle Edward leave to act in his stead, although it will not hurt to speak to my father when we are all at Broadhurst," Jane related conspiratorially.

Receiving Mr. Gardiner's consent was but a matter of a few minutes. When a joyous Andrew Fitzwilliam took his leave, he was half of a hopeful and happy, officially courting couple.

~~~~~~~/~~~~~~~

As Jane had given him leave to disclose all to his parents and brother, Andrew did so after informing them he was courting the lady. His family sat in surprised silence for some minutes. "William is going to kick himself in that arrogant arse of his. Sorry, Mother, when he finds out who they are and how much wealth they have," the Colonel broke the silence.

"You are not to mention anything to him," the Earl cautioned his younger son.

"I know, Father," Richard threw his hands up in surrender. "No one allows me to have any fun," he added with mock petulance.

"She is my friend's granddaughter," the Countess repeated.

"Not by blood, but fully accepted as one by the De Melvilles, and do not forget her Uncle Wes and Aunt Marie," Andrew pointed out.

"Why can I not fall in love with such an heiress!" Richard asked rhetorically.

"All I want for you, son, is that you fall in love with a good woman, regardless of fortune," the Countess told her younger son.

"Miss Bennet has four siblings?" the Earl confirmed.

"Yes Father. Miss Elizabeth is next in age, the one our cousin slighted, then Longbourn's heir Tom, Esther, and the baby is Mark, who will have Netherfield one day," Andrew informed his father.

"They are the owners of the two town houses to the right of Matlock House that are leased out?" the Earl asked in wonder.

"Right opposite Darcy House," Richard smirked. "It is my dream to see William be taken down a peg or two. I love my cousin as well as a brother, but some of his notions are decidedly snobbish, and this from a man who treats his servants and tenants so well!"

"When do we meet the lady?" the Countess asked.

"My apologies, Mother. In my excitement I very nearly forgot. Mrs. Gardiner invited all of us to join them for dinner on the morrow," Andrew relayed apologetically.

"I will send a note over now with our acceptance," his mother responded with alacrity, and made her way to her study to pen the missive.

After the brothers departed, the Earl sat next to his countess. "I have heard from the heir to Brookfield. His uncle passed recently, and he is keeping his word to us as far as the sale goes. Out of respect for his uncle's passing we will finalise the sale after Easter."

"Reggie, that is the best news! I cannot wait for the day when our Richard never has to return to war!" a gleeful mother stated. The Earl kissed his wife before taking his leave of her as he had correspondence to attend to in his study.

~~~~~~~/~~~~~~~~

"Caroline, I cannot believe that you were insensible enough to try and compromise Darcy, and I still do not know why you are here and not at Netherfield. If word gets out that you were in bed with a servant, you will never be able to show your face in society again. What were you thinking?" Bingley demanded.

"He only danced with that Bennet nobody, and I want Pemberley," Miss Bingley stamped her foot like a petulant child.

"I should have told you this long ago, Caroline. Mr. Darcy will *never* offer for you. If word of an attempted compromise gets out, you will be ruined, and he will still not marry you. As it is, if you approach him again, he will cut you; I am to inform you that you are not to call at any of his homes! It is time you accept reality and move on. Now again I ask, why are you, Louisa, and Hurst in Town? You know I plan to return to ask Miss Bennet, my angel, for a courtship, do you not?" Bingley stated.

"She has ties to trade and an inconsequential family! She will do nothing to raise me, I mean you, in society, and she does not love you. She will accept you for your fortune only," Miss

Bingley related spitefully.

"What do you know of the lady's feelings; you hardly spent any time with her?" Bingley asked.

"If you do not believe me, ask Mr. Darcy, for I heard him say the same!" Miss Bingley turned on her heel and stormed out of the study.

Deep down, Miss Bingley knew that once her attempted compromise failed it was the end of her dream of becoming Mrs. Darcy, but to hear what her brother related still made her blood boil. She slammed her chamber door with as much force as she could muster then proceeded to throw a tantrum of epic proportions. Nothing breakable survived her snit.

VOL 1, CHAPTER 11

"**M**r. Bingley is here to see you, Mr. Darcy," Killion, Darcy House's butler announced to his master, who was sitting at his desk in the study working on correspondence.

After Miss Bingley's attempted compromise, Darcy was not sure he was ready for Bingley's excuses, but the years of friendship won out. "Show him in please, Killion," Darcy relented.

"Darcy, it is good to see you," Bingley was his affable self, trying his best to ignore the problem between them.

"Coffee, Bingley?" Darcy offered.

"No thank you, I partook at Curzon Street before I departed," Bingley responded. Even Bingley was not myopic enough to miss the displeasure in his friend's mien. "I have spoken to her. It caused a massive tantrum as I feared, but there is no excuse for her sinking to the level of trying to compromise you."

"It is appreciated that you *finally* conveyed my message to her. Do you not see that had you done so the first time I asked it of you that we may have avoided the whole unpleasant situation?" Darcy took a deep breath. "I should not have been such a gentleman and merely hinted at my lack of interest. We have been moving inexorably to the point we arrived at this past Friday night. She is lucky that my man was the only servant aware of her actions. If it were widely known, the talk would have been broadcast abroad and your sister would be ruined!"

"That is what I told her when I spoke to her, Darce. You have the right of it, and I should have spoken to her without delay. You know how I hate confrontations," Bingley owned.

"Bingley, you are my friend, and it is not easy for me to say this to you. As the head of your family, there will be times when you have to do that which is unpleasant; all men do. If you had been diligent in your care of your sister rather than coddling her, both of your lives would have been far easier. Her behaviour will never gain her entry to the first circles, while at the same time that same behaviour hurts your position in society. Your older sister is not much better, but at least she is not your responsibility any longer."

"Where does that leave us, Darce?" Bingley's frown deepened.

"Unless you can check your sister, I will have no choice but to make a public split from you. That is not my choice, but I will not have your sisters use my name to wheedle invites any longer. If she is with you, do not bother coming to my homes as you will not be admitted in her company. When do you plan to return to Netherfield?" Darcy asked. As soon as he mentioned his friend's leased estate, he saw a fine pair of green eyes in his mind's eye.

"I will be returning alone. My sisters and Hurst followed me to Town. They departed Netherfield hours after me and Caroline tells me that she had the house closed. I must return to my angel," Bingley smiled as he thought about the beautiful Miss Bennet. "Do you know that my sister lied to me and told me that Miss Bennet does not love me, that she would only accept me for my fortune," Bingley scoffed. His face fell as he saw his friend's serious look and that he did not dismiss his sister's claims.

"There was a time that I would have agreed with your sister, as loath as I am to own that, on both points. I too would have indicted Miss Bennet of being a fortune hunter who was using her feminine wiles to increase your ardour. I no longer think that…" Bingley perked up, "…however, I am sure that she does not love you. She may not even like you overly much," Darcy laid out the harsh facts for his friend.

Bingley's face fell and he looked like a puppy who had

been kicked hard in the stomach. "Why do you say that?" Bingley asked quietly.

"Before I elucidate for you, tell me what signs you saw from Miss Bennet that signalled her regard for you?" Darcy asked.

"She smiled at me." Bingley noted hopefully.

"She smiled at everyone." Darcy countered.

"She would always sit and talk to me in company," Bingley insisted.

"Bingley, you would go to her every time that you saw her, would you not?" Bingley allowed it was so. "You were loquacious, but did Miss Bennet ever respond beyond the bare minimum? Did she ever cross the room to talk to you?"

"She was just being modest." Bingley was defensive.

"Think about it honestly, Bingley. Look at the ball. Miss Bennet was present when you proposed the event, was she not?" Bingley nodded. "Why do you think it was that there was only one set open for you, none of the significant ones?" Darcy highlighted for his younger friend.

"She did not want to dance them with me!" Bingley fell back in his chair, his expression crestfallen. "She was not merely being modest, was she?"

"I am afraid not, Bingley. You saw what you wanted to see in your latest angel. In my opinion, you still have some maturing to do. My hope for you is that you start to see more than the physical attributes of women. Once you do that, mayhap you will find your match, my friend," Darcy said compassionately.

Shortly after that conversation ended, a dejected Bingley departed his friend's house.

~~~~~~~/~~~~~~~

When Bingley flopped down behind the desk in his town house on Curzon Street, he saw that an express from Mr. Phillips in Meryton had been delivered while he was with Darcy. He broke the seal, assuming it was about the house being closed up after only two months. The more he read, the more apoplectic he became.

Bingley's butler came when his master loudly summoned to him. "Are my sisters here, Tushman?"

"They are in the drawing room with Mr. Hurst, sir," Tushman replied. Letter in hand, Bingley strode directly toward those he had asked after, relieved they were at least in the house.

The three occupants did not pay attention to his arrival until he slammed the door behind him. "Charles, why would you do such a thing?" Miss Bingley scolded.

Bingley took a deep breath, effectively stopping the eruption of temper that was just below the surface. "When you closed up the house, were you abusive to servants, including the housekeeper and butler, sisters?"

"They were not performing their duties as we directed," Miss Bingley's superior air proved the truth of the assertion.

"And you struck one of the maids?" Bingley confirmed.

"She talked back, but how would you know, Charles?" Miss Bingley asked.

"How indeed. Allow me to read this letter for you, it will clear things up," Bingley growled.

"We are going to see dear Georgiana this afternoon..." Miss Bingley did not complete the sentence.

"You are barred from Darcy House, or have you ignored the truth again as you seem to do far too much? Sit and listen!" Bingley commanded. With her pinched look firmly in place, Miss Bingley sat.

24 November 1810
Meryton

Mr. Bingley:
It is my solemn duty to inform you that pursuant to clause 10.4 of your lease you are evicted as of the above listed date and the £5,500 for the remaining ten months has been forfeited as you have contravened the abovementioned clause after a final warning was issued.
Offences:

Miss Bingley struck Millie Jackson in the face.

Both Miss Bingley and Mrs. Hurst were verbally abusive to the servants for not closing the house with enough speed after they were given no notice of the task beforehand.

In addition, you are liable for £572 due to breakages of art work, mirrors, and furniture. Clause 15.10 of the lease you signed lists your responsibility for breakages, and the final pages of the lease was a full inventory of furniture, fixtures, and artwork that were present and in good order when you took possession of Netherfield Park. I direct your attention to your signature on all pages, including the inventory.

It gives the landlord no pleasure to enforce the terms of the lease, but they will also not shy away from protecting their investment.

Sincerely,

Franklin Phillips, Esq

"Every last brass farthing will come out of your dowry!" Bingley yelled.

"You cannot do that to me! That would leave me with less than fourteen thousand pounds!" Miss Bingley screeched.

"The time to consider the consequences was before you caused me to lose over six thousand pounds!" Bingley shot back. "You were WARNED, Caroline!"

"Louisa was there with me!" Miss Bingley tried to shift part of the blame.

"Caroline Bingley!" an outraged Mrs. Hurst exclaimed.

"I think it is time that the Hursts moved back to their own home," Bingley stated without emotion.

"Now hold on, Bingley," Hurst attempted to protest.

"*NO*, Hurst. For too long you and my sister have lived off my largess. That all ends today. You have your own town house, *use it!*" It seemed that the eviction from Netherfield had been the impetus for Bingley to take a stand and grow a backbone with regards to his family obligations—at least temporarily. "I will give you a sennight to be gone from my home, and, as of today, my liquor cabinet will be *locked!*"

~~~~~~~/~~~~~~~

"William," Georgiana Darcy entered her brother's study. "Did I see Mr. Bingley depart?"

"You did, Gigi. Are you ready to leave for Pemberley by Thursday? That way we will arrive home on Saturday and not have to spend the Sabbath on the road," Darcy asked his sister. He was happy to see the stay at Matlock House had helped her immensely. She was still shy but seemed much stronger and was not prone to bursting into tears spontaneously as she had been for the first month after the near debacle with Wickham.

"William, who are the Bennets?" Georgiana asked as she seated herself opposite her brother.

"How do you know about the Bennets?" Darcy asked, surprised at his sister's mentioning their name.

"You mentioned Miss Elizabeth in every letter that you wrote me from Hertfordshire, William. Sometimes more than once in a single letter. Do you not remember what you wrote to me? You are not *that* old," she teased, a clear indicator of her improvement.

"I did? Ahem. She is the daughter of an inconsequential family with no wealth and low connections. They possess a smallish estate neighbouring the one that Bingley leased. I cannot think why I would have mentioned her name in a letter," Darcy attempted to cover the gaffe.

"You mean letters, brother. Is Miss Jane Bennet her sister?" Darcy's eyes opened wide. Surely, he had not mentioned her!

"Did I write her name as well?" Darcy asked, not imagining another possibility for his younger sister to have heard Miss Bennet's name.

"No, William, you did not mention it. When I first told them that you had mentioned the name of a lady, Andrew mentioned something about being attracted to a lady with that family name. I had forgotten about that until on my last day with Aunt and Uncle Fitzwilliam, I heard them discussing Andrew's decision to call on a lady named Miss Jane Bennet.

157

When I entered the sitting room, they must have changed the subject as I never heard her name again," Georgiana informed her brother.

Darcy was gobsmacked. Had Miss Bennet somehow sunk her talons into his older cousin? Was that why Bingley's fortune was of no interest to her when a much larger one, not to mention a title, was in play? He decided a call to Matlock House was necessary. "Gigi, I have been remiss in greeting our aunt and uncle; I will go see them now." Darcy stood abruptly.

"William, it is close to dinner time. Would not a call during calling hours be better?" Georgiana could not account for her brother's strange behaviour. Since she had moved back into Darcy House, it had seemed like some great issue was weighing her brother down. When she had asked what was troubling him, William had dismissed her concerns. And now this. What was it about her brother and the Bennets?

Darcy's walk was much shorter than he planned. As he exited his front door, he saw the Matlock town coach pull away from in front of his uncle's house. It turned in the square and passed him on its way toward the connecting road. He could see all four of the Fitzwilliams in conversation within, though none of them noticed him. He watched as the vehicle made a turn out of the square. With nothing left to do that night, Darcy turned and walked back inside of his house.

~~~~~~~/~~~~~~~

"Grandmother, grandfather, it is so good to see you!" Jane exclaimed as Lord and Lady Jersey were announced at Gardiner House.

"We received your note, granddaughter. How could we not join you to celebrate your courtship with young Hilldale," her grandfather enfolded her in a hug. "Does he know the truth? I assume so if we were invited tonight."

"He does, for I could not start our courtship off with a lie. Where are my uncles, aunts, and cousins?" Jane asked.

"Both Wes and Marie and their families had previous engagements that they could not easily break. We did, however, find one person we thought you would like to see," Jane's grandmother smiled cryptically.

"Hello big sister!" Jane heard and whirled around, opening her arms for her brother Tom to receive a welcoming hug.

"Tom! I did not know that you had arrived from Oxford already!" Jane exclaimed happily.

"I arrived at Jersey house not two hours ago and asked our grandparents not to mention my presence as a surprise to my *much* older sister when they accepted Aunt Maddie's invitation," Tom explained. "Hello Aunt Maddie, Uncle Edward," Tom greeted the Gardiners as Jane released him from her hug.

"Only yesterday you agreed to a courtship, and today I find you in the arms of another man," Andrew teased as he and his family entered the drawing room.

Introductions were quickly made by Andrew of his parents and brother to Jane. Lord and Lady Matlock were impressed by Miss Bennet's poise, and the Colonel thought his brother a lucky ████. "This young man is my brother Tom. He arrived at our grandparent's house from Oxford some hours ago. I was not aware of the scamp's presence," Jane glared at her brother with mock indignation.

"Hello, Elaine," Lady Sarah greeted her friend, who had not noticed her and her husband standing in the background during their introductions to her granddaughter.

"Sarah, Lord Cyril, I did not see you. How are you?" Lady Elaine greeted her long-time friend warmly.

"Matlock," Lord Jersey acknowledged his colleague from the Lords.

"Jersey," Lord Matlock returned and the two wandered off into a corner to talk.

"Tom," Madeline Gardiner called her nephew over, "if you have some time, the children would love to greet you in the nursery."

"I will go up and greet them soon, Aunt. It is good to see you and Uncle Edward again," Tom gave his aunt a kiss on the cheek and excused himself from the company to go see his young cousins.

"I understand that you do not want my dour cousin Darcy to know the truth of your family at this time," the Colonel, who had asked to be called Richard, reiterated.

"Please, Richard. It was not just his slight of Lizzy, but we got the idea that he did not approve of us as we were too far below him. We would prefer that he not know the truth for now," Jane explained.

"If a betrothal is announced?" Richard pushed.

"Then he will be in for somewhat of a surprise," Jane contemplated. "Mayhap he will learn not to make assumptions about people based on their perceived wealth and connections."

"Jane, Lilly and Eddy tell me you promised to read them a story before they go to sleep tonight," Tom reminded his sister on his return to the drawing room.

"When the sexes separate after dinner, I will go and fulfil my promise," Jane smiled sweetly at her brother, the pleasure of the thought impossible to hide.

The butler announced dinner and the diners flowed into the dining parlour, ignoring precedence. Tom Bennet found a seat next to Richard Fitzwilliam and was entertained by his tall tales from the continent, as was his sister who was seated opposite him and next to Andrew. Andrew warned them to take his brother's stories with a grain of salt, and Richard, in turn, put on an exaggeratedly aggrieved look.

At the summation of the repast that was enjoyed by all, Jane kept her promise to her cousins. When the men re-joined the ladies, Jane was one of the last to perform. Andrew discovered that she was beyond proficient on the harp and that her mezzosoprano voice was that of an angel's. It was rather late when the guests returned home after spending a most enjoyable evening with family and friends.

~~~~~~~/~~~~~~~

"A missive arrived from Edward this morning," Bennet informed his family as they broke their fasts. "Our Jane has accepted a courtship with Lord Andrew Fitzwilliam."

"And he is nothing like his disagreeable cousin?" Elizabeth was cynical.

"Lizzy, I thought that you had let your anger for Mr. Darcy go," her mother asserted. "What purpose is there to hold onto your prejudices against him? Even if Jane marries the Viscount one day, you will not be forced into Mr. Darcy's company if that is your choice. Just know that he is close with his Fitzwilliam cousins, so you have to decide if you are willing to cause a rift in the family because you refuse to move on."

"I suppose it is rather selfish of me, is it not mother? For some reason, his slight affected me more than it should have," Elizabeth owned.

"You know what I think, Lizzy? I think that your visceral reaction was because at some level you are attracted to Mr. Darcy, so his slight of you has become far more than it should have," Mrs. Bennet stated with a knowing look.

Before Elizabeth could deny her mother's assertion, let alone with the vehemence it deserved, her father changed the subject. "At least you were not blind enough to fail to see that wastrel Wickham for what he is," Bennet stated.

Wickham had tried to call on Miss Elizabeth a number of times with no success. The final time, Bennet had the officer shown to his study. Wickham had been his normal, overconfident self—that was until Bennet had spoken.

"Mr. Wickham, do you think yourself an intelligent man?" Bennet asked.

"Why yes, Mr. Bennet, I do." Wickham had puffed up like a game cock.

"Would an intelligent man keep calling on a lady who was never home to him, or would that indicate an overblown sense of self?" Bennet asked, watching Wickham as he went still.

"Miss Elizabeth and I had a good connection," Wickham attempted to salvage the situation.

"Is that what you thought? Why do you think that my daughter had her mother and me, and others in the family, stationed

behind you when you spun that pack of horse manure to my daugh-
ter?" Bennet asked pointedly.

Wickham pasted a smile on his face in hopes that he would be
able to charm his way out of a situation that was not going the way
he had hoped. "Why would I, who saved a lady at the expense of
myself, lie to your daughter?"

"Because that is not what happened, is it? The only way that
you would help anyone but yourself was if there were a big reward
in it. Additionally, you have all the hallmarks of a coward. I have
had you investigated, Mr. Wickham. Based on what my investiga-
tor reports, any number of fathers or brothers of young maids that
you have ruined or creditors that you have run out on would have
happily given you the injury you claim was received due to altru-
istic actions on your part. I still do not know how you managed
to fool your late godfather; however, it seems the son saw you for
what you were!"

"Darcy! Damn him! If he is to blacken my name, then I will tell
the world..." Wickham's anger burned hot as Bennet cut him off.

"Mr. Darcy has not mentioned your name to me. From the
first, my daughters found you wanting. It was easy for them to see
that you are a practised liar—practised but not particularly good
at it unless one is predisposed to believe your lies, and I was listen-
ing to your balderdash. Do you know how many times you contra-
dicted yourself? I gave up counting after ten. My daughter had
taken your measure but had decided she would hear what lies you
would spew so that you would not spread them to someone more
inclined to listen."

"B-but I was denied the living at Kympton," Wickham in-
sisted.

"Did you take orders? I have a living in my gift, and I would
not give it to one who had not taken orders. If the church was your
desired profession, why did you not take orders and look for an-
other living or a curacy? I will tell you why not—it was too much
like hard work for you. You are a profligate wastrel who wants
things to be given to him without work. You wasted the education
that the elder Mr. Darcy gifted you. How he did not hear about your

escapades at Cambridge I do not know. I assume his son cleaned up after you to spare his father's feelings, because, unlike you, he actually cares about others.

"The biggest lie of all was your claiming that Mr. Darcy is jealous of you! Anyone with a modicum of intelligence can see that you are the one who is jealous of Mr. Darcy. If you set foot on my land again, I will have you arrested for trespassing. You are being watched, now get out and never return!" Bennet commanded as he dismissed the man, inwardly satisfied with his being so stunned.

Bennet had sent a copy of his investigator's report to Colonel Forster who immediately demoted the man to private, and had him watched at all times by four men to make sure he never left the encampment.

The Bennets had supplanted Darcy as Wickham's main enemy, and he swore vengeance. He did not realise that, in addition to his militia minders, he was watched at all times by men employed by Mr. Bennet.

~~~~~~~/~~~~~~~

Darcy presented himself at Matlock House while the family were breaking their fasts. After he greeted his family, he got right to the point. "Gigi mentioned that she heard some talk of a Miss Jane Bennet in connection to Andrew," Darcy opened. "I am not sure how Andrew has been taken in, but she has no connections other than to trade and is a fortune hunter who spurned Bingley for the bigger prize of a Viscount."

Andrew was about to jump up and strike his cousin, but his father placed a restraining hand on his son's arm. "William, do you think your judgment is wiser than *all* of ours? I would be extremely careful with the next words out of your mouth. Andrew is courting the lady with *our full support*! Before I continue, tell me, William, how many times have you had a conversation, meaningful or otherwise, with the lady?" Darcy's uncle asked pointedly.

"I...er...that is..." Darcy scanned his memory to come up with an answer.

"It is never, is it not?" the Earl said correctly, and Darcy nodded, suddenly not as sure of himself as he had thought. None of them were on his side of the matter, but his pride would not allow him to retreat from his position so hastily. "So how were you able to gain these *insights* of yours, William? Did you visit her home? Is her family a disgrace? What is it, William?"

"They have no wealth or connections!" Darcy blustered.

"Are you saying that unless people have wealth and connections, they must be fortune hunters, that one's character depends on social standing?" Lord Matlock was well known for his skills as a debater and was enjoying the chance to use the skill on his pompous nephew. "Does that not make you a fortune hunter if all you care about is wealth and connections? Is that really what my sister and brother taught you, William? What of your Aunt Catherine, my sister? She is high born, wealthy, and connected, but look at her behaviour. If my sister is not a fortune hunter, then I know not who is." His uncle gave him the gimlet eye while the Countess and her younger son smiled at Darcy's discomfort. Andrew, Darcy realised, was still seething.

"Doing my duty to my name and lineage does not make me a fortune hunter," Darcy bit out sharply. "My father..."

"Told you to do your duty to your estate and your name, and you misinterpreted his words to think that you were meant to think meanly of those below you, William. Before I forget, you call it duty, but choosing a wife based on fortune and connections alone is the very definition of a fortune hunter. Most in the *Ton* are exactly that. Is not marriage a business arrangement for most? Is that what your late parents wanted for you? It was your father's great regret that you took his words to you as you did. He always intended to speak to you about it, but he died suddenly, before he could explain his definition of filial duty to his only son."

"He said that I misunderstood his meaning?" Darcy asked softly.

"He did. Now I have a question; you derided Miss Bennet's

connections to trade, did you not?" the Earl asked, leading Darcy to the point he wanted him to see.

"Yes, one uncle is a solicitor, and the other is actively in trade," Darcy returned.

"What about all of the connections you have to trade, William?" his uncle asked insightfully.

"I do not have such low connections," Darcy denied primly.

"So you are not friends with Bingley? You do not invest with Gardiner, and you do not earn money from trade?"

"That is different!" Darcy insisted.

"You arrogant horse's arse!" Andrew could not remain silent any longer. "Is it different because it is the *high and mighty* Fitzwilliam Darcy, and the same rules do not apply to you?"

Darcy was taken aback by the ferocity of the anger the normally amiable Andrew directed at him. *'Could I be the one who is wrong? Am I the arse that Andrew called me?'* Darcy asked himself as he began to doubt all of his former assertions. *'I have a lot to think on.'*

"Before you turn tail, William, do you think that I, who, like you, has been escaping fortune hunters since I came into society, would suddenly fall for one? If you ever call the honour of the woman I hope to make my wife into question again, so help me I will call you out. I will leave you with this. We, all of us here, know *all about* the truth of Miss Bennet's fortune and connections!"

"William, you plan to depart for Pemberley on Thursday, do you not?" the Earl asked. Darcy, unable to find his voice, only nodded. He felt his gut clenching like he had been kicked in the stomach by Zeus—multiple times! "Come see me on Wednesday morning; we have much to discuss." Darcy nodded, bowed to his family, turned on his heel, and took his leave without another word.

"That was harsh of you, Andrew, a horse's arse?" Richard chuckled.

"He deserved it," Andrew asserted. None of his family said

anything in opposition.

VOL 1, CHAPTER 12

"**P**apa, I received a missive from Jane in which she asks me to join her in Town. Aunt Maddie added to her letter assuring me that I am more than welcome at Gardiner House," Elizabeth requested.

"As long as your mother has no objection, for my part you may go. Yes, Lizzy, I am aware that Tom is in Town, and you are keen to see him and quiz him about his studies. And you know Robert has returned to Ashford Dale, so he is not in London with Tom," Bennet teased his second daughter.

"Very amusing, Papa!" Elizabeth replied with mock affront. "You know very well that I see Cousin Robert as another *younger* brother! I will seek Mama out before you unleash your *supposed* levity on me again." Elizabeth exited the study before her father could reply, soon finding her mother in the morning room.

"Mama, I have been invited to London," Elizabeth handed her mother the missive. Although not the most patient of the Bennet children, Elizabeth curtailed her natural inclination and did a credible job of waiting for her mother to complete reading and render her verdict.

"You have asked your father?" Mrs. Bennet confirmed and Elizabeth nodded to agree she had. "His answer was…?"

"I may go as long as you do not object, Mama," Elizabeth's gave her mother a pleading look.

"I see no reason why not, Lizzy. Let me discuss something with your father before you accept the invitation and decide on travel plans." Mrs. Bennet kissed Elizabeth's cheek and made her way to the study.

"Welcome, my love. I assume that you added your approval of Lizzy's desire to join Jane at the Gardiners?" Bennet asked.

"There is no reason why Lizzy cannot join Jane, though it made me think of something. We have not seen Tom since the term break, and I am sure that Esther and Mark are just as keen to see him as we are. In addition, my parents do not leave for Broadhurst for another ten days, and you will be able to have a little *chat* with Jane's suitor before we depart for the holidays," Priscilla's eyes twinkled at the idea of what that conversation would include.

She was well aware that Andrew Fitzwilliam was not one of the lordlings often found gallivanting about with the immoral members of the *Ton*. Nevertheless, it would not be a bad idea to meet him and his parents before Christmastide.

"You are out-thinking me yet again, my love. This is one time that I will not object to making a trip to London," Bennet said enthusiastically. He was interested to see how the future Earl of Matlock would bear up under his scrutiny.

"I will write to Maddie and Mama and let them know. If Gardiner House is not ready to receive all of us, we will stay at Jersey House." Priscilla took some parchment and waited for her husband to mend a pen for her before she wrote the two expresses.

~~~~~~~/~~~~~~~

"As if it were not bad enough for Charles to abandon us, you will not believe what I saw on Bond Street today, Louisa! I will allow you one hundred guesses, and still you would not guess correctly." Miss Bingley's voice was shrill and even more cutting than normal.

"Do not be arduous, Caro. Just tell me, please," Mrs. Hurst requested in a subdued voice. Without Charles to show them through doors that Mr. Darcy opened for him, their life was boring, for there were no invitations of which to speak.

"Well," Caroline huffed, not liking the tone her sister now addressed her with, "I was walking toward Madam Chambourg's to beg, ahem, I mean to see if she has an opening for us yet. As I approached the store, who should step out of a carriage as if she owned the place? *Miss Jane Bennet*! She was with Lady Marie, the Marchioness of Holder, and Lady Isabelle, Viscountess Westmore! That fortune hunter must work as a paid companion when she is in London. Can you believe it, Louisa?" Miss Bingley crowed.

"And she had the gall to speak about us being tied to trade when she is nothing but a glorified servant!" Mrs. Hurst perked up with the news. There was nothing like a feeling of superiority to banish the malaise she had felt since the confrontation with their brother.

"We have to tell Charles before he makes a fool of himself. Oh, and yes, we must visit dear Georgiana to make sure Mr. Darcy knows just how low that family is. I am sure he will offer for me once we help him expose the Bennets for who they really are!" Miss Bingley felt exuberant, certain that such news would put everything to rights again.

<center>~~~~~~~/~~~~~~~</center>

"Jane, dearest, the one who was gawking at us when we entered the modiste, the woman who looked like an uncoordinated peacock, was that the infamous Miss Bingley?" the Marchioness of Holder asked as they rode back to Gardiner House in one of the Holder carriages.

"Yes, Aunt Marie, that was one half of the supercilious sisters," Jane sighed. "If I never saw any member of that family again, it would be too soon. You know that her disgusting behaviour towards the Netherfield servants caused her brother to be evicted, do you not?"

"Your Uncle Wes mentioned something to that effect a few days ago," Jane's Aunt Isabelle noted for all in the carriage. "Did it not cost the brother ten months' rent?"

"It did, Aunt Issy. Unfortunately, the one warning they received went unheeded. I am not surprised as, even from my short acquaintance with that family, it appears that they all seem to share the trait of seeing and hearing only that which is pleasing to them," Jane related disapprovingly.

"Does that woman still chase Mr. Darcy like a hound after the fox?" Lady Marie asked.

"Even with his rudeness and slight of Lizzy, not even he deserves that fortune hunting, social climbing harpy on his trail. You would have to travel far to find others as vulgar as those two. In the short time I was around them, I lost count of how many times they managed to make mention of the amount of their dowries. They would have died had they discovered that any one of us have more individually than they do combined!" Jane's normally calm voice had a thread of disgust which said far more to her aunts than any of her words had thus far.

"When your courtship becomes common knowledge, they will have apoplexies!" Lady Isabelle giggled at the thought.

"If they dare start any rumours about you, or any of my nieces or nephews, I will see them run out of Town and never able to return!" Lady Marie got herself riled up at the thought of anyone causing harm of any sort for her little sister's children. Her husband and mother had been required to step in to keep her from marching over to Darcy House to give the arrogant master of Pemberley a piece of her mind.

"I am sorry that Allie was not able to join us today, Aunt Marie," Jane said to deflect her aunt before she told the driver to head to Curzon Street, though the thought of it held enough appeal. She smiled as she pictured the expressions of both Miss Bingley and Mrs. Hurst when she was announced to be the niece to such as her aunt.

"Allie had plans with Lady Lydgate that she could not cancel. You know how my youngest loves to spend time with her cousins," Lady Marie smiled as she thought of her mischievous daughter, Alicia.

"When will Uncle Stan return from Holder?" Jane continued to distract her aunt, ignoring her Aunt Isabelle when she smiled behind her hand, for she was quite cognisant of what their niece was doing.

"He had much to do at the estate, so he will join us at Broadhurst for the holidays. And Jane, I am sufficiently calm now, you may stop your diversions," Lady Marie smiled in true amusement at her niece.

"You knew," Jane winced dramatically as if she was upset to be so easily seen through.

"I did, and I appreciate your efforts, though I own I would very much like to be near when those sisters you call supercilious learn the truth!" Lady Marie took her niece's hands. "When it comes to defending my family, I am a lioness at times, and I need to take a breath or have one forced upon me. Thank you for your assistance, Jane."

"Did you say that you invited Lizzy to join you?" Lady Isabelle asked.

"I did, Aunt Issy, and I anticipate an answer when I arrive back at Gardiner House. I know that she cannot wait to see Tom again," Jane confirmed.

After thanking her aunts for a fruitful outing, Jane found Aunt Maddie in her sitting room with a letter in hand. "Your mother replied, Jane. You may read it," Mrs. Gardiner handed her niece the missive.

6 December 1810
Longbourn

Maddie,

We are taking your invitation to come anytime literally. We will arrive on the morrow by eleven. Thomas has agreed to stay until Monday or Tuesday. Lizzy will remain with you until we all meet at Broadhurst.

If our coming on short notice is not convenient, you know that we are able to be hosted with my mother and father so do not put yourself out to ready the house, but we will at least stop for tea, even should moving to Jersey house prove best for you. Would you please invite the Fitzwilliams so we may meet the young man who is courting Jane? If you are able to host us, dinner may prove long enough for Thomas to take his measure and feel like he has given the young man enough of the evil eye to allow his daughter his blessing.

Sincere regards,
Priscilla

"I am guessing that once Lizzy was coming, Mama and Papa could not pass up seeing Tom and meeting Andrew. They will like him and his family, of that I am certain. Papa disdains the typical members of the *Ton*; thankfully the Fitzwilliams are nothing like that," Jane related.

"I am only put out that she thinks I would allow someone else the pleasure of having you all in residence." Mrs. Gardiner huffed, smiling when Jane laughed and went to read to her cousins. While she did, her aunt sent a note to Matlock and Jersey Houses inviting the Fitzwilliams and De Melvilles to a family dinner to be held on Saturday. Affirmative replies were received from both families.

~~~~~~~/~~~~~~~

Georgiana Darcy did not understand why her brother seemed so melancholy. Normally, no matter if he succumbed to ennui or not, heading home to Pemberley restored his mood almost as soon as they were on the road headed north.

In all of his adult life, Darcy had never before been prone to this level of introspection, but his actions had been called into question starting the day that he had unwisely tried to substitute his judgement for Andrew's and among other things had been called a *'horse's arse!'* Ever since that disastrous and officious attempt to interfere with his cousin's choice of a lady, the questions had not stopped running through his head.

And while he had been facing some uncomfortable truths, none of his questions had prepared him for the meeting he had had yesterday with his uncle, the Earl of Matlock, the day before his departure from London.

Darcy arrived at Matlock House at ten where the butler showed him directly to his uncle's study. "Sit, William," his uncle commanded, and an uncomfortable silence had prevailed while the butler brought coffee to the men. Both were sitting with a steaming mug of the dark liquid in their hands when Lord Reggie, with no preamble, asked a question that rocked Darcy to his core. "William, who do you think you are?"

"I am sorry, Uncle, but what do you mean?"

"It is a simple question, William. Let me rephrase it. Do you think that you are always correct, that everyone should bow to your will the way that spineless friend of yours does?" Darcy felt like his uncle had slapped him. "For you to come into my home and start offering unsolicited advice as if you are an expert is the height of hubris! As far as I know, Andrew never requested your opinion about Miss Bennet, so what made you think that you had the duty or right to give it?" The Earl challenged his nephew.

"I-I was trying to protect Andrew." Darcy did not need to see the cynical look on his uncle's face to know that his excuse held no water. What was far more shocking was that he would soon learn that his uncle was only getting started.

"You must think all of us are simpletons who would be taken in by the first pretty face that smiles at Andrew! Tell me, William, how many years have you spent observing Miss Bennet in all facets of life to be able to make your impeccable judgements? You must know every facet of her character to be so sure of yourself. You did after all call her a fortune hunter, did you not?" Darcy cringed as he remembered that this was not the first time in the recent past that unwise words of his had been thrown back at him.

"The family is not wealthy and have no connections and those they do have are in trade," Darcy replied feebly.

"No connections? What do you call my, make that our, family? Again I ask you, William, how did you make your judgements, or is everything, as I believe it is, based on assumptions?" the Earl lambasted his nephew, demanding an answer for which he knew there was no defence. "In my book, William, you are a hypocrite! Your friend, the one you were visiting, is a tradesman's son!"

"I had no idea that Andrew was going to be taken with Miss Bennet when I was in Hertfordshire," Darcy's excuses were getting weaker and more desperate as he ignored his uncle calling him a hypocrite.

"William, Andrew met Miss Bennet months ago at her uncle's house, and again when she volunteered at Haven House."

"Andrew went to Cheapside?" Darcy asked in wonder.

"For an intelligent man, you are exceptionally dim, Darcy. You have been to the uncle's home, and, as Andrew pointed out, you invest with her uncle as well!"

Darcy lost his colour. "T-the uncle is Edward Gardiner?"

"The very same, and a man who is extremely protective of his nieces and nephews, especially the one that was tolerable but not handsome enough to tempt you! What kind of gentleman are you, William? You, who are so concerned with upholding the Darcy name, degrade it when you go around giving offence as you do!"

"I was thinking about Ramsgate and Gigi. Also, I expected everyone to be talking about my wealth." Darcy dropped his head into his hands, unable to face the ire of his uncle.

"So you do not have to behave like a gentleman if you have other concerns? That gives you the right to slight the young lady who will more than likely be Andrew's sister? Tell me, William, when exactly did you apologise for your boorish behaviour during the rest of your stay?" the Earl asked pointedly.

"I-I, err, I..." Darcy spluttered.

"You thought it below you to apologise to those you decided were not worthy. Miss Bingley and your Aunt Cat are both wealthy, are they not?" Darcy's eyebrows pinched together with a look of confusion as to what point his uncle was now trying to make. "Correct me if I am wrong, but did you not say that you thought Miss Bennet a fortune hunter because you think her family is not wealthy?" Darcy nodded, sure that he knew the point his uncle was about to make. "Explain Miss Bingley and Aunt Cat to me! Did Miss Bennet behave like either of them?"

"No, no, she did not. She was always proper. I was, I am still, fighting against an attraction to Miss Elizabeth." Seeing his uncle's incredulous look, William explained the way he was captivated once he really looked at the lady and his subsequent interactions. "Apparently, I allowed my pride and prejudices to cloud my vision."

"You believe yourself well on the way to being in love with a woman who you insulted yet did not have the decency to apologise to, either her or her family, even though they kept using your words of your insult in conversation with you?" Darcy nodded. "You do realise that your actions were not those of a gentleman, do you not, William?" Then his uncle added, "Given your concentration on wealth and connections, are you not a fortune hunter, William?"

"I am beginning to see that quite clearly, Uncle Reggie. I always thought I was behaving in the way that I had been taught to act. I have been hunted..." Darcy began to say.

"Do not use that as an excuse, William. Andrew had been hunted longer than you, but have you ever seen him be rude to anyone, to slight a person regardless of their standing, or act like a spoilt schoolboy who did not want to do something? Let me answer for you, no you have not!" The Earl paused and then looked at his nephew. "Before I forget, do you know why Miss Elizabeth was sitting out when you slighted her?"

Darcy was about to give his assumption but stopped himself. "I do not."

"Did you not notice that there were far more ladies than men present?" Darcy shook his head, his disgust with himself building painfully in his chest by the moment. "The Bennet ladies, as well as most in the neighbourhood, all sit out two dances so that no one will be left without a partner for the evening! Miss Bennet explained it to us when we had the pleasure of meeting her."

"I am a cad, am I not?" Darcy winced, his head again dropping before his uncle in clear defeat.

"Before I answer that, you said the other day that you were doing what your father taught you. This is not what George Darcy wanted for you, William. Did your mother not talk to you about how she wanted you to choose your wife?" Darcy swallowed dryly as he nodded that she had. "Your father wanted the same! He, like your mother, wanted you to marry for love rather than wealth and connections. What need have you for more wealth and connections, William? Is Pemberley having a financial crisis I do not know about?" Darcy shook his head mutely. "William, you are a gentle-

man, and the Bennet girls are a gentleman's daughters; you are equal. You are a paradox to me sometimes, my boy. You are the best master and landlord and will do anything for those who depend on you, but at the same time you sometimes behave like a lout.

"No, William, I do not think you a cad, but you need to examine yourself. At this moment, I see more of my sister Catherine in you than your mother and father. If you want to be like her that is your choice, but you will be a very lonely man unless you are able to change," the Earl stated grimly.

"I have seen that in myself, and no, Uncle Reggie, Aunt Cat is the last person in the world I want to emulate. I clearly see the need to change and will take the time while at Pemberley for the winter to work on myself before I make my annual visit to Rosings Park. When or if I am in the company of the Bennets again, I will make a complete apology. As I look at my behaviour now, with the clarity you have given me, I cannot view it without feeling abhorrence at my actions." Darcy promised quietly. The Earl stood and walked to where his nephew was sitting.

"Being able to honestly acknowledge the error of your ways is the first step on a journey that only you will be able to take. I look forward to seeing the man that emerges from that journey, William." The Earl had extended his hand in a gesture of family and support, and Darcy had appreciated the gesture. After greeting his aunt, Darcy returned to his house and sat alone in his study late into the night thinking of a great many things he wished were not his to consider.

If Darcy had felt like Zeus had kicked him after Andrew took him to task, for the whole of that night he had felt like he had been stampeded by a large herd of horses, and they had come back for a second trampling!

The conversation with the Earl had accentuated the fact that it was time to revaluate his life and the way he interacted with others, and after a night of reviewing years of interactions, Darcy reached a decision. The first step would be making a full disclosure to his sister. She had worked hard to recover after Ramsgate, and that hard work was yielding tangible results. Now it was his turn, he would have to improve himself and failure was not an option! At the first stop of the morning, Darcy requested that Mrs. Annesley ride in the second coach, disclosing to both that he wanted to discuss something particular with his sister.

~~~~~~~/~~~~~~~

"Mark!" Tom exclaimed as his little brother ran towards him and was enfolded in his older brother's welcoming arms as soon as he scampered out of the coach, ruffling his hair affectionately. "Father, Mother, Lizzy, Esther," Tom greeted each family member as they alighted from the conveyance.

"Mark, my dear, do you think I can have a turn to hug Tom now?" Their mother asked laughingly as she watched her youngest cling to his brother.

With Mark's desire to be in his brother's company barely assuaged, he was reluctant to do so, but he stepped aside so that Priscilla could hug her oldest son, followed by Elizabeth and Esther. Bennet brought up the rear and clapped his heir on the back. Jane was waiting on the steps patiently to greet everyone understanding that after not seeing Tom for some months, the family would want to greet him first.

"You have been very coy, Jane," Elizabeth accused her smiling sister. "I understand that you met your Viscount many months ago, and in all that time you never mentioned a word to me!" Elizabeth linked her arm with her sister's as the family proceeded indoors.

"Andrew is not *my* Viscount, Lizzy. It has only been a few days that we have been courting," Jane explained. "When we first met, I was impressed by him. He is not one of the dandies or popinjays that populate the *Ton*. And he is the farthest thing from a rake that you will ever meet."

"Oh Jane, I am so happy for you. Never have I seen you so animated about a man before. If you like him, that is enough for me. How did he take it when you revealed our true situation to him?" Elizabeth asked hopefully.

"It changed nothing for him! He had been adamant

about wanting to court me when he knew only the reported information, and when he learned the truth, he agreed that it did not change anything in his eyes." Jane teased her sister into a laugh. "He is such a good man Lizzy," Jane smiled one of her ethereal smiles that showed her pleasure.

The Gardiners were inside and welcomed the arriving Bennets to Gardiner House. Robert Jamison, who had been given leave not to return home yet, was waiting in the drawing room and was warmly greeted by the rest of the Bennets. "You will meet Jane's young man and his family on the morrow. We are having a family dinner, and yes, Priscilla, your parents as well as Wes and Isabelle will be here." Seeing Priscilla's look of concern, Maddie Gardiner added, "Marie and Stan have a previous engagement. I did not have much time to organise the dinner as it was."

Jane and Elizabeth met in their shared sitting room after the latter had washed and changed. "Please tell me that the Fitzwilliams have not told Mr. Darcy the truth of our connections and wealth," Elizabeth asked.

"Not a word, Lizzy, I promise you," Jane consoled her sister. "Andrew called his cousin a horse's arse," Jane chortled into her hand.

"I do not disagree, but why call his cousin that?" Elizabeth's inquisitiveness demanding that she know all.

"Mr. Darcy advised his cousin that I was a fortune hunter who was not interested in his friend Bingley because I had my eye on the *bigger prize* with a title thrown in. Andrew told him that should he ever call my honour into question again, he would call Mr. Darcy out!" Jane related, seeing Elizabeth was immediately spitting mad.

"Who the hell, sorry Jane," Elizabeth was chagrined that in her pique she had used unladylike language. "Mama has been telling me I should not be so harsh in my judgements of that proud, disagreeable, and arrogant man, but then he attempts this! It just reinforces my opinion of him!"

"What has Mr. Darcy done now?" Their mother asked,

sighing, as she joined her daughters. Jane calmly related all to her mother, including that Mr. Darcy had been called on the carpet by the Earl before he and his younger sister departed for Pemberley.

"You see, Mama, this only proves what I think about the man is correct!" Elizabeth insisted.

"Elizabeth, what religion do we claim?" her mother asked.

"Christianity, of course." Elizabeth frowned, able to see the path her mother was taking, but unwilling to walk it.

"And is not forgiveness one of the central tenets of our faith?" Priscilla asked.

"It is, Mama, but he has not apologised for any of the offences he has perpetrated against one of us, either in Hertfordshire or here in London." Elizabeth countered the insinuation that she should grant forgiveness when it was not asked for.

"How many times have you been in company with him for more than a minute or two other than during your dance, when, by your own admission, you were doing whatever you were able to in order to discompose the man? You were the *only* lady he danced with at our former tenant's ball. Are those the actions of a man who does not find you tolerable enough to tempt him?" Priscilla challenged her daughter to consider the facts, not just her emotions with regards to Mr. Darcy.

"I suppose I will have to reserve judgement until I see him again. Mama, I have a question," Elizabeth waited for her mother to grant permission before asking. "When Jane becomes betrothed and the veil is lifted on our true position, how will I know if Mr. Darcy is truly contrite or is only apologising because of our wealth and connections?"

"That, my daughter, will require your vaunted intelligence to help you make a judgement. Personally, I do not think him that kind of man, but you will have to decide for yourself, when and if he makes his apologies," Priscilla kissed her middle daughter on the cheek.

~~~~~~~/~~~~~~~

"Sed, I do not like the look of your pallor!" Lady Rose observed with concern.

"Rose, if I am to meet the heir, I must go to London earlier than we planned. I think that I will not be the one who makes the tour to the rest of our properties and businesses. As much as I want more time with you, my love, this is something that is beyond my control," the Duke wheezed as he spoke quietly to her.

"Will you be able to travel in the winter?" Lady Rose worried.

"There is little choice in the matter. I am determined to meet my heir, so it must be this way. A Bennet will hear an apology from a Rhys-Davies for the injustices of the third duke. Let us see if we can wait until late February before we have to depart. As long as there is no significant worsening, we should be able to enjoy a little more time together at Longfield Meadows," the Duke managed a thin, wan smile, secretly believing it was no more than a wish, but he did not want to disabuse her of it before the holidays.

"Is that why you agreed to return home, Sed? You could feel your symptoms progressing?" the Duchess asked softly.

"After all of these years together you know me too well, my dear wife. I will wait patiently at heaven's gate until you join me one day so we may be reunited. However, I hope it is not for many years in the future. How many who have had arranged marriages can boast a love like we found, Rose?" the Duke asked tenderly.

"Very few, I dare say," the Duchess agreed. "Sed, have you informed your friend Jersey that you have an heir?"

"I will write anon, my love. He was extremely helpful in the fruitless search before I turned to the letter. I hope to see him when we are in town, I will reveal the identity of the heir when we are sitting face to face."

"And it will be good for me to see Sarah again, for it has been far too long. She has been a good friend over the years. I regret that we have not seen them for many years," the Duchess lamented.

With his plans set, the Duke wrote a missive to Sir Randolph Norman to apprise him of the accelerated timetable for his visit to London.

VOL 1, CHAPTER 13

"**L**ord Matlock, Lady Matlock, Lord Hilldale, and Colonel Fitzwilliam, Mr. Thomas Bennet, Lady Priscilla Bennet, Miss Elizabeth, Master Tom, Miss Esther, and Master Mark. The young man at the end is Master Robert Jamison, a cousin of the Bennets. Lord Reginald and Lady Elaine Fitzwilliam, the Earl and Countess of Matlock, Lord Andrew Fitzwilliam the Viscount Hilldale, and the Honourable Colonel Richard Fitzwilliam." Gardiner made the introductions.

"Please, call me Matlock," the Earl allowed as he shook Bennet's hand.

"Bennet for me," Bennet returned the welcoming gesture, gratified that his first impression of the Fitzwilliams was positive. They seemed to be down to earth, showing no evidence of improper pride; they were simply warm and friendly.

"It has been many years since I have seen you in society, Lady Priscilla," Lady Elaine noted. "I believe it was during one of your seasons over twenty years' past."

"You are correct, Lady Matlock," Priscilla agreed with a smile as she glanced at her husband.

"If our children have their way, we will be family; you must call me Elaine," the Countess insisted.

"So this is your sister who was not *handsome enough* to tempt William," the Colonel chuckled. "Not to embarrass you, Miss Elizabeth, but my dour cousin must have been suffering an apoplexy that caused him to speak the opposite of the truth that night." He bowed in her direction.

"Jane mentioned that you are an incorrigible flirt, Colonel," Elizabeth teased him in return, thankful to note that from what she could tell, unlike Mr. Darcy, his relations were all people she would enjoy knowing.

"Guilty as charged, Miss Elizabeth, guilty as charged," the Colonel owned with a grin.

"What is my much younger brother up to now?" Lord Andrew asked in feigned despair as he brought Jane a glass of sherry.

"You are not exactly an old man, Andrew. I am but two years younger than you!" his brother shot back.

"I was referring to your maturity, not your physical age!" Andrew ribbed.

"My brother would have you believe that I am never serious," the Colonel displayed mock outrage.

"Miss Elizabeth, please allow me to apologise for my cousin's behaviour when he was in your neighbourhood," Andrew stated.

"Lord Hilldale, you have naught for which you need to apologise. Not only were you not there, but you cannot control what someone else does. As you have no part in the offence, you have nothing for which to be forgiven," Elizabeth replied. "Please call me Elizabeth, or Lizzy as most everyone does."

"You are of course correct, Elizabeth, please call me Andrew." He agreed, grateful that none of the Bennets held the actions of his cousin against his family.

"And I am Richard," the Colonel added. "Did I hear talk of Hunsford?"

"Yes, our distant cousin just returned to his parsonage there. He will be married to our good friend Miss Lucas next month, and I will visit her around Easter," Elizabeth relayed.

"If I know our Aunt's requirements for her parsons, then this one could not be much to boast of," Andrew chuckled. The sisters told the brothers about their cousin's stay and betrothal to Miss Lucas, and both brothers were much diverted when the embargo on talk of his patroness was shared.

"Grandmama, Grandpapa, Uncle Wes, Aunt Issy!" Mark exclaimed as the De Melvilles arrived.

"How are you, Scamp?" Lord Jersey asked his youngest grandchild.

"Very well thank you, Grandpapa. I am bringing Calista with me when we visit Broadhurst," Mark reported with pride.

"I look forward to meeting her," Lord Jersey replied as he ruffled Mark's hair affectionately leaving the lad to try and pat his locks back into some semblance of order.

"Aunt Issy, will we be seeing our cousins at Broadhurst?" Esther asked hopefully.

"Yes, all three of my children will be present, as will Aunt Marie and Uncle Stan and their two," Lady Isabelle promised her niece.

The Gardiner's butler announced dinner and the company moved into the dining room with precedence being ignored among friends and family. The repast, all four courses, was both delicious and plentiful as Madeline Gardiner rightly prided herself on setting a good table. When the diners were sated, Mrs. Gardiner stood and led the ladies to the drawing room where tea and coffee awaited them. Once the ladies exited, Andrew requested that Bennet join him at the unoccupied end of the table.

"I appreciate that you bestowed authority on your brother-in-law to act in your stead, but I want to make sure that you do not have any questions or concerns that you would like to discuss with me," Andrew offered.

"If your interest in my Jane had begun *after* you discovered the truth about our family, this discussion would have been vastly different. As it is, I know your interest did not wane, no matter how much of our *reported* information Gardiner shared with you. I have heard nothing but good of you from my wife's parents and siblings. As long as you respect my daughter, and should you two choose to marry, that you will be a good husband to her, there is no more that I need to know at this point." Bennet raised his glass of port to his daughter's suitor, who returned the gesture with his snifter of cognac. "Besides, I have Randolph and James investigate those who get close to my family."

Andrew raised an eyebrow. "I trust there was nothing too scandalous in my past," he quipped.

"As I have not ordered my daughter to break the courtship, that is a safe assumption," Bennet returned. "Though I own that even more than them, I trust my daughter's intuition; she is not one to suffer fools."

"Your second daughter would not allow me to apologise for William's...," Andrew saw the confused look as he changed the subject. "Sorry, you know him as Darcy, and she would not allow me to apologise for his rudeness and arrogance while in your neighbourhood."

"Very astute of my Lizzy, though she often is. You cannot apologise for that which you are not responsible. Let me ask you something now, sir. What is Mr. Wickham to your family?" The way the younger man bristled at the mention of the name was most telling to Bennet.

"How do you know that libertine's name?" Andrew asked shortly.

"He is a member of the Derbyshire Militia who are quartered in Meryton currently," Bennet shared.

"Do you object if I ask my brother to join us?" Andrew requested and Bennet waved away the chance to object.

Once the two had returned and settled, when the older brother mentioned Wickham's name, the look that Bennet noted on the Colonel's face was murderous. "Was my cousin Darcy aware that the miscreant is in Meryton?" Richard asked with steel in his voice.

"I believe so," Bennet told him.

"He should have..., never mind. How did the blackguard come to your notice?" Richard 's frown deepened, and he assessed Bennet anew.

Bennet related all to the brothers, including the gist of his daughter's conversation and her complete disbelief of close to every word out of his mouth. "I have run him off my land as he seemed not to get the message after he had called a half dozen times and was told that my daughter was not home for each of his visits. He was never admitted to my house except for the instance when I warned him off. Also, I had him investigated and turned the results over to the Colonel, who demoted the liar to a private."

"He has sealed his own fate," Richard said with satisfaction.

"In what way?" Bennet asked. Richard and Andrew related the truth of Wickham's assertions regarding the living, and about the wastrel's life of debauchery, gambling, and dissipation. "Lizzy had the right of it—a kernel of truth cloaked in sheaves of lies," Bennet whistled softly. "If your cousin holds over two thousand in the man's vowels, why is he not languishing in Marshalsea for the rest of his days?"

"Part of it is a misdirected sense of honour toward his father. William, or Darcy, was reticent to act against his father's godson out of love for his late father. That was until this past summer," Andrew stated.

"Miss Darcy!" Bennet exclaimed before he caught himself.

"How could you know about Ramsgate?" Richard asked in alarm.

"I knew not what, where, or why. Well, the where certainly until this instant. I had my investigators do an extensive check on Charles Bingley prior to his being offered a lease on Netherfield Park. As your cousin would be with him and acts almost like a father figure for the man, he was investigated peripherally. All the report said is that there was a possible incident with Miss Darcy," Bennet informed the brothers.

After swearing him to tell no one outside of his wife and older children, and only if necessary, Andrew and Richard told Bennet about Ramsgate and Miss Darcy's near ruination. When they were complete, Bennet sat for a moment in silence. He knew that had it been one of his own daughters, he would not have rested until the libertine was in the ground. "Now I understand the reaction that Lizzy reported when your cousin saw Wickham in Meryton. It also explains, at least partially, his mood at the assembly in Meryton," Bennet stated thickly.

"As he has contravened William's conditions for his freedom, I will be taking a little ride to Meryton on Monday morning," Richard stated menacingly, and that was the moment that Bennet understood no matter how jovial the younger Fitzwilliam could be, he was not one to get on the bad side of.

"Father had a long chat with William the day before he and Gigi, Miss Darcy, departed London. I think it may be beneficial to talk to him about William, if you would like," Andrew suggested.

"I heard my name used in vain," Matlock said as he approached his sons and Bennet, and Andrew repeated his suggestion his father and Bennet talk, so an appointment for Monday was made for Bennet to attend the Earl at Matlock House.

The men soon joined the ladies and younger children in the drawing room where the Fitzwilliams, who had never had the pleasure before, were amazed by the talent of the three Bennet sisters, especially the middle sister when her voice swelled for a solo. Her family all looked on in pride while the Fitzwilliams sat in open-mouthed stupefaction before the applause drowned out all.

~~~~~~~/~~~~~~~

The freezing temperatures and the light dusting of early snow did nothing to reduce Darcy's pleasure at being back at Pemberley as he sat atop Zeus inspecting some tenant homes with his steward, Mr. Edwin Chalmers. Darcy quickly authorised all of the repairs, then parted with his steward and pointed his horse back towards the manor house.

Working with the steward on tenant issues reminded Darcy of his recent conversation with his Uncle Reggie, more accurately labelled as a raking over the coals. The more he considered the whole of the conversation, from being asked who he thought he was, to a clarification of what his parents wanted for him, the more he was ashamed at how abhorrent his behaviour had been both in appearance and deed. He faced the truth of his former behaviour fully. Regardless of his reasons and justifications, his behaviour had been decidedly ungentlemanly.

At the time, he had tried to deny the charges that he was hypocritical to himself, but he could no longer hide from that truth—even Gigi had called him out on that score as he remembered their conversation when they spoke in the carriage on the way home.

After minutes of silence while his sister had waited patiently for him to talk, Darcy finally told her all. He left out nothing. He did not miss the look of displeasure when he told her of his slight of the second Bennet daughter. When he told her how he had attempted to dictate who his cousin should or should not court, his sister's eyes had grown as large as saucers.

Gigi had not interjected and had, in fact, held her peace until his recitation, which ended with their uncle's admonishments, was complete. She took some time to contemplate before she addressed him. "Uncle Reggie is correct, brother; you have practised a level of hypocrisy. I have never understood how you would sit by silently when Miss Bingley and Mrs. Hurst would disdain those in trade while they are from trade! *How could you think landed gentlefolk below you when you were being hosted by the son of a tradesman? If I did not know you better, I would agree with Uncle that you could be deemed a fortune hunter.*

"You accepted Mr. Bingley as a friend, but what of his connections that you used as a foil for your objections to the Bennets? In the past, I have heard you state it is not money which sets one's position in society, but that seemed to be the measure you used with the Bennets?" Georgiana shook her head. "It is hard to reconcile what you have told me with the image of you as the perfect brother. Like me, William, you have erred, and also like me, you should have known better."

"I am starting to understand that Gigi. I have a lot to work on, and after my visit to Aunt Cat at Easter, I will journey to Hertfordshire to apologise to all of the Bennets and hope they will see it

in their hearts to forgive me. I fear I have lost the only woman that I have loved, and whom I still love. I will not blame Miss Elizabeth if she never wants to see me again after the way I behaved toward her family, most especially toward herself," Darcy lamented.

"William, the only way you will know that for sure is if when you have worked on changing those things that give offence so readily and you return to Meryton to apologise. If she is not willing to even listen to your apology, then she is not the one for you," Georgiana had offered her opinion gently, but that only underscored the truth of her words.

"When did you become so wise, Gigi?" William asked.

"I was forced to look at my part in the near debacle at Ramsgate and acknowledge it. Only after a lot of introspection was I able to start to work on being a better person in general, which was for me also changing my thoughts toward myself to be both kinder and more truthful. It is this I believe you also have begun to do. You have started to acknowledge your faults, and I am well aware that our aunt and uncle see this as the way to begin to make meaningful change. It is also precisely the correct first step, of which we are now both aware." She smiled a little ruefully when her brother had nodded his agreement. For his part, he had been impressed at how much his sister had matured since escaping the clutches of George Wickham.

As Darcy handed Zeus off to a groom, he fervently believed that his sister's wise counsel was correct. The time had come to take a long, hard, and unvarnished look at his life; it was now the time to make course corrections. What Gigi said about Miss Elizabeth resonated with him. He was determined that the next time he saw her he would be worthy of her company, though he would not delude himself that she would be waiting with open arms to welcome him back. He would have to work to earn both her trust and her respect. Once he had that, he could try for more. Fitzwilliam Darcy had never been afraid of hard work!

~~~~~~~/~~~~~~~

"Would you like coffee, Bennet?" Matlock offered.

"No thank you, Matlock. I enjoyed some before I departed from Gardiner House. I understand that Richard collected copies of the vowels and is on his way to Meryton?" Bennet stated.

"Yes, he took Andrew for company. They told you what that bastard tried to do to my niece?" Matlock got riled up each time he thought of how narrowly disaster had been averted, exhaling slowly to control his ire when Bennet nodded.

"Andrew told me that you had a long conversation with your nephew before he departed for the north. Has he always been the way he was in Meryton?" Bennet asked.

"Conversation? I mostly spoke and he mostly listened. But to answer your question? No, he used to be an exceptionally good and considerate boy; he still is with his tenants and servants. Do not get me wrong, he is as honourable a man as you could hope to find and is fiercely loyal. He has never dallied with *any* lady and is neither a dandy nor a rake. He was so different before he came out in society and the hunt for his hide began. The fundamental truth is he was never outgoing like my boys, but he also was neither arrogant nor rude." Matlock then related pertinent parts of his *conversation* with Darcy to Bennet.

"My wife told Elizabeth that there may have been more to his behaviour at the assembly," Bennet offered easily, proud of his wife's excellent intuition.

"Yes, he had reasons to be upset, but none of them excuse his behaviour that night, or any other time he was rude or dismissive," Matlock asserted. "Also, you should know that he is in love with your second daughter."

It took Bennet a few moments to snap his jaw closed after the shock of that revelation. "He hides his feelings rather well," Bennet replied sardonically. "My daughter felt that the few times they were in company together, that he was looking at her to find fault."

Matlock gave a sage nod. "My nephew is adept at retreating behind his mask and he becomes inscrutable. The irony was that he was worried he would excite expectations he felt his duty to his name would preclude him from fulfilling. He is in for quite a shock when he eventually learns the truth."

"If he wants Lizzy to look at him as anything but a pride-filled, arrogant man, there will be a lot of grovelling involved!" Bennet chuckled. Was he ready to part with two of his daughters if Darcy ever succeeded in winning Elizabeth's heart? That was not exactly what he had expected to have to consider this day.

~~~~~~~/~~~~~~~

"Colonel Fitzwilliam, to what do I owe the honour of a *bona fide* war hero visiting a humble militia colonel?" Colonel Forster welcomed his visitor to his office. "Welcome, Lord Hildale."

"Thank you for the welcome, Colonel Forster; please call me Fitzwilliam. I am here about a man who, I believe, was an ensign in your unit, a wolf in sheep's clothing."

"Are we talking about one George Wickham, by any chance?" Forster asked. "*Was,* is correct. He is no longer and officer; the man is a private!"

"Then he has been up to his usual nonsense?" the Viscount drawled.

"I never had a good feeling about him, not even the day he joined my unit. He spun a tale that I surmised to be cock and bull about how he saved some maiden and ended up with his bent nose and missing tooth," Forster informed the brothers. "Then he ran afoul of a Mr. Bennet, who had the man investigated, turned over the report to me, and I promptly demoted him. I do not want a libertine as an officer, even if it is the militia."

"You were right to doubt him; he was caught trying to abscond with a tender-aged girl by a relative of hers who gifted him a facer for his trouble. We have come to take him off your hands. He has an extremely long engagement to fulfil at Marshalsea," Fitzwilliam shared. "I suggest you have his tent searched at some point; he has been known to *borrow* items that do not belong to him."

"Carter!" Forster called. "Where is Private Wickham?"

"He is asleep sir; he had night duty last night," Captain Carter reported succinctly.

"Show Colonel Fitzwilliam, Lord Hilldale, and all those accompanying them to Wickham's tent," Forster ordered. Carter guided the brothers, the bailiff, and his men to the private's tent. He was about to call out to Wickham to announce their arrival when he was stopped by the Colonel.

"Thank you, Captain, we will take it from here. You are dismissed," the Colonel ordered quietly.

Wickham's rifle and bayonet were quietly handed to one of the men with the bailiff, and once they made sure that there were no more weapons in the tent, the brothers tipped the cot over and Wickham ended up face down on the hard ground with a thud.

"*What the bloody hell!* Get out of my tent!" Wickham yelled, not seeing his antagonists as yet as he tried to push himself up from the dirt.

"Now, Georgie Boy, is that the way to welcome *old friends!*" Richard 's sardonic reply cut through Wickham's tirade.

At first Wickham thought it was a nightmare, at least, he did until a boot to his posterior rudely reminded him of reality. "W-why a-are y-y-you h-h-here?" Wickham managed to stammer.

"Were you not given a very specific warning by my cousin of what your fate would be if you attempted to blacken his name again?" the Colonel asked as he towered over the cowering and snivelling shell of a man.

"I have not," Wickham attempted to prevaricate as he searched for a way out of the trouble he had once again caused for himself.

"Are you trying to tell me that all of the Bennets who reported hearing you are lying and you, who would not know the truth if it took a bite of your arse, are to be believed?" Lord

Andrew pointed out sceptically.

"How w-would you know the bloody Bennets?" Wickham could see the writing on the wall. He would either be dead before the sun set that day, or, more likely, on his way to Marshalsea, which in many ways was worse than death. "Ow!" Wickham exclaimed as the Viscount gifted him with a kick in his arse.

"Watch how you talk about the family of the lady I am courting!" the Viscount warned the wastrel.

Of all the bad luck Wickham had in his life, this took the cake. He had taken a chance, believing that the Bennet daughter hated Darcy! Instead, he had chosen a lady who herself, or one of her sisters, was being courted by the prig's bloody cousin!

"If it were up to me, I would run you through and leave you to the carrion. However, I agree with my father and brother. The rest of your miserable life locked up in Marshalsea will let you experience some of the pain you thought naught about dispensing to those around you. Perhaps you will be lucky and annoy the wrong one in the gaol, and he will instead send you to hell early," Richard growled.

Wickham decided to play his last card as he stood up. "If I were you, I would have me sent to the Americas in first class with a good amount of money to start with," Wickham added to his list of many misdemeanours as he attempted to use blackmail to save his hide. "Never knowing who I will talk about Miss..." Whatever he was about to say was lost as both Richard and Andrew's fists slammed into him. Richard connected with Wickham's mouth and dislodged four more teeth, while Andrew drove his blow into the bastard's stomach with all the force he could muster.

The combined force of the blows drove Wickham into the wall of the tent and out the other side as the pegs gave way. When Richard reached him, he was lying in own vomit, having cast up his accounts from the force of the brothers' blows. Richard lowered himself to his haunches, so he was close to the blubbering man's ear.

"If you *ever* mention that name again, even in passing, I will hear of it. I will use all the techniques of interrogation that are used by any army in the world on you for days before I finally allow you to die! Everything that has befallen you is by your own hand! You had better pray that you never see me again," Richard whispered menacingly to the prostrate man.

Wickham did not doubt that Richard Fitzwilliam meant every word of his threat. He had played what he thought was his trump card, and it had backfired on him in the worst way. The Viscount turned to the bailiff. "This rubbish is yours now; please remove it to Marshalsea, and the journey may be as painful for him as you please."

The man nodded to two of his burlier men who lifted the blubbering man to his feet. His hands and legs were well and truly secured with manacles and chains, then he was roughly tossed into the back of a cart. Once they had him in it, his chains were locked to an iron ring in the bed of the cart, and soon it was moving out of the encampment while Wickham's former comrades in the militia watched with disgust, relieved that the blight on their regiment was finally removed.

Per Colonel Fitzwilliam's suggestion, Colonel Forster had Wickham's belongings searched after the man had been carted off. A number of missing items, including Denny's and Saunderson's purses, were recovered. Forster thought over the merit of pressing further charges, but as the man would never be able to get out, he decided that his languishing in Marshalsea for the crimes he had already committed was punishment enough since his men's money was returned almost in its entirety.

VOL 1, CHAPTER 14

The morning that the four Bennets - the parents and their two youngest children - were to return to Longbourn, Bennet and his wife asked the two eldest daughters to meet them in the sitting room attached to their suite.

"Your father and I want to share some information with you, a few items actually. Lizzy, you remember I said although it was not an excuse for Mr. Darcy's behaviour, that there may have been pressures we were not aware of?" Priscilla asked.

"I remember, Mama, and I was trying to let it go, but he tried to interfere with Jane's courtship," Elizabeth returned irritably.

"When I met with Lord Matlock yesterday, he shared the following with me and authorised me to inform you, so long as you are able to promise you will repeat what I am about to tell you to no one," Bennet said, satisfied when both swore they would not repeat what they were told to any living soul. Bennet proceeded to tell them what had been related to him about Wickham's interactions with Darcy and his attempt at Ramsgate. Neither parent was surprised when their compassionate daughters quietly cried for the pain Georgiana Darcy had experienced at Wickham's hand, though they had not met the young lady. "I did not trust that man, but I never imagined him so bad!" Elizabeth exclaimed.

"That is one of the additional things we needed to share with you. He will never be able to hurt Miss Darcy or anyone else ever again," Priscilla assured her outraged daughters. "Andrew and Richard had him thrown into Marshalsea. His stay there will be a lifetime in duration."

"How would any of us have reacted, given everything Mr. Darcy has been through? No, Lizzy," Bennet said when his second daughter attempted to speak. "It of course does not excuse his being rude or the improper pride he exhibited. It does, however, allow us to understand what led to that behaviour. His uncle says the same, that as a gentleman he should have behaved better," Bennet stated.

"All we are asking of you is if or when Mr. Darcy apologises, that you will be open to hearing him, Lizzy. Your father tells me the Earl related that in the meeting with his nephew, before the Darcys' departure for Derbyshire, he saw understanding and acknowledgement of wrongdoing from Mr. Darcy. Evidently, the man was genuinely contrite. He began to examine his own behaviour with a critical eye.

"Lizzy, your father and I expect from you the same as we do any of our children, and that is that you keep an open mind next time you are in company with the man. Do not forget, he knows not the truth of our situation. If he approaches us beforehand to make his contrition known, that will be very telling. It would mean he is more like Andrew and less like his Aunt Catherine," Priscilla added, directing her comment the younger of the two.

"How I react when I next see him, I do not know, but this I can promise you all. I will keep an open mind, and if he is genuine in his contrition? Who knows, we may even become indifferent acquaintances," Elizabeth smiled.

"That is all we ask of you, Elizabeth," her father affirmed.

"It is good that the neighbourhood is rid of that terrible man, Mr. Wickham," Jane opined. "So much evil wrapped up in one man."

It was not long after that the four Bennets took their leave of the family; it would not be a long separation as they would all be together at Broadhurst in ten days.

~~~~~~~/~~~~~~~

"What does Richard's letter tell?" Georgiana Darcy asked her brother.

Brother and sister, along with Georgiana's companion, were in Pemberley's music room, where Georgiana had been entertaining her brother, when the missive was delivered. "He has done what I should have after Ramsgate," Darcy informed his sister without dismissing her companion, as Mrs. Annesley was fully aware of what had occurred the past summer.

"What do you mean, William?" Georgiana asked.

"Wickham will never be able to harm another, for Richard and Andrew have had him thrown into Marshalsea. You remember I told you he was a member of the Derbyshire Militia quartered in Meryton near the Bennets' home and the one Bingley used to lease?" Darcy reminded his sister.

"Yes, but please tell me he has not hurt another, especially not one of the Miss Bennets?" Georgiana responded with concern.

"No Gigi, he was not able to hurt anyone in the area. Evidently, he told his lies about both of us to Miss Elizabeth Bennet, and she did not believe a word of it. When the families met in London, Mr. Bennet told our family that Wickham was in Meryton and all about his attempts to ply his normal trade, which were roundly rebuffed. It is another mark against my character, Gigi. I cared more about keeping our private information private than I did the protection of the innocents from that wastrel," Darcy berated himself.

"He was not able to harm anyone, you said? I would love to meet Miss Elizabeth, as she was not taken in by him at all. If only I had been so discerning." As happened still, though more rarely, Georgiana became maudlin as she remembered how she had been fooled by Wickham.

"Gigi, you were but fifteen at the time, and I wrong-headedly thought I was protecting your sensibilities by not telling you the truth about him. Miss Elizabeth is five years older than you were and did not remember him fondly from her childhood. If anyone should feel guilt it is *me*. Out of a warped sense of duty to father, I never told him what his god-son had become, and because of it, I cleaned up after the man for far too long," a melancholy Darcy relayed.

"When I was at my lowest, did not all of you tell me there was naught I could do to change the past, William?" Georgiana asked, not surprised when Darcy nodded. "I suggest you take your own advice; learn from your mistakes and look to the future. Remember what Mrs. Annesley told me—if we do not learn from our errors, we are doomed to repeat them," Georgiana told her brother firmly.

"I am in awe of how wise and strong you are, baby sister," Darcy smiled for the first time since the conversation began.

"William, may I accompany you to Rosings this Easter?" Georgiana asked changing the subject.

"Gigi, are you sure you want to face the dragon?" His sister had never been willing to accompany him and Richard before as she was terrified of their aunt who she called the *old dragon*.

"Yes I am, William; I desire to see Anne again. It has been far too long, and I cannot hide from Aunt Catherine all of my life. If you can face your ███████ I can face the dragon," Georgiana claimed encouragingly.

Darcy was pleased with the maturity and poise his sister displayed. Richard would be at Rosings park as well, so Gigi would have both her guardians to protect her if needs be.

~~~~~~~/~~~~~~~

"Did I not tell you to betroth yourself to the oldest of the Bennet daughters?" Lady Catherine demanded in her imperious manner once Collins had proudly reported that he had obeyed her by returning a betrothed man.

"Their father refused me permission to approach any of my fair cousins, your beneficence," Collins bowed low for the fourth time since being admitted to the great lady's presence.

"Well, in that case, I suppose I can forgive you for your not following my orders to the letter, but do not let it happen again. You say that this Miss Lucas is a demure lady? Good. When you return from your wedding in January, I will begin to instruct her on how to run your household as it should be," Lady Catherine dictated.

"She will only benefit from you most gracious condescension." Collins bowed again.

"You say you met my Anne's betrothed in Hertfordshire?" Lady Catherine inquired.

"I did, your Ladyship." Collins did not dare repeat her nephew's assertion that he was not betrothed to Miss Anne de Bourgh. "I humbly request a sennight away from my duties after Twelfth Night for my wedding."

"You may have your time. Here is a draft of your sermon for this Sunday, it is on the distinction of rank." Lady Catherine handed the page to a footman to pass to her simpering parson, who she then dismissed after inviting him to dinner some evenings later.

Collins felt the compliment of an invitation to Rosings keenly. He had wondered why it seemed no one from the neighbourhood visited his patroness or that she did not make visits to her neighbours, but never asked the great lady about her reasoning about the situation, knowing she would not appreciate him questioning her about a subject unless she introduced it herself.

~~~~~~~/~~~~~~~

Miss Bingley was most displeased. Three times she had attempted to gain access to Darcy House to relay her intelligence about the Bennets, and each time she had been turned away by the butler, who told her that the family was not home. Yes, the knocker was down, but that had never stopped Miss Bingley before.

After her latest rebuff at Mr. Darcy's home, she and her sister had visited their brother at his town house. "Charles, would you believe that Mr. Darcy's butler keeps claiming that he is not home for me to visit my dear friend, Georgiana?" Miss Bingley whined. It had taken a few days of whining and manipulation for her and her sister to get Charles to allow them back into his house, to visit at least, and she was certain he would address this for her.

"Caroline, are you truly that delusional? Do you not remember what I told you about Mr. Darcy, and his warning about using Miss Darcy's familiar name?" Bingley asked.

"I am sure he did not mean any of that, Charles; he was in a bad mood being close to the Bennets and that insipid neighbourhood. I did us a favour by ensuring we never have to return so Miss Bennet cannot trap you in her tentacles," Miss Bingley stated, her nose elevated as she relayed her superior opinion.

"Darcy is no longer in Town, and he meant every word he said to both of us. Darcy never wants to be in your company ever again, Caroline! There was only one thing Darcy agreed with you about, to a certain extent. He said Miss Bennet does not love me; in fact, he went further and helped me see she never sought my company. It was all in my own head; I was seeing what I wanted to, just like you do with the Darcys." Bingley became wistful, as he did each time he thought about the angel who had no interest in him.

"It is just as well. Do you know I saw Miss Bennet in Town working as a paid companion for the Marchioness of Holder and Viscountess Westmore? It is appropriate that you have given up on that woman!" Miss Bingley crowed triumphantly.

"I would advise you not to spread any unsubstantiated rumours, Caroline. You are already in a precarious position after your ill-conceived attempt to compromise Darcy. If you instigate rumours, it will only bring unwanted attention to you. Would you like to marry Darcy's valet?" Bingley tried to curb his sister—for once.

"Why did we not receive an invitation to Pemberley for Christmastide?" Miss Bingley asked, changing the subject without addressing anything her brother said.

"Unless it is for me alone, and my friend is sure you will not wheedle your way into the carriage, there will be no more invitations for either of you," Bingley looked at each sister pointedly, "ever again."

As much as she hated to admit it, Miss Bingley accepted that spreading a rumour would not do her any good, and self-service was the easiest way to have her agree to anything. May-hap it was time to consider other gentleman as marriage partners? There was always Darcy's cousin, the Viscount! Sadly, her resolution to give up her chase of Mr. Darcy did not survive the night!

~~~~~~~/~~~~~~~

With the unscheduled ride to Meryton to deal with the miscreant and normal family obligations, Andrew Fitzwilliam had not been able to spend as much time with Jane Bennet as he would have liked. The time the couple did have together was thankfully outside of the attention of the *Ton*.

The most public event they had shared was a ride along Rotten Row, hours before the fashionable time. The courting couple had been accompanied by Richard, Elizabeth, Tom, and Robert Jamison in addition to two grooms. That, coupled with the cold, made sure that even had they been seen by anyone with a penchant for gossip, no one would have given a group of six riders a second glance.

As far as Andrew was concerned, the time they did spend together reinforced his opinion that Jane was the perfect woman for him. Although he was in no hurry to push for a betrothal, the last thing he wanted was for Jane to feel pressured. His feelings for Jane Bennet were decidedly tender, right on the precipice of love. They would have three weeks far away from the prying eyes of society while in Essex. Andrew did not know the state of Jane's feelings for him, but that she was not indifferent to him was obvious.

And as far as his cousin Darcy was concerned, he was encouraged by the letter he had just received from Pemberley.

15 December 1810
Pemberley

Andrew,

I will make my apologies to you in person when I see you, but in the meantime, all I can say is that you had the right of it! I was a horse's arse!

When I see the Bennets again, it is my intention to beg their forgiveness for my boorish behaviour. The more I examine the way I behaved, the more I feel abhorrence at my actions.

I was becoming a male version of Aunt Cat, believing my judgement reigned supreme, regardless of how few facts I had to support my assertions. I have written to Uncle Reggie, Aunt Elaine, and Richard to express my sincere contrition, but to you I owe more than that.

As it was, none of my concerns were based in fact. If I truly had concerns about Miss Bennet, then I should have spoken to you in private, and presented them as my opinion, not as fact! When, or if, I am allowed into her company again, I will make my apologies directly to her. I saw absolutely no evidence to support my proclamations, and yet I felt it my right to do so.

I allowed my over-inflated pride and belief in the infallibility of my opinions to overrule how I was taught to behave as a gentleman. As such, there are many amends that I need to make.

I clearly see the hypocrisy in my life, which was pointed out to me at Matlock House, and again by Gigi when I was honest with her. As much as it cut me to the quick when it was said to me, I truly was behaving like one of the fortune hunters that I despise.

Unlike before Ramsgate, I have not hidden anything from Gigi in a misguided attempt to protect her, and consequently my little sister has shared some sage advice with me. I honestly believe that if Gigi can recover as she has from her near ruin in the summer, I can certainly amend my behaviour, though she has less to regret. My little sister is an inspiration to me.

That only leaves me to beg your forgiveness, Andrew. I stand ready to apologise as many times and to whomever I need to until everyone I have offended sees that I am sincere, but this one I wanted to express first as I have long considered you not just a cousin, but more a brother and friend. I am working to correct the flaws in my character that led to my behaving thusly, but I ask should you find it necessary, do not hesitate to call my actions into question again. I request that you do it soonest, so I may check my-

self before you must call me a horse's arse again!

Regards,
William

Andrew appreciated the sincere and full apology contained in his cousin's letter and believed that he was moving heaven and earth to correct his character flaws. Whatever else William could be called; liar was not one of them.

As he walked into his parents' sitting room, he saw each of them reading their own letter. When they both completed their reading, his father looked up. "Welcome son. Is that from William, too?" the Earl pointed to the pages in Andrew's hands.

"It is, Father; he told me he wrote to all of us separately. It is an excellent start that he has made, and I, for one, believe he will achieve his aim of improving himself," Andrew stated, as he sat down after giving his mother a kiss on her proffered cheek.

"We agree, Son; both your mother and I remarked after our first reading that it seems like William is finally making the changes that could only enhance his own future happiness," Lord Matlock shared. "I wondered after that meeting we had if I had been too harsh with him."

"Given the results, I do not believe so, Reggie," Lady Elaine squeezed her beloved husband's hand. She understood how hard it had been for her husband to take William to task. They had acted as surrogate parents to the two Darcys since George Darcy had joined Lady Anne some five years ago. Darcy, a young man of one and twenty, had been left with not only the responsibility of the Darcy estates and properties, but the guardianship of a young sister who was almost eleven at the time. The saving grace was that George had made Richard coguardian, so in that, at least, not everything rested on William's broad shoulders.

"If William succeeds, he will become the man our late brother-in-law was sure he could be. Will you allow Jane to see the letter, Andrew? There is no entreaty from William not to do so is there?" Lord Matlock asked.

"There is not Father. I think when I see her later today, I will tell her about it and give her the choice if she would like to read it or not," Andrew stated.

"You learn fast, Andrew. Take it from years of experience it is better to canvass the opinion of a strong woman and not make assumptions on her behalf." Andrew saw that while the words were meant for him, that his father was looking at his mother as he spoke, causing her to light up with love and pleasure.

~~~~~~~/~~~~~~~

Once Andrew offered, Jane read the letter from Mr. Darcy. "Your father must have taken him to task in a great way for it to have wrought the desire to change so fundamentally in your cousin. My family will be vastly pleased to know he has seen the error of his ways and intends to apologise, and this before he is aware of our true situation." Jane thought for a few moments of her younger, and most stubborn, sister. She had promised her parents to have an open mind, but Jane decided reading the letter could only help soften Elizabeth's opinion on the matter of Mr. Darcy. "Andrew, would you permit Lizzy to read this?"

"As I have offered for you to read it, there could be no reason to refuse the same for Elizabeth," Andrew agreed easily. The other slight disclosure of Darcy's being in love with Elizabeth could not but be assisted by the man's words. Being the unwitting party would mean Darcy would owe him a future favour should he win the object of his affection. It was always satisfying when Darcy owed him rather him owing Darcy, for it made life so much more fun.

"Mrs. Ponsonby, please have a footman summon my sister," Jane requested, and not too many minutes later Elizabeth joined them. Jane opened the topic by explaining about the letters that all four Fitzwilliams had received. When asked if she would like to read the letter, Elizabeth answered in the affirmative.

"He does seem sincere, does he not?" Elizabeth confirmed while she blushed at the allusion to herself in the letter. Her companions nodded, ignoring her reaction to the words about her in the letter. "I will reserve final judgement until I hear from him in person, but it pleases me that he is working to correct the faults he sees in his character," Elizabeth said softly. "That he is able to acknowledge his faults shows great strength of character."

"And he is willing to make changes and apologise without any knowledge of our true situation. Mama was correct, Lizzy. There is more to Mr. Darcy than we thought," Jane pointed out to her younger, headstrong sister.

"I, too, was wrong, which mother has reminded me more than once. After his slight, I interpreted every word he spoke and each of his actions through the lens of my prejudice against him," Elizabeth owned.

"If Gigi—that is what we call Georgiana—had been physically hurt, William would never have forgiven himself. As it was, he blamed himself for the trauma she suffered, even though his decision to make a surprise visit to Ramsgate gave him the chance to intervene and save her. You will not find a more loyal man to those he cares for, and that includes his servants and tenants. As soon as he moves past the arrogance and pride that became part of his mask, you will see a completely different facet of the man," Andrew explained about the man he knew and loved. "He will be the same in essentials but will be more pleasant to be around."

"Has he always been this way?" Elizabeth asked.

"No, he was much more easy going before he came out in society and was chased by every debutante and their mothers, and some fathers as well. He, like Gigi, was always shy, so he created a defence to try and ward off the huntresses. We call it his 'mask.' Even as he was when you saw him, had you seen him at Pemberley with no social pressures, and without worrying about his sister's recovery from her situation, you would not have recognised him as the one you met in Hertfordshire," Andrew related to the sisters.

"I suppose we all wear a mask of some sort in public," Elizabeth said thoughtfully. "We hide our wealth and connections to protect us, which, now that I think on it objectively, is just a different form of mask from the one your cousin chose."

"You are correct to a certain extent. The difference is while I wore a mask in society, as did your family, we were not overtly rude, nor did we give offence wherever we went. William could have protected himself while still being a gentleman in every respect. There is no good excuse for his behaviour, but that is the part I believe he is correcting in his character," Andrew smiled ruefully.

"If Mama had not stopped me that night at the assembly, I would have spread the story of Mr. Darcy's slight to all who would have listened. I know I am quick to temper and sometimes act without thought; just as he has to correct certain aspects of his character, so do I," Elizabeth offered introspectively, gazing into the distance as she considered this.

"None of us is perfect, Lizzy," Jane soothed.

"Except for you, Jane," Elizabeth teased.

The three chatted for a while longer until it was time for Andrew to take his leave. They decided to ride in the park again in a few days to get in at least one more ride, weather permitting, before they decamped for Broadhurst.

VOL 1, CHAPTER 15

"Charlotte, it is so good to see you again." Elizabeth welcomed her friend once she had greeted her parents, Esther, and Mark after the Bennet travel coach arrived at Broadhurst.

"Eliza, I have missed you ever since you absconded to go gallivanting around Town. With both you and Jane gone, there were few friends to visit," Charlotte teased her dearest friend.

"I do not *gallivant*," Elizabeth returned with mock effrontery.

"Has your betrothed been writing to you, Charlotte?" Elizabeth asked with a smile.

"Yes, I have heard much about the great Lady Catherine de Bourgh, but little about himself and my future home," Charlotte replied hollowly.

"Do not be mawkish. After all, he is soon to be your husband, then you will be able to start pointing him in a better direction!" Elizabeth smiled knowingly.

"Will you stand up with me, Eliza? It will be a small ceremony without a wedding breakfast. He wants us to return to Hunsford as soon as may be so we may pay our respects to Lady Catherine before all else," Charlotte beseeched her friend.

"What about Maria? Will she not be put out that you have asked me?" Elizabeth worried.

"You know that with over ten years between us I am more like a second mother to her. Also, knowing how close we are, it was she who suggested you," Charlotte assured her friend.

"If that be the case, then it would be an honour and a pleasure to stand up with you, my friend," Elizabeth accepted.

"How proceeds your courtship, Jane?" Charlotte turned to

her other favourite Bennet sister.

"Well, I think," Jane's cheeks grew pink with her blush.

"When do we get to meet Lord Hilldale?" Charlotte prodded.

"The Fitzwilliams arrive Thursday. Have you set a date for your wedding yet?" Jane asked to move the focus from her courtship—for now. She had no doubt that Charlotte would interrogate her fully later.

"Yes, we will marry on Friday, the eleventh day of January. That will give me some time to recover after the return trip from Essex. My mother will make sure all is organised while I am here." Charlotte realised one who she expected to see was not present. "I see Tom, but where is Robert?"

"His father had an accident on the estate—a minor one, but it has incapacitated him for some days, so Robert returned to assist with running of the estate until his father recuperates. He was to leave in time to arrive at Ashford Dale before Christmas Eve, so he will not return to Broadhurst," Jane related.

"Eliza, your attitude toward a certain gentleman from Derbyshire seems to have softened somewhat, or am I reading too much into your letters?" Charlotte asked before they entered the manor house.

"You are not wrong, Charlotte; I will tell you more later. After you greet grandmama and grandpapa, Jane and I will show you to your chambers. They happen to be right next to ours!" Elizabeth took her friend's arm as they made their way to the drawing room where their grandparents were welcoming the other four arriving Bennets.

~~~~~~~/~~~~~~~

"Have you heard back from Sir Randolph yet, my love?" Lady Rose asked.

"I have, Rose. A letter arrived this morning, and you saved me having to seek you out to inform you," the Duke replied lovingly.

"Are you going to tell me what he said?" his wife teased

with a glint in her eye and the playful look he still loved to see even after all these years.

"He will send a letter to Thomas Bennet in mid-February requesting he and his wife come to London on an urgent matter that will impact his and his family's future. As things stand now, I would like us to leave Longfield Meadows by Monday, the eighteenth day of February. The meeting will be set for the following Monday, so we will not have to push too far each day. I think rather than the normal three to four days, with longer and more frequent stops, a Saturday arrival in Town is likely," the Duke explained his intentions. "In addition, I requested that Sir Randolph's investigators prepare a report on the heir and his family, so we have some knowledge of them before the meeting."

"That sounds like a sound plan, Sed," the Duchess agreed. "Did you send a letter to our distant cousins to notify them that there is a legitimate heir?" Lady Rose enquired.

"Yes, love, I wrote to the Regent and his mother. I made a suggestion to him about the defunct earldom of Meryton as well. I am waiting for a response," her husband replied.

"What is it that you suggested, Sed?" She asked, listening intently and truly pleased with what her husband had proposed.

"If I could beg your indulgence, allow me to address a serious subject, my love." The Duke took his wife's hands gently in his, pre-emptively soothing her by rubbing the back of her hands with his thumbs. "As much as I would like to return to Longfield Meadows, my Rose, I believe when I leave it will be the last time I will see our estate. No, my love," he placed his finger on his wife's lips to stop the violent objection she was about to make then retook the hand he had relinquished. "You know in your heart it is naught but the truth. Do not let me see my wife make my death much harder on herself by denying reality."

"My promise to you notwithstanding, your leaving me will leave a hole in my heart that will never be able to be filled."

The Duchess could no longer hold back the tears that had been threatening each time she contemplated her beloved husband's death.

"Remember, Rose, I am not leaving you. My time in the mortal world is coming to end, and not by my design. Please never forget, I will always be with you right here." Lord Sed reached out and gently placed his hand over his wife's heart.

~~~~~~~/~~~~~~~

After an enjoyable evening filled with the convivial company of family, Charlotte, Jane, and Elizabeth met in the latter two ladies' sitting room. "I hope you will first ease my curiosity for how your opinion of the proud and disagreeable man that we met in Meryton changed, Eliza," Charlotte opened the conversation.

"There are a number of reasons I have changed my opinion and am determined to see him anew. It started with my mother..." Elizabeth related her conversations with her mother, and, to a lesser extent, her father. She told Charlotte that she now knew although his behaviour was not acceptable, Mr. Darcy had a valid reason for his pique at the assembly. Even if her promise prevented her from disclosing the reason, she wanted to assure her friend of its existence. She also pointed out the man was being chased relentlessly by Miss Bingley and her indecorous behaviour, which alone would cause any man to snap at someone without cause.

Then, without referring to the details contained in Darcy's letter, Elizabeth informed Charlotte that he had apologised in writing and intended to do so in person as soon as he was in company with the Bennets again. As he knew nothing about their wealth and connections, such an apology meant he was sincere.

"What precipitated this change of heart in Mr. Darcy?" Charlotte asked in genuine surprise.

"His family," Jane replied. "The Viscount called him a horse's, um, posterior." Jane rolled her eyes at their amusement of her checking herself, for it was just the three of them. "He tried to warn Andrew off, claiming that I was a fortune hunter. Andrew took exception." Jane smiled sweetly.

"He did not!" Charlotte tutted and both Bennet sisters nodded emphatically. "He apologised for his attempted interference?"

"Indeed he did, most sincerely. His failed high-handed interference with our courtship led to his uncle, the Earl of Matlock, taking him to task about this and many other misconceptions under which Mr. Darcy was living," Jane stated.

"Does this mean I will not see a Jane or Eliza set down delivered to the man?" Charlotte asked, only half teasing. While Elizabeth would administer a set down more often, still not many times and all had been well-deserved, if Jane were spurred into action, it was a wondrous thing to see.

"Unless he deserves one, no, I am afraid not," Elizabeth smiled at her friend.

"Your suitor and his family arrive the day after the morrow, Jane. I am looking forward to meeting the prince among men who was finally able to excite the interest of Miss Jane Bennet," Charlotte teased a blushing Jane.

"Unlike the puppy who was evicted from Netherfield, Andrew sees me, not only my face. He is decisive and does not need others to make his decisions for him. Where Mr. Bingley is a boy, Andrew is all man," Jane stated succinctly, leaving no doubt in Charlotte's mind that her friend's heart was deeply engaged.

She envied the Bennets that they had the freedom to accept a man of their choice. Not for the first time, Charlotte wondered if she had been too hasty in securing Mr. Collins. She was as sure as she could be that he was not a vicious man, but as she read each letter from her betrothed, she began to see the task of turning him away from his reverence of his patroness would be much harder than she originally thought.

~~~~~~~/~~~~~~~

The next day, the Phillips, Westmores, and Holders arrived. Lady Alicia Carrington arrival was highly anticipated by

Esther as they were the same age and the closest of cousins. Wes and Isabelle's son and two daughters were spending the holidays with their spouses' families, as were the two Carrington sons. Lord and Lady Jersey shared for those who were unaware that they were on the cusp of becoming great-grandparents as the older of their son's daughters was with child.

Dinner that night was a boisterous affair with so many family members enjoying each other's company. To their delight, the two older Gardiner children had been invited to join the adults for dinner. The two youngest had not been sanguine about being excluded, but a story from Cousin Lizzy diverted them so they soon forgot why they had been upset in the first place. The Gardiner children loved stories from any of the cousins, parents, aunts, or uncles; however, if there were ever a choice, Elizabeth would be chosen. Her reading was the most animated, and she made different voices for each character in the story.

As would be expected, there were many musical performances that night. The highlight was the penultimate performance, when the three Bennet daughters sang together. As usual, Elizabeth was asked to close the night, and she sang a Scottish folk song in the original Gaelic. Whether one understood the language or not, there was no mistaking the quality of the singer's voice.

~~~~~~~/~~~~~~~

The two Darcys helped in the decoration of the manor and had fun doing so. It had been many years since Darcy had felt so relaxed. He was always more comfortable at Pemberley than anywhere else, but he had never felt quite like he did now. The more he identified his objectionable behaviour and took steps to not repeat it, the more he found his spirits lifted.

Darcy's uncle's intelligence that he had misunderstood what his father meant by duty to his name had lifted a weight, he had not been aware he was carrying, off his shoulders. Once he accepted the rectitude of his uncle's words, Darcy was able to accept his mother's charge to him those many years ago was what *both* his parents desired for him. He finally understood his beliefs had been a non sequitur. He had many amends to make, those he owed to the Bennets only the start.

Now that he was able to look at his actions through the eyes of others, he saw how the impression he had given in Hertfordshire had been so offensive, and if he were ever to be granted his heart's desire of Miss Elizabeth Bennet, there would be much apologising and begging involved. He would have to allow the lady to see all of him and the mask would have to be permanently banished.

When he looked back on his time at Netherfield, as he began to see his actions from other people's perspective, he finally understood the cold reception he had received in the neighbourhood. He belatedly realised they cared not a whit for his wealth or connections; he had been evaluated and found wanting by standards of decency. Darcy had been blinded to the truth by nothing but his own pride and belief in the infallibility of his opinions.

Bingley had come to see Darcy later during the day that Uncle Reggie had torn into him—just before Darcy's departure from Town. He had not been in a humour to deal with Bingley again, but when he saw the distress his friend was in, Darcy had relented.

Bingley had informed his friend of the eviction from Netherfield, and his intention to recoup the funds from his sister's dowry. Darcy applauded his friend's decision, though in the back of his mind he doubted Bingley's ability to resist his sister's manipulation. Once Bingley had vented and informed Darcy that he had told the Hursts and his sister to leave his townhouse, Darcy had been impressed.

Unfortunately, he had been proved correct though he wished it were not the case. In Bingley's last letter, from what he was able to decipher, his friend had told him he would only take half of the money from his sister, and they were all living at the Bingley town home again. And there had been a not too subtle hint for an invitation for all of them to Pemberley near the end of the mess of a letter.

Unlike Bingley, when Darcy decided, he stuck to it. As much as it was a shame, they were at cross purposes, and when Darcy examined the friendship, he saw the proverbial fork in the road which they had reached. He was guardian to his sister; he did not need another ward, which Bingley was more of than a friend. When he returned to London, he would break with Bingley. It was not something he would do via the post—it would be face-to-face.

Darcy decided to put the unpleasant thoughts of the Bingley siblings out of his mind until he returned to London, a few weeks prior to his journey to Kent.

~~~~~~~/~~~~~~~

"Charles, our invitation to Pemberley must have been lost in the post," Miss Bingley insisted. "You know that our friend Mr. Darcy would never want us to be on our own at Christmastide, and it is just too far to Scarborough!"

Miss Bingley had known how it would be. Once her brother cooled down after the initial indignation of being evicted, she and Louisa had gone to work on him. They had begged his pardon, though not meaning one word of it, but so long as he believed they did, all was well. First, they had manipulated him into inviting them back to his much more comfortable town house than that of the Hursts'. After a few days of words dripping with honey, Miss Bingley was exceedingly proud she had convinced her brother it was only fair they should split the cost of the loss from Netherfield; he was the master of the estate after all.

Her plan was to work on him, with Louisa's help, so that, in the end, it would cost her nothing. Her current machination was to convince her brother they should depart for Pemberley. Once Mr. Darcy saw her superior self without the distraction of any Bennets, he would forget about his words and her attempted compromise and would finally offer for her.

"I do not know, Caro. I did not think there was any ambiguity in Darcy's edict that he would not welcome you into any of his homes," Bingley answered, less sure of himself than he was before; the backbone he discovered after the eviction seemed to melt away.

"Charles, when you were angry you sent us away, but when you calmed you welcomed us back, did you not?" Louisa assisted her sister.

"I suppose..." Bingley acknowledged haltingly.

"Louisa, I am of a mind about something. Do you not remember the other day that was so tedious with constant rain that a soaked missive was delivered?" Miss Bingley dissembled.

"Yes, sister, I do, how could we forget about that?" Mrs. Hurst aided the lie.

"You know, Charles, now that I think upon it, the writing did look like that of Mr. Darcy. I am sure that it was the Darcy seal. What would he think if you ignored an invitation from him?" Miss Bingley played on the fact her brother would hate to snub his closest friend.

"Truly? Why did you not mention it before?" Bingley asked.

"When we tried to dry it in front of the fire so we could open the letter, it fell out of my hands, and before I was able to retrieve it the fire had claimed it. I was embarrassed that I had been so clumsy with an obviously important communication that I put it out of my mind until we had this discussion." Miss Bingley smiled internally; she knew she had just gotten her way, and she was not wrong.

"Then it must be so; we will leave on the morrow and arrive by Saturday, the day before Christmas Eve," Bingley decided. The sisters left the drawing room to begin supervising their packing.

"Caro, what if Mr. Darcy will not receive us?" Mrs. Hurst asked when they were alone.

"He is too much of a gentleman not to, but if he does not, I will feign illness and he will have no choice!" Miss Bingley cackled.

The next morning, the Bingley carriage departed Curzon

Street as early as they had planned. It was one of the rare occasions that Miss Bingley did not want to be late and make an entrance.

~~~~~~~/~~~~~~~

The night before the Fitzwilliams travelled to Broadhurst, Lord Matlock and his wife decided to reveal the purchase, which would close as soon as the mourning period for the deceased master of Brookfield was completed; that would happen during the morrow's journey.

The next morning a fresh topic was broached. "Richard, you know it has long concerned us that all of the Matlock estates are entailed, and we were not able to give you one to allow you an alternate profession than the army," his father opened.

"Father, I am well aware that had you been able to do something, you would have," Richard responded easily.

"We are now, my son," Lady Elaine told her younger son.

"But how? As you just stated, the Matlock estates..." His father cut him off.

"Not a Matlock estate. You remember old Mr. Brookfield of Brookfield?" Lord Matlock asked, not surprised when his son allowed that he did. "He recently passed away. His heir is a distant cousin and master of a large estate in Devon. I met him when the late Mr. Brookfield was already extremely ill, and there was no doubt that the end was coming. When he mentioned that he did not want to keep an estate so far from his own, I asked him to contact me when he became master and was ready to sell. We agreed on terms and a price more than a week ago. Around the time of your trip to Rosings Park, the money will have been transferred and the estate will be yours," Lord Matlock informed his son with much pleasure.

"Father, Mother, Andrew, I do not know what to say. To say I am grateful would be an understatement! I thank you many times over. You know how much I love to work with horses and have always admired the breeding programme at Brookfield!" Richard exuberantly thanked his family.

"You know I was against this, do you not, brother," Andrew ribbed his brother good naturedly.

"Against it, indeed. I know as the heir you would have co-signed on a transfer this large, so do not try me, brother. I will accept this gift now, but you must allow me to repay the cost from the annual profit," Richard insisted.

"You would devalue our gift by wanting to repay us a non-existent debt?" his father asked. "The Matlock coffers are quite healthy, and even a large outlay such as this barely dented our wealth. What is the purpose of all of that money if we never use it, and on an expenditure as worthy as this?" Lord Matlock challenged his younger son.

"In that case, I have no choice but to graciously, as much as I am able to be gracious, accept this most generous of gifts," Richard grinned.

"You will resign your commission after Twelfth Night will you not, Richard?" Lady Elaine asked hopefully.

"Mother, I understand your desire that I leave the army soon, but my medical status will not be reviewed until June, so there is no need to worry about the possibility of me returning to the war. As soon as the sale is final, I will resign and sell out; you have my word of honour," Richard compromised.

An hour later, the Matlock coach turned from the main road onto the one that led towards Broadhurst.

~~~~~~~/~~~~~~~

Thomas and Priscilla Bennet were amused as they watched their oldest glance at the clock every few minutes. They shared knowing looks; all the signs pointed to Jane's heart being engaged far more than she had admitted to any of them, even Elizabeth. During the time they had to observe Andrew Fitzwilliam during their short stay in Town, the Bennet parents judged the Viscount's heart was engaged also.

Broadhurst's butler informed the master that carriages were approaching the house. Knowing their granddaughter was waiting and would not rest easily until she greeted her suitor, Lord and Lady Jersey led the party to the front of the house just before the arriving vehicles came to a halt.

Charlotte Lucas felt a tinge of envy as she watched Jane's whole being light up as a tall man with sandy blonde hair alighted from the coach. It was a safe assumption that he was the Viscount, as the first man to exit was much older and the last was in uniform. She correctly guessed that the officer was Colonel Fitzwilliam, of whom she heard both Jane and Eliza talk.

After greeting the hosts and Mr. and Mrs. Bennet, Andrew made straight for Jane with his smiling brother following. "It is very good to see you again, Jane," Andrew said gallantly as he bowed over her hand and bestowing a soft kiss on it.

"And you, Andrew." Jane felt like she was whole again as soon as she saw Andrew and realised it was like half of her was missing when she was away from him.

"While those two are lost in their own world, someone should greet you, Richard," Elizabeth smiled.

"Hello, Lizzy; I trust you are well. Will you introduce your friend, please?" Richard requested. The young lady next to Elizabeth was intriguing to Richard. She was not a classical beauty, but there was something about her he could not put his finger on.

Elizabeth, knowing what an incorrigible flirt Richard could be, made sure he understood that Charlotte was not fair game in the introduction. "My pleasure Richard. This is Miss Charlotte Lucas of Lucas Lodge, a neighbouring estate to Longbourn. She will soon be my cousin as she is betrothed to Mr. Collins." Elizabeth introduced them, surprised when Charlotte gave her friend a scathing look. "Charlotte, this is Colonel Richard Fitzwilliam, brother to the one over there who is not aware that we are in the same part of the realm as he is. When he is not lost in my sister's eyes, he is Andrew Fitzwilliam, Viscount Hilldale."

"Did you call me, Lizzy?" Andrew became aware of the fact there were others present in addition to Jane.

"I think Lizzy was trying to introduce you to Charlotte. Andrew, this is our particularly good friend from home, Miss

Charlotte Lucas."

"Pleased to meet you, Miss Lucas. I am sorry I was distracted," Andrew said in greeting.

"You are not sorry, brother; you are besotted!" Richard teased, earning a punch on the arm for his trouble.

"I hate to pull you away from my granddaughters and their friend, Andrew and Richard. Let us enter the house and you may re-join us after you change," Lady Sarah said, receiving sheepish looks from both brothers.

Notwithstanding that she was betrothed, Richard wanted to get to know Miss Lucas better, but remonstrated with himself that he would need to be careful to not cross any lines of propriety.

VOL 1, CHAPTER 16

"Your Jane looks very happy with her suitor," Lady Sarah said as she sat with Marie, Isabelle and her youngest, Priscilla, in her sitting room one morning a few days later.

"She is, Mama, and it was like my meeting Thomas, happenstance. Our carriage was disabled in just the right place, and I found the love of my life; Jane happened to be at the Gardiners one day when Andrew called. As far as I know, neither has declared love for the other, but I do not believe it will be too much longer. If things happen as Thomas and I believe they will, they will have a very felicitous marriage," Priscilla opined.

"Cilla, is Charlotte Lucas not betrothed to that halfwit you described—the parson at Hunsford?" Lady Marie asked.

"She is, Marie, why do you ask?" Priscilla enquired.

"Because, sister dearest, have you not noted how much time Richard spends talking to her? Where you find one, you more than likely will find the other," Lady Marie smiled widely.

"Neither Richard nor Charlotte would ever breach propriety!" Priscilla stated vehemently.

"I am not saying they have or will, merely that they seem to enjoy one another's company. If Charlotte's husband-to-be is half as bad as you and Thomas have described him, she will be in want of some sensible conversation," Lady Marie clarified.

"Do not forget," Lady Sarah reminded, "she will be subjected to Lady Catherine's *infinite wisdom*. I hope for her sake she will be able to tolerate the attempted officious interference from the self-proclaimed *great lady*."

"Did I hear Jane say that young man, Darcy, has finally

apologised for slighting our Lizzy?" Lady Isabelle asked.

"Yes, Issy, that too is true." Priscilla turned to her mother. "Has Lord Matlock told Papa of his taking his nephew to task, Mama?"

"Not yet, no, but I am sure I will hear all about it when we retire tonight as the *older* men are all spending the day in the library together. It must be nice to be young. I understand Charlotte and my grandchildren are on a ride with the Fitzwilliam brothers. It is too cold for my liking," Lady Sarah admitted.

"Our husbands are with Papa and his group in the library," Lady Marie shared. "A ride in this weather was not attractive to them either. Something about wisdom increasing as bones age."

"The riders will not go too far or fast as Lilly and Eddy Gardiner are with them and they have not graduated from ponies yet. Everyone needs to be back at the house early so they will have time to prepare for Christmas Eve dinner. I understand from Maddie that her two eldest children will join us for the midnight service to welcome Christmas in the chapel tonight," Priscilla stated.

"Come, daughters; let us go join the other ladies in the drawing room." Lady Sarah rose and led her daughters out of her sitting room.

~~~~~~~/~~~~~~~

Just when there was nothing to be done about it, Charlotte Lucas finally found herself attracted to a man. While she would not do anything to act on her preference. She had no idea if the Colonel, Richard, had any tender feelings for her, but she was at last feeling what it was like to fall headlong into love. She permitted herself this one chance she would have to experience love, albeit unrequited. He was funny, highly intelligent, and well built. In other words, everything that her soon-to-be husband was not.

Even if he harboured feelings for her, there was naught she could or would do about it. Mayhap Elizabeth had been right; she had been too hasty to secure a husband when she had essentially proposed to Mr. Collins. Charlotte would no sooner bring the shame of a broken betrothal on her parents, brothers, and sister than she would stop breathing.

For his part, Richard was conflicted. Everyone was aware that he enjoyed harmless flirting and that he was never serious about looking for a wife. The possibility of being sent off to war had been all too real. Thanks to the disclosure on the way to Broadhurst, he would soon be leaving the army. Not only that, but he would have the six thousand clear per annum that Brookfield profited. He had gone from poor second son to a highly eligible bachelor.

Like Andrew, Richard would never be able to feign interest in some society bride who cared more about seeing and being seen than the important things in life. Just his luck to start losing his heart to a lady who was no longer available. Worse, next time he saw her she would be Mrs. Collins, married to that buffoon to whom his aunt had awarded the Hunsford living.

"Have you noticed how compatible Richard and Charlotte are?" Jane asked as she rode alongside her suitor.

"It is new for me to see Richard being serious around a woman and not his usual playful and harmlessly flirting self. It is a pity the lady is already spoken for," Andrew replied. "To speak of a topic much closer to my heart, remind me to thank your grandmother for inviting us here this year. Before you revealed your connections to me, I thought I would not see you for weeks, until we returned to London. I prefer not spending so long a time separated from you, Jane."

"I feel the same way about you, Andrew. I have already thanked my grandmama for her wise choice of friends to invite this year," Jane smiled ethereally.

"When Mr. Gardiner was enumerating all of the reasons I should rethink my request to call on you, until I understood his purpose, I was worried you were already taken," Andrew admitted.

"And I thought you would never consider me with my reported lack of wealth and connections. It pleases me that we were *both* wrong," Jane said.

"Are you reconciled that our courtship will be known to the *Ton* when we return to London? There will be no more peace and quiet when we attend events. I know how much your family values its privacy and being unknown to the *Ton*," Andrew asked.

"Yes, I am. We knew there would come a day when it would be hard to continue hiding from society after we began to court. My father is becoming used to the idea that his life will not be as peaceful as it was before." Jane had been worried about the scrutiny her courting would place on her family's future, but both of her parents had assured her that her happiness was worth that and more, and they could see Andrew made Jane happy.

"It is time to return," Tom informed the group of riders. "Grandmama will not be impressed if we are not ready in time for Christmas Eve dinner."

At that pronouncement, the riders dutifully turned their mounts and commenced the less than one-hour ride back to the stables.

~~~~~~~/~~~~~~~

"Douglas, Pemberley's butler, entered the master's study. "Mr. Darcy, there is a carriage approaching the house."

"Who could it be?" Darcy wondered aloud, for he was not expecting anyone. The Fitzwilliams were in Essex, and Lady Catherine rarely left Rosings. Travel as far as Derbyshire was almost unheard of, and certainly not in winter. "I will accompany you to the courtyard, Douglas."

Darcy was standing just inside the front door when he identified the conveyance as it turned into the courtyard. "What in tarnation is Bingley doing here? And *with* his sisters!" Darcy was beyond furious that his weak-willed friend had taken such a step. "Douglas, get our burliest footmen out there, now. Besides Mr. Bingley, *no one* is to exit that carriage!" Douglas gave a short nod and quick bow, calling out to the three nearest footmen with their instructions and told them to inform the four men on duty in the courtyard of the same.

"What did I tell you, Charles; Mr. Darcy is waiting for us," Miss Bingley crowed.

When the conveyance came to a halt, it was then that things started to go other than she expected. Bingley stepped out and was about to hand his sister out when a burly footman closed the door on her, and five others positioned themselves so that there was no way for the occupants of the carriage to alight.

"What is the meaning of this?" Miss Bingley screeched. Bingley felt a sinking feeling in his stomach and realized that he might have well and truly erred. That realization was re-inforced when he saw the thunderous look of fury on Darcy's mien.

"Follow me, *Mr.* Bingley," Darcy barked out.

~~~~~~~/~~~~~~~

"Caroline, what have we done? Not only will Mr. Darcy not allow us in his house, but he will not allow us to set foot out-side of the carriage," Mrs. Hurst worried.

"He will once he hears his future wife is ill," Miss Bingley asserted.

"Are you really that delusional? Rather than going to Scar-borough from here, Bingley needs to drive you directly to Bed-lam!" Hurst shocked his wife and sister. He had known this was a fool's errand, but he was willing to allow his wife's and sister-in-law's lies to play out. He had hoped Bingley had finally found the gumption to check Caroline, but as soon as his anger cooled it was more of the same.

"What do you know? You are but a waste of space!" Miss Bingley responded with vitriol.

"I am not the one that lied to my brother to follow a delu-sion. You were the only one who was not able to see the hints that Darcy gave you. He did not desire you for *anything*. Even after you were told in no uncertain terms that even had your compromise succeeded, he would not offer for you, you gave free rein to your delusion rather than moving on as you said that evening when you thought me asleep!" As Hurst turned to his wife, she cringed, for she could not mistake his expression as anything but anger. "Louisa, I am finally asserting my authority as your husband. We will hire a carriage in Lambton and join my family at Winsdale. *Alone!*" Hurst raised his hand to stay any objection from either sister.

"You cannot..." Miss Bingley tried to say, ignoring his warning look and his warding off.

"Shut up, Caroline!" Hurst commanded, satisfied when Miss Bingley's jaw shut with a clack. "Until and unless I am satisfied that your sister has learnt how to behave like a lady, you will not see her again. And until your brother grows a pair of balls, excuse my language, we will not see him!" Hurst allowed his words to sit for a minute. "Do you understand, Mrs. Hurst?" His wife nodded wordlessly. Miss Bingley wished she had something to throw.

~~~~~~~/~~~~~~~

Once the door to Darcy's study was closed, Bingley made to sit in the chair he had used in the past when he had joined his friend in the study. "Did I invite you to sit, *Mr.* Bingley?" Darcy asked menacingly.

"But Darcy..." Darcy cut Bingley off before he could utter another word.

"Only my *friends* are allowed to address me thusly. One who blatantly disregards what I tell him is no friend of mine. Did I or did I not expressly tell you that your sisters would not be allowed in any of my homes again, and if they were with you, neither would you?" Darcy demanded.

"Yes, but Caroline..." Bingley tried to justify the unjustifiable.

"Miss Bingley what? Manipulated you into coming here without an invitation?" Darcy saw his guess was correct.

"B-but she and Louisa said you sent one that was wet in the rain and then..." Bingley stopped as the realisation hit him. "You never sent any post, did you?"

"I did not. I was waiting to see you in Town face-to-face

so I could do what I must do now. All connection between us is at an end. I will not acknowledge you if I see you in public. If you or your sisters try and approach me or *any* member of my family, you will be given the cut direct. I will have word disseminated that there is no connection between us, and neither you nor your family may use my name to gain admittance to the first circles. If any of you attempt to use my name, I will hear about it and know how to act. You are to return to your carriage; my men will escort you off my land and you are never to return. My good opinion, once lost in this fashion, is lost *forever!*"

"B-but why?" Bingley barely managed to squeak it out.

"Why? Are you as delusional as your younger sister? Did I not warn you that if you did not assert control over Miss Bingley not only would she ruin both you and herself in society, but you would lose my friendship as well? Or did you ignore me then as you did everything else I said about your sister? Do not answer; I do not care to hear any more excuses. Leave. *Now!*" Darcy commanded in his best Master of Pemberley voice as he rang for his butler.

"Douglas, escort Mr. Bingley to his carriage. He is to enter and none within are to exit. As soon as the door closes, have him escorted from my land. If he or either of his sisters ever arrive here without a written invitation from me in hand, have them arrested for trespassing." The butler bowed and escorted an almost catatonic Charles Bingley from the study.

It did not please Darcy to break with his friend of more than five years in the manner that he had, but he was left with little choice. There was a light knock on his study door as Georgiana entered. "Are you well, William?" she asked concerned with the look of anguish on her brother's countenance.

"I will be, Gigi, I will be." Darcy assured his sister as he enfolded her in his arms for a much-needed hug.

~~~~~~~/~~~~~~~

When their brother entered the coach, he looked like a broken man. As soon as the vehicle exited the internal courtyard, four outriders took station to comply with the master's order to make sure its occupants departed Pemberley forthwith.

As the gates of Pemberley closed behind the Bingley coach, two outriders continued to follow it in order to make sure there was no attempt to return. "You will not believe how that slob," Miss Bingley pointed a bony finger at Hurst, "spoke to me!"

"Be quiet, Caroline! Just silence yourself. There is nothing you have to say that I want to hear. Your lies have cost me my best friend! I was too weak to see through your lies and enforce what Darcy, no, *Mr.* Darcy, told me, and now it has cost me everything. We are to be at Scarborough for the foreseeable future," Bingley stated as melancholy set in.

Hurst informed his brother-in-law that he and his wife would be exiting in Lambton. When the coach reached the inn in that town, Bingley hit the ceiling with his stick. Once the Hursts exited and their trunks were unloaded, the two remaining Bingleys began their silent journey north.

Hurst decided to rent a room for the night and asked the landlord to arrange for a hired carriage to depart in the morning. The next morning, just after sunrise, the Hursts were on their way to his family estate in Yorkshire.

~~~~~~~/~~~~~~~

A few days after Christmas, the Duke of Bedford whistled as he read the report he had commissioned on the Bennet family. Ironically, it was prepared by the same investigators that performed the task for Bennet when he ordered investigations.

In the fourth Duke's letter there had been no mention of the property the first Tom Bennet had inherited. The Bennets were wealthy, and not only that, connected to close friends of the Duke and his wife. The Duchess entered the study and did not miss the incredulous look on her husband's face. Before she could ask a question, the Duke wordlessly handed his wife the report.

"No!" Lady Rose exclaimed with something approaching

glee. "Is this correct?"

"When have you ever known Norman and James's investigators to err my love?" He grinned.

"Of course you are correct, Sed. The first wife died, and he married little Priscilla! Do not look at me so; I know she is not a little girl any longer." Lady Rose could not believe the coincidence, and how fortuitous it was that her friend's daughter would be the next duchess!

"They have excellent connections, and it says here the oldest daughter, the only one from the first marriage, is being courted by Matlock's son Andrew, Viscount Hilldale. Also, it seems that Sarah and Percy have accepted her as a granddaughter as much as any of their others by blood. Besides you, my love, they will have many who will be able to help and guide them through the shark-infested waters of the *Ton*. I am pleased. Thomas Bennet has a son, no *two* sons. The Bedford dukedom will live on for at least two more generations. As there is a second son, I will have to amend my request to Cousin George," the Duke added thoughtfully.

"I agree, my love. It is a good way to honour the first Tom Bennet and his long-suffering mother. I cannot wait to see Sarah's face when she finds out that her younger daughter will be a duchess before Marie. I wish it were not so, but it seems to be the will of God." Lady Rose had tears in her eyes as she thought of her husband's approaching death. The Duchess dried her eyes as though she had not been crying endlessly. The Duke was saddened by her tears, which continued to fall as she read the report. "It seems your heir does not enjoy London and its so-called *polite society* any more than you do, Sed." She smiled up at him.

"I did see that, love. The report does not tell me all there is to know about the next duke, but I can see that he is a good man, one who cares for his family. For the first time since I opened that letter, I believe that this seat will be filled by a worthy man—one who cares more about people than wealth, power, and connections. We need more peers of that ilk." Lady

Rose felt some hope that her husband might last longer than they suspected, as he seemed to relax now that the stress of worry about his heir lifted.

With more of a spring in his step, the Duke sat down at his desk and wrote a letter with an amended request to his cousin.

~~~~~~~/~~~~~~~

Bingley unceremoniously deposited his sister with their spinster aunt, Mathilda Bingley, their late father's youngest and strongest willed sister, the day he arrived in Scarborough. After meeting with his aunt, he departed without a word to Caroline.

On Monday, the final day of the year 1810, Bingley arrived at his aunt's house just after ten on a cold morning. His aunt practically dragged Miss Caroline out of bed and made sure she was downstairs rather quickly; Caroline obeyed as her aunt was not above using her cane as encouragement to motivate her wayward niece.

"Have you finally come to your senses and come to retrieve me, Charles?" she asked as she flounced into the parlour.

There was no answer from Bingley, who did not talk until his aunt closed the door and sat herself down. "Thank you for your time aunt, and for putting up with my ungrateful and delusional sister."

"How can you speak to me thusly..." Miss Bingley closed her mouth as her aunt raised the cane.

"Need I remind you that I instructed you to remain silent until and unless asked to speak?" Miss Bingley warned.

"I am releasing your dowry to you. After today, I want nothing to do with you, Caroline. Your delusions and lies, and yes, my own weakness, allowed you to exploit me and cost me the friendship of a man that I liked and respected. You will never have the opportunity to manipulate me again.

"Where you live is up to you but know that you will have only five hundred pounds per year to live on with the remainder of your dowry in the four percents. I have deducted the money you cost me by causing me to be evicted, as well as your overspending and the breakages you caused in my house in Town.

"Darcy did not make an idle threat. It is well known among the *Ton* that he broke with me. If you, in particular, try to use his name or any of his family's names, it will be against his express wishes. You have made your bed, Caroline; now you must lie in it. If you have any questions, I will remain another five minutes to answer them. If you start to screech and berate me, I will leave immediately," Bingley stated with a finality in his tone that shook her to her core.

"How much dowry remains?" Miss Caroline asked carefully.

"Twelve thousand pounds." Seeing his sister's horrified look, Bingley explained, "You know about the six thousand. Yes, you thought you manipulated me to cover part of your debt, did you not? The further two thousand indicates my generosity, given your continual overspending of your allowance and the items you destroyed every time you had one of your tantrums."

"May I withdraw more than the interest?" Miss Caroline asked, hopefully.

"Yes, the money is completely under your control; however, remember this, sister *dear*—the more principal you access, the less there will be to live on, and neither I nor Hurst will replenish your funds if you fritter them away. So, unless you find some man who has not heard of your reputation as a social climbing, fortune hunting shrew, you will have a hard time finding a husband. Mayhap you should consider a tradesman." Bingley stood before his sister could retort.

He thanked his aunt and left her house, finally coming to terms with the fact that he too had a lot of growing up to do.

VOL 1, CHAPTER 17

January 10, 1811

Collins arrived in Meryton the day before his wedding. His cousin had refused his request to stay at Longbourn, so even though his venerated patroness had granted him a sennight off, he delayed his coming to the day before to avoid the expenditure of staying more than one night in the Red Rooster Inn.

As there would be no wedding breakfast, there was a celebratory dinner at Lucas Lodge the night before the wedding. Jane and Elizabeth had returned from Town the Monday before the wedding so they could spend some time with Charlotte beforehand.

When they arrived at Lucas Lodge, they found the soon-to-be bride sitting in the chamber which had been hers since her father left his trade and purchased Lucas Lodge after being knighted by the King. Charlotte, who had claimed she was not a romantic, was in love. She had not meant for it to happen. Richard had been a perfect gentleman, never crossing any lines, as she had not either, but it had happened all the same.

They had spent much of their time in one another's exclusive and well chaperoned company over the holidays. He challenged her, and she him. Neither pandered to the other, and, above all else, Richard respected her. He was interested in what she had to say, requested her thoughts on many issues, and yet often they had just sat in companionable silence and took comfort in the fact that they were together.

Charlotte had come close to breaking her engagement. Richard had never asked that of her, had not even hinted at it, and should she have done so, it would have been of her own volition had she taken that drastic step. But the banns had been read, and the shame and ridicule her family would have endured would not allow her to follow her heart's dictates.

Charlotte had always considered her views on marriage, those she had learnt at her mother's feet, were the correct ones, while her friends Jane and Eliza and their fanciful dreams of true love, mutual respect, and felicity were childish indulgences. Too late, Charlotte knew they had the right of it while she was the one with the wrong expectations of matrimony.

She had thought herself so clever when she had gotten the simple Mr. Collins to marry her by effectively proposing to him. All she had seen was security and a home of her own. Charlotte had known from the first time she spoke to Mr. Collins that her husband-to-be was ridiculous and a sycophant, but she believed she would be able to manage him. Through his letters, she was learning that the way he revered his patroness, as if she were a god who had descended from the pantheon walking among the mortals, would make it almost impossible to redirect.

It was all too late now anyway; in the morning she would marry the man. In less than twelve hours she would be Mrs. Collins. The one bright spot on the horizon was Eliza had agreed to arrive in mid-March and remain a little over a month, departing after Easter in mid-April. Charlotte was in true anticipation of seeing how her friend would deploy her scintillating wit when Mr. Collins's patroness displayed her lack of education and tried to *advise* Eliza on subjects of which the great lady knew nothing.

Charlotte's mother had given her a short talk, telling her to endure her husband's attentions as best she could. Most of the time had actually been used to give Charlotte stratagems on how to avoid the marital bed. The night before her wedding, Charlotte Lucas dreamt of Richard Fitzwilliam, much as she had every night since she started falling in love with the man.

~~~~~~~/~~~~~~~

The soon-to-be ex-colonel had a fortnight's leave from his training duties with the Royal Dragoons. Knowing that he was in love with a lady who was about to be married and wanting to make sure he was not close enough to ride to Meryton to object, Richard rode to Pemberley to be with his cousins. As much as his heart yearned for the lady he loved; his honour would not allow him to act on his feelings.

"Richard, why are you so forlorn?" Darcy asked. It was the night before *her* wedding and the cousins were sitting in the master's study with snifters of brandy.

Before he answered, Richard had to check himself. He had to be careful how much he revealed. He realised that with Andrew courting Jane, he could be truthful about his problem without revealing where they had been. "I met a friend of Jane's and Lizzy's with whom I fell in love. There is only one slight problem, which is, she is already betrothed."

It cut Darcy to the quick that Richard was allowed to call the lady of his dreams by her familiar name, even though he understood they were just friends having spent time together while keeping an eye on the courting couple. "Which of their friends? Not the one who is engaged to the sycophantic parson of Aunt Cat?"

"Yes, Miss Lucas, Charlotte," Richard confirmed.

"Please tell me you did not…" Darcy started to ask.

"Good heavens no! What kind of cad to you think me? A Wickham? I would never dally with a gentlewoman's affections! We were always in the company of others and never once did we come close to breaching propriety. Before I knew where I was, I was in love, truly in love, with a woman for the first time. No, not in lust, and not puppy love. She is marrying an imbecile tomorrow and all is lost," Richard lamented his unrequited love.

"At least she bore your company with equanimity. Miss Elizabeth rightfully hates the very sight of me!" Darcy stated hollowly.

"Not quite anymore, William," Richard consoled.

"What do you mean?"

"Your letter to Andrew, the one similar to those you sent to Mother, Father, and me," Richard hinted.

"Yes, what about my apology letters?" Darcy frowned at the reason they needed to be written, not that they were being brought up.

"Andrew allowed Jane and Lizzy to read his as you never stated it should be held in confidence. If you meant what you said in the letter, then I would predict your exit from the doghouse!" Richard felt a little better as he saw the pleasure suffuse his cousin's features. "I am not sure I should tell you this, then again, no one told me not to."

"What Richard, tell me what?" an expectant Darcy demanded.

"Lizzy will be at Hunsford from about the middle of March until a week or so after Easter. She is to visit her good friend, who will be Mrs. Collins at that point."

"What say you we write to Aunt Cat and tell her we will arrive on the twentieth day of March?" Darcy asked keenly.

"You know what she will assume at our coming early do you not?" Richard warned.

"I care not what she thinks! The first time she brings up my non-existent engagement to Anne, I will not leave it with us being at cross purposes. I will inform her in terms she will not be able to misconstrue that the match she desires between Anne and myself will never take place. Do you know that idiot man called Anne my betrothed at the ball Bingley held before he was evicted from Netherfield?" Darcy scoffed at the parson's temerity.

"I heard about Bingley losing his lease and rent," Richard said absentmindedly thinking of his lost love.

"How would you know that information, Richard?" Darcy asked somewhat suspiciously.

Richard realised that he could answer the question without having to dissemble too much or giving away information he had been requested to keep to himself for the time being.

"When we were at Lord and Lady Jersey's estate, the landlord was present. Do not ask, he does not want his name widely known," Richard stopped the question on the tip of his cousin's tongue.

Darcy tried to probe for the name a few more times, but his cousin would not budge. The subject changed to Bingley and the breaking of the friendship. Richard agreed there was no other option after what had happened with Bingley showing up at Pemberley uninvited with his sisters in tow. That night, Richard was well and truly in his cups trying to block out the thoughts of despair that perturbed him. The woman he loved would be married to a buffoon in a matter of hours.

~~~~~~~/~~~~~~~~

The morning of her wedding, Charlotte awoke to resignation that she had crossed the Rubicon; for in a few short hours she would be a married woman. To console herself, she held tight to the fact that she had, after all, met the goals of matrimony she had set for herself. Was he decent and respectable? Yes. Did he have a good home over which she would be mistress? Yes. Would she no longer be burden on her parents or her brother in the future? Yes again.

But no matter how many times she went through the list it did not dispel the forlorn feeling that she was about to make the biggest mistake of her life. She had chosen in haste when she thought it was her one opportunity; now her suspicion was she would repent at leisure for the remainder of her life. As much as she wished it otherwise, she would walk down the aisle on her father's arm.

At nine, Charlotte met her father and made the ride with him to St. Alfred's Church in Meryton. As she stood in the vestibule, a maniacal urge to run struck her, but she resisted it and was soon walking up the aisle to where Eliza was standing, ready to assist her. Franklin, Charlotte oldest brother, was standing up with her betrothed as he had had no friends or family he could call on after Mr. Bennet had demurred when offered the *honour*.

When her father placed her hand on Mr. Collins' arm and kissed her on the cheek, a single tear escaped. Only Elizabeth, who was facing her friend, noticed it drop. The couple stood before Meryton's minister as he conducted the marriage rites. When he asked if anyone had cause to object, Charlotte held her breath, hoping for a voice which did not ring out. She recited her vows in a monotone that proved strength of will and no pleasure, and then, after the final benediction, the register was signed, and Charlotte was Mrs. William Collins.

Elizabeth was one of the few who knew that Charlotte loved Richard, and she suspected that her love was returned. As much as her heart ached for her friend and for Richard, she had to respect their fortitude and honour in not creating a scandal. Elizabeth was the last person that Charlotte hugged outside the Church.

"Promise me again that you will come to visit me, Eliza, for I need something I able to look forward to," Charlotte beseeched her friend. She had not wanted to release Elizabeth from the hug, for when she did, she would have to depart.

"You have my solemn word, Charlotte," Elizabeth reiterated.

"We need to be on the road, my dove," Collins intoned, and Elizabeth did not miss the roll of her friend's eyes at the endearment.

With one last farewell to her family, Charlotte, with her husband, boarded the small, hired carriage that would bear her to her new home.

~~~~~~~/~~~~~~~

The next morning, Richard was sitting in the dining parlour with his cousins nursing a headache from his overindulgence the night before. He looked at his pocket watch as he had done many times that morning and his shoulders fell lower than any watching had believed they could fall. It was done, she was married.

"Richard, William tells me I will meet the famous Miss Elizabeth when we are at Rosings," Georgiana stated happily. It had been heart-warming to see how happy her brother was at the prospect of seeing the lady again and that Miss Elizabeth was willing to hear his apologies. He was even willing to endure more time in their aunt's grating presence in order to see the lady. Georgiana was sure if her brother did not already love the lady, he was well on his way.

"Yes, that is correct." What Richard did not say was they would also see the new Mrs. Collins. He did not know how he would use *that* name when addressing Charlotte.

"Do you think Miss Elizabeth will like me?" Georgiana enquired shyly. "Will she not think me a silly girl when or if she is informed of my folly?"

"Gigi, she already knows, and the *only one* she is angry with is that seducer who is now languishing in Marshalsea, not you. She said the same as all of us when we told you although you should have known better, the fault lies with Wickham and his paramour alone. Knowing about what happened did not change her desire to meet you, if anything it increased it," Richard assured his ward.

"I told you that did I not, Gigi? She would blame the one that deserves the blame and not you," Darcy added his assurances.

"How is Andrew's courtship proceeding?" Georgiana asked, feeling much better after hearing what her cousin and brother said.

"If he had not had to return to personally tend to problems at Hilldale and Snowhaven, I believe he would have proposed to Jane," Richard opined. "That is another way to say his courtship is proceeding anon."

"What problems?" Darcy asked.

"A fire at Hilldale. I believe two tenant cottages were severely damaged, but thankfully with no loss of life. At Snowhaven, I believe there are some sundry tenant issues. Andrew volunteered to work with both stewards as he had to be at Hilldale, thus saving my father the journey," Richard explained.

"Will I get to meet her as well?" Georgiana enthused.

"Sooner or later you will, Gigi," Darcy confirmed.

"What is *reported* of their wealth and connections does not give you pause any longer William?" Richard prodded.

"Not at all. Like Andrew, I have more than enough of both. I know how wrong my thoughts were, and I believe I have put the prideful, arrogant man I used to be in the past. I will take every precaution to ensure he will not rear his ugly head again," Darcy replied with conviction.

~~~~~~~/~~~~~~~

Charlotte was happy with her new home. It was built from the same grey stone as the church it was attached to. There was a dining parlour, sitting room, her husband's study, and a back parlour—which she chose for her particular use—as the principal rooms on the ground level. Up the stairs to one side were the master's chamber, her own was opposite and across the hall. There were also two small guest chambers.

The first bone of contention was when on gaining her chambers, Charlotte immediately removed the shelves from her closet, so she was able to hang her gowns. Her husband had protested most vehemently and remonstrated with her on the subject of Lady Catherine's displeasure. She had listened calmly, and then as cool as could be asked where, if there were shelves in her closet, her gowns were to be hung. Her husband had spluttered for but a little while before turning on his heel and leaving her be.

When he had asked when he should come to her, she had claimed her monthly indisposition. She knew she could not put him off for too long, but whatever reprieve from what she was sure would be a distasteful act with her husband, she would take with open arms.

When she was finished breaking her fast, her husband called out for her, sounding somewhat agitated. "Mrs. Collins where are you!"

"Here, Mr. Collins," Charlotte answered calmly as she stepped into the sitting room.

"Come, my dove, we must not be late for Lady Catherine. She is expecting us, and she cannot countenance those who are not punctual!" Collins worried.

After a walk of no more than fifteen minutes, her husband was huffing and puffing with exertion, and she was privately amused that he was sweating profusely with so little exercise. As they walked, between his breaths, he still managed to extol the magnificence that was the manor house before them, especially the cost of the glazing and chimney pieces.

The butler, who Charlotte judged was seventy if he was a day, led them ploddingly into her ladyship's drawing room. Charlotte had never imagined such a gaudy and ostentatious display of vulgar, ill-advised taste could exist let alone she would ever view it.

Seated in the middle of the room was a lady Charlotte judged to be above fifty, with angular features and a severe coiffure, seated on a gilded, throne-like chair on a raised platform.

She had seen her husband bow low before, but not as low as this. His nose was mere inches from the ground, and Charlotte could not fathom how he did not tip over. Charlotte curtsied—normally. She was sure her husband would not be happy that she did not genuflect as she would to royalty, but she would not regardless of the remonstration.

"Lady Catherine, I am most humbly appreciative of your beneficence and cond..." The lady cut off his speech.

"Yes, yes, Mr. Collins. Introduce me to your wife at once and stop babbling like a fool." Charlotte schooled her features so she would not burst into giggles.

"Lady Catherine de Bourgh, my wife, Mrs. Charlotte Collins. Mrs. Collins, the Right Honourable Lady Catherine de Bourgh." Collins made one of his low bows again, this time fighting to keep upright.

"You look like a pleasant sort of girl who will fit as a parson's wife, and one who did not think too highly of yourself as to refuse my clergyman as his cousins did. As my instructions have been followed, I am sure you found the parsonage to your liking, Mrs. Collins!" Charlotte smiled to herself; for it was a statement, not a question.

Before she could answer, her husband interjected. "I must humbly beg your pardon, your beneficent ladyship. Mrs. Collins removed the shelves from her closet that you had instructed me to place." He bowed again.

Before her ladyship had a chance to give her lecture, Charlotte spoke. "My husband must have misunderstood your instructions, your ladyship, as no one with good sense would instruct one to place shelves in a closet leaving no room to hang clothing that needs to be hung up." It was said with an innocent voice.

"Mr. Collins, how could you have misunderstood me so? Shelves in a closet where clothing should be hung! Do you think me a dimwit that I would advise such a thing?" Lady Catherine bellowed at the cowering clergyman. Charlotte had just discovered the perfect way to work on her ladyship while preserving the lady's ego. Her mother and friends would enjoy her letters most thoroughly after all.

"I...er...yes...no..." Collins did not know how to answer without giving offence to the last person in the world that he wanted to offend.

"You will come for tea in two days," Lady Catherine ordered and then dismissed the sweating man and his wife with a wave of her hand. On their walk back to the parsonage, Charlotte was light of step while Collins was reeling, still not understanding what just happened to get him admonished when he was certain he had done all exactly as his patroness had instructed.

VOL 1, CHAPTER 18

Mid-February 1811

The journey to London had been far more arduous than the Duke of Bedford had hoped it would be. Rather than arrive before the sabbath, they had finally arrived at Bedford House on Russell Square on Monday afternoon, the eighteenth day of February. The stop for the sabbath had helped the Duke fortify himself for the last leg of the journey.

The Duchess was terribly worried about her husband. He was sweating more than she had ever seen, and he tired so quickly. As much as she wanted to deny it, she knew her Sed would not be with her in the physical world for many more months, or weeks for that matter.

On Tuesday morning, a runner was dispatched to the offices of Norman and James with the instruction to invite Mr. and Mrs. Bennet to a meeting at their earliest convenience. The runner returned with the message that the express would be on the way to Longbourn by the time that he relayed his message.

The couple were gratified the Regent had agreed with his cousin's suggestion and request. As hoped, the patents naming Thomas Bennet as the Marquess of Birchington and Earl of Meryton were waiting for them at home, along with the patents for the new Marquess's second son to be named the Viscount of Netherfield and heir to the earldom of Meryton.

The third Duke's failure was now fully realised. Not only was a Bennet to carry the Bedford line forward, but the Bennet earldom had been revived. All that was left was a note from Sir

Randolph informing them of the date and time of the meeting.

~~~~~~~/~~~~~~~

Priscilla Bennet entered her husband's study with a questioning look, amused to find him equally bemused when she walked in to see he was staring at an express. "Is it bad news Thomas? Not one of our children?" Priscilla asked as she had imagined the worst on the way to the study, as all mothers do.

"No, no, my love, nothing like that. We need to hie to Town again; on the morrow I think," he said as he handed the express to his wife who read it.

19 February 2011
Norman and James, Inns of Court, London

Mr. Bennet:
In this matter I am representing another client, who I am not at liberty to identify yet. It is requested that you send an answer with the courier to let me know when you can meet me here at your earliest convenience.
All I am at liberty to say is that this meeting will greatly affect you and all of your family for, I believe, the better.
Sincerely,
Randolph Norman, Sir

"I agree, Thomas, we must to London. Should we bring Mark and Esther with us?" Priscilla asked.

"Yes, of course. With Jane and Lizzy at the Gardiners, they will not object to a few more Bennets." Bennet hated not knowing what this momentous thing was that would affect his family, but it was only a day or two, and if he trusted those he had long done business with. If they said it was for the better, he would put faith in that. And all would be known in but a day or two.

The courier returned to the law offices with the answer, and another was dispatched immediately with the information to the Duke. The meeting was set for Thursday morning.

~~~~~~~/~~~~~~~

"Mama, Papa! What brings you all to Town?" Jane asked

when her parents and siblings entered the drawing room at Gardiner House close to midday on Wednesday.

"We have a meeting at Norman and James," Bennet answered honestly.

Given that their father had meetings with his barrister and solicitors from time to time without prior notice to them, neither of the two older Bennet sisters gave the surprise visit another thought.

"When will Andrew return to Town?" Priscilla asked.

"Around the time Lizzy departs for Hunsford, Mama," Jane replied dreamily as she thought about her suitor.

At Broadhurst, Jane had recognised she had fallen in love with Andrew and was fairly certain he felt the same about her even though neither had made a declaration to the other. She believed that, had he not been called away to deal with the issues at his and his father's estates, she would already be betrothed; now it was down to the details as their hearts had already determined their paths. Rather than feel missish about his absence, she respected Andrew's devotion to duty and looked forward to sharing them with him.

~~~~~~~/~~~~~~~

After dinner, the Bennet and Gardiner parents were seated in the latter's sitting room. "You have no idea what this is about?" Gardiner asked as he held up the note.

"None whatsoever," Bennet owned.

"There is no point in us speculating," Priscilla pointed out. "We will know soon enough as we are to be at Sir Randolph's chambers at ten."

"As usual, Cilla, you make eminently more sense that I," Bennet kissed his wife's hands. Not long after, they went to bed and talked about nothing at all though they shared all in their hearts.

~~~~~~~/~~~~~~~

When the Bennets were shown into the meeting room at Norman and James, they saw Sir Randolph sitting at the head of the table. To his left was an older couple who Bennet did not know, but a memory stirred for Priscilla though she could not place it. The chief solicitor, Mr. James, was also present, along with two clerks and a man that neither Bennet recognised.

"May I introduce the Bennets, your Grace?" Sir Randolph asked, and the man he referred to nodded his head. "Your Graces, it is my honour to introduce Mr. Thomas and Lady Priscilla Bennet. Mr. and Mrs. Bennet, their Graces, the Duke and Duchess of Bedford, Lord Sedgwick and Lady Rose Rhys-Davies." Bennet bowed and Priscilla curtsied.

"Lady Rose, it has been well over twenty years. I did not recognise you," Priscilla relayed as she and her husband sat.

"Think nothing of it, Lady Priscilla. I see you are looking well," Lady Rose returned.

"Why are we here, Sir Randolph?" Bennet asked when he saw the greeting had concluded, more confused now than he had been when he had received the express from the barrister.

"All will become crystal clear, Mr. Bennet. I believe that you should start by reading this letter. It is a faithful copy of the original that is extremely old. We have it in document preservation if you need to see the source." Sir Randolph nodded and a clerk placed the copied letter in front of the Bennets, who together read it in silence.

12 October 1670
Longfield Meadows
Yorkshire

If you are a direct descendant of Tom and Karen Bennet and you are reading this letter, then the worst has come to pass and there are no more heirs who bear the name Rhys-Davies. I am sure that this will come as a shock to you, so allow me to explain fully.

My name is Sedgwick Rhys-Davies IV, the forth Duke of Bedford. I had, no, I have a brother who was born Thomas Rhys-Davies. Our late mother was Esther Elizabeth Rhys-Davies, née Bennet. She was the only child of the last Earl and Countess of Meryton, Lord Thomas and Lady Horatia Bennet, who both died in 1651. As I am sure you know, the earldom died with the last earl.

We were happy, my brother Thomas, sisters Amelia and Elizabeth, and I growing up. For some reason, known only to him, the third Duke who was my father, did everything in his power to separate me from Thomas, starting when he sent me to Eton at the age of thirteen. From that point on, I almost never saw my brother.

When it was his turn to go to school, my father sent Thomas to Harrow. Where I attended Cambridge, he was at Oxford. As I grew older, my father took every opportunity to denigrate Thomas in my eyes and mould me in the image that he wanted me to fit. To my everlasting shame, I succumbed to my father's manipulation for too many years.

For me, the last straw was when my father claimed that Thomas had stolen an inheritance from our mother's father that was supposed to be mine. Like my father, all I saw was the supposed theft and that I would not be receiving my due.

The next and last time I ever saw Thomas, who was calling himself Tom (I believe because my father hated that shortening of his name), was at our mother's funeral where I treated him like an enemy and not as I should have—as a brother.

When I first went to Eton, I would write to Thomas and he to me. Suddenly the letters stopped, and my father told me that he had begged Thomas to write to me, but my brother refused as he was jealous that I and not he was the heir.

Over the years I started to note behaviours in my father which I could not reconcile. He bartered my sister Amelia to an aged Earl for money. He told me he disowned my brother, but for his own reasons never filed the paperwork to make the break irrevocable. My youngest sister Elizabeth disappeared one day, and my father hardly lifted a finger to try to recover her. He told me that had someone tried to ransom my baby sister back to him, he would refuse to pay!

He bribed me with her dowry being retained in our coffers, so I overlooked his callous reaction at that point. I still feel mortification at succumbing to his manipulations so easily. In the year after his death, when I had Tom investigated, I discovered that Elizabeth was alive and well, living with Tom and his wife in Hertfordshire.

SHANA GRANDERSON A LADY

My father was taken from us in May of 1669. Some months after his death, I was searching through the attic for something from my childhood for my son whose wife was with child, their first child, when I discovered a trunk buried in the corner at the back of the attic.

It contained all of the letters that I posted to Thomas, he to me, and also between my mother and brother. Once I started to recognise the cruelty in my father, I suspected that he had intercepted the letters. Thomas had never refused to write to me, and my father had lied!

Once I made the discovery and the depths of my father's evil cruelty were proved beyond doubt, I was too embarrassed to reach out to Thomas. I knew full well that he had taken our mother's maiden name before she married and was known as Tom Bennet. After all my father had visited on him and my little sister, I decided to leave them be in peace.

Now to the crux of the matter for writing this letter. For whatever reason, over the years, we Rhys-Davies have had small families. It is conceivable that at some point in the future there will be no heir, which is also only true if my brother's direct descendants have all died out, and as you are reading this letter, it is you.

Before you tear up this letter and refuse the title of Marquess of Birchington if a Duke still lives consider this, I do not ask— and charge my descendant to honour this—for you to change your name from Bennet to Rhys-Davies! In my mind, it will be poetic justice for the Bedford dukedom to be carried forward by one of my brother's descendants.

My father's pride, I believe, stopped him making his disowning of my brother irrevocable, which means that his improper pride has directly led to you reading this letter.

On behalf of all who have ever born with the family name Rhys-Davies, I offer my sincerest apologies for the cruelty perpetrated by my father.

Lord Sedgwick Rhys-Davies IV
Duke of Bedford

No one in the room spoke allowing the new marquess and marchioness to assimilate the words on the page and, as they did, Thomas Bennet racked his brain. He had extensively studied his family history; he now understood why there was no direct line between the last Earl of Meryton and Tom Bennet. He had always assumed that it was some sort of error, but after reading the letter he at last understood. He could not have found a connection which never existed.

"Why now, your Grace?" Bennet asked.

"First, I echo my ancestor's words and apologise for the actions of the third duke." The elder duke offered, and Bennet held up his hand.

"You are not responsible, your Grace," Bennet wanted his point of view understood on that score. "I do not hold you any more responsible for the despicable actions of that man than I would any random man on the street."

"You are magnanimous. As I am technically an uncle, or at least a cousin, may we dispense with the *your graces*. I ask you to call me Uncle Sed, or, failing that, Lord Sed." He relaxed when both Bennets nodded their agreement.

"Please call me Aunt Rose or Lady Rose," the Duchess requested.

"As to why now, my Rose and I never had any children gifted to us, and I am not long for this world. I had hoped for more time to get my affairs in order, but that will not be the case. I am told that my heart is weak and will not hold out much longer. My only regret is that I did not open the letter earlier than I did," the Duke explained.

"If I read this correctly, I am a marquess, and, with your passing, soon a duke?" Bennet asked nervously.

"There is one more matter, my Lord," the man who the Bennets had seen and had been silent said. "I am Lord Oscar Timken, assistant to the Lord Chamberlain. I serve at the pleasure of the Regent. The Regent has reconstituted the Earldom of Meryton in you, Lord Birchington. The secondary title, Viscount Netherfield, is bestowed on your son Mark. As your older

son will become the Marquess when you ascend to the dukedom, your younger son will become the Earl of Meryton at that
time."

"Thomas, it seems that we cannot hide from the *Ton* any
longer!" Priscilla stated, still very much in shock at the revelations of the Bennet's unknown connections.

"So it seems, my love. Your Gra—Lord Sed, you were born
to this, you were trained and had years to learn your duties and
obligations. It seems that I have a short time to do the same.
How…" The Duke held up his hand.

"What you say about the time I had to prepare is the
truth, Thomas… may I call you Thomas?" He smiled in appreciation when Bennet nodded his approval. "That being said,
you will not be on your own. I will teach you what I am able
to until I am called home to God. My Rose," he indicated his
wife, "is committed to help you in any way she can. You have
your mother and father-in-law, your brothers and sisters-in-
law, and their families who will all be able, and I suspect, will
also be more than willing to help and advise you as needed. If
that were not enough, with your oldest being courted by Lord
Hilldale, I have a feeling that the Matlocks will be available to
assist as well," the Duke pointed out.

"What Lord Sed says is nothing but the truth, Thomas. We
will not be wanting for people willing to be of service, but it is
also true that you are one of the most capable and intelligent
men I have ever met, so once you accept this is our new reality,
you will learn with all haste," Priscilla assured her husband.

Bennet looked at Sir Randolph "I assume that Lord Sed
used the same services I do in order to discover so much about
us!" Bennet smiled wryly.

"As you say, my Lord," Sir Randolph confirmed, not fully
able to check his smile.
"How do we proceed?" Bennet asked.

Lord Timken stood and excused himself, as his part in
the meeting was complete. "The timetable of the revelations is
very much up to you," Lord Sed stated. "I do suggest that un-

less you have a pressing need to return to your estates that you remain in Town so we may spend as much time together as we are able with my health restrictions," the Duke looked to his wife. "We have much to go over. The list that the clerk is handing you enumerates my, soon to be your, holdings."

With a nod from the Duke, a clerk laid some papers in front of the new Marquess. Bennet and Priscilla read quietly, both of them just managing to catch their gasps before they escaped as they perused the list of the assets of the richest dukedom in the realm. "A shipping line, ship building yards, *seven* estates! Good lord, the income from all combined plus the investments is north of two hundred thousand per annum! The profit is not much below that mark. And additional millions in liquid assets? What would one do with all of this in a hundred lifetimes?" Bennet asked rhetorically as he read the list before him with disbelief.

"As I said, there is a *little* to go over," the Duke said sardonically. "Would you and your wife like to discuss all of this tonight, and, if agreeable to you both, we can meet at Bedford House at the same time as today on the morrow? With my difficulty travelling, that would conserve my energy." the Duke requested.

Bennet looked at his wife who gave a nod. "We will be there, Lord Sed. We ask that, until we decide about how we want this information disseminated, not a word is mentioned outside of this group. We will ask for advice from some family members, but we are assured of their discretion," Bennet asked. The request was agreed to by all.

~~~~~~~/~~~~~~~

"Thomas, until we have made some final decisions, can we not tell the children? This news will change their lives forever and curtail much of their freedoms," Priscilla stated in the carriage on the return to Gardiner House.

"Absolutely, my love. I want you to know with you at my side as my marchioness and then duchess, I know that all will be well," Bennet told his beaming wife just before he kissed her soundly.

On their return to Gardiner House, the Bennets requested that the Gardiners invite the Jerseys and Matlocks to dinner, telling them that their attendance was urgently needed. Maddie Gardiner sent the notes without prying as to the reason for the urgency, surmising when the Bennets were ready to tell them, they would.

Priscilla sent a note to her sister to request that she invite her children for dinner and to stay the night with their aunt and uncle. Both the Countesses of Jersey and Matlock accepted on their husband's behalf, and Lady Marie issued the invitation, sending one of her carriages to bring the Bennet siblings to Holder House.

For the first time, the eight parents alone sat in the drawing room together. Once the butler served aperitifs to all, he left and closed the door securely after himself.

"I am going to read a letter that we were given at Norman and James today. Please hold comments and questions until I have read all of it," Priscilla requested and received nods from the six who were unaware of its contents.

The more she read, the more obvious was the shock which grew to amazement for their family, or soon to be family, in the case of the Fitzwilliams. When Priscilla finished, Bennet took advantage of the quiet to hand a list of assets to each of the other three couples. The stories about the third duke and his avarice and pride were legendary, so neither the De Melvilles nor the Fitzwilliams were overly surprised at the revelations of his cruelty. As the new information was digested, there was silence until Gardiner spoke first.

"You are the Marquess of Birchington?" Gardiner confirmed.

"Yes, except I am also the Earl of Meryton, and Mark is Viscount Netherfield," Bennett added.

"Prinny has revived the Earldom and allowed Mark to inherit, he will be the earl one day," Lord Cyril stated, still trying to assimilate all of the revelations.

"Actually, Papa, Mark will be an earl sooner rather than later." Priscilla proceeded to explain the health of the current Duke of Bedford, and how Mark would become the Earl when Lord Sed passed, and her husband became the new Duke.

"And before our nephew woke up, he thought you were so far beneath him!" Lady Elaine smiled at the irony. "I would give anything to see William's face when he finds out."

"You know we are here to assist you with whatever you need do you not, Thomas?" His father-in-law assured him. "Do not forget that we can enlist Wes and Issy, and Marie and Holder. They will be more than willing to lend their hands."

"Lady Rose will be with us as well," Priscilla pointed out. "When I saw her today, Mama, she looked familiar, but it was not until we were introduced that I remembered her."

"She will be bereft when her husband passes; and I want to add that she will have as much support from me as she will take as well," Lady Sarah stated fervently.

"Gardiner and Maddie, may we impose on you for the foreseeable future? Both of our townhouses are being leased. If it is an imposition, I am sure there is room for us at Jersey House." Bennet looked to the Gardiners.

"You know you are welcome as long as you desire to stay, *my Lord*," Maddie offered with a tease.

"That will take some getting used to. Cilla and I discussed it on the way back. Unless Lord Sed passes before Easter we would like to keep this news private until the term break when Tom returns from Oxford," Bennet informed the group.

One and all concurred with the Bennets' decision and agreed they would not break their confidence.

The next day, after their four offspring returned from their Aunt Marie's, Bennet and Pricilla explained that there was far more business in town than they first anticipated, and they would be residing with the Gardiners until everything was completed to the satisfaction of all parties involved. It was not a lie but rather an omission.

The End of Volume 1

VOL 2, CHAPTER 1

Mid-March 1811

Miss Caroline Bingley was not a happy person. While it was true, she had long since been unhappy as her aims to gain the status as Mr. Darcy's wife were denied at every turn, her banishment and being abandoned by her siblings were the latest in her long line of failures. Now, stuck living with her spinster aunt in Scarborough, unhappy did not even begin to describe her state.

To her displeasure, her forty-some pounds of interest each month was sent to her aunt who took some for board, lodging, and breakages, before the remainder was turned over to Miss Caroline. She had written letters *ad nauseam* to both her sister and brother without a single response. After almost three months of exile, she was starting to realise she had pushed her siblings too far this time.

She had been so sure her gambit to convince her brother to take her to Pemberley would bear fruit, but the exact opposite had been the result. She missed London terribly, but none of her *friends* had extended invitations, regardless of how she hinted in her letters, and she would not give in and institute an establishment for herself in Town, as that would be like pasting a label on her forehead that read: 'On the Shelf.'

What she could do, she had no idea, but she scoured the gossip rags and society pages each time she was able to lay her hands on them to be on the lookout for an opportunity that she could take advantage of.

~~~~~~~/~~~~~~~

The last month had seen Lord Sed deteriorate significantly, but he still spent as much time with Thomas Bennet as possible to acquaint him with the running of all of the Bedford holdings. In the last month, the stewards of all of the Bedford estates, along with the Birchington estate, had been to London to meet with the Duke since his final rounds had been cut short and he had been unable to reach those estates. The final one was the steward of the estate in Ireland that bred horses. He had departed a few days previously.

Respecting Bennet's desire not to disclose himself as the heir as yet, to give his children as much time as possible to be carefree, in all of the meetings with the stewards and the managers of the other Bedford assets, Bennet had been introduced as an associate of the Duke's.

Tom Bennet would arrive in London at the end of March. Elizabeth, who had left for Hunsford a day earlier, would be retrieved before she planned to return. The others were in London, including Jane, who was once again happier than ever, as Andrew had returned a sennight ago.

The two earls and his brothers-in-law had been an immense help as Bennet learned from the Duke while Gardiner had been advising him on the matters of business. One irony for them both was that Gardiner was also a client of Bennet's now, as he exclusively used Dennington Line ships for his import and export business.

The same could be said for Priscilla Bennet who, in addition to Aunt Rose, as she now called her, and the two countesses, her sister and sister-in-law were always willing and able to assist. It had only been a month, but Thomas and Priscilla Bennet believed that although it would be daunting, the tasks ahead no longer seemed insurmountable. The vast library at Bedford House had ensured Bennet had fallen in love with the home. They had access to Birchington House on Grosvenor Square, but until the investiture the Bennets preferred to remain at Gardiner House.

Thankfully, with Jane busy with her suitor and Elizabeth on her trip to Hunsford, the two oldest Bennet daughters, who under normal circumstances would have noticed something was up with their parents, had been sufficiently diverted. If they had asked their parents direct questions neither would have prevaricated, but thankfully they were busy with their own lives.

Esther did notice something out of the norm but knew that when there was something to tell, her parents would do so, and she too was busy spending time with her cousin Allie and helping with Mark and her young Gardiner cousins.

~~~~~~~/~~~~~~~

The previous day, Lord Andrew Fitzwilliam had gained Bennet's approval for a private interview with Jane. As yet, neither he nor Richard had been informed of the massive changes about to effect the Bennets' life.

He arrived at Gardiner House at exactly ten and was shown into Gardiner's study. Bennet, having informed Gardiner of the approval for the interview, was well aware what the Viscount was about and had his butler summon his niece. "You have ten minutes, and the door will not be closed," Gardiner stated as he left the couple alone.

"Jane Francine Bennet," Andrew began as he sunk to one knee and took her hands in his. "I find that I am irrevocably in love with you. It was not love at first sight, but I felt an attraction to you like I had never felt for another from the first. You are strong, intelligent, compassionate, generous, and if all of that were not enough, you are the most beautiful woman I have ever beheld. I respect, esteem, and love you, Jane, and I know there is none other for me. Jane, will you grant my fondest wish and agree to be my wife?"

"Andrew Reginald Fitzwilliam, I, too, am in love with you and could never marry anyone else. There is no other man for me, so yes Andrew, a thousand times yes, I will marry you," Jane responded as she beamed and blushed with absolute joy and pleasure.

Andrew was so pleased he felt like he was floating on the clouds. He stood and slowly slipped a ring onto Jane's forth finger. It was a gold band, adorned with a huge sapphire and not-so-small diamonds on either side of the blue stone which he had chosen because it matched Janes eyes. He then drew Jane to himself, and she lifted her head, indicating that she did not object to being kissed. The first kiss was soft and sent tingles of anticipation through both. The next was a lingering kiss as his tongue gained entry to her mouth and they truly tasted one another for the first time.

Not wanting to risk the ire of her uncle, Andrew took a step back, though their hands were intertwined as their foreheads rested one on the other. There was a sharp knock on the door and Gardiner waited a moment, giving them time to separate fully.

When he entered, and before Andrew could request anything, he could tell he had been accepted by Jane. "Bennet gave me leave to convey his consent and blessing to this union. Welcome to the family, Andrew. I believe you will be very happy, Jane," Gardiner intoned.

"Thank you, Gardiner. Will Bennet place the announcement, or should I?" Andrew asked, keen to shout his good fortune from the rooftops.

"Bennet had a request. He asks that you wait until the end of the month for the official announcement, as Tom will be here, and he also plans to bring Lizzy home early." Gardiner conveyed Bennet's requirement. "Your mother is here with Jane's mother and grandmama; and I am sure they would be happy to hear your news."

Jane and Andrew entered the drawing room and Jane immediately noticed one lady she had not met before; she was an older lady of perhaps sixty. "Jane, my dearest Andrew, welcome. Andrew, I think you know my good friend, Lady Rose, the Duchess of Bedford. Rose, this is my oldest granddaughter, Jane," Lady Sarah covered so Jane would not question the Duchess being present.

"By the ring on your finger, I take it that my son has finally done the smart thing and asked for your hand in marriage?

The ring was most becoming on my late mother, but it looks like it was made for you, Jane," Lady Elaine enthused.

"I requested Jane's hand and she accepted me. Her uncle bestowed her father's consent and blessing," Andrew reported to exclamations of joy from all of the ladies.

"Welcome to the family, Andrew," Priscilla hugged her future son-in-law while Lady Elaine returned the favour by enfolding Jane into her arms. Jane hugged her grandmama and Aunt Maddie and accepted best wishes from the Duchess.

"It is about time, Andrew," his mother teased as she playfully swatted her son on the arm. All talk of duties of a duchess were forgotten for the afternoon as the talk turned to weddings.

~~~~~~~/~~~~~~~

Charlotte Collins had been overjoyed to welcome her good friend to her home the previous day. Charlotte had endured two months of marriage to her husband, but it felt more like years than months. A week after taking up residence at the parsonage, Charlotte had finally relented and allowed her husband to have his way with her.

She had expected pain and blood, there was neither. Collins had come into her darkened room, lifted her night dress, climbed on top of her, and grunted and sweated as he moved around, seemingly without purpose. Charlotte could not help but notice that her husband sweated profusely with any activity that he partook in. She had felt something small and soft push against her leg, then after the longest two minutes of her life there had been a little sticky discharge, and, soon after, Collins had thankfully departed leaving his mortified wife to clean her leg.

Her management of her husband, for the most part, was successful. The hardest part was his unbridled reverence of his patroness. Whenever needed, Charlotte would employ her successful strategy of getting Lady Catherine to reverse an edict, making it look as if were the lady's intent the whole time. It was not lost on Charlotte that Miss Anne de Bourgh seemed to be highly amused when the rector's wife was able to manipulate her mother to reverse some of her ridiculous edicts.

Whenever Miss de Bourgh rode out in her pony drawn phaeton, she would make a point of stopping and asking Mrs. Collins to join her; Mr. Collins would never object as he would never slight his patroness's daughter. A firm friendship had grown between the two, and although Miss de Bourgh was sickly, she had a keen sense of humour and enjoyed her time with Mrs. Collins exceedingly.

Charlotte had convinced her husband to spend an inordinate amount of time in his garden or his study and, for the most part, other than meals she hardly saw him. She had been mortified on behalf of her friend when, on her arrival, Collins had attempted, in a not too subtle way, to point out all of the manifest advantages one of his cousins could have enjoyed had they married him, completely insensible of the insult to his own wife.

Charlotte and Elizabeth were sitting in the former's parlour when the portly, sweating man burst in with exuberance. "My dove, Cousin Elisabeth, you will never guess the honour that will be bestowed on you on the morrow. My most esteemed patroness Lady Catherine de Bourgh's most estimable nephews and niece are to arrive, and we have been doubly honoured as we are invited to dine at Rosings the following evening for dinner. What an honour you will have, cousin, to be in the company of one so high born!" Collins had babbled. Both Elizabeth and Charlotte did their level best to not burst out laughing, and Collins was certain that their reactions proved their pleasure of the honour of being in her ladyship's company.

Elizabeth had been concerned before she saw Charlotte, worrying that she would find her picture of abject misery. Elizabeth knew that Charlotte had fallen in love with Richard and he in his turn with her. She had been relieved to find Charlotte, if not happy, then at least content. Elizabeth was impressed at how, for much of the day, Charlotte managed to keep her husband anywhere but in her company.

After Collins departed the parlour and had closed the door, Elizabeth looked to her friend. "Charlotte are you able to be sanguine about Richard's arriving on the morrow?" Elizabeth asked gently.

"I am well, Eliza. I am a married woman now, so we may meet as indifferent acquaintances," Charlotte was trying to convince herself as much as her friend, and they both knew it.

"Indifferent indeed," Elizabeth returned softly.

"Eliza! Behave yourself!" Charlotte demanded with mock effrontery. "More importantly, how do you feel about Mr. Darcy's coming?"

"He is welcome at his aunt's home. If he follows through with his intent as he wrote in the letter to Andrew, I will accept his apology as long as I see genuine change and not the proud, haughty man from Hertfordshire. As long as he is not, I see no reason why we cannot begin anew," Elizabeth stated evenly. "I am very much looking forward to meeting Miss Darcy."

The two discussed those arriving on the morrow, and then Elizabeth went for a walk in the grove that led from the parsonage into Rosings Park. She enjoyed being able to take a solitary ramble, as Mercury was not with her, so she made do with as many walks as she could.

~~~~~~~/~~~~~~~

The three cousins were sitting in Darcy's comfortable travelling coach as they departed the rest break at Bromley. Darcy had been in Town for a full fortnight prior to the departure. He had not been aware that most of the Bennet family were in residence at Gardiner House.

He found out the night before they departed when Andrew handed him a letter from Miss Bennet for Miss Elizabeth. It was at the dinner that Darcy learnt that Andrew was betrothed to Miss Bennet, and for Bennet family reasons the announcement would not be made public until after the beginning of April. He had been sincere in his wishes to his cousin.

As he sat, almost lulled to sleep by the rocking of the conveyance, he could not help but smile when he thought of the pleasure of delivering his apology and the letter to Miss Elizabeth. He was also just as keen for Miss Elizabeth to meet Gigi as his sister was to meet Miss Elizabeth.

At the other end of the rear facing seat was the Honourable *Mr.* Richard Fitzwilliam. The sale of Brookfield had become final almost a week previously, and as promised, the day his father handed him the deed to the estate Richard had gone to see General Atherton and resigned from the army. The sale of his commission had been finalized the day before, and Richard had been relieved that it was finished before they set out for Kent.

As much as he was looking forward to taking up residence at his estate, he was doubly so to see Charlotte Lucas, no, not Lucas, Collins, again. He was fully aware she was forbidden fruit, and unlike Adam and Eve, he would not succumb to temptation. He had far too much honour to ever dishonour anyone's wedding vows regardless of his heart's yearning for Charlotte.

He told himself he wanted to assure himself she was well, that the buffoon was not mistreating her in any way, and his aunt was not making her life a misery, though he felt certain Charlotte would be able to manage his aunt better than most. Regardless of her pronouncements to the contrary, their aunt was not the smartest person of their acquaintance. She had more wit than Mr. Collins, but that in itself was an exceptionally low threshold to meet.

Georgiana Darcy could not wait to arrive. It was not her aunt or Anne she wanted to see—although she did like Anne and corresponded with her—it was Miss Elizabeth Bennet that Georgiana wanted to meet most of all. The fact the lady knew about Ramsgate and *still* wanted to make her acquaintance boded very well for their becoming friends, despite there being five years between them.

As the coach passed the parsonage, the parson seemed to be on the lookout for them and bowed so low as they passed that the occupants were sure he had planted his face in the grass. "What was that?" Georgiana asked.

"That, Gigi, was one Mr. Collins, Aunt Cat's latest in a line of sycophantic and vastly stupid clergymen she has installed at Hunsford," Richard informed his young cousin, his tone not so very acerbic as his thoughts. He grinned when Darcy smirked at him, for it was naught but the truth.

"Do you suppose he was seeking worms in his lawn?" Georgiana giggled.

"Georgiana!" Darcy warned, although his smile let his sister know he was not upset at her irreverent remark.

"Come now, William," Richard called to his cousin, "Gigi merely spoke the truth, and we always want her to speak the truth, do we not?"

"I have no issue with the truth, as long as she keeps it respectful while she tells it," Darcy retorted.

"Here we go into the dragon's lair," Richard teased Gigi as the carriage come to a halt under the portico at Rosings.

The three arrivals stopped by the drawing room to make their obligatory greetings to their relations. "Fitzwilliam, Richard, Georgiana, you are late!" Lady Catherine claimed.

"No, Aunt, we are not," Darcy responded shortly.

"Is your betrothed not looking good..." A shocked Lady Catherine was speechless as her nephew dared interrupt her by raising his hand.

"Aunt—Lady Catherine—I have been remiss in making myself clear in the past, and I will not make that mistake again. Anne and I have *never* been, nor will we *ever* be, betrothed!" Darcy stated with unmistakable steel in his voice. Before his aunt could respond he turned to Anne and gave her a wink that his aunt could not see. "Anne, have I *ever* proposed to you?"

"No William you have not," Anne said, trying to supress a smile at this finally coming to a head.

"Do you desire to marry me, or anyone for that matter," Darcy asked.

"Anne does not know her own mind, I will..." Lady Catherine was astonished when her nephew raised his hand once again to demand her silence.

"As you are not the one asked the question, you will refrain from answering." Darcy warned her calmly, the undertone of warning not missed by any in the room.

"No, I do not. I see you as nothing but a cousin, and I know full well that my body would not allow me to perform any marital duties, as bearing a child would kill me as surely as if I had been shot," Anne stated evenly. "Mama, I know why you want me to marry William. In a month I will be five and twenty and I *will* take control of my inheritance."

"You are too frail for the rigours of running this estate," Lady Catherine grasped at the last straw she had now that the one she had been pulling on broke.

"My body may be weak, Mama, but my mind is fully capable. You know that Uncle Reggie will support me in this!" Anne knew by using her uncle's name her mother would say nothing further. Her uncle was the only one who could easily bend her mother to his will.

"Aunt, I know no promise was ever given by my mother, and my father also refused your entreaties for a betrothal. Please stop embarrassing yourself by claiming otherwise. Come, Gigi, let us go change before we deliver the letter." Darcy turned and he and his sister left the drawing room, leaving a shocked Lady Catherine asking herself what had just happened to all of her well thought out plans.

"Anne, if you would like to come with me, can I have your company for a few minutes before we complete the task we were charged with? I would dearly love it as I hardly ever see you." Georgiana went to Anne and kissed her cheek.

"Go, Gigi. I will be here for mother to explain what her options are after next month as discussed with Uncle Reggie. I will see you later." Anne kissed Georgiana's cheek and smiled in contentment as she walked away.

It was only after the door closed that Lady Catherine realised she had not been addressed again and they had turned to

Anne rather than herself. "Now, mother, it is time for a discussion I have long planned to have with you. You will remain quiet until I ask you questions. Do I make myself clear?" Anne stood and looked down at her mother as she closed in on her. "Do not make this more difficult on yourself. I have had many years of difficulty and would happily consign you to the dower house should you not agree to the following terms. The first will be to cease all talk of my marrying cousin Darcy. The second..."

~~~~~~~/~~~~~~~

The three cousins walked enthusiastically to the parsonage. Luckily, they had missed Mr. Collins who was on his way to see his patroness. And even better, though they would never know, he would be asked to wait until the conversation in the parlour was finished to Miss de Bourgh's satisfaction. It was a wonder they were able to have so much time without him, or just the amusement of Miss de Bourgh to ensure that Mrs. Collins was reprieved that day of his company and able to enjoy that of her favourite cousins instead. "Welcome, Mr. Darcy, Colonel," Charlotte saw Richard shake his head, "Mr. Fitzwilliam. I assume this young lady is Miss Darcy?" Charlotte smiled warmly at the young lady and indicated her guests should sit.

"Mrs. Collins and Miss Bennet, may I have the pleasure of introducing my sister, Miss Georgiana Darcy. Georgiana, Mrs. Charlotte Collins and Miss Elizabeth Bennet." Darcy turned to Elizabeth. "Miss Elizabeth please allow me to apologise for my behaviour in Hertfordshire, especially for my slight at the assembly. I shudder to think of how I behaved and have hopefully started to become a man who my sister would be happy to claim as her brother." Darcy did not miss the questioning look on both ladies, but he shook his head. "A story for another time. It is also true, as you now know Miss Elizabeth, I had other concerns on my mind." Miss Darcy coloured. "However, none of that excuses my not behaving as a gentleman should. Please know, not only should I never have uttered those offensive words, but I have long known that they are the opposite of the truth as I saw it soon after, and still see it.

"Regardless of your wealth and connections, I should have judged you on the strength of your character alone. Had I done so, I would have seen you are one of the better, actually are among the best people of my acquaintance. I humbly beg your forgiveness, and truly hope we can start again, Miss Elizabeth." Darcy waited as he watched Miss Elizabeth for a sign—any sign, she did not despise him.

Elizabeth arched an eyebrow. "How can I not forgive you, Mr. Darcy. I believe your apology sincere, and as I think we may be cousins one day, yes, I too would like it if we may begin again," Elizabeth granted. "Is that a letter from Jane I spy in your hand?"

"It is. Miss Bennet charged me with placing it in your hand." Darcy handed the missive over to its intended recipient.

"Open it, Lizzy, we know what it says," Richard teased.

Elizabeth broke the seal and opened the page as fast as she was able, and quickly read the short note within. "Jane and Andrew are to be married!" she exclaimed.

"You see, your forgiving me was most timely as we *are* to be cousins," Darcy quipped.

The three cousins remained a further quarter hour before they departed. Elizabeth was surprised, pleasantly so, to discover that Mr. Darcy had a dry sense of humour, and she was fast on her way to liking Miss Darcy very well.

VOL 2, CHAPTER 2

The next morning, before she had to endure breaking her fast with her arduous cousin who ate more food than any other three people combined, Elizabeth took a refreshing walk in the grove. It was not just the amount of food which her cousin consumed that disgusted Elizabeth, but the manner in which he consumed it. It was as if he could not insert enough food into his mouth to satiate his apparently voracious appetite, and if that were not bad enough, he thought nothing of conversing with his mouth full, which sprayed food in all directions. It was within moments of sitting at the table with him in the parsonage that she understood why Charlotte sat at the opposite end of the table and had placed Elizabeth next to her.

When Elizabeth thought back to the visit they had received the previous day from the two Darcys and Richard, she had to admit the recollection brought not a little pleasure. Mr. Darcy had changed and changed for the better. She liked Miss Darcy and was hoping they would spend much time in one another's company while both were here in Kent and beyond.

Elizabeth knew from what she read in Andrew's letter that, at least when it had been written, Mr. Darcy held her in a certain amount of tender regard. She was at a loss when she tried to divine when and how that could have happened given the limited and contentious interactions in Hertfordshire. She turned when she heard a horse approaching her; discovering Mr. Darcy as if her very thoughts had conjured him.

"Good morning, Miss Elizabeth," he greeted as he dismounted.

"And a good morning to you, Mr. Darcy. Who is this fine

fellow?" Elizabeth asked, allowing Darcy's stallion to sniff her hand. She had an apple with her that she had intended to eat, but when the big black animal sniffed her pocket, she offered it to him on the palm of her hand and he happily munched on the treat.

"It is Zeus who just charmed you out of your apple, Miss Elizabeth," Darcy laughingly informed her. "Did you not bring your black and white stallion with you to Kent?"

Elizabeth was impressed he seemed to have being paying attention to her enough to know what Mercury looked like. "I was not sure there would be anywhere to stable Mercury, so he remains at my uncle's house in London. Does it shock you that a lady would choose to ride a stallion rather than a more docile mare?" she challenged. She had forgiven him but wanted to push a little to see if the haughty, proud man would make an appearance.

"Not in the least, Miss Elizabeth. If Gigi, that is what we call Georgiana, ever wanted one, and so long as she could command him, I would not object," Darcy replied, impressing his walking partner. As they ambled along, he offered his arm and Elizabeth rested her hand on it lightly, his stallion trailing behind them like a dog following his master.

"Andrew and Richard informed us of Miss Darcy's nickname. As we are to be cousins, do you not think we may dispense with formality, and you call me Elizabeth or Lizzy?" Elizabeth offered, which elicited a smile from him like she had never seen before. If it were only the smile it would be pleasant enough, but he revealed his dimples to her for the first time.

'My, he is handsome when he smiles, and those dimples! I suppose he was always handsome, but I refused to see it before,' Elizabeth admitted to herself.

"In that case, please call me William as my family does," Darcy responded, grateful at being granted the privilege to use her familiar name.

Darcy guided them to a glade, and they sat on a bench near the side of the pond. "As we are soon to be family, I find

UNKNOWN FAMILY CONNECTIONS

that I must reveal some information to you we keep hidden for the same reason you employ that infamous mask of yours," Elizabeth told him.

"You are not poor, are you?" Darcy had finally pieced pieces of the puzzle together while in town after the multiple admonishments, unsurprised when Elizabeth nodded. "All of the signs were there, but I refused to see what was before my eyes as it did not fit with my preconceived notions. How blind and arrogant I was!" Darcy berated himself.

"What clues did you ignore?" Elizabeth teased him into a less frustrated state of mind.

"First of all, the horses! The sheer number of them, and more importantly the quality. There is no poor country squire I know of that has more than one carriage. I almost dismissed the thought the night of the ball until I saw that both were pulled by matched pairs rather than farm horses. I was distracted by a true beauty that night," he looked directly at Elizabeth who blushed lightly, "so I may be excused from not fully considering my thoughts about the horses," Darcy commented, causing Elizabeth's blush to darken. "I always prided myself on my perspicacity, but it seems I had none where you and your family are concerned."

"It is not just the wealth," Elizabeth revealed. Darcy turned to hear the rest, a sinking feeling in his stomach that the wealth was the least of it, and the glint of amusement in her eyes proved it was so even before she continued. "Jane's mother was the daughter of a solicitor when my father fell in love with her. She was taken from them but days after Jane's birth. My father met my mother by chance just longer than a year later. They courted, married, and a year later yours truly made her appearance into the world."

"Then I assume your connections are wider than the Phillipses and Gardiners?" Darcy asked carefully, almost dreading the answer.

"One could say so. Before she married my father, my mother was *Lady* Priscilla De Melville." Elizabeth smiled when

Darcy's expression changed to stunned disbelief.

"Your grandparents are the Earl and Countess of Jersey? Your uncle is Viscount Westmore, and the Marchioness of Holder is your aunt?" Darcy laughed; a full belly laugh escaped before he had a chance to stop it. "Good Lord, if Miss Bingley and Mrs. Hurst would have had any idea who your family was, they would have been kissing your feet!" He grinned.

"Which is exactly why we never corrected what is reported. I must return to watch the feeding at the menagerie. That was not kind of me, but my cousin's way of eating..." Darcy lifted a hand to prove he understood without Elizabeth finishing her excuse.

"William, before we go our separate ways, you must allow me to apologise," Elizabeth added, much to Darcy's surprise.

"I fail to see how I am due an apology when the offence was all given by myself," Darcy asserted.

"It has been pointed out to me that I am quick to judge and slow to forgive. I said uncharitable things about you. However, my mother made me consider things that I had refused to, as it was much easier to paint you as the villain," Elizabeth admitted.

"Although I do not believe you need to beg my pardon, you have it nonetheless. I find there is little I would deny you." Before Elizabeth could formulate an answer, he carried on to change the subject so she could not correct him out of his hopes just yet. "I told you I would provide an explanation of the split from Bingley. When we next have time to talk, I will make good on my promise. Before I forget, may I bring Gigi to visit you later this morning?"

"Any of you would be welcome any time you choose to visit," Elizabeth replied so pointedly, he grinned at the acceptance of them all by the ladies who held the hearts of himself and his cousin in their gentle hands.

They walked back towards the parsonage and the two separated before they could be seen from the house. Darcy mounted his horse and turned Zeus back towards Rosing's stables, while Elizabeth walked toward the front gate of the parsonage.

~~~~~~~/~~~~~~~

Tongues were wagging in the *Ton*. Lord Hilldale had been seen at multiple events, always with the same blond beauty on his arm. It quickly became evident that the Viscount was courting the unknown lady and would soon propose to her or already had done so, depending on the version one heard. It was discovered that she was a Miss Bennet of Hertfordshire.

Lady Elaine smiled as the number of morning callers increased significantly; those just seeking information receiving far less than they hoped. The Countess confirmed that her son was courting a young lady, and they had the full support of both families. The news that the eligible, but elusive, Lord Andrew Fitzwilliam was off the marriage mart was a blow to many a debutant and their matchmaking mothers. They lamented that such a prize as Viscount Hilldale was now courting in earnest, and from what they could glean from the little known about the lady, she was a country miss without any reported fortune or connections.

For their part, Jane and Andrew ignored the gossiping members of the *Ton* and revelled in one another's company. With both sets of parents' approval, the couple selected the first day of May as the date they would marry from Longbourn. The more time the two spent together, the more their love grew.

~~~~~~~/~~~~~~~

"I understand my great-niece is to wed Hilldale on the first of May, is that correct?" the Duke asked after Bennet had seated himself in Bedford House's library with his relative.

"There is something I need to ask you, and it is rather a delicate subject," Bennet asked tentatively.

"What to do about the wedding should I die before it has taken place?" the Duke guessed.

"Yes, exactly. We do not want to disrespect your memory, so I would appreciate some guidance from you on this," Bennet requested of the man he now considered an uncle.

"It is simple. Unless it is within a few days of my death, they must get married. What would be a better affirmation of life than a wedding? There is a circle of life, and mine may be ending, but I do not want the world to stop when I go. Rose and I have spoken about this, and she has my wishes in writing. If I am gone by then—in case any jealous harpies of the *Ton* try to use the wedding so soon after my passing against you, she will be able to step in," the Duke informed his heir. "Now, when does your son arrive from Oxford?"

"Tom should return by the last Friday in March, Uncle Sed. Why do you ask?" Bennet was curious, for the man canvassed subjects quickly enough to sometimes even lose him. After being able to follow the four women in his house in conversation, that was impressive.

"My cousin, well, *our* cousin, would like to meet you and your family. Will your daughter in Kent return to London the same day so you will be able to reveal the connections between us to all of them?" the Duke enquired further.

"Yes, I will send a coach there to collect her that Friday morning. She will not be happy to have her time with her friend curtailed," Bennet grinned ruefully. "Did I tell you that Mr. Darcy followed through and apologised completely?" The Duke shook his head. "He did, and without knowing of our true situation, believing it to be as was reported before you and I met. It seems what Matlock told us about his nephew is all correct."

"At least you know that his interest in her was before he knew of anything, never mind what is about to be revealed. I met his father, Mr. George Darcy as he was. We transacted some business, and he was an exceptionally good man," the Duke related.

Bennet knew that there was always more that he would have to learn once he became duke, but the two men did not use all of their time just teaching and learning. Bennet had grown very fond of his uncle in the short time that he had known him, and for the Duke it almost felt like Thomas Bennet was the son he was never granted.

~~~~~~~/~~~~~~~

Miss Caroline had begun having thoughts that she had never allowed before, for she had started to ask herself why she was an anathema to practically everyone she knew. At first, she reasoned the blame to be all on others as was her habit, but once she had moved past the self-pity, she was forced to try something she had never done before. She looked at herself and her behaviour through the eyes of others.

The more she considered them, the more her own shame proportionally increased, for how she had acted was wanting in many ways. Having been denied entry to Pemberley, she had started with her interactions with Mr. Darcy. As she became more honest with herself, she was forced to admit that it was obvious that Mr. Darcy had never wanted anything to do with her. Rather than look at her as a possible wife, he looked on her with true abhorrence.

And now that she saw it for herself, she searched for reasons for her behaviour. She was able to trace much of it back to the seminary that she boasted had made her an estimable lady. She and Louisa had been looked down upon and derided for their roots in trade by daughters of the *Ton*. Rather than take the way she had been treated as an exemplar of how *not* to treat others, Miss Bingley realised she had aped the behaviour, which had led to her belief in her superiority, and as she was wealthy she could behave exactly as the girls had toward her— except her own behaviour had been far worse.

She could see how she had blatantly cared for none but herself and her own wants, and she had never considered, nor wanted to consider, the consequences of her behaviour. She had known Mr. Darcy was serious in what he said to Charles, but she had wanted him, so she had not cared who got hurt to further her aim or how much she had had to lie or manipulate others to get there.

She knew her brother was weak-willed, and rather than

help him, she had played him like a violin. Miss Bingley was then forced to also admit to herself that she had never cared about Louisa's feelings. She treated her sister somewhat better than she had her brother, but only as long as Louisa did her bidding.

She finally was forced to allow that Jane Bennet had shown clear signs she had no interest in Charles, but not being willing to admit that their money did not impress her, she had fed her brother's misconception that she cared for him even while railing against her, as it helped her control him.

Miss Bennet had always been a lady, even when she reacted to the barbs being fired at her. Miss Bingley could not but remember the look of disgust that had flashed across the lady's features when Miss Bingley had boasted about her dowry, and how vulgar she felt as she reviewed the memory of it. The regret was crushing, and that night, for the first time in almost a decade, Miss Bingley cried herself to sleep.

She began to accept she had been the author of her problems—nobody else. She did not know how she would begin to atone for all she had done, but she was sure of one thing, she had to make the attempt. She was determined to try, even though she did not expect something in return, not even forgiveness, though she hoped some measure was granted. By the time she woke up the next morning, her resolve had weakened significantly.

~~~~~~~/~~~~~~~

Mr. and Miss Darcy, along with Mr. Fitzwilliam, were admitted to the parsonage by the bowing and scraping, ridiculous parson. "What an honour..." he started, about to launch into a sycophantic welcome speech, when his wife rescued the guests.

"Welcome, please join Miss Elizabeth and me in the parlour for tea," Charlotte invited. Collins was left spluttering as the three followed his wife without a glance in his direction.

Elizabeth smiled warmly and patted the seat next to her for Miss Darcy to join her. "It is good to see you again, Miss

Darcy," Elizabeth welcomed the young girl.

"Please call me, Georgiana, or Gigi, Miss Elizabeth, we are practically family already," Georgiana invited.

"I agree, Gigi, as long as I am Lizzy to you," was her pleased response.

Before Georgiana could reply, the huffing and sweating Mr. Collins entered the parlour. "My dear, is it not time for your visit with Lady Catherine?" Charlotte asked deftly.

With one of his low bows, her husband exited the room, pausing only to appreciate his wife for entertaining his guests. The front door was heard closing not long after. Charlotte smiled as peace descended on her home, and her guests politely coughed to stop themselves from bursting into laughter.

The former colonel was still fighting an internal battle. He loved Charlotte, but all he could be forever more was a friend. At least he had just been reassured that she knew how to redirect her husband, so it seemed that she did not have to suffer the buffoon's company very much.

"Now that my cousin has departed, please tell us what happened to cause a break with Mr. Bingley," Elizabeth requested.

Darcy readily complied as he no longer wanted secrets between himself and those in the room, including Mrs. Collins, as it was obvious the love she and his cousin shared was not of a weak variety. He explained how he had tried to advise his friend to take Miss Bingley in hand after her attempted compromise of himself, and the ill-fated trip Bingley had been manipulated into taking to Pemberley. When he completed his recitation, both Charlotte and Elizabeth agreed there had been no other choice.

"That is why Jane was never interested in him. Papa had had him investigated before he rented Netherfield, and the report presented an irresolute man," Elizabeth informed the group.

"Wait, your father is the landlord of Netherfield Park?" All the clues he had seen when he resided with Bingley suddenly made sense.

"Did I not mention that this morning, William?" Elizabeth asked innocently.

"No, *Elizabeth*, you did not. You acknowledged you were wealthier than known and who your connections are," Darcy's arched brow brought out a delightful smile from her, and he would be glad to learn her secrets for the rest of his days, should he be so fortunate.

"May I tell him about the town houses, Lizzy?" Richard asked and Elizabeth nodded. "You know the two houses opposite Darcy House that are leased out?" Richard asked.

"They belong to the Bennets?" Darcy asked in genuine surprise.

"They do," Elizabeth explained the part of the story she knew about an ancestor winning five acres and allowing the land to become part of Grosvenor Square in return for the houses.

The housekeeper knocked on the door and entered at Charlotte's answer. "Miss Anne de Bourgh, mistress."

"So this is where all my cousins are hiding?" Anne asked irreverently as she sat down next to her friend. "Your husband is commiserating with my mother while she gets used to the new reality which is less than a month away."

Anne explained the terms she had laid down in return for her mother not being banished to the dower house, and Darcy was most pleased at the embargo on talk of the phantom engagement. "I am sorry we left to change and missed the fun," Richard stated with a grin.

"As I am determined to redecorate and make my house a home, what should I do with all of the gaudy pieces my mother bought?" Anne enquired.

"I think I know someone who could help you with that, Miss de Bourgh," Elizabeth told the frail young woman.

"That is Anne to you, Miss Elizabeth," Anne responded airily.

"Well then, *Anne*, it is Elizabeth or Lizzy *to you*. You are not aware yet, but we will soon be cousins." Anne looked at both of her male cousins with raised eyebrows.

"It is neither of us, silly goose," Richard teased her with his long-used term of endearment when they were together as children. "Lizzy's older sister is betrothed to Andrew."

"This is rich," Anne giggled. "Mr. Collins had been telling Mama about your low connections and how you are a poor family of no consequence. I have not been to Town for many a year and am not educated on the latest fashions, but even I can see your clothing is of high quality. You may be a lot of things, but I suspect poor is not one of them."

"May I tell Anne who your grandparents are?" Darcy asked Elizabeth, his eyes alight with mirth.

"So William knows?" Richard looked questioningly at Elizabeth.

"Not before he apologised," Elizabeth stated succinctly. "Go ahead William."

"The Earl and Countess of Jersey!" Darcy said grinning.

"How?" Anne asked. Elizabeth briefly explained her family history to Miss de Bourgh, who was fully laughing by the end of the retelling. "I am sure my mother will make some insouciant comment to Mr. Collins's "informed" statement about your family. Please do not reveal the truth until then. I cannot wait until she finds out your sister will be her niece and will soon rank above her."

Elizabeth readily agreed to her new friend's request. "Eliza, I think you should wear a Chambourg creation tonight, I know you have some with you," Charlotte advised.

"You have some gowns here that Madam Chambourg created?" Georgiana asked excitedly.

"I do, Gigi. Would you like to see them?" The younger girl nodded emphatically. "While I am gone, why do you not tell William and Richard how you got Anne's mother to order your husband to remove the shelves from the closets?" Elizabeth suggested with a tinkling laugh. It was music to Darcy's ears, the same laugh which had made him really look at Elizabeth for the first time.

Anne had her cousins in stiches as she told the story from her perspective. Richard was happy that it seemed Charlotte was able manage his aunt as well as she did her husband. After the two descended from viewing Elizabeth's gowns, the three cousins departed for Rosings. Elizabeth promised that the next time she and Gigi were in London at the same time, she would take Gigi to Madam Chambourg's for her own special fitting.

~~~~~~~/~~~~~~~

Not long after the party from Rosings departed, a most agitated Collins returned. "My dove, Miss Elizabeth, you will not believe what an infamous way Miss de Bourgh is treating her mother!" He was indignant for his *poor* patroness.

"In less than a month, Miss de Bourgh turns five and twenty, and Rosings becomes her property." Charlotte said pointedly. As Mr. Collins sputtered she added, "I would listen to the daughter and not the mother, if I were you. After all, in a few weeks, Miss de Bourgh will be your patroness and it would not do to alienate her, would it, husband?"

Mr. Collins became still as the wheels turned slowly in head and he returned to his study without another word. No matter how he tried, he could not think of a way not to support his patroness fully without ignoring his actual patroness' wishes.

VOL 2, CHAPTER 3

"**C**ousin Elizabeth! What are you wearing?" Collins was horrified. His cousin was wearing a dress that seemed to be of far better quality than those his patroness wore.

"Did you not tell me to wear the best gown I brought with me, Mr. Collins?" Elizabeth asked innocently.

"Mr. Collins, you know how much Lady Catherine hates tardiness, and if you send Eliza up to change now, we will be late, which will lead to your patroness being most displeased with you," Charlotte redirected her husband's attention.

"You are of course correct, my dove, let us depart forthwith," Collins led the charge towards the front door as his wife and his cousin donned their outerwear and followed him.

It was not long before they caught up with him, as he was huffing and puffing, unable to maintain his initial pace. Elizabeth pretended not to notice sweat was dripping off the hapless man and was impressed that Charlotte did the same. Between gasping for breath, he attempted to deliver a dissertation on the many wonders of Rosings Park and its mistress.

After handing their outerwear to a footman, the ancient butler showed the guests into the drawing room. The first thing Charlotte noticed was the absence of Lady Catherine's throne, and the second was that the lady seemed to be in high dudgeon over the eroding of her perceived power.

Collins introduced his cousin and began to apologise for her dress. "Mr. Collins, are you insensible?" Miss de Bourgh asked, silencing the silly man mid-sentence. "Elizabeth is dressed perfectly; it is not her fault my mother has refused to update the style of our dresses for some years now. Please

SHANA GRANDERSON A LADY

allow me to be the judge of *my* guests mode of dress or anything else!" Seeing her mother was about to interject, Anne directed a quelling look at the lady, and the protest withered before it was spoken. A sharp look from his wife silenced Collins on the subject as well.

Collins was having a hard time grasping what was happening around him. He could not understand how no one venerated his patroness as he did, how it could be that her daughter was usurping Lady Catherine's *power,* and how Lady Catherine was seemingly unable to stop it. Rather than commanding the room with her wise pronouncements, his patroness was sitting subdued in a way he had never seen before.

The butler announced dinner and Mr. Darcy offered his arm to Elizabeth, which she accepted without hesitation. Richard escorted his cousin and aunt, one on each arm, while Collins followed his wife and Miss Darcy, who seemed to find something they needed to discuss as he approached them to offer his services to escort them into dinner.

As soon as they sat, Lady Catherine gained her voice and started to quiz her parson's cousin, for she had not missed the way her nephew looked at the lowborn woman. Her dream of a match between him and her daughter had been squelched. Although the match was apparently dead, she would not allow him to throw himself away on some floozy with no wealth or connections.

Lady Catherine opened her attempt to cow the country miss, certain in this she would have success, for Mr. Collins had assured her these Bennets were uneducated and uncouth. "My rector informs me that your mother is the daughter of a country solicitor." Said rector nodded even as he shovelled large pieces of roast beef into his mouth.

"I am afraid Mr. Collins is misinformed, your ladyship," Elizabeth responded pleasantly. She noticed Anne was going to warn her mother off, but her friend stopped when Elizabeth gave her a slight shake of her head.

"What is the meaning of this? Mr. Collins, did you lie to

me?" Lady Catherine demanded.

"I would never do such, your beneficence," Collins managed, sending only a *little* of his food spraying on the tablecloth in front of him.

"My answer was, Lady Catherine, that my cousin was *misinformed*, not that he lied. Like many," Elizabeth looked from her to Darcy at whom she smiled. "Mr. Collins made an assumption, and never bothered to ask the pertinent questions."

"Stop speaking in riddles girl!" Lady Catherine demanded.

Before Elizabeth could answer, Anne decided to join the fray. "Mama, did you know you will be aunt to Elizabeth's sister soon?"

"Anne, of what nonsense do you speak? Neither Fitzwilliam or Richard is betrothed, and they would not connect themselves to one with what Mr. Collins told me is less than a three-thousand-pound dowry!"

"I am afraid Anne is correct. *Andrew* is, in fact, betrothed to Miss Jane Bennet, who has a dowry many times larger than the amount Mr. Collins reported," Richard informed his aunt.

"What?" Both Collins and his patroness exclaimed simultaneously.

"To which part, Aunt?" Darcy asked.

"How much does your sister have?" Lady Catherine demanded.

"As I am sure you are aware, it is vulgar to discuss such things in polite company," Elizabeth demurred.

"I am his nearest relation, it is my right to know his concerns," Lady Catherine blustered.

"My parents will be interested to know that you are Andrew's nearest relation, Aunt," Richard stated.

The more upset his patroness became, the more agitated Mr. Collins became on her behalf, though unlike her, he sought solace by adding more to his fork as he considered how best to assist her. "How can my brother allow his son to marry one with no connections other than in trade?" Lady Catherine demanded indignantly.

"My sister has the same connections as I do, as my mother accepts her as her own, as do our grandparents, aunts, and uncles," Elizabeth stated evenly.

"What are you going on about? Oh, that is correct—you mentioned something about your sister's mother," Lady Catherine remembered, an off-hand wave proving she believed them as insignificant.

"Yes, my sister's mother was taken from her days after Jane was born. My father married my mother, the natural mother of myself and my younger siblings, two years later. As I said, Jane is accepted as a daughter in all ways by Mama. You may have heard of her before she wed my papa, *Lady* Priscilla De Melville," Elizabeth related calmly, schooling her amusement as she watched Lady Catherine's eye's bulge.

"Y-your g-grandparents are the Earl and Countess..." Lady Catherine's jaw clamped shut, unable to even say it.

"Of Jersey, I think you were trying to say, Mama," Anne added for her mother. "Which would make her one aunt and uncle a marchioness and marquess, and the others a mere viscount and viscountess."

Collins could not believe that he, and even worse, his patrpness, had been taken for fools. Forgetting he had a mouth full of food, he took a deep breath so he could make his displeasure known, except no sound came out as he drew the food into his windpipe.

No one was looking at him, and so none of the diners were aware there was a problem until they heard his head slam onto the table followed by his corpulent body tipping his chair over as he crashed to the floor.

Richard was first out of his chair and also closest to Collins. The rest of the diners stared for a moment and then everyone started moving until Richard, who had been trying to find a pulse or any sign of breathing, shook his head.

"Anne, please take the ladies with you to the drawing room and have the butler send for the doctor and the magistrate," Darcy urged.

"Do I need to remain?" Mrs. Collins asked.

Richard walked up to Charlotte and looked her in the eye. "There is nothing that can be done, Charlotte. He is gone."

Charlotte gave him a small smile of relief even as she nodded and followed the ladies to the drawing room. As she walked in, she heard Lady Catherine say, "I will have to appoint…"

"Under no circumstances will you be appointing another clergyman to the living at Hunsford, Mother. You have about as much theological knowledge as an uneducated child, so your days of writing ridiculous sermons about the distinction of rank are *over*! If you would like to move to the dower house and live on one hundred pounds a year, just mention once more you that will appoint another one of your sycophants to the position! It is time for Uncle Reggie to be invited to Rosings. I will write to him now," Anne rounded on her mother angrily. It was partly her callous disregard for the man lying dead in the dining parlour, and partly that her mother still tried to challenge her authority at every turn which had angered her much, but she would handle this.

"There is no need to bother my brother, Anne." Lady Catherine showed fear for the first time. She was well aware that her brother, as executor of the Sir Lewis's will, could make any decision he saw fit and there was naught she could do about it.

"I *am* requesting Uncle Reggie's presence, Mother. One more word, and you will find yourself barred from Rosings the day I turn five and twenty. Just in case you would consider it, know my will is filed with *my* solicitor. If I die or am incapacitated, Richard will inherit, and we both know he would not be manipulated by you," Anne challenged her mother to gainsay her again.

As much as Lady Catherine liked to have control of everything, she would never harm her own daughter, and the fact Anne thought it a possibility shook her to the core. As the shock reverberated throughout her being, Lady Catherine truly looked at her daughter. Anne saw something she could not ever remember seeing—a look of deep regret and tears in her mother's eyes.

"I would never harm you, Anne. I am mortified I have acted in a way that leads you to believe I am capable of such a despicable act. I love you, Anne. Go, write to my brother," Lady Catherine replied softly.

Anne watched as the fight went out of her mother and she seemed to visibly age in front to her. She told Elizabeth, who was holding Georgiana tightly, and Charlotte, that she would return forthwith, then made her way to the study to write to her uncle.

~~~~~~~/~~~~~~~

The doctor confirmed what was already obvious to the two cousins, Mr. Collins was deceased. When asked for his opinion on the cause of death, the doctor opined the clergy-man had choked on food which had stopped his ability to breath. The magistrate was informed of the doctor's findings, and it was over. There was no need for an inquest as the prob-able cause of death was accepted.

Once the two men departed, Richard instructed the butler to have some footmen take the body to the icehouse until they had spoken to his widow about burial arrangements. It took four footmen to move the heavy body, and then the cousins joined the ladies in the drawing room. While Darcy went to sit with his sister, Anne, and Miss Elizabeth, Richard sat near Charlotte.

"Did your husband have any family other than the Ben-nets?" he asked gently.

"Just my family through marriage," Charlotte answered without any trace of sadness. She was feeling guilty that she felt nothing for the man who had died—only relief. "Richard, do I have to mourn him?" she asked quietly.

"My belief is mourning is a deeply personal ritual, so it would be up to what you feel." Richard hoped his words helped.

"In that case, I will give him the same length of time we were married. One month full mourning and one month half,"

Charlotte decided. "When my mourning is complete, we need to talk, Richard," Charlotte spoke plainly and Richard nodded, offering a private smile that proved he felt the same.

"Anne, may I use your study? I must send an express to my father," Charlotte asked.

"Anything you need, Charlotte," Anne replied.

"I will accompany you Charlotte, I need to write to my father as well," Elizabeth stated.

~~~~~~~/~~~~~~~

Miss Caroline had hardly slept in days. The more she considered her behaviour, she discovered her actions were perceived as wanting by others who she needed to impress. She looked at the pile of correspondence on her dresser, it was obvious she did not have one true friend. The realisation was as hard to swallow as was the acknowledgement of others seeing her behaviour as despicable. Then she started to rethink things, had it been her behaviour, or were others simply jealous of her?

She did not know if any of the recipients would believe her words, or even read her letters, but she had to write to them. She started with her brother, then one to her sister and brother-in-law. She wrote both to Mr. Darcy and his sister. In each of the letters, she laid out the offenses she believed they held against her and begged their pardon for any she had forgotten.

The last letter she wrote was to Jane Bennet. She apologised seemingly sincerely, laying out her behaviour and acknowledging the wrongs she believed would be held against her. It grated on her to write to the country miss, but one never knew when she might be of use. Not being aware that Miss Bennet was in Town, the letter was posted to Longbourn, where it was forwarded to Gardiner House in London with the post on the day it was received at the Bennet estate.

By the time Miss Caroline sought out her Aunt Mathilda and requested an audience, she had already decided she was the one who was wronged. She only needed those around her to believe she had changed if she were to have a chance to achieve her aims. "Aunt, I have come to see how selfish and damaging my behaviour has been, and I now understand why Charles and Louisa want nothing to do with me. To say I used to behave selfishly is an understatement," Miss Caroline showed contrition she believed her aunt would want to see.

To say her aunt was surprised would not go far enough. She was also sceptical but decided to give her niece the benefit of the doubt—for now. The older Miss Bingley thought mayhap the change was genuine, until her housekeeper delivered the tea service, and her niece thanked the servant politely. He aunt noticed that although she said the words, there was a look of distaste her niece did not hide fast enough not to be noticed.

"Caroline, it pleases me vastly that you have started to see your actions through the eyes of those they affected, but I have to ask. Why now, and not last month, or even last year?" her aunt asked pointedly.

"You know how Mama and Papa indulged me before their accident do you not, Aunt?" Miss Caroline repeated what her aunt and others had said over the years. Her aunt nodded her agreement. "I was always given anything I wanted, even if it were something belonging to Charles or Louisa. I was spoiled and never had any consequences for my own actions or behaviour. I learnt the wrong lessons at the seminary and exploited Charles and Louisa, who I knew liked peace." Miss Caroline said more of what she believed her aunt wanted to hear. "Until first being kicked off of Pemberley's lands, Charles losing his friend, and my living here, I had never had to suffer the consequences of my choices. This time, no amount of lying or manipulation changed the result. At first, I blamed everyone else, but I eventually had an epiphany—I am the problem and only I can make the decision to change, to attempt to repair some of the damage I wrought. I need your help, Aunt," Miss Caroline asked softly, looking down at her hands. Inwardly Caroline Bingley thought she had delivered a stellar performance.

"With what, Caroline?" Miss Bingley asked. Initially, she

had almost started to believe her niece, wanted to believe her until she saw the calculating look as Caroline glanced down. When added to the look of distaste her niece had directed toward the housekeeper, it was clear this was an act.

"I need to learn to be worthy of the name Bingley again. I care not if Charles, Louisa, or any of the others I wrote to believe me or ever forgive me. I need to learn to forgive myself! Will you help me, Aunt Matti?" Miss Caroline used the name she used to call her aunt before she had started to become the person others found so objectionable. She would deal with this situation, then show them all how wrong they were.

"Yes Caroline, I will help you."Miss Bingley pulled Caroline to herself and enfolded her niece in a hug as Miss Caroline decided that tears would make her performance that much more believable. No other method had succeeded in getting her back into society, what had she to lose?

After Caroline returned to her chambers to *reflect* on her past behaviour, her aunt shook her head slowly. She sadly accepted her niece's attempt at manipulating so many was indicative of the fact that she was long past redemption.

~~~~~~~/~~~~~~~

The courier Anne had dispatched with the expresses to Town and Meryton made his first stop Gardiner House on his way to Grosvenor Square, only to find that, to his luck, two of the recipients were present. The Fitzwilliams were there with the Bennets, as they often were with the planning of the wedding.

After the betrothal, the Bennet and Fitzwilliam parents had met with Jane and Andrew and informed them of the impending change. Neither indicted them for not informing them sooner, understanding Jane's parents wanted to give their children a last little bit of normal life they were used to before the change that would bring about a new normal.

"Cilla, we must leave for Rosings," Bennet informed his wife. "Is the courier still here?" Bennet asked. The Gardiner's butler confirmed the man was eating in the kitchens as he was tasked with waiting for any replies.

"Us too, Bennet. we must leave for Rosings as well. My niece needs me to help assert her rights. Why are you needed there?" Lord Matlock asked quizzically.

"My cousin, the one Richard calls a buffoon, has choked on his food and is deceased. I was his only family. I am sending an express to Longbourn with instructions to make one of my travelling coaches available to Sir William Lucas and his family. They are Charlotte's family," Bennet clarified. "I am sure Sir William and Lady Lucas will want to be of comfort to their daughter; it has been but two months since the wedding."

"I am not sure if this will be a tragedy or a blessing for Charlotte," Priscilla wondered aloud.

"Jane, will you and Andrew accompany us?" Lady Elaine asked?

Jane looked at Andrew who nodded. "Yes, Mother Elaine, we had already determined to be among the party as I would not leave Charlotte in such a moment as this, and Andrew is pleased to assist his cousin in any way she needs."

"What say you, Bennet? Shall we depart at first light on the morrow?" Lord Matlock asked. Bennet agreed, and a note was dispatched to Bedford House.

~~~~~~~/~~~~~~~

Charlotte and Elizabeth had accepted Anne de Bourgh's invitation to move to Rosings from the parsonage with little encouragement. Anne provided maids to assist with the packing of the friends' trunks and footmen to load them onto a cart. Charlotte thanked the housekeeper and other two servants for their service for the short duration she was the mistress as she left the parsonage for the final time.

She had no regrets about never seeing the house again. It represents two wasted months of her life. Try as she may, she could feel nothing but being grateful she was no longer married to Mr. Collins. She suspected that Richard's honour would keep him from approaching her for many months as he did not know how she felt about him, and she was sure that the last thing the dear sweet man wanted to do was feel like he was pressuring her.

Knowing that, Charlotte made a decision. She had approached a man once, and although he was not a bad man, they had been as incompatible as two people could ever be. This time she knew that she loved the man and was as sure as she could be, without any verbal declaration, that her love was returned. She would not engineer a proposal like she had with her late husband. However, before she and Richard went their separate ways, she would make sure he knew how she felt. After that, it would be up to him.

Charlotte thought it was providence that the two traits she found most distasteful in her husband—his sycophantic veneration of Lady Catherine and his eating habits—in the end were the keys to her freedom. She had thought she would have a lifetime to regret her hasty decision to marry Mr. Collins, but she had been rewarded with clemency as she had had just two months to regret.

"Do we need to dye any of your dresses black, Charlotte?" Elizabeth asked as the two friends walked toward the manor house arm-in-arm. Elizabeth hugged Charlotte's arm tighter as she and Jane knew the truth.

"I suppose I should, although I will only be in deep mourning for a month," Charlotte replied thoughtfully.

"Was it so very bad, being married to him?" Elizabeth asked.

"He was never vicious, but it was almost as if I was a parent directing a child rather than a wife to a husband. We had *nothing* in common, but I did learn one valuable lesson from my short marriage to him," Charlotte informed her friend.

Elizabeth stopped walking, causing Charlotte to do the same. "What did you learn?" she wanted to know.

"You remember how I always vociferously argued against your and Jane's notions of matrimony and how to select a partner for life?" Charlotte asked as Elizabeth nodded. "You heard my opinions on the subject more times than you cared to, but I now realise you and Jane had the right of it. I was the one who was wrong!" She owned.

"What a hard way to learn the lesson, Charlotte. However, if I am not mistaken, the love you and Richard share will be an even greater treasure for you both." Elizabeth smiled.

The two recommenced their walk toward the house with Charlotte blushing. "Yes Eliza, I am still in love with Richard." Charlotte revelled in the verbal confirmation from her friend that Richard loved her.

"What will you do about it? He returns your feelings, but he will not allow himself to approach you yet," Elizabeth said.

Charlotte told her friend of her intentions, which Elizabeth felt was a solid plan of action. They both blushed in pleasure when they found Darcy and Richard waiting for them under the portico to make sure that they arrived safely. "Has everything you wanted to keep been packed?" Richard asked.

"Yes, thank you," Elizabeth responded for both of them.

"I noticed the cart arrive some minutes ago," Darcy informed them. "Before I forget, and I was remiss not to tell you this when I made my apology to you in person Elizabeth, when I have the chance, I will ride to Meryton and make my apologies to all in the neighbourhood to whom I was rude and dismissive, starting with your father, Mrs. Collins."

"Please do not address me with *that* name Mr. Darcy. Please address me as Charlotte, as I have no desire to be reminded of the folly that was my marriage," Charlotte requested, all the while looking at Richard as she spoke.

"In that case, Charlotte, please call me William," Darcy gave her a half bow.

"My father and our neighbours will appreciate your willingness to show true contrition to those you were reputed to consider so far below your station, William," Charlotte opined.

"I cannot but agree with Charlotte's opinion," Elizabeth added. "It is noble of you to do so, William."

"It is gratifying that you approve, Elizabeth. Your approval is not easy to win, so the winning of it means much to me," Darcy smiled, revealing his dimples to Elizabeth and the rest of the party.

Although he schooled his features, Richard felt extremely relieved, a feeling of pleasure coursing through his body. Seeing her initial reaction to the buffoon's death, he had momentarily worried that Charlotte felt more than she evidently did. He had gained some measure of hope when she asked about mourning periods, but that had been nothing to what he felt now. She had looked directly at him as she spoke, delivering an unambiguous message. He would give her the two months, then he would present himself and press his suit.

"Are you four ever going to enter the house?" Anne called out playfully from the door, both she and Georgiana smiling at their conversation. "I have placed you two next to Gigi's suite and those two reprobates," Anne playfully indicated her mock affronted cousins, "are being moved to a guest floor."

"You never allow us to have fun!" Darcy teased her as he used to before her mother tried to force them into marrying, where there were no more than cousinly affections.

"How is your mother, Anne?" Elizabeth asked as they all walked into the house.

"Unnaturally quiet," Anne reported. "Something changed last night, though I am not sure what, or if it is a permanent change. For that, we will have to wait and see. All I know is she has not tried to issue one order since the drawing room."

"Will you finally pension poor Mortimer?" Richard asked, referring to the septuagenarian butler.

"Yes, I am meeting with him today. The poor thing. Mother refused to pay him a pension, forcing him to work years beyond what he desired. He and his wife will receive a spacious cottage, and I will give them fifty pounds a month for the rest of their lives," Anne related.

"That is most fair, Anne. After all of his years of service to the de Bourghs, it is nothing less than he deserves," Darcy agreed. "Do you have a replacement in mind, Anne? And what about the fact that your mother did not pay fair wages?"

"I do have a replacement. The underbutler will do a creditable job of it, and he is more than thirty years poor Mortimer's junior," Anne replied. "And yes, I am aware of my mother's habits. All will be put to rights."

Elizabeth was impressed, it seemed what she had heard about William and the way he treated servants had been true. The more that she was near *this* William Darcy, the more she became drawn to him. She was starting to feel as if they could, in fact, become good friends. For now, Elizabeth was not quite ready to think of anything beyond that.

"Have you heard back from our relatives, Anne?" Charlotte asked.

"The courier returned in the early hours of the morning; my maid handed me the response from my Uncle who will arrive later today. Here is one for you Charlotte and for you Lizzy," Anne handed each their missive as they sat in the drawing room.

Elizabeth opened hers and read out loud:

21 March 1811

Lizzy, your mother, Jane (yes, Andrew too), Esther, Mark and I will arrive on Friday, the day after I dated this missive. I must be there at the burial as the only known relative of the unfortunate man. Uncle Edward will accompany me in case he can be of assistance. We will be travelling with Andrew and his parents.

We have much to discuss.

Your loving father.

"I wonder what my father means by *we have much to discuss*?" Elizabeth wondered aloud.

"You will know in a few short hours, my impatient friend," Charlotte quipped. "My father tells me that yours provided one of the Bennet travelling coaches and they will arrive this afternoon."

"In that case, we need to prepare for an invasion of Fitzwilliams, Bennets, and Lucases," Anne teased.

Anne summoned the housekeeper to have chambers prepared, and then found her mother and informed her they were about to receive many guests. Lady Catherine just nodded her understanding, still deep in thought since her epiphany the night before.

VOL 2, CHAPTER 4

The coaches for the Fitzwilliams and Bennets from London arrived a little after eleven. After the arriving family members had washed and changed, they made their way down to the drawing room to meet the rest of those in residence at Rosings Park. The first order of business before the travellers went to change was for those who had not been able to do so yet to personally to wish the betrothed couple happy.

Before they could enter the drawing room after changing, Elizabeth requested that her parents, Jane, and Andrew follow her to a parlour. Bennet and Priscilla looked at one another with raised eyebrows when Elizabeth stated, "William, Mr. Darcy that is, apologised to me for his behaviour in Hertfordshire. He made no excuses and told of his intention to apologise to all of you when he has the chance. The apology was made *before* I revealed our true situation to him. I disclosed the truth to him because his entreaty to pardon him was entirely sincere," Elizabeth related. She saw that both of her parents were giving her knowing looks. "No need to gaze at me with that 'I told you so' look!"

"I am proud that my cousin has endeavoured to change the parts of his character that were wanting," Andrew stated with pleasure.

"What have you learnt from this, Lizzy?" her mother challenged.

"Not to be so quick to judge, and to not allow my prejudices and conjectures to stop me from considering the facts," a chastened Elizabeth responded.

"It seems that Mr. Darcy is not the *only* one to learn and

grow from all of this," Bennet added sardonically.

"Papa, I almost forgot. He intends to ride to Meryton when he is able and apologise to everyone he offended," Elizabeth informed them.

"That would be most of the four and twenty families in the neighbourhood," Jane pointed out.

"Should we join the others?" Priscilla asked, taking her husband's arm and leading the way when he nodded.

In the drawing room, Anne was introduced to Mr. Gardiner, who Richard told his cousin was the man Elizabeth had spoken of to help her dispose of any unwanted items. The two agreed to talk later when Anne would be able to show Gardiner more of the house and the items which she wanted to be rid of.

"Did we miss anything?" Bennet asked as they joined the rest.

"Only my obtuse cousin eating crow and apologising to my uncle and aunt," Anne related with a smile. It was not every day that she was witness to her once-haughty cousin humbling himself.

"You seem to be making somewhat of an apology tour, Mr. Darcy," Priscilla quipped.

"It is nothing less that I must do, Lady Priscilla," Darcy bowed to the Bennet matriarch.

"Lady Catherine," Priscilla acknowledged the silent lady. She could not remember a time that she had ever seen the woman not trying to command any room she was in.

"Lady Priscilla," Lady Catherine replied calmly.

"Before I start, this young lady," Darcy pointed to where his sister was standing with Elizabeth, "is my sister, Georgiana, whom we all call Gigi." Darcy then turned to face Lady Priscilla. "As you have succinctly pointed out, your ladyship, I am on my *apology tour* so..." Darcy apologised to all of the Bennets. After again congratulating her on her betrothal, he especially apologised to Jane for his misguided attempt to interfere in his cousin's courtship of her. He also related a brief synopsis of his break with the Bingleys.

After looking to his wife and oldest daughter and receiving nods, Bennet addressed Darcy. "On behalf of my family, I accept your apologies without reservation. And as we will soon be family, please call me Bennet. Now to…" Before Bennet could carry on with what he wanted to say, Lady Catherine stood, still not looking anyone in the eye.

"With your approval, Mr. Bennet, I have something I would like to say," Lady Catherine looked to Bennet questioningly, and he nodded as it was her house of residence, to be asked at all was shocking. "Like Fitzwilliam, I owe all of you many apologies, except I think I have far more for which to beg your pardon."

"No reason to fight over which of you have committed more offences," Lord Matlock teased, trying and lighten the sombre mood a little.

"It is not lost on me that for many years I have been dispensing unwanted and wrongheaded advice. I was aware of what I was doing, but I felt that it was the best way to control those around me. It was a vain attempt to remain relevant. Rather than learning the facts, I pontificated without regard for anyone else. Sometime while growing up, I forgot what Mother and Father taught us, Reggie, and in its place, I told myself that my rank made me right, regardless of the facts." Her brother had to pinch himself to make sure he was awake, as he had *never*, not in his wildest dreams, thought he would ever hear these words uttered by his sister.

"As much as I welcome your words, Cat, what happened to cause this level of self-examination in you?" Lord Matlock asked as the rest of her relatives watched, none as surprised as their Anne.

"After Collins passed last night, Anne said something that shocked me to my very core," Lady Catherine's eyes teared up as she again considered it.

"Was it that I thought you might harm me to keep control of Rosings?" Anne repeated the question when she got no response, paying no attention to the aghast looks of surprise on the others' faces.

"That is it exactly," Lady Catherine confirmed, trying to blink away the tears in her eyes.

"Oh Mama, I did not mean to wound you so." Anne went to her mother and hugged her.

"No Anne, it is I who owes the apologies, not you. Were it not for what you said, there is no guarantee that I would have been able to see what I had become. That I was so bad, so grasping, and so much of a fortune hunter that my own daughter thought I would harm her for gain? It was the blow I needed. I am not sure if I can be forgiven, but I am deeply sorry. And if it will make it easier for you, Anne, I will remove myself to the dower house today," Lady Catherine offered with all sincerity.

"That is not needed, Mama. All I ever wanted was to have a good relationship with you, which was impossible as things were. I, for myself, forgive you and look forward to discovering the person that my mother can truly be," Anne hugged her mother and kissed her cheeks, both crying tears of relief.

"On behalf of the rest of your family, you are forgiven, Lady Catherine. More importantly, I have missed you, Cat," her brother hugged her next, using his handkerchief to dry her tears. "It seems that most of what I was needed for is already taken care of. Bennet, do you know if your cousin had a family plot somewhere?"

"Not that I am aware of. And given the split that was caused by his grandfather in our family, the Bennet graveyard would not be appropriate," Bennet shrugged, smiling sadly at Charlotte.

"Then he will be interred in the Hunsford Church's graveyard," Anne decided. "Charlotte, did he leave anything for you?"

"I have my dowry as he had not yet spent any, I believe he may have one hundred pounds saved from his time at Hunsford," Charlotte replied.

"That money will all stay with you, Charlotte. We will pay

any costs to have him buried," Bennet stated with finality.

Charlotte knew the Bennets well enough not to argue when Mr. Bennet decided something like he just had. It would be foolhardy, for he would allow none to gainsay him. "On behalf of my family and myself, I thank you for your continued generosity, even if my family is not aware how much we are in debt to the Bennets."

"Jane, Lizzy, did either of you tell Charlotte?" Bennet asked.

"They said nothing to me, Mr. Bennet, I suspected all on my own that the scholarships to Oxford were from you, though until you confirmed it right now, I was not sure," Charlotte blushed a little at the subterfuge she had employed. Rather than be upset, Bennet was impressed at the effective use of her wit.

"Do we need to notify the parishioners so they will know when the funeral is?" Bennet asked Anne.

"It is doubtful many of them would come, as Mr. Collins was not well liked." Anne looked apologetically at her friend and Charlotte waved her concerns away.

"My late husband's faults were well known to me. I managed him as well as I could, but there were some areas where I was not successful in steering him onto a new course," Charlotte smiled cynically.

"The same way you steered me when you needed me to change one of my nonsensical pronouncements that Collins took as gospel?" Lady Catherine quirked an eyebrow.

"You knew?" Anne asked in surprise.

"Not at the time. My ego would not allow me to admit, even to myself, that I was so easily managed. When I started to think about everything, I was able to see what you had done so skilfully," Lady Catherine genuinely smiled at Charlotte.

The admission by Lady Catherine broke the serious mood in the drawing room, and there was a smattering of giggles and laughs, none as sweet as Georgianna's. "As we do not need to wait for anyone else, let us have the funeral conducted on the morrow. Did Collins have a curate?" Bennet asked.

"He was too tight fisted to take on one. When he travelled, the curate from St. Anselm's in Wye would conduct services and be paid the minimum possible. Mr. Bamber is loved by the parishioners in this parish who, I would wager, would have been happier had Mr. Collins never returned each time that Mr. Bamber filled in for him," Anne explained. "In fact, he is my first choice to offer the Hunsford living."

"If that is settled, there is something momentous I must share with my family," Bennet stated. Seeing Lady Catherine, Anne, the two Darcys, and Charlotte stand to leave, Bennet stayed them. "You are all family, or will be soon, and so as long as you can promise me that until the official announcement is made you will not talk to anyone not in this room on the subject, you are welcome to remain. Those who had started to stand sat down, all vowing that what was said would not leave the room.

"It started about one hundred and fifty years ago..." Bennet read the copy of the letter the fourth duke wrote. He then went on to relate what took place in the meeting at Norman and James, and all that had been happening since. He ended by telling his middle daughter that Jane, along with Andrew, had only been informed after the betrothal so they would understand why there would be no public announcement yet.

Elizabeth was the first to recover from the shock of the revelations. "Papa and Mama, you are a Marquess and Marchioness now, like Uncle Stan and Aunt Marie," Elizabeth confirmed.

"That is correct, Lizzy. And you, Jane, and Esther now hold the honorific of Lady, Tom a Lord, and this scamp," she pointed at Mark," is Viscount Netherfield," Priscilla replied. "We will not use the titles in public until the Royal Decree is published on the day of the investiture. It is planned for the second day of April, as long as Uncle Sed is still with us." Priscilla realised that those who had just been informed knew not who she was talking about. "Uncle Sed is Lord Sedgewick Rhys-Davies, the current Duke of Bedford."

"In my arrogance, I thought I was above all of you, when, whether you knew it or not, you were always far above me! Andrew, 'horse's arse,' sorry ladies, does not begin to cover how arrogant I was," Darcy shook his head in rueful regret.

"You were told nothing of our connections, the ones we knew about before today, or our wealth, because I did not want you to make amends only because of those things. You alone decided to make changes and you apologised before you knew any more than you did in Meryton, which is why we have all forgiven you completely," Elizabeth corrected him. "You cannot go back and change the past, and you agreed we should all begin again. Chastising yourself for the past will achieve nothing other than making you melancholy."

"When my parents arrive in a few hours, they will be most appreciative to receive your apology, William," Charlotte pointed out.

As Darcy shook off his maudlin mood, he turned to Bennet. "You have my apology for making it about me when you had just relayed life changing news, Lord Birchington."

"Nothing to apologise for, and I am still Bennet until the investiture. Then it will be Birchington, I suppose," Bennet returned.

"Wait, I will be like Uncle Wes, also a Viscount?" Mark asked in wonder.

"For a short while. When your papa becomes the Duke of Bedford, you will become the Earl of Meryton," his mother clarified.

"So like Grandpapa and Uncle Reggie?" Mark put it in terms he could understand easily. "Will I have to call mama and papa your Grace?"

"Only when you misbehave," Bennet teased his youngest.

"When does Tom arrive in London, Papa?" Jane asked.

"By the last Friday in March, which is why the investiture is set for the second of April. That, and we did not want people to think it was a prank for the first day of April," Bennet smiled wryly.

Lady Catherine who had been silent up to this point looked at Bennet. "Is the Bedford dukedom not the wealthiest one on the realm?" She asked. It seemed Lady Catherine's interest in wealth was not completely banished just yet.

"That is true," Bennet answered without giving any details.

"Papa, just how wealthy will we be?" Esther asked. The shocking information seemed to have no end of revelations.

"I will be happy to discuss that with you at another time," Bennet deferred the question.

After more questions about where they would live and when they would move, the discussion returned to more mundane matters, though the disclosures were never far from anyone's thoughts. Not long after, the new butler announced the midday meal.

~~~~~~~/~~~~~~~

Miss Carolinehad been sitting with her aunt when the papers had been delivered. As she always did, she read the society pages first. She saw a particular entry that made her blood boil, but she schooled her features and politely excused herself from her aunt's presence. Her aunt did not miss the deep look of displeasure before her niece tried to hide it.

The article that had destroyed her equanimity and caused something to snap deep within her was the one that officially announced that Lord Andrew Fitzwilliam, Viscount Hilldale, was courting one Miss Jane Bennet of Longbourn in Hertfordshire. The fury that she felt was nothing like she had ever felt before.

How was it that the insipid blond who smiled too much had captured Lord Hilldale? Was she not a companion when in Town? She had hied to her chambers as she would not have been able to maintain her countenance before her aunt. Miss Caroline focused all of her vitriol and ire on Miss Bennet. Mayhap the chit would believe the letter she had written to apologise and would allow her near her person? She would manipulate the Bennet girl to help gain her way back into society's good graces!

Miss Caroline smiled as she made her plans. She chastised herself for the momentary weakness of thinking herself the problem, but she did know if she were to succeed in getting back to society, possibly even Mr. Darcy's good graces, she had to project the contrition that would be expected of her.

As soon as Miss Bingley had been taken by her performance, she knew it was her way back and she was sure that, regardless of what she had written to Charles in the letter she sent, that he would soon restore her funds and she would again be able to manipulate him, just as she had always done.

If she had ever been around the former Colonel Fitzwilliam, she would have heard him relate how a plan seldom survived first contact with the enemy.

~~~~~~~/~~~~~~~

Bingley was visiting Winsdale, the Hurst's estate in Yorkshire. He was seated in a parlour with his sister and brother-in-law. "Have you read Caroline's letters, Louisa?" Bingley enquired. "I myself have consigned anything from her to the fire."

"As have we," Mrs. Hurst reported. "That scheme to get us to Pemberley uninvited was the last time I will ever assist our youngest sister with any of her machinations." Then she added. "Charles, I need to apologise for my part in the lies you were told. I thought it would be harmless, but I never imagined the cost would be your friendship with Mr. Darcy."

"I was as weak as you were when it came to Caroline's manipulations, Louisa, so we both bear guilt, me more so. I should have checked her a long time ago." Both Hursts were impressed by the apparent maturation of their brother. The time apart had all of them making changes for the better after having been confronted with the need. "There is no one to blame but myself for the loss of my friendship. I should have known better. In fact, I *did* know better."

"Did you see that Jane Bennet is being courted?" Mrs. Hurst asked her brother.

"Yes, I am aware of that. She was never for me and, as evidenced by her suitor, she was meant for far better than myself," Bingley reflected.

"I received a letter from Aunt Mathilda where she gave her opinion that although Caroline at first seemed sincere about changing, she quickly detected that it was not so. Our sister still thinks no one sees through her manipulations," Mrs. Hurst stated changing the subject again. She shook her head in sorrow for the sister she had lost.

"I too received a similar missive and wrote back warning our aunt not to be fooled," Bingley agreed quietly.

"What are your plans for the future, Charles?" Mrs. Hurst asked.

"I have decided to leave the Kingdom and travel to the Americas. I have heard so much about New York. It is reported to equal, or even exceed London in size. Tradesmen are not looked down upon in that country. There, class is more along the lines of wealth, so I will do well. I would be pleased if you two would come with me," Bingley invited.

"But I am the heir to Winsdale," Hurst objected.

"You have a younger brother, do you not?" Hurst nodded. "In that case, if you left the estate would still have an heir," Bingley reasoned.

After a lengthy discussion, Hurst agreed to approach his father and present the subject. "My father says he is sure Jack will do well by the estate and wishes us well," Hurst related when he returned.

Ten days later, after putting all their affairs in order, the three boarded a Dennington Lines ship in Liverpool bound for the Canadas. From there they would travel overland to New York. Before they boarded the ship, Bingley posted a letter to his aunt for their sister from both himself and his older sister.

~~~~~~~/~~~~~~~

Once the Lucas parents and Maria had washed and changed, they were introduced to all of those in residence at Rosings. Shortly after the introductions and a most appreciated apology from Mr. Darcy, Sir William agreed to help Darcy when he arrived in Meryton in contacting those who were to be apologised to. Bennet then requested Sir William and his family to join the Bennet family in the library.

"What do you intend to do now, Charlotte?" Lady Sarah Lucas enquired of her daughter.

"While I am in mourning, which will be only two months complete, my plan is to reside at Lucas Lodge, unless that is inconvenient for you." Charlotte expected one or both of her parents to object to the shortened mourning period, but neither uttered a word in opposition.

"You are most welcome, Charlotte, but what would you do after the two months?" Sir William asked. Sir William, as was his wife, was relieved his daughter had escaped her marriage relatively unscathed. Not long after getting to know the hapless man, Lady Lucas, even with her unromantic views on matrimony, was worried for her daughter's sanity, living with such a man. She was once again free, so if she chose to mourn for but a week, neither parent would have attempted to gainsay her.

"After the two month's mourning, Jane and Eliza have invited me to reside with them in Town or, when they are not in town, at one of their estates," Charlotte explained cryptically. If her parents had questions why their daughter would be staying at a neighbouring estate to Lucas Lodge, neither verbalised them.

With his daughter's future decided, Sir William turned to his friend and enquired after the plans for the funeral and was informed that the ceremony would proceed on the morrow. Sir William was told that the curate from St. Anselm's in Wye would arrive by eight and the service would commence soon after.

Once talk of his late son-in-law's funeral was concluded, Sir William made to rise, but Bennet asked him and his wife to remain. Bennet asked Esther to take Maria with her and to go amuse themselves for a while.

After the younger girls had left with Mark in tow, Bennet informed the Lucases of all of their news, including Jane's betrothal. Once Bennet, with help from his wife and daughters, had completed the tale, Sir William and Lady Lucas sat still, almost in a stupor.

Sir William had always felt the honour of his knighthood keenly and had insisted that everyone, good friends like Bennet included, address him by his title. Here he was sitting with his friend who was a marquess, soon to be a duke, who was not insisting that he be addressed as anything but Bennet.

It highlighted for Sir William that he may have let what was, in fact, the most minor of honours go to his head. Bennet saw the emotions roiling within his friend and rightly guessed the reason. "Once it is official and we are in public, I give you leave to call me by my title if that will make you feel better," Bennet joked. His friend's levity helped settle Sir William, who along with his wife wished the Bennets well on their pending elevation and Jane on her betrothal.

"Did you say once you are the Duke that Mark will be the Earl of Meryton?" Lady Sarah asked, regretting that Maria was not closer to Mark Bennet in age, or that she did not have a daughter younger than Maria.

"He will be," Priscilla responded, amused at the wish for she would have had the same thought if their situations were reversed.

~~~~~~~/~~~~~~~

Early the next morning Mr. David Bamber conducted the funeral rites for Mr. Collins in front of a small congregation. Besides the men resident at Rosings, there were only two other men who came to pay their respects, and one of them was the manservant who worked at the parsonage. There was a short service at the graveside as Mr. Collins was laid to his eternal rest. After the internment, the six men, along with the curate, walked to the manor house to break their fasts.

After the meal, Anne asked Mr. Bamber to meet her in her study where she offered, and he gratefully accepted, the living.

He related to Miss de Bourgh that gaining the living would allow him to marry his ladylove, a Miss Julia Swift. He had not wanted to marry until he could offer her a good home and a secure future.

Once word was disseminated throughout the parish that the new rector was the former curate who was already well loved by the parishioners, there was much relief and joy, and the following Sunday's services were well attended by the smiling parishioners.

VOL 2, CHAPTER 5

"Lizzy, I had intended to send for you in a few days so you and Tom would be here for the investiture and the announcement, but Collins's death brought us all to you instead. You did not think we would bear all of the scrutiny of the *Ton* and not allow you your part in the pleasure, did you?" Bennet smiled sardonically where he sat in the library at Rosings with his daughter.

"I thank you for my share, Papa, but I would happily forgo *that* pleasure, although I suppose I must be with the rest of the family when we meet the royals. Are they our family now, even though the connection is through the Duchess?" Elizabeth asked.

"It is a tenuous connection at best, as you correctly state. Aunt Rose is the one related to the royals by blood. The truth is that it all depends on them. If they recognise us as family, it will be so," Bennet explained.

"When do we decamp for Town, Papa?" Elizabeth asked. "I assume we want to be back before Tom arrives?"

"We depart on Monday. Uncle Gardiner is currently making an inventory of all of the *objets d'art* and useless furniture Miss de Bourgh wants to sell. He is sure he can recover close to full price for her selections as he has many clients who enjoy displaying such gaudy items." Bennet shared. "Some of his men will return next week to catalogue and remove the objectionable pieces."

"I am in amazement at the changes in Lady Catherine. Anne's statement must have shaken her to the core to cause such a radical change in her behaviour in such short a time," Elizabeth opined.

"That is true, Lizzy. You never know what will force a person to see their behaviour towards others. Thankfully, most change their course when confronted as Lady Catherine was, but there are those who will let nothing shake them from their path," Bennet stated sombrely. "Unfortunately, I think Miss Bingley falls into the latter group. Until Darcy told us what occurred at Pemberley, I would have hesitated to say something so dubious even about her, but no longer." Bennet stood. "I need to discuss something with your mother; enjoy your book Lizzy." Bennet kissed his daughter on the forehead and left the library.

There was almost a collision in the hall outside the of library as both Bennet and Darcy were deep in thought and not paying attention to where they were going. "Ah, Bennet, I am sorry, I was wool gathering and almost bowled you over," Darcy gave a half bow.

"We both have an equal share in the blame, Son, for I too was not paying attention to my surroundings," Bennet allowed.

"Then I will take chance as providence and say it was fortuitous, this running into you. I would like to request your permission for a private interview with Miss Elizabeth, Sir," Darcy said, his fate now officially out of his own hands.

"You may speak to her now if you like; she is reading in the library. Before you do, I will send my girl's companion to sit in with her. You will be observed but not heard, and the door will remain open," Bennet stated. He hoped that Darcy was not foolish enough to propose to Elizabeth yet, she was not ready for that step, with him or any other.

Darcy waited patiently in the hallway until Mrs. Ponsonby joined him, then entered the library after her, waiting as the companion found a seat in the corner out of earshot. Realising that Elizabeth was engrossed in her book, he cleared his throat to let her know she was no longer alone. "Do you mind if I sit, Elizabeth?" he asked when she looked up smiling at him.

"I do not mind," Elizabeth indicated the wingback chair

where her father had recently sat.

"I apologise if I am disturbing your reading, you seem engrossed with..." Elizabeth held up the book for him to see the cover. "*Robinson Crusoe*. It is one of my favourites," Darcy revealed.

"You are interrupting my reading, but it does not follow said interruption is unwelcome. It is also one of my favourites, I have read it several times before," Elizabeth shared.

"It pleases greatly me to hear that my interruption is not unwelcome. Your father granted my request to speak to you alone." Darcy said evenly. Elizabeth's eyebrows raised in question as she placed the book on the table between them. "I think you have gleaned from my letter that I have tender feelings for you, Elizabeth," he began.

"Yes, I now know you do, but just because your feelings are thus, it does not follow mine are as well. Or did you think I would swoon as the great Fitzwilliam Darcy has bestowed his regard?" Elizabeth bit out, falling back to her old habits and assuming that which he had not said.

"I am well aware my feelings for you are not returned, Elizabeth. It is but days since you agreed we could begin again. Trust me when I tell you ever since Uncle Reggie's verbal evisceration, I question my ability to convince anyone of anything. If I gave you the wrong impression, I am profoundly sorry and I will leave now and allow you to return to you book." Darcy made to stand but was stayed by Elizabeth's hand on his arm.

"Please stay, William. In this instance, it is I who must beg your pardon. My mother has pointed out my propensity to be too hasty to make judgment based on assumptions, and that is what I just did. You asked a question and my answer to it should have simply been 'yes.' Instead, I reacted as if you had asked much more than you actually did, I know of your having a regard for myself. It seems we both will have to work to reduce misunderstandings between us," Elizabeth stated with deep contrition.

"Then I will continue with what I intended to say, with

your permission." He waited, relieved when she nodded her acceptance. "I *know* it is too soon for you to have any tender feelings for me, and in truth I am lucky that it seems you no longer *dislike* me. You know I had these feelings before what you revealed to me the other day and certainly before the earth-shaking news your father delivered. So at the very least you may acquit me of my affection being borne of the knowledge of your wealth and connections," Darcy laid out.

"There is nothing in that statement with which I would argue." Elizabeth allowed. Darcy drew his hand across his forehead in a dramatic gesture as if he were wiping sweat from his brow. The effect was a smile from Elizabeth that reached her eyes.

"Whew!" Darcy feigned great relief then again sobered. "Only *if* you agree, I would like for us to get to know one another better. If I thought you would accept a courtship..." Seeing she was about to interject, Darcy raised his hand to stay her reply. "But as I am sure you are not yet ready for that step; I am requesting your permission to call on you so we may get to know one another better and hopefully reduce the instances of misunderstandings between us."

"It is good you stopped me," Elizabeth owned. "I was about to tell you I thought you presumptuous when you were not. In fact, you were just the opposite. Yes, William, you may call on me, as I too would like to get to know the real you. I am sure you are cognisant of the fact there will be many demands on our time after the investiture?" Darcy nodded. "I am not a prognosticator so I cannot tell you what will be in the future, but I believe we are making progress on a good start," Elizabeth stated evenly.

"I have another request, Elizabeth, though it is not about me or us," Darcy qualified, earning him a tinkling laugh. How he loved to hear her laugh, and to be the cause of it was even better. "It is about Gigi. You know what she has been through." Elizabeth nodded. "She is much recovered but still shy, and it is hard for her to make new friends. I have observed that she feels more comfortable with you and your sisters than any other friends I have noted previously. Her affinity is especially with you. My request is that when you are able to do so, please visit her and include her in activities with you and your sisters. I believe it will do her self-confidence a world of good," Darcy asked fervently.

"That is an easy request to grant as it was already my intention. I believe she will do very well with Esther and Ally," seeing his quizzical look, Elizabeth clarified. "Our cousin, Lady Alicia Carrington, my Aunt Marie's daughter who is almost the same age as Esther. She has a good heart and is not spiteful."

"Thank you. It warms my heart that Gigi has been accepted so readily by all of you. She is aware that you know of Ramsgate, and it makes your friendship all the more special to her." Darcy stood. "I need to inform your father that you have permitted me to call on you in case he objects. I think he thought me addlepated enough to be about to propose!"

They both shared a laugh at what a mistake that would have been, and Darcy took his leave to seek out Elizabeth's father.

~~~~~~~/~~~~~~~

"Caroline, please join me in the drawing room," Miss Mathilda Bingley called up the stairs to her niece.

Caroline Bingley was not in a good mood. Not *one* response to any of her letters had been received. How could that be? Surely, she had used the correct words to make herself seem sincere and garner sympathy at the same time. It must be something with the post! She had seen no notice in the paper of there being an issue with the post, but perhaps the bag with her letters had been misplaced and the letters were taking longer than normal to be delivered.

As Miss Caroline descended the stairs, she affected the sweet look she had seen Miss Bennet use to enamour her brother and then entered the room where her aunt was waiting for her. Once she sat, her aunt wordlessly handed her a letter. Caroline's smile brightened at receiving a reply at last, certain her efforts were about to be rewarded when she saw it was in Louisa's handwriting. She started to read:

22 March 1811

Caroline,
I am writing this letter for Charles so you will be able to read the missive.

By the time you are reading this, we will no longer be in England. We have left the Kingdom permanently.

A stream of invectives flew out of Miss Caroline's mouth, a number of which her aunt had never heard before and was uncertain she wanted to know how her niece had. "What is this nonsense? I am always able to manipulate them, so just what is going on here?" Miss Caroline's façade had slipped, and she was again revealing her true self as she read on.

I have spoken to some of our former acquaintances in town and can faithfully report that, just as your letters to us, your letters to them were consigned to the fire. Do you not realise your behaviour has made you, and all of us by connection to you, persona non grata? *Are you truly so delusional you think Charles, Harold, or I believed one word that you wrote, Caroline?*

Your days of working on us are over, and as you will never know where we are, you will never again be able to cause havoc in our lives. Since you were sent to our aunt, I now have a good and felicitous relationship with my husband who no longer needs to feign being in his cups or asleep!

If only you had had the capacity to change, Caroline, we would have happily taken you with us. It is unfortunate that you never learned to care for anything but your own selfish and delusional desires! We choose *to no longer live that way.*

As sad as it is to admit, we are all happier without you, for your attempts to gain your own way always made our lives miserable.

I pray you one day find true happiness, no matter how much I doubt your being able to.

Louisa.

"Bitch!" Miss Caroline screeched, ripping the letter and angrily throwing the pieces into the fire. Her aunt smiled at the symmetry, for the same fate had befallen the letters she had sent in her attempt to gain her wish of returning to society. All, except of course the one addressed to Jane Bennet which was waiting for her at Gardiner House.

"Were you not wanting to make amends for your past mistakes, Caroline?" Miss Bingley asked with feigned concern, for two could play the game, and she had much more time to affect being sincere.

"Why should I make amends when I did naught wrong?" Miss Caroline spat back, slamming the drawing room door on her way to her bedchamber to start scheming all over again.

~~~~~~~/~~~~~~~

Having been told he needed to come to London alone due to some necessary family business, Tom arrived on the final Friday in March. After a long soak in a steaming bath, he changed clothes and joined the family in the private sitting room.

To say he was surprised might not convey the full depth and breadth of his reaction. As they had with his siblings, his parents allowed him to read the copy of the letter which had started the Bennets on this whole new path in life.

Tom was similar in character to his oldest sister. He seemed easy going, even biddable, until someone tried to convince him to do something he knew was immoral or would hurt another. It was then the antagonist would find out just how hard it was to manipulate Tom Bennet. As he read the letter, his anger toward the long dead third Duke was palpable and the Bennet heir took exception on behalf of his namesake and all his ancestors for whom the avaricious and cruel Duke had caused so much pain and heartache.

Initially, he had not been interested in meeting the current Duke, but he owned that he could not hold the man

311

responsible for what was done by one evil man long before the man in question was born. Tom accepted the logic of his thoughts and agreed to join the family for dinner at Bedford House after church services on the morrow.

He listened with awe as his parents explained their new position in life and the immense wealth it came with. He was warned to be on his guard for false friends, and, of more immediate concern, huntresses who would view him as the ultimate prize given he would be the heir to a dukedom and the biggest fortune in the realm outside of the royals.

Then Tom was allowed to address what he had only done by letter, giving Jane a long, congratulatory hug as he expressed his belief in her future felicity. He was also impressed that Mr. Darcy had started to make amends, had even apologised to the Lucases, and was currently in Meryton making his apologies to all whom he had offended. Darcy would arrive back in town by the evening, and he and his sister would join the Bennets and Fitzwilliams at Bedford House after church.

"You have a higher rank than me, little brother, do I need to genuflect to you," Tom teased as he ruffled the young Viscount's hair.

"Leave off!" Mark complained, trying to flatten his hair back into place.

"When Papa becomes the Duke, you will be a Marquess which, I believe, ranks above an Earl," Elizabeth interjected.

"That is true! Enjoy it while it lasts scamp!" Tom grinned at Mark, then hugged him. He knew his brother missed him when he was away, and he missed being with his siblings as well.

"Let us enjoy the last few days of anonymity," Bennet sighed.

~~~~~~~/~~~~~~~

If Mr. Darcy had made his amends to those he offended in Meryton on the first day of April, they would have thought the man was making a fool of them. The combination of the fact it was not the fool's day, the sincerity of his speeches, and that Sir

William Lucas organised the central meeting, made sure all of his apologies were accepted graciously.

After he had completed his apologies to the members of the neighbourhood, Darcy presented himself at the militia encampment and sought out the officers he had sat with during the dinner he had attended with Bingley, and to whom he had been rude and dismissive. He particularly wanted to apologize to Colonel Forster for not informing him of Wickham's vicious propensities as soon as he became aware the man was in the unit.

As part of his amends, Darcy covered any debts and debts of honour Wickham had owed to his fellow officers. Darcy was wholly forgiven for things, which any man had done on occasion, when they too are having a rough week. By the time he left, the officers, who thought they would never see their funds again, were singing Darcy's praises at a dinner he had left funds to pay for at the inn. He appreciated their reaction, even if it was not the reason he had helped.

His last stop was Mr. and Mrs. Phillips, who he found preparing to depart for Gardiner House. Darcy rode alongside their carriage until they reached the house on Portman Square, then took his leave with a tip of his hat and rode on to Darcy House.

~~~~~~~/~~~~~~~

Lady Rose hosted the dinner, but the Duke was conspicuous by his absence. His illness was in its end stage, so he was bedridden. Bennet took Tom in to meet Uncle Sed. Tom felt ashamed that he had ever thought to blame the sick man he found before him for the actions of an evil ancestor.

Lord Sed beckoned Tom over so he could see the next Marquess. "Fine looking lad," the Duke managed with difficulty.

"Thank you, your Grace," Tom responded.

"Uncle Sed," the Duke countered in a wheeze that somehow still was an order, which made Tom grin down at his newfound uncle.

After Tom left, Bennet introduced his three daughters and

youngest son to the Duke. Other than give them a smile and a nod, Lord Sed said nothing as it was too much of an effort to speak. Seeing the Duke was starting to fall asleep; Bennet and his children departed the bedchamber to join the rest of the family. The Fitzwilliams and Darcys had arrived while he was with the ailing Duke, so it was then Tom finally met Miss Georgiana Darcy who his siblings had long been sending him updates about. He was fascinated by the shy young lady who sat between Elizabeth and Esther.

Richard took pity on Tom and introduced him to the Darcy siblings who were to be his cousins when Jane and Andrew wed in a little more than a month. Tom took an immediate liking to Darcy, who asked to be called William, a feeling that was reciprocated by Tom as he requested the same of Darcy.

Before Tom could enter the discussion between his sisters and Miss Darcy, the De Melvilles and Carringtons arrived, and he watched Ally join the group with Miss Darcy. Much to Tom's consternation, with so many present he never found an opportunity to talk to Miss Darcy while they were at Bedford House that evening.

Georgiana had heard about the three Bennet daughters' proficiency with their instruments and of their singing, but she was not prepared for the effect caused when their three voices rose in unison. It felt as if she were glimpsing what heaven would sound like. But when Elizabeth played and sang in solo, Georgiana was certain she was hearing an angel perform.

As she had promised William she would, Elizabeth included Gigi in any plans being made for the younger ladies. Darcy could not have been happier at the pleasure that suffused his sister's face each time she was included. Georgiana made her pleasure known to her brother when they returned home.

Not long after the final performance, the guests took their leave, all of them reaffirming they would see one another on

Tuesday at St. James Palace.

~~~~~~~/~~~~~~~

It was somewhere between two and three Monday morning when there was an insistent knocking on the front door of Gardiner House. When Gardiner opened the door, accompanied both by his butler and Bennet, there was a footman in the livery of the Duke of Bedford standing with a black edged letter in his hand.

He bowed to Bennet, "Your Grace," he intoned, then handed the notice to the eighth Duke of Bedford, the first in the line to bear the name Bennet, as Lord Sed had gone to his final reward. Bennet thanked the man who was now his footman, asking him to convey the family's condolences to the Dowager Duchess.

"I knew it was coming, Thomas, but my goodness, you are a duke!" Gardiner stated, nodding at Phillips when he joined his brother and Bennet to be of assistance were he needed. They had previously determined not to inform the Phillipses for, as harmless as his wife was, they knew the instant she was privy to the information all of Meryton would have been as well.

"You are a *WHAT*, Bennet?" Phillips asked stupefied.

"Come sit, Frank, we have a lot to tell you," Bennet pointed at a chair in Gardiner's study. The more he heard, the quieter Phillips was.

~~~~~~~/~~~~~~~

The news that the Duke of Bedford was deceased was abroad first thing Monday morning. It was known there was an heir of the same bloodline, but none outside of their small circle knew who it was. Members of the *Ton* who were clamouring for intelligence were disappointed, for they too would have to wait like everyone else for the royal decree on the morrow and the reported investiture of the new duke and his family.

VOL 2, CHAPTER 6

Monday morning, just after nine, the Countesses of Jersey and Matlock; Lady Priscilla Bennet; Marchioness Holder; and Viscountess Westmore were shown into the receiving room at Bedford House. Lady Rose, who had been sitting with her husband's body until the ladies arrived met them, sadness evident in her mien.

"We are so sorry for your loss, Rose," Lady Sarah commiserated. "We are here to help with whatever needs doing."

"Thank you, Sarah, all of you," Lady Rose said sadly. "Even though I knew his passing was inevitable, it does not make it any easier for me. I will always wish my Sed was still with me."

Just then the butler announced Princess Elizabeth, who was followed by her retinue. "Cousin Rose, please accept the deepest sympathies of our entire family," the Princess conveyed as the rest of the ladies gave deep curtsies to Queen Charlotte's daughter. "Will you introduce us to those we do not know?"

Lady Rose introduced the only lady the Princess had not met. "Your Royal Highness, Princess Elizabeth, I present to you the new Duchess of Bedford, her Grace, Priscilla Bennet."

The new Duchess curtsied as the Princess inclined her head in acknowledgement. "It would have been preferable to meet our new cousin under better circumstances. You will accompany your family to Buckingham House this afternoon will you not, Lady Priscilla?" Lady Priscilla nodded, very well understanding that it was not a question, as their meeting with the royals had been accelerated by events beyond the control of any man. "When will the late Duke be transported to Longfield Meadows?" The Princess directed the question to Lady Rose.

"As investiture will take place today, we hope to depart on the morrow, Your Royal Highness," Lady Rose replied.

"In that case, we will take our leave." The Princess offered her hand to both Lady Rose and Lady Priscilla to kiss and departed, her retinue following her out.

As Lady Priscilla watched the Princess depart, she considered all of the changes that had occurred the instant that the seventh Duke died. As much as they had tried to prepare since the first meeting at Norman and James, it was still overwhelming. They had all hoped there would be a few months at least until Thomas became the new Duke. It was not to be.

Lady Sarah saw the overwhelmed look on her daughter's face. "Do not forget, we are *all* with you, Priscilla, and we will *all* help you, as well, Rose."

"Aunt Rose, I am sorry to take away from you on this sad day, I just was not prepared to see the Princess and be introduced as the Duchess. It did not enter my head until you introduced me with this new title," Priscilla looked at the Dowager Duchess contritely.

"There is no time for recriminations now, Priscilla," Lady Rose lifted her chin. "There is much to do if we are to depart Town on the morrow. Thank goodness it is still cool enough for the transporting of Sed to Yorkshire."

Lady Elaine indicated herself and Lady Sarah as she said, "Rose, go and sit with your Sed and let our husbands make all of the arrangements. I will remain with you while the rest of the ladies return to Gardiner House to assist the Bennets. Sarah," Lady Elaine looked at her friend, "will you send our husbands to Bedford House as soon as may be? There is much to do, as we will all accompany the Bennets to the investiture this afternoon. Rose, I am sure they will understand if you are not present."

"I gave my word to Sed, and I will do what needs to be done; so yes, I *will* attend Buckingham House." None of the ladies tried to argue with the Dowager Duchess, for giving their word to their husbands was a promise they always tried to keep themselves. The departing group each hugged Lady Rose and conveyed their personal sympathies before they departed.

~~~~~~~/~~~~~~~

When Priscilla returned to Gardiner House, she found her husband in the study with her father, Lord Matlock, Gardiner, and Phillips. "How is Aunt Rose this morning, Cilla?" Bennet asked quietly.

"She is as well as can be expected." Priscilla turned to her father and Lord Matlock. "You two are expected at Bedford House to help make arrangements. Elaine remained with Aunt Rose. Princess Elizabeth paid her condolences on behalf of the Royals, and we are to be at Buckingham House at two. I thought I was prepared for all of this, but when Aunt Rose introduced me as the Duchess of Bedford, I was overwhelmed for a moment."

"It was a natural response, Cilla," Bennet soothed as he drew his wife into his arms. "We expected to have some time to adjust after the investiture; we no longer have the luxury."

"My son-in-law has the right of it, Daughter," Lord Jersey added his support. "Do not forget you are surrounded by those who love you and will assist you and Bedford in any way possible."

Even though the messenger had addressed him as *your Grace*, hearing the name Bedford used by his father-in-law drove home the change which had occurred to his family this morning. Tom was the Marquess of Birchington and Mark, not yet twelve, was the Earl of Meryton!

"We must away, Jersey, my wife awaits us," Lord Matlock stated, reminding all of the first task that was also of utmost importance. He led the way to those who most needed them.

"I assume your primary estate will be Longfield Meadows in Yorkshire?" Phillips enquired.

"That is a safe assumption," Bennet agreed quietly.

"What about Longbourn and Netherfield?" Phillips asked.

"We need to change my will, Phillips. Mark will have both estates now and," he looked at his wife, "what say you, Priscilla that we no longer lease out Netherfield? More money is the last thing we need."

"You will hear no objection from me, Thomas," Priscilla agreed. "Although we will spend time in Yorkshire, for my part we will not abandon Longbourn. I suggest that, until Mark is of age, we reside at Longbourn for a month before the season. With the easy distance to London, if we need to escape the machinations of the *Ton* now and again during the season, it is close by."

"Who will criticise a Duke and his family if they forgo part, or even all of a season?" Bennet smiled wryly.

"What of the girl's dowries?" Gardiner asked.

"Now, as we have what is for all intents and purposes unlimited wealth, we will increase the amount for all three. Priscilla and I will discuss that, but there is no need to make a decision right away," Bennet stated.

"Have the children been informed?" Priscilla asked.

"Not without you by my side, Cilla. With all of the activity, they likely have guessed or at least know something has happened, and Jane was woken by the messenger banging on the door this morning. But by now they know we will tell them what they need to know when we are ready," Bennet explained.

"Let us not delay, Thomas," Priscilla suggested.

The Bennet children were found in the breakfast parlour, along with the two older Gardiner children and their two aunts. Gardiner nodded to his wife who asked her two children if they had eaten sufficiently, and when they agreed their mother ask them to return to the nursery.

"As I am sure Jane has informed you, there was a messenger who arrived in the early hours of this morning," Bennet began. "His sad duty was to inform us that Uncle Sed had passed away." Bennet did not miss the realisation on the faces of his four older children as they assimilated the meaning of his words.

"Had we not believed, or at least hoped, Uncle Sed would live for some more months?" Elizabeth asked. She had only met her late uncle once, but had felt affection for the kind, old man.

"That was the hope, Lizzy. We also prayed for him to recover, but unfortunately those prayers were not answered, and God called him home," Bennet said softly.

"Papa, does that mean you are a duke and Mama is a duchess?" Mark asked carefully.

"Yes, son, it does," Priscilla told her youngest.

"Does that mean I am Mr. Meryton now?" the young boy pressed.

"Not *Mr.* Meryton, but *Lord* Meryton. Do you remember the discussion at Rosings when you asked if you would be an earl like grandpapa and Uncle Reggie?" Bennet reminded his son, smiling sadly when Mark nodded. "That is what has happened today."

"Tom is like Uncle Stan now?" Mark verified.

"Yes, Tom is the Marquess of Birchington, and your sisters are all Ladies now," Bennet confirmed.

"I know my sisters are ladies!" Mark exclaimed in confusion.

"Not ladies as in girls, Mark. You know how grandmama, Aunt Marie, Aunt Elaine, and Aunt Jacqui all have the honorific Lady before their names?" His mother asked.

"Because you are a Duke, my sisters are Lady Jane, Lady Lizzy, and Lady Esther?" Mark verified.

"Yes, son, you understand now," Bennet smiled at his youngest. Mark was a smart boy; but like all of the family, he was bewildered by the speed of the events. Even though they had known Uncle Sed was sick, they had counted on having some time after the investiture which had originally been planned for the morrow.

"We are all to be at Buckingham House by two, which means we will arrive at least a quarter hour earlier. One does not keep the royals waiting, even if it is their prerogative to have us do so if they choose," Priscilla informed her children. As she considered the enormity of what lay ahead, she remembered something the Princess had said. "Thomas, I forgot to tell you Princess Elizabeth called us *cousins*. It seems the royals will accept us as such, even though it is Aunt Rose who is related to them by blood."

"You met one of the Princesses, Mama?" Esther asked in awe.

"So shall you, all of you, this afternoon. Not just one, but some of her sisters and brothers, the Queen, and the Regent," Priscilla informed all of her children.

"On the morrow, we will be part of the convoy of coaches that will escort Uncle Sed back to the primary ducal estate, Longfield Meadows in Yorkshire," Bennet told their children.

"We will not be living at Longbourn any longer?" Esther asked in concern. "How will I see Maria?"

"There will be times when we reside at Longbourn, but it will no longer be our primary estate." Bennet went on to explain what he and their mother had discussed in the study earlier.

"Charlotte will be my guest," Elizabeth informed her younger sister, "I am sure if you ask Mama, she will be more than happy to invite Maria to visit us as well."

To her youngest daughter's relief, Priscilla agreed with Elizabeth's words. "Your father and I have much to arrange. Please be ready to depart no later than one," Priscilla instructed her children as she dismissed them. All stood and departed the breakfast parlour with the exception of Tom, who had been silent through the whole discussion.

"Father, Mother, will I remain at Oxford?" he asked carefully. "When I spoke to Uncle Sed, he told me how all of their family went to Cambridge, but I am loathe to leave all of my friends."

"You will remain at Oxford, my son," Bennet assured him. "Thanks to the third Duke's cruelty, all Bennet men from the original Tom Bennet until you have attended Oxford, so I see no reason to change the tradition."

"Other than the fact of our elevation, we are and will be the same people we were before, and we will *never* expect you

SHANA GRANDERSON A LADY

or your sisters and brother to *ever* give up a friendship based on rank or fortune. It may be the way of some in the *Ton*, but it will *never* be our way!" Bennet stated forcefully.

A much-relieved Tom left his parents, aunts, and uncles in the breakfast parlour. Bennet turned to both couples. "What I just said to Tom very much applies to you as our family of long standing and new. Nothing will change between us; I wanted to assure you of that in case you were wondering."

"We know your and Priscilla's characters too well to have ever considered that as an option," Gardiner grinned. "However, it is most gratifying to hear you affirm it."

~~~~~~~/~~~~~~~

"Lizzy, what should I do with this letter I received from that wretched Miss Bingley? I have been debating whether to read it for entertainment or just consign it to the flames," Jane asked breezily as she glanced to where she had dropped it for later consideration.

"It may be amusing to see what the superior sister has deigned to say to you, *Lady* Jane," Elizabeth teased her as the two sat in their shared sitting room.

"In that case, I will read it aloud so we may both be diverted," Jane replied as she broke the seal.

20 March 1811
Thistledown House
Scarborough

My friend, Miss Jane Bennet,

"Really, is the woman so very obtuse?" Jane shook her head.

I have realised that my behaviour may have been objectionable to those who witnessed it. I am sure you understand the compliment of one of my stature apologising to one so decidedly below me, so I trust that you will pardon any offences against you.

"Jane, the woman must be insane! She claims that she wants to apologise but insults you at the same time," an incredulous Elizabeth stated.

"It is not worth dignifying the rest of her drivel by reading it," Jane said with disgust as she tossed the missive into the fire. "If that harridan tries to approach me I will give her the cut direct!" Jane exclaimed.

"If you did not, I would think your brain addlepated!" Elizabeth teased.

"Can you believe I will marry Andrew a month from today? Oh," Jane's lips formed a perfect 'O,' as the facts of the day hit her. "We will have to postpone the wedding for at least two months; we cannot marry so soon after Uncle Sed's passing." Jane was distraught at the thought but felt there was little she could do as their uncle who had just so instrumentally changed their lives had passed.

"Before you change anything, Jane, let us ask Mama and Papa," Elizabeth suggested, leading her sister out and finding their parents in the study with Uncles Gardiner and Phillips.

"Jane, what is it?" Priscilla asked, concerned that her daughter was carrying the weight of their Uncle Sed's death unduly when she saw that Jane looked decidedly unhappy. She was the one who bore unhappiness the best of them.

"It is selfish of me to ask, Mama, but what about my wedding? Will we not have to postpone it?" Jane asked softly. "It is just that..." she swallowed around the lump in her throat, "if I had had my desire, we would have been married already!"

"There is no need to postpone your nuptials, Jane," Bennet smiled, relieved she was already brightening with hope.

"How is that to be, Papa?" Elizabeth asked, knowing Jane would want to understand all but was unable to ask herself as she scarcely dared believe it possible.

"Uncle Sed was aware he might not be with us when you marry, Jane, so he directed, verbally and in writing, that if he was taken before the first of May, unless it were within a sennight of his passing, you were to marry Andrew as planned. He wanted to reaffirm life and the joy of continuing the lines of our families, not death," Bennet explained to his daughters. "I apologise for my being so remiss; I should have informed you and Andrew as soon as Uncle Sed made his wishes known."

"You and Mama had so much to consider at that time, so of course you are forgiven, Papa," Jane hugged her father, and a much happier daughter exited the study with Elizabeth.

As they departed, the butler informed them the Fitzwilliam brothers had arrived and were in the small parlour. "Lady Jane, Lady Elizabeth," Andrew and Richard bowed as the ladies entered the parlour, followed by Mrs. Ponsonby who seated herself in a corner unobtrusively. "Richard and I wanted to convey our sympathies for your family's loss," Andrew spoke on behalf of both brothers. "I do not want to discuss matters today, but, when possible, I would like to discuss an alternate date for our wedding, Jane." He stated quietly as he took her hand.

"Do you want to change the day? For I do not, and Uncle Sed did not want us to. But if you want to postpone, I understand, sir." Jane's smile grew wider as he stared at her in incomprehension, relieved of his primary worries when his Jane explained the late Duke's wishes. Now the only thing she was not sure of was from where they would marry.

"My assumption would be Longbourn, Jane," Elizabeth opined. "Notwithstanding Uncle Sed wanting you to marry without delay, doing so at the estate where he lived would, in my opinion, not be acceptable."

"I agree with Lizzy," Andrew offered. "Unless your parents want it otherwise, I propose we keep the wedding at Longbourn. It is, after all, where you grew into the woman I love."

"Andrew, at least wait until Lizzy and I are not present before you act so besotted," Richard ribbed his brother. "We understood from Father, before he departed to join Mother at Bedford House, that the investiture is this afternoon?"

The sisters confirmed the same. Just then, Darcy and Georgiana were announced. "We just heard and wanted to convey our sympathies," Georgiana stated as she hugged her soon to be cousins.

"Please pass our sympathies on to their Graces," Darcy

bowed. "And if there is anything I may be of assistance with, it will be my honour and my pleasure, my Ladies."

"It was bad enough when Andrew used our new honorifics, in private can we please stay with 'Jane' and 'Elizabeth'?" Jane requested after a slight nod from her sister.

"Unless of course you would like to be Mr. Darcy to us again," Elizabeth teased with an arched eyebrow and Darcy raised his hands in mock surrender. "Would you join us at Buckingham House this afternoon?"

"Is that not only for family?" Georgiana asked.

"Are you not family, or soon to be so?" Jane asked.

"In that case, we will be happy to witness the investiture," Darcy promised, smiling as he watched Georgiana's excitement grow.

The sisters informed them of the time their mother said they needed to arrive.

~~~~~~~/~~~~~~~

Before they entered the chamber, the Lord Chamberlain had explained how they should present themselves to the Regent and what would occur, and exactly at two, the Bennets and their family and friends were ushered into the receiving room at Buckingham House by the Lord Chamberlain. In the centre along the back wall were two thrones, the Regent sat in one and Queen Charlotte in the other. To their left and right were a half dozen smaller thrones, some of them filled by Princes and Princesses. The walls to the left and right were lined with some of the highest-ranking peers of the realm.

The arriving party genuflected to the royals. "Rise," the Regent intoned. Bennet, Tom, and Mark walked forward to a point and kneeled. The Regent stood, and, after receiving a ceremonial sword from a page, moved his corpulent body to stand in front of Bennet, tapping him on both shoulders with the dull blade. Tom and Mark then received one tap each. After handing the sword back, the Regent sat and the three rose.

"Your Royal Majesty and your Royal Highnesses, I present to you Lord Thomas and Lady Priscilla Bennet, Duke and

Duchess of Bedford; Lord Tom Bennet, Marquess Birchington; Lord Mark Bennet, the Earl of Meryton; Lady Jane Bennet; Lady Elizabeth Bennet; and Lady Esther Bennet." Each one bowed or curtsied as the Lord Chamberlain presented them to the royals.

"Cousin Rose," the Queen recognised the Dowager Duchess first as was most appropriate. "We are most sorry to hear about our cousin's passing. We wish you our deepest sympathies." Lady Rose curtsied to Her Royal Majesty. "Lady Priscilla, it is good to see you back in society even for this sad reason." The Queen looked to Lady Sarah and Lord Cyril. "We note your youngest was well hidden in the wilds of Hertfordshire."

Next the Queen turned her attention to the three Bennet daughters. "Once the mourning period for our late cousin is observed, we invite you to take tea with us and some of our daughters. Word of the musical prowess and talent you possess has reached our ears, and we would like to hear you exhibit. We understand we need to wish you happy, Lady Jane and Viscount Hilldale."

After a few more questions directed at the Matlocks, Jerseys, Holders, and Westmores, the Queen dismissed them with a flick of her fan. The group backed out of the receiving room as was expected.

No sooner had the courtiers who had been present at the investiture departed, the rumours about the Bennets began to circulate. Outside of the royal family, no one quite understood how an unknown family had come to be one of the most powerful in the kingdom, but all were going to search for answers. They would, for the most part, never gain anything beyond that which the family desired them to know.

VOL 2, CHAPTER 7

At the same time the late duke was being carried home to join his predecessors in the family crypt, the papers dated the second day of April arrived in Scarborough. As was her wont, Miss Caroline Bingley ignored the rest of the paper and went directly to the society pages. What she saw almost caused her heart to stop:

"The Duke and Duchess of Bedford are pleased to announce the betrothal of their oldest daughter, Lady Jane Francine Bennet of Longfield Meadows to Andrew Fitzwilliam, Viscount Hilldale. The Viscount's parents, the Earl and Countess of Matlock, join the Duke and Duchess in wishing the couple joy."

There was a second announcement below the one announcing the betrothal that was no less shocking:

"Lord Cyril and Lady Sarah De Melville, the Earl and Countess of Jersey, wish their granddaughter, Lady Jane Bennet, and Andrew Fitzwilliam, Viscount Hilldale, well on their betrothal."

If that were not bad enough there was one more:

"Lord Stanley and Lady Marie Carrington, the Marquess and Marchioness of Holder and their children, and Wesley and Jacqueline De Melville, Viscount and Viscountess Westmore, and their children, wish their niece and cousin, Lady Jane Bennet, and Andrew Fitzwilliam, Viscount Hilldale, well on their betrothal."

Caroline Bingley was certain she was inside a nightmare! How could this be? Jane Bennet, *Lady* Jane Bennet was a niece, not the companion! And what was this nonsense about a duke and duchess? If the paper had been dated the first day of April, Miss Bingley would have been certain that it was some elaborate prank.

She snatched up the rest of the paper and there, on the front page, was the royal decree. The Bennets were in fact the new Duke and Duchess of Bedford! The elder brother was the Marquess of Birchington, the younger an Earl, Lord Meryton, and the three daughters were, in fact, Ladies!

Her stomach roiling, she dreaded what the article below the announcement might say; but Miss Bingley read each word carefully:

"My dear readers, this reporter has been granted exclusive information about the new Duke and Duchess of Bedford and their family. When the courtship between Lady Jane Bennet and Viscount Hilldale was announced, there were many uninformed members of society who dismissed Miss Jane Bennet as a fortune hunter, those kinder believed her an unknown country miss without connections or wealth! The truth bears no resemblance to those conjectures.

"Mr. Bennet's first wife perished soon after giving birth to Lady Jane. After an appropriate mourning period, Mr. Bennet married his second wife, Lady Pricilla De Melville, the meeting a happy accident, as they tell it. The rest of the children, starting with Lady Elizabeth Bennet were the product of that union. Miss Bennet is declared to be a granddaughter by Lord Cyril and Lady Sarah De Melville, the Earl and Countess of Jersey, and a niece by the Lady Marie Carrington, Marchioness of Holder and Wesley De Melville, Viscount Westmore and their spouses."

Miss Bingley stopped reading, too flabbergasted to assimilate anything else that was written. The mother, the one Miss Bingley had disdained as being a solicitor's daughter, was, in fact, the daughter of an *Earl*! After the shock wore off, Miss Bingley was furious that *Lady* Jane had so lied to her, replaying their conversation at Netherfield in her mind to pinpoint exactly when and how. She was dismayed when her memory proved that Miss Bennet had answered the questions she had been asked honestly and had only not corrected her own misconceptions erroneously drawn. Through her anger, Miss Bingley could see she had been played for a fool of her own making. The clues had all been there, but she had refused to see them. To avoid considering her own folly, she chose to continue reading:

"As you can see, dear reader, Lady Jane's connections are those anyone would dream of having, even before the elevation! As to her and her family having no wealth and she a fortune hunter? That too was mistaken conjecture, for the family owns two estates in Hertfordshire, Longbourn and Netherfield Park, and two townhouses on Grosvenor Square. This reporter can affirm this was the truth *before* the new Duke attained his title and all the holdings associated with it.

"Dear reader, you may ask why the Bennets did not boast about their wealth and connections as so many in society would and do? The reason why the misconceptions about their wealth, connections, and property were never corrected was a simple choice collectively made by all in the family: It was done to keep fortune hunters and false friends at bay."

As she lowered the paper, Miss Bingley remembered the deference the Bennets were paid by the Netherfield servants and the quality of their dresses and gowns. When she thought about it now, she realised she had never seen any of the Bennet women in the same outfit more than once! To her horror, she realised the dresses she had thought were copies of Chambourg Creations had been the real thing! If only she had not been so blinded to the truth! She would have pushed Charles at Jane Bennet with all of her might, arranging a compromise of her rather than attempt one herself, though she might have tried for the eldest son too, not the untitled Mr. Darcy. She, Caroline Bingley, could have been closely related to a Duke and his family, if not the wife of a future duke! She read on:

"I am sure many of my readers are saying: 'All of the above is remarkably interesting, but how did Mr. Thomas Bennet inherit the dukedom of Bedford without being a Rhys-Davies?' Let me as-

sure you, my readers, that the new Duke, the former Mr. Bennet, is a direct descendent of the Rhys-Davies.

"How, you ask? Circa 1665, Lord Thomas Rhys-Davies, brother to Lord Sedgwick Rhys-Davies IV, the forth Duke of Bedford, decided to honour his mother's family, the former Lady Esther Bennet, by changing his name to Tom Bennet. His late grandparents, Lord Thomas, and Lady Horatia Bennet, the last Earl and Countess of Meryton, had been lost to an influenza outbreak.

"The selfless act of becoming Mr. Tom Bennet assured the Bennet line did not die with the Earl and Countess. Over the years, and because of a ruined family bible, the knowledge of the connection was lost. Thankfully, however, a letter written by the fourth Duke was discovered by the seventh Duke some months ago which enumerated the hitherto unknown family connection, and so the two branches of the family were finally reunited.

"The seventh Duke passed on the last day of March without any children of his own, which led to the passing forward of the title to the eighth Duke. The royal historians have studied the records, which is why there was a delay in announcing the connection, and found His Grace, Thomas Bennet, is, in fact, a direct descendant of the Rhys-Davies line, and therefore is the rightful heir to the title.

"The Duke and Duchess's eldest son, Lord Tom Bennet, is the new heir and the Marquess of Birchington. In his wisdom, our Regent has revived the earldom of Meryton. When his father ascended to the dukedom, Lord Mark Bennet, at the ripe old age of eleven, became the youngest earl in the realm.

"The royal family wish their cousins, the Bennets, well in their new roles!"

After she had finished reading the article, Caroline Bingley did not move for some minutes. But once the stupor wore off, the first question she asked herself was how the Bennets' elevation could be used to her advantage. It was time to formulate a plan!

~~~~~~~/~~~~~~~

The article that had stricken Miss Bingley and had led to the thoughts of opportunities lost, had been carefully crafted and sanitised by the family, with the approval of the Queen, before they departed for Longfield Meadows with the late Duke's remains. The family wanted to be sure the story they wanted the *Ton* to know was the one being told rather than leaving it to the speculation of the gossips to fill the vacuum of no information.

The effect on members of the *Ton* was exactly as intended. The Bennets had connections the rest could only dream of, and, if the rumours about the wealth of the Duke of Bedford was even half of what was reported, they were the wealthiest non-royals in the realm! Any thoughts of denigrating the *upstart* who had dared to take Viscount Hilldale off the marriage mart swiftly died.

The change of focus was *not altruism,* but a much more avaricious reason: Lord Hilldale was nothing compared to the jewels the four unmarried Bennets were now they were out of hiding and ready to join society. A marquess, who would one day be the ninth Duke of Bedford; an earl, young but never too young to draw up a betrothal contract; and two Ladies—Elizabeth and Esther—who all knew would have magnificent dowries.

Before the seventh Duke was even in the ground, the matchmaking machinations of the *Ton* were beginning in many a household.

~~~~~~~/~~~~~~~

It was a windy day in April when Charles Manners-Sutton, The Most Reverend Willowmere, by Divine Providence, Lord Archbishop of Canterbury, conducted the funeral services for the late Duke. The royals were represented by Prince Frederick, Duke of York and Albany, and his sister Princess Mary, Duchess of Gloucester and Edinburgh.

The Princess remained sitting with her cousins, Lady Rose, and Lady Priscilla, while the Prince attended the service and interment with men. After the interment, if anyone had noticed the new Duke and those with him studied the former Dukes' resting places skipped that of the third Duke, no one commented on the obvious.

Darcy stood back as he watched his Grace say a personal goodbye over the grave of the freshly laid-to-rest duke. He had been surprised and honoured when he and Gigi had been invited to accompany the family to Longfield Meadows as part of the convoy that brought the seventh Duke home for the final time. They had been told *all* family was included, even soon-to-be family.

Although now was absolutely not the time to advance his suit with Elizabeth, Lady Elizabeth, he corrected himself, he could not be anything but happy at how their friendship was proceeding. He thought back with pleasure to the leg of the journey on the second day of travel when both the younger Bennet sisters had accepted an invitation from Gigi—which he may or may not have suggested—to ride with the two Darcys.

After the break for the midday meal, Darcy and Gigi had welcomed Elizabeth and Esther Bennet into his carriage to ride with them and Mrs. Annesley. He and the companion sat on the rear-facing bench as Darcy noted how happy Gigi was to be joined by the sisters on her forward-facing seat.

Esther and Gigi, who had become even closer, were rapt with one another's conversation, which Darcy could not repine as it allowed him to talk to the object of his affection. "Let me reiterate how sorry I am for your family's loss, Lady Elizabeth," Darcy had opened.

"William, do I need to go back to calling you Mr. Darcy? Did you forget what I previously told you? Regardless of what has happened to my family, I am still just Elizabeth!" she had insisted. "I am sad to have lost Uncle Sed before I really got to know him, we only met once before he passed. I am becoming close to Aunt Rose, and I know she feels his loss keenly. I believe they were married for more than two score years. She puts on a brave face, but the pain is plain to those who look."

"I know it is not the same, but I still feel the pain of losing

*my mother, and then without warning, six years ago, my father,"
Darcy was subdued as he thought about his beloved parents. "My
apologies Elizabeth. I become melancholy when I think about them
and losing them."*

*"You have nothing to apologise for. Your feelings are just and
natural," Elizabeth had stated with warmth in her voice, and she
had leant forward and squeezed his hand in support.*

*"To his credit, Father started to educate me on running Pem-
berley and our other estates from a young age. Once I was at Cambridge, each time I returned home for a term break or holiday he
would give me more responsibility. Thanks to his foresight, when I
had to take over for him, I was more or less prepared. I would have
preferred, however, to take the reins many years later than I was
forced to do so," he added almost wistfully. "It was not only the
estate and other properties, but I also had to be both father and
mother to Gigi. Thank goodness, at least in that, my father had the
good sense to make Richard a co-guardian alongside me. It would
have been too overwhelming for me without Richard's assistance."*

*As he was speaking, Darcy had seen a definite softening in
Elizabeth's features. "It must have been exceedingly difficult for
you. Not only the loss of your father, but all of the demands of the
estate, the other properties, and a young sister. Couple that with
the way you have been hunted by those who desired your fortune
and connections, I begin to understand why you felt the need for
your mask. A lesser man barely at his majority would have broken
under that sort of pressure." Elizabeth had paused as she cogitated.
"None of this, as we have discussed, excused your behaving in a
fashion not becoming of a gentleman, but it helps me to better
understand you as you were then."*

They had then spoken about books, both prose and poetry,
and Darcy remembered how he had revelled in finding when
they disagreed, they would debate, and if they were not able to
reach agreement, there was no rancour. They simply agreed to
disagree unless or until one or the other could prove her or his
position to be the superior one.

Darcy knew, as surely as he drew breath, the conversation

in the carriage had made a substantial change to their relationship. He would patiently wait for the three months of mourning to pass to make his request for a courtship. He would not
even allude to it till then. He was however reasonably confident that when he did make his request, it would be met with a
more positive response than had he attempted to request more
than to call on Elizabeth in the library at Rosings Park.

Once the Duke had completed his goodbye to his predecessor, he joined the rest of the party of both family and
friends who would soon be family, as the group walked slowly
back towards the manor house.

~~~~~~~/~~~~~~~

Prince Frederick and Princess Mary visited with the family for an hour after the men returned and then departed with
their retinues to return to their homes. By the next day, thankfully for Lady Rose and the Bennets, all guests except family
and their closest friends had left.

Elizabeth was amused as she watched her Aunt Hattie's
mouth fall open in awe each time she saw a different part of
the house, especially when, on the third day after the funeral,
Mrs. Loretta Sherman, Longfield Meadows' housekeeper, gave
the new Duchess, her daughters, and a few of the visiting ladies a tour of the manor house.

It did not take Elizabeth long to realise that this house
dwarfed both Longbourn and Netherfield combined. In her estimation, the gigantically huge ballroom had more room than
Longbourn itself. There were three conservatories, six dining
parlours of varying sizes, more drawing rooms, parlours, and
music rooms—yes three of those—than Elizabeth had ever imagined, let alone seen.

The family floor, not counting the extensive master suite
that, out of deference to Lady Rose, the new mistress requested to skip for the tour, had thirty double suites with two
bed chambers and a shared sitting room each. If that was not
enough, there were ten single suites, each with its own sitting room. There was an enormous nursery that, in addition

to the children, could house up to ten nursemaids. Elizabeth had wondered at the reason for the size given what they had been told about the Rhys-Davies traditionally small families, but the housekeeper admitted she too had wondered. If all of that was not enough, there was a music room, an art studio - the housekeeper explained that the Dowager Duchess loved to paint - and two-family sitting rooms on the floor. In the back west corner were the schoolrooms with chambers for companions, tutors, and governesses.

Above the first floor were three guest floors, each one contained thirty double and twenty single suites, a music room, and a sitting room. The only guest floor that was different was the fourth floor, the highest of the guest floors, as rather than the twenty single suites there was a guest nursery and chambers for companions, tutors, governesses, and nursemaids.

There were two more floors above—the attics, yes *two* attics, which housed the servants, one floor for female and one for male servants, which could only be accessed from the servant's hallways. On the new mistress's insistence, Mrs. Sherman led the party to the first of the two housing the single females. The Bennets were impressed—each room was comfortable and furnished well.

The last stop on the tour was the library, where they were met by the Duke, Darcy, and some of the other men. To her father's delight, the library made the one at Bedford House look like a closet space. She knew the room was impressive when Darcy admitted, with ribbing from both Andrew and Richard, that it was larger even than Pemberley's vaunted library. Darcy confided in Elizabeth he had seen almost twice as many first editions in this library than was in his own.

As she meandered in the library, Elizabeth judged it was above, and larger than, the ballroom. There were comfortable seating areas set up for reading, some with four wingback chairs and a table, a few with two chairs and a table, and others with two armchairs, a settee, and a table. As she was looking at a section that housed first editions of the Bard's works, she sensed someone was behind her.

Elizabeth turned to discover Darcy staring reverently at the books. "I have always desired first editions of Shakespeare's works but have not been so lucky as to acquire any yet," he sighed with desire as he looked at the treasures.

"I suppose you will have to invent reasons to visit," Elizabeth teased.

Darcy took her comment as another positive sign—an incredibly positive one. "Richard had the right of it in his jesting. My library *is* smaller, though not by as much as he suggests," Darcy avowed staunchly. "My library has three levels to it, if one were to factor the extra area the two upper levels add, it is about three quarters the size of your library here."

"So the opposite of what Richard intimated?" Elizabeth asked with arched eyebrow. It amused her that William felt the need to defend the size of his library. "Silly me, I always thought that size does not matter, for is it not the quality and variety of the books?"

Darcy looked anywhere except at Elizabeth after she used the unintentional double-*entendre*, and he felt the heat radiating from his ears. "Are you well William, you look a little flushed?" Elizabeth asked innocently. Seeing the saucy look that she gave him, Darcy realised she knew exactly what she had said and what it referenced, and Elizabeth also achieved her aim—for William never tried to defend the size of anything he owned to her again.

~~~~~~~/~~~~~~~

"No, Aunt Rose, you are *not* moving to the dower house!" Priscilla insisted. "Until we met it was just you and Uncle Sed, and as he is awaiting your company elsewhere! He has allowed us time with you, so you are not alone. In the short time since we met," Priscilla indicated her husband and children, "and again for myself, you have become our family and we yours. It would please *us* if you would select one of the two bedchamber suites on the family floor. We want you with us, not three miles away!"

"If that is how you all feel…" Lady Rose saw nods from all of the family except Mark who stood before her and took her hands.

"Please say you will stay, Aunt Rose," he beseeched.

"How can I refuse the Earl of Meryton," Lady Rose teased him.

"Then you will remain with us, Aunt Rose?" Elizabeth confirmed. Like the rest of the family, she had grown to love her new aunt in short order.

"It seems I have been overruled," Lady Rose responded with a smile.

"That is good. Aunt Rose, you know it is not only love that was the genesis of my request, but it was also pragmatism as I need your help—as much as you are willing to give," Priscilla smiled.

"If this old lady may be of use, then so be it," Lady Rose returned, appreciating them for making her part of the family, and not allowing her to wallow in grief.

"Pish-posh! You are not an old lady, Aunt, for you are more spry than some half your age," Jane challenged.

"Thank you, Jane dear, it is kind of you to say so," Lady Rose emoted.

"We need to depart on the morrow, Priscilla," Lady Sarah informed her daughter. "You know your father must return to the Lords."

"It is the same for us," Lady Elaine stated. "Reggie needs to return to the House as well."

"Aunt Priscilla," Georgiana attracted the Duchess's attention. "William has asked me to invite you to make a stop at Pemberley on your way back to Town. He is sure that Uncle Thomas will enjoy seeing our library."

"Please thank William on our behalf. I will confer with my husband and let you know before you depart on the morrow. As long as you know we will not be able to break our trip by more than a day or two, dear." Georgiana allowed that she was well aware of the fact.

Elizabeth felt the compliment keenly. She was sure the invitation was issued so she could see Pemberley and realised she was hoping her father would have no objection to making the detour on their return to Town.

Later that evening, to the delight of both Elizabeth and Darcy, the invitation was accepted.

~~~~~~~/~~~~~~~

The morning before the Fitzwilliams departed, Jane and Andrew were walking in the extensive rose garden, which was in bloom, with Mrs. Ponsonby trailing them. "I will miss you, Jane," Andrew stated.

"And I you, Andrew. We will arrive in Town in the next sennight as I do not believe we will sojourn at Pemberley for more than two or three days. Papa needs to be inducted into the House of Lords before the end of the session, so he will not dally for long regardless of how attractive the library is," Jane opined.

"And it is less than three weeks until we marry, after which we need not be separated again. I am counting the days," Andrew promised quietly as he kissed the underside of each wrist he held reverently.

"Andrew!" Richard called as he strode into the rose garden. "Sorry Jane, but it is time for us to depart."

Jane walked to the drive with her betrothed holding tightly to his arm, then joined her parents and siblings in seeing the Fitzwilliams, Darcys, the grandparents, and their aunt and uncle depart. Once they carriages had disappeared from view, it was only the Bennets and Aunt Rose in residence in the mansion.

VOL 2, CHAPTER 8

Miss Caroline Bingley was obsessed with the formulation of a plan to coerce the lady she considered biddable and demure, Lady Jane Bennet, to smooth the way for her return to society. In her opinion, the one she needed to be wary of was the next youngest Bennet, Miss Eliza.

That lady had committed the ultimate crime of attracting Mr. Darcy with her *fine eyes*, something for which Miss Caroline would never forgive her. While there had been no reply to the letter of *apology* she had sent Lady Jane, Caroline could not imagine that sweet, pliant Jane Bennet would not read her letter, nor would she doubt the sentiments professed therein.

Knowing that as fact, a plan began to form in her mind. Miss Caroline was sure the Bennets would be in Town for the remainder of the season, so she would have to go to London. As much as she did not want to do it, she would ask the solicitor her brother had left in charge of her diminished dowry for help. If only Charles had not turned tail and run before she had wheedled more funds out of him, or at least gotten him to rent her an establishment in Town. She would also need to hire a companion so no one could question her respectability.

She now knew the Bennet ladies were clients of Madam Chambourg. She would have to maintain a vigilant watch of the entrance to the shop so she could come across them by *chance*, then she could start her campaign to manipulate and control the meek Lady Jane Bennet. Being so naïve in the ways of society, she would need guidance, after all. Miss Caroline believed her plan was infallible, much as she had when she lied to manipulate her brother into making the ill-fated trip to Pemberley before Christmas. One would think its failure would give her pause, but that, too, required the ability to recognise that they were fallible.

The first step was to visit Mr. Huntington, the solicitor. She asked her aunt for one of the maids to accompany her, to which Miss Bingley agreed. The solicitor told her that he had contacts in London who would find her apartments. He asked Caroline in which location she wished to live and determined the cost. Ignoring her brother's admonition about spending her principal, she threw caution to the wind and told the man that she wanted to be as close to Mayfair as could be, even in that exclusive neighbourhood if possible. She also charged the man with finding her a suitable companion, preferably one who had previously worked for other members of the *Ton*.

Mr. Huntington agreed to have the requested information if not in a sennight, then at most, a fortnight. Hoping to speed up the process, Caroline Bingley decided she would hie to London in a hired carriage with a lady's maid she would hire for herself and informed him he could reach her at Grenier's Hotel until she he had located a place of her own. She also decided to take the task of advertising for a companion herself.

On her return to her aunt's house, she found MIss Bingley relaxing in the drawing room. "Aunt, I have decided to return to society. I have been too long without polite society." Miss Caroline knew she was insulting her aunt but did not care, as she would not need her again. "I have *many* friends in Town and will soon be a darling of society yet again," she boasted.

"Good luck, Caroline," Miss Bingley replied, hiding her amusement in her small smile.

The next day, with a new maid in tow, and after having paid twice the going rate to hire a carriage, Caroline Bingley was on her way to London.

~~~~~~~/~~~~~~~

Darcy and his sister waited happily to welcome their guests. The three large coaches with the Bedford arms emblazoned on the doors pulled to stop in the internal courtyard at Pemberley. His footmen efficiently placed the steps and opened the doors of the conveyances.

The Duke handed out his Duchess and then the Dowager Duchess down from the lead vehicle. The three Bennet daughters exited the second. Darcy expected the Marquess and the Earl to exit the third, but it was only the latter, the others his governess and tutor.

"Welcome Bennet and to you all," Darcy intoned as he shook Bennet's hand. "Did your older son remain at Longfield Meadows?" he asked.

"Tom returned to Oxford the day after Easter. He did not want to miss any more lessons than those he already missed when he left a few days before the start of the Easter break," Bennet explained.

"How long will you break your journey to Town?" Darcy asked as they climbed the stone stairs to the front doors. He did not miss that his sister was gaily chatting away with the three Bennet sisters like they had not seen each other for months. It warmed his heart to see Gigi so happy.

"Two nights," Bennet replied. "As much as I never intended such a life for myself, there is much to be done, and my father-in-law and your uncle are eagerly waiting to introduce me in the House of Lords so I may be inducted into that august body. My wife and daughters will be returning to Longbourn to prepare for the wedding after a short sojourn in Town. Delaying it is not an option, or my daughter may cause a scandal by making for Scotland with your cousin just when we are becoming known."

"At least you understand the situation well." Jane smiled at her father. "And yes, we are to Longbourn after a visit to Madame Chambourg's," she added. She had made her decisions about her wedding gown before the late Duke's passing, so this stop was expected to be a final fitting, knowing Madame intended to send a seamstress to Longbourn for any last-minute repairs or alterations.

Once all were in the entrance hall, Darcy introduced his

housekeeper, Mrs. Reynolds, asking her to show everyone to their chambers then have someone show them to the Rose drawing room once they had refreshed themselves. Mrs. Reynolds curtsied and led the guests up the grand staircase to the family wing. As they were to be family in a short time and he and Georgiana had been treated as such with the invitation to Longfield Meadows, Darcy had not thought it presumptive.

Elizabeth had been vastly impressed by what she had seen of Pemberley on the drive from the gatehouse. William's estate was about two-thirds the size of Longfield Meadows, just as he had described one day when she had asked. A smile suffused her face when she remembered that she would not tease him about the size of one of his possessions again after her comment in Yorkshire.

The old growth forests had impressed her on the drive to the manor house, which had glowed gold as the midday sun hit the façade made of the signature Derbyshire stone. The house was well placed on rising ground on the far side of the valley. As she admired the vista from the carriage while they descended into the valley, she could not think of another estate she had seen where nature had done so much, and the awkward tastes of man had so little counteracted the beauty of mother nature.

Pemberley's manor house, while somewhat smaller than the manor house on their estate in Yorkshire, was the second largest house she had ever seen. It was an extremely comfortable home, nothing like Rosings Park had been before Anne and Uncle Gardiner started emptying it of all of the objectionable pieces. There was no question as to the quality of the furnishings, but it was understated elegance. One of the things that Elizabeth had appreciated in their new estate, and what was also evident here, was that everything was meant for comfort rather than to show wealth or status. She had a much healthier appreciation for that after her visit in Kent, before Anne had begun to assert her rights.

As Andrew and Richard had told her those many months

ago, William was most comfortable at his estate, and she discovered they had possibly understated the effect. She was even more impressed with the man she found here. He was completely at ease and had a kind word to say to all, even if they were the lowest of servants, her parents, or anyone in between.

She would be dissembling to herself if she said she was not beginning to develop tender feelings for William Darcy. Elizabeth was sure his honour would not allow him to propose a courtship until the three months of mourning were completed. It was not the same situation Jane and Andrew claimed, as they had been betrothed and had set a wedding date before the late Duke's passing. In fact, they had done so before the Duke had entered their lives and changed their entire existence.

After dinner that evening, there was no separation of the sexes. The servants were used to hearing the little miss play music, as she practised for many hours when in residence, but none had ever heard the sounds that emanated from the music room that night. There had been a choir of angels followed by one on her own which rose above any other they had heard.

"Thomas, have you noted the way our Lizzy looks at William now?" Priscilla asked as the two climbed into bed that night.

"And the way he looks at her? Yes, Cilla, I am not blind, so I have not missed the looks each gives the other when they believe they are unobserved," Bennet stated.

"At least we do not need to question whether it is our rank and connections that has attracted William," Priscilla opined.

"You have the right of it, Love. Darcy is a good man, and if he is Lizzy's choice, you will hear no objection from me," Bennet conceded. "It does not hurt that his library is as magnificent as advertised. Not that I have a dearth of tomes in our own libraries. I own not a library but *libraries*." He grinned.

"Yes, dear," his wife smiled. She blew out the last candle and snuggled into her beloved husband's arms.

~~~~~~~/~~~~~~~

Thanks to an express sent by the solicitor in Scarborough placing a notice in *The Times* that a lady was seeking a companion, on her second day at Grenier's Hotel Miss Bingley interviewed four ladies. She felt one's characters stood out above the rest, so she hired Mrs. Karen Younge without researching her references, as she remembered that Miss Darcy had once had a companion with a similar name. If only she had paid more attention to the inane chatter of the mousey brat, but Mrs. Younge claimed to have never worked for the Darcys, so Miss Bingley did not inquire further about the possibility again.

Mrs. Younge had learnt her lesson after she discovered how much Wickham had been using her. She had heard nothing from him for months and months until she started to receive beseeching letters for help from Marshalsea. When she did not respond right away, the letters turned crueller in tone. After one particularly abusive letter, she had begun to consign them unopened to the fire. Thankfully, he seemed to have received the message and had ceased writing letters to her.

She had used fake characters to gain this job, but she was determined to act as she should going forward. A few days after being hired, Mrs. Younge accompanied her mistress to a house close to Mayfair which was owned by a widow who was offering one floor for rent.

Miss Bingley approved of the apartment and paid Mrs. Beatrice Ralston, the owner, for two months. She had comfortable chambers for herself and a smaller chamber for her companion. As the house had a mews that was not used because Mrs. Ralston did not keep a carriage, Miss Bingley contacted her solicitor's man in London and had him purchase her a conveyance and two horses, asking him to hire a coachman and footman on her behalf. She cared not that she was continuing to expend her capital, as she was sure that once her plan had started to work, she would be snapped up by a man of means, perhaps even Mr. Darcy, if he had finally come to his senses. She vowed to make him ask twice after the words hurled in her direction the night she accidentally had gone into his room.

To be safe, in case the Bennets returned to Town before it was reported in the gossip columns, Miss Bingley and her companion took teas at a little teashop on Bond Street with a good view of those coming and going from Madame Chambourg's shop.

~~~~~~~/~~~~~~~

While Bennet relaxed in the library with the latest offering by the scandalous Lord Byron in his hand, his wife and children accompanied Darcy and Georgiana on a ride up a bridal path that offered a fine view of the estate. On a clear day, one could see the Peaks in the distance.

Elizabeth had been impressed with the extensive stables at Pemberley and the amount of quality horseflesh. Luckily, the Darcys owned enough horses trained for side-saddle, which they had not expected as it was only he and Georgiana in residence most of the time. After about an hour and climbing in single file up the steep path, they reached a plateau which offered a view that was better than advertised. "That way," Darcy pointed to the southwest, "twenty-five miles is Andrew's estate, Hilldale. Snowhaven, my aunt's and uncle's estate, is fifteen miles southeast of us, and Richard's Brookfield is ten miles west," Darcy pointed.

"William, this view is everything you and Gigi told us it would be and more," Priscilla enthused. "I am sorry we could not convince Thomas to join us."

"Are those the Peaks?" Mark asked, pointing to the shimmering view due west in the distance.

"They are," Georgiana nodded, her smile brightening at the chance to share this special spot with their family. They already were family to her and would be able to claim as such soon. "We are lucky it is a clear day today and they are not hidden by clouds." After so many years of relative solitude on the estate but for their Fitzwilliam family, the recent past had been a particular pleasure for herself and, she was sure, her brother.

"William, your estate is everything you said and so much

more. It is so peaceful up here," Elizabeth stated, her horse resting next to the stallion Darcy was riding. Zeus has been left in Town, so he was riding Dylan, a younger horse who had been broken and trained in the last six months.

"It pleases me you think so, Elizabeth. This is a place I come to when I want to think. I spent a lot of time here in this exact spot last December after my uncle's set-down," Darcy owned.

"I am sorry; it must have been painful for you," Elizabeth empathised.

"It was both needed and deserved. We would not be friends if I had not received the kick in the a...pants Uncle Reggie delivered," Darcy admitted.

"And we would not have been friends if my mother had not made me think about my behaviour," Elizabeth acknowledged. "If I behaved as I used to, I may have missed the truth of the man you are, William."

"We promised to begin again, so let us not argue who owns the bigger fault for the past, especially as it is clearly me!" William teased.

"When did you start coming to this beautiful place to think?" Elizabeth complied with the suggestion they move forward.

"After my mother passed," Darcy replied. "I used to dismount and scream at God, asking why He took my mother. I believed as I was closer to heaven here, my voice would be easier to hear, such was the working of my mind at eleven."

"You were Mark's age. It was not just sad occasions that brought you here, was it? I would hate to think that this place is associated with only sadness for you," Elizabeth stated softly.

"No, Elizabeth, happy occasions more than sad ones brought me here, one of the happiest being today and our sharing this place with...friends." As he spoke, he looked directly into her entrancing eyes. Elizabeth understood his message clearly.

The spell was broken when someone noted it was time to return to the manor house.

~~~~~~~/~~~~~~~

Lady Marie Carrington and her sister-in-law Jacqui had been to Madame Chambourg's to check on their niece's dresses and gowns. As they exited, they could not miss the burnt orange monstrosity on the woman walking on the other side of the street.

"Is not that the pretentious social climber, Miss Bingley?" Lady Marie whispered to her sister-in-law as they entered their carriage.

"I believe it was. Did we not leave word she is *persona non grata* in society after what William told us about her behaviour in Hertfordshire?" the Viscountess asked sweetly.

"I thought our brother Thomas' investigators reported that she was banished to Scarborough," Lady Marie wondered.

"We will make sure to warn our nieces that the harpy is in Town. Not even Esther, who generally likes everyone, can stand the sight nor, I dare say, the smell of that woman. Mayhap they will not be unfortunate enough to see her as they will only be in Town for two days before heading to Longbourn," the Viscountess speculated.

"I have the feeling she is lying in wait for our nieces. Given what we know of her, she must be salivating to be in their company now that the truth of their situation is public." Lady Marie offered her estimation.

"Then I think we need to speak to Mother Sarah and Lady Elaine even before the Bennets return to Town." Lady Marie could not have agreed with her sister more.

~~~~~~~/~~~~~~~

"I am sure Thomas will take steps to protect all of his children now they have become the focus of many machinations by those who care only for connection and fortune. I will, however, recommend he add guards to whomever he intends to assign to each of my grandchildren," the Earl of Jersey stated with purpose at the meeting with the Fitzwilliams, Carringtons, and his son Wes and wife Jacqui.

"I think I may be able to assist in this, Lord Jersey," Richard stated.

"Just Jersey, young Fitzwilliam," the Earl allowed.

"There are a good number of my ex-soldiers looking for work. Good, ferocious men who could work as footmen-guards. There are two I specifically have in mind, Biggs and Johns, and believe me the name *Biggs* is an understatement. Both men look like walking mountains but are deceptively fleet of foot and have the reflexes of a cat. I could have twenty or more as soon as Bennet gives the go ahead," Richard informed the group.

"Jersey, do you believe Bennet will think it presumptuous if my son reaches out to have the men ready to meet with him when he arrives in Town the day after the morrow?" Lord Matlock asked.

"I do not believe so, Matlock. In fact, I think it a sound plan, and as a grandfather am willing to overrule his objection should he attempt one. I rather think both my daughter and son-in-law will be grateful, as they place the safety and security of their children above all else. Remember what they let people believe for years just to stave off fortune hunters and false friends like that Bigley woman," Lord Jersey opined.

"Bingley Papa, the Bingley woman!" Lady Marie said with a smile.

"Who cares what her name is so long as she does not get near our nieces and nephews," Lord Holder stated with asperity.

"Do you think she would try and harm one of them?" Lady Sarah asked with concern.

"You never know with one as delusional as she is, which never gets better, only worse for one who would attempt to manipulate her whole family into thinking Darcy had not meant his warnings. It may be she only wants to use them for her social climbing endeavours, but I would rather we were safe than sorry," Andrew added. "If she tries to harm my

Jane..."

"She is not, by any means, the only potential threat. With the wealth they have, they are targets for all kinds of unscrupulous people looking to gain wealth the easy way," Richard pointed out, his strategic mind thinking three steps ahead about how best to cut off any avenues which could be attempted.

"*No one* will be allowed to harm Jane or any of her siblings, Andrew," his father assured him. "Richard, make the contacts and have the men at Bedford House by Friday morning. Twenty, forty, whatever you think best."

Everyone felt easier knowing there was a plan of action to protect the Bennets. Just like the late Duke had predicted, the Bennets were surrounded by friends and family determined to protect them and see that they succeeded.

VOL 2, CHAPTER 9

The Bennets and Lady Rose arrived at Bedford House in the afternoon of Thursday, the eighteenth day of April. They were met by John and Maude Cox, the butler and housekeeper, who had all of the servants lined up in the entrance hall to welcome the new Duke, Duchess, and their family to Bedford House. The Dowager Duchess was welcomed warmly, but the senior staff were too well trained to look to her for instructions any longer.

The master suite had been made over per the instructions Lady Priscilla had left the first time she had visited the house. The three sisters had chosen chambers on their first and only visit when they met the late Duke. Elizabeth and Esther shared a suit, each with her own set of chambers on either side of the sitting room, while Jane had chosen the suite next to them.

Elizabeth would have shared a suite with Jane, but given the latter's impending nuptials, the arrangement made the most sense to all of them. Each also had her own French lady's maid who had their mistress' trunks unpacked, and their dresses and gowns hanging in the large walk-in closets before the sisters even reached their chambers.

Mark was in the nursery down the hall from the rest of the family.

Lady Rose had a large two bedchamber suite which she had chosen before they had departed London. The Bennets had offered her the choice to remain in the master suite, but she had declined, citing that she could not reside in those chambers without her beloved Sed.

The knocker was down and would remain so as the ladies would depart for Hertfordshire on the coming Tuesday. The

Duke intended to follow on Thursday, the day after his induction into the Lords. The butler had been instructed the family was not at home to any visitors except family and a few friends who were on a selective list provided.

An hour later, the butler announced the Earl and Countess of Matlock, Viscount Hilldale, and the Honourable Mr. Richard Fitzwilliam. They joined the family in the family sitting room and were followed shortly by the Earl and Countess of Jersey.

"We need to discuss some safety measures with you for not only yourself but all of your family, Bennet," Lord Jersey began. He very carefully laid out the conversation they had the day his daughters had seen Miss Bingley watching Madame Chambourg's modiste shop like a cat expecting fresh cream. He then ceded the floor to Richard.

Richard reported he had more than thirty men to choose from, and if Bennet needed to see more it could easily be arranged. "The two who, in my opinion, should be hired regardless of who else you choose are Biggs and Johns." Richard followed this pronouncement with his reasoning for his suggestion of those two particular men.

Bennet looked at his wife who nodded, he was to act immediately. "What time will they be here on the morrow, Richard?" he asked. "As for the two huge men, tell them they are hired. Jane must be at Madame Chambourg's in the afternoon, and I would prefer at least the two of them were with the ladies when they accompany Jane."

"What about livery?" Lady Sarah asked.

"If we do not have anything that fits their size, Mama, we will order some fabric and have it made up in a matter of days," Priscilla responded.

"There is no need to wait, my dear," Lady Rose informed them. "There is ample fabric here for the livery and we have a seamstress on staff. If Richard can have them here this evening, they will have a set of uniforms waiting for them in the morning."

"If that meets with your approval, Lady Priscilla, I will

send a message and have them here in the next hour, two at most," Richard stated.

"That is perfect, Richard, thank you," Priscilla averred. Richard moved to the escritoire, wrote his note and had it dispatched.

"Do you really think Miss Bingley is insane enough to cause Jane physical harm?" Elizabeth asked.

"Possibly not, but there will be more threats than just her, and I would rather have too much protection than not enough," Bennet told his daughter. "Once word of your dowries is leaked, you will be targets for any and all fortune hunters. Your mother and I have decided to add to each of your dowries an additional two hundred thousand pounds."

"Papa, that is too much!" both Jane and Elizabeth chorused while everyone else was shocked into silence.

"It is but a small portion of the wealth we now possess," Priscilla clarified.

"Mama and Papa, there are so many that are in need," Esther spoke up. "I would like my original dowry donated to charity. I do not want to speak for my sisters, but even without what I want to donate, I think there will be more than enough of a dowry." She noted dryly, a small smile proving it was rhetoric and Elizabeth smiled as she took her sister's hand.

"I agree with Esther," Elizabeth stated.

"As do I. If you agree and allow us to designate where the funds go, I want mine to go to Haven House," Jane decided.

Bennet looked at his wife and they communicated wordlessly. "It shall be as you girls desire, and yes, Jane, you each may choose which charity or charities are to receive the largess."

"I have always been proud of you three," Lady Sarah said as she hugged each granddaughter in turn, "but never more so than now."

"Your donation will fund Haven House for twenty years, Jane!" Lady Elaine exclaimed with tears in her eyes. She was the chairwoman of the committee that ran the home for young girls who had been used and abused both physically and sexually. "Thank you, Jane; I cannot wait to tell the committee to whom we are indebted."

"It must be anonymous, Mother Elaine," Jane used the new title that Lady Elaine had recently asked her to use.

"Then anonymous it will be," Lady Elaine agreed.

"Aunt Elaine," Elizabeth called. "Did I not hear talk that you wanted to open some houses like Haven House in other locations in the country?"

"We recently were discussing just that, Lizzy," Lady Elaine nodded.

"In that case, I would like my donation to be used for that purpose," Elizabeth stipulated.

"And mine!" Esther added.

"Thomas and I will match the contributions of our daughters," Priscilla pledged.

Lady Elaine was speechless, for in a matter of minutes her committee had just received three hundred thousand pounds so they would be able to fund many, if not all the houses they had dreamed of.

"As much as I hate to return us to reality, we need to continue our discussion on the safety measures for not just the young ladies and your sons, but all of you, Bennet. Your wealth could make any of you targets for unscrupulous men," Richard stated when the conversation had lagged for a moment.

"Richard, I trust you implicitly, so tell us what you suggest." Bennet nodded his leave.

"If it were me, I would hire a cadre of footmen-guards and outriders. When all or some of you move from place to place, you want your carriages to be the *least* attractive target to any brigand who fancies himself a highwayman. I would suggest the assistant drivers and postillions all be guards as well." Richard paused as his words sunk in. "When any of you are out and about in Town, the two men I just wrote to should be with you, as well as two to four more. The size of the party would determine the number. If any of you go for a ride or ramble on her own," Richard looked pointedly at Elizabeth given her habit of solitary walks at Rosings Park, "then Biggs, Johns, and two more footmen-guards should be your escorts."

"It will be as you suggest, Richard, so I believe we may need to see more than thirty men," Bennet opined.

"There is no shortage of good men who would love the work after they have completed their service to King and country. With such a large force, you will need a commander," Richard added.

"I take it you have one in mind?" Bennet surmised.

"In fact I do. He was a Captain and was injured when he fought alongside me at Corunna. His injuries have healed, but they were bad enough for the army to place him on half pension. His name is David Burnett, and I would, and in fact *did* on more than one occasion, trust him with my life," Richard informed them.

"If he is in London, will I be able to meet with him on the morrow?" Bennet asked with the intention to offer him the position on that recommendation alone.

"He is, and I believe so," Richard confirmed.

As the rest of the Bennets listened to the conversation about the security measures being put in place to ensure their safety, it was brought home to them once again just how much their lives had changed.

~~~~~~~/~~~~~~~

Lady Catherine de Bourgh hardly recognised Rosings Park's manor house as the same one she used to rule over with an iron fist only weeks before. Gardiner's men had returned, catalogued all her daughter wished removed, and had promptly taken all of the items and artwork Lady Catherine had been so proud of, certain they were a testament to their wealth and status. Now that she had been jarred back to reality, she was able to see it all through her daughter's eyes and was forced to admit the way she used to decorate was instead classless.

According to Anne, they would attend Andrew's wedding

at the end of the month, and then they would use the funds from the sales of the items that had thus far been removed to place an order with Chippendale's for new furniture. As the new pieces arrived, the remainder of the pieces to be replaced would be carted to Gardiner and Associates for sale also.

The most difficult of her dreams to give up had been the union between Anne and Fitzwilliam. As hard as it had been for her to give up her dream, she now had no doubt neither of the principals would ever unite. Lady Catherine had at last accepted that Anne's decision was to never marry.

When the then *Miss* Elizabeth Bennet had been a guest of her late parson, she had not missed the looks her nephew Darcy had bestowed on the lady when he thought he was not being observed. She had come close to berating the country miss, it had been on the very top of her intentions that very night until the dinner when she revealed who her family was. That and the next day's revelations convinced Lady Catherine that, if the two ever made a match, it would truly increase the family's stature rather than the degrading she would have erroneously professed.

They were still a sennight from Anne's five and twentieth birthday, but her daughter had been mistress of the estate since that fateful night. Lady Catherine had always thought Anne as weak in mind as she was in body, but Anne had proved the fallacy of her beliefs many times each and every day since then. Rather than feel rancour that her position had been usurped, Lady Catherine felt a deep pride in her daughter.

~~~~~~~/~~~~~~~

When the news of the Bennet's elevation initially reached the environs of Meryton, the population thought it an elaborate Bennet hoax, for they all well knew their friend and neighbour enjoyed a good prank. But once the royal decree was seen with the accompanying article, the realisation sank in; it was all true.

After the news was publicised, Sir William and Lady Lucas confirmed that Bennet had disclosed the truth to them when they collected Charlotte from Kent. Said daughter was pleased her month of full mourning was rapidly drawing to a close, and she would be almost halfway through her half mourning when she attended Jane's and the Viscount's wedding breakfast. She was also gratified that she was not relegated to attend only the ceremony in the church as full mourning would have required.

There was little or no time which passed during these hours that Charlotte was not thinking about Richard, where he was and what he was doing. Her love for him had grown to a stout, irrevocable love, and she was counting the hours until she saw him again.

She was most pleased her mother had accepted the invitation for Maria, and consequently herself, to travel north with the Bennets after the wedding, almost joyous to learn she would be leaving Meryton a fortnight before the originally planned departure.

All three Lucas ladies were helping with the wedding preparations in Meryton and Longbourn as a way of assisting the new Duchess. Lady Lucas was surprised at the need to occasionally remind Charlotte to concentrate but was glad to see her daughter smiling when she thought no one was observing, as her mind appeared to be thinking of a certain former colonel.

~~~~~~~/~~~~~~~

The prior evening, Richard had accompanied Biggs, Johns, and former captain Burnett when they met the Bennets. Both huge men accepted the position with gratitude and were immediately sent to see the seamstress to measure them.

When the Bennet parents met with Mr. Burnett, he impressed them greatly. They conferred for hardly any time before offering him the position. The former captain started that very morning, and his first task was to assist Bennet with interviewing the men Richard had organised as potential employees.

Based on Bennet's acceptance of his recommendations,

Richard added a further fifteen men, and each one of the five and forty men had been hired. The men, some of whom had found no employment since their return from risking life and limb for King and country, and others who only had menial jobs that paid but pennies a month, could not have been happier, for their new positions paid them seven pounds a *month*. For some, it was what they had been used to earning in a full *year*.

The men would have been loyal to the Bennets no matter what they paid, but the amount paid purchased a fierce loyalty. Two former lieutenants were hired, one who would be in charge of the outriders and a second who would be in charge of the footmen-guards, including those who would be placed on the carriages.

Biggs and Johns, who had both been sergeants, reported directly to Mr. Burnett, as did the two former junior officers. The seamstress and three maids, who helped her as needed, were far busier than they had ever been sewing uniforms for all of the new men.

~~~~~~~/~~~~~~~

Just before ten, Georgiana arrived, as she was included in the expedition to Madame Chambourg's. Not long after, the Carrington coach arrived with Lady Marie. Ally and Aunt Jacqui had also joined their party.

As the new Duchess was busy working with her predecessor, she had chosen not to join the shopping expedition, for there were many logistical details when one adds almost fifty men to their household. Their Aunt Marie's conveyance was large, but not large enough for seven ladies to avoid having their skirts crushed and wrinkled. Jane and Elizabeth rode with their aunts, while Esther, Gigi, and Ally rode in a Bedford carriage.

"Do you think Miss Bingley will be lying in wait, Aunt Marie?" Jane asked placidly as they started moving.

"I suspect she will be, yes," Lady Marie averred. "You have naught to worry about. If her intention is malevolent, there are

SHANA GRANDERSON A LADY

those huge men on the back of our carriage, as well as two of the burliest footmen from Bedford House."

"Those two seem very gentle, but, like our Jane, if you anger them, or in this case threaten their charges, I have a feeling you would not like to experience the consequences," Elizabeth opined then looked at her older sister. "When you read the portion of her *apology* letter, you said you would give her the cut direct. Is that still your intention, Jane? I will take my lead from you."

"It is. Do not forget we need to protect Gigi. She told us how the harpy used to fawn all over her in an attempt to impress William," Jane reminded her companions.

"She will receive the same protection as any other member of the family!" the Viscountess insisted. Not many minutes later the coach started to slow as they approached Madam Chambourg's.

~~~~~~~/~~~~~~~

Miss Bingley was beginning to think her daily vigil was yet another waste of time when she saw Lady Marie's conveyance halt in front of the modiste's shop. It was closely followed by one Miss Bingley recognized as a Bedford vehicle.

She sat up straight. "Mrs. Younge, be ready to move when they...my friends exit the modiste's." Miss Bingley's eyes were fixed on the entrance of said shop.

"Whatever is your pleasure, Miss Bingley," Mrs. Younge replied. Each subsequent day she had sat with her mistress staring at the shop opposite gave Mrs. Younge a growing suspicion that her employer was not entirely stable.

Miss Bingley watched with envy as Lady Jane and the hated Eliza were assisted out of the Carrington coach by a huge, lumbering footman. They were followed by the Marchioness of Holder and Viscountess Westmore. Her eyes widened even more when she saw who stepped out of the trailing carriage. She identified the youngest Bennet, Lady Es... something, then there was a young lady she did not know, who was followed by none other than Miss Georgiana Darcy!

What a boon! The chit thought she liked her! It was proof she would succeed as now there were two ladies who would welcome her inclusion in the group. She watched them enter the shop. Miss Bingley was so fixated on the group across the street that she did not notice how her companion had blanched with shame when she saw Miss Darcy.

~~~~~~~/~~~~~~~

"Janie, you look like a fairy princess," Elizabeth gushed. Jane had requested Elizabeth stand up with her, which Elizabeth had accepted joyously even before her sister had managed to finish the sentence. As such, she was in the room with Jane for the fitting. Her sister wanted most of the others to see her gown for the first time when the vestibule doors opened at Longbourn's church.

"Thank you, Lizzy! It seems to me there is no further alteration needed," Jane opined as she watched herself in the mirrors as she turned side-to-side.

"It is perfect for you, Jane; it reflects your character well. Gorgeous with hidden depth." Elizabeth hugged her sister gently; for she did not want to damage the gown.

"Did you notice the orange monstrosity in Bentley's Tea Room across the street?" Jane asked quietly.

"It was hard to miss, Jane," Elizabeth laughed, "and my eyes were as punished this time as they had been every other time we were forced to endure her company!"

"The woman has the temerity to think she can advise me! I would sooner call her a wit." Both sisters laughed so brightly even the Madam smiled at them.

"While you change, I will go speak to our aunts," Elizabeth stated, and Jane nodded her agreement as two of the assistants assisted her out of her wedding gown.

"Gigi," Elizabeth sat next to the younger girl, "did you notice what is prowling outside the store, no doubt to bump into us by *chance*?" Elizabeth asked, as she nodded her head in the direction of the objectionable woman.

"Yes, I am aware of—well, whatever it is. William has told

me to give her the cut direct if she approaches me in public and he is not with me. I am sorry if..." Before Georgiana could complete her statement, Elizabeth took her hand and squeezed gently as she softly shushed her friend from saying anything further, to help her manage her distress.

"As we will do the same, there is no need to apologise. She must be the most obtuse woman in the world," Elizabeth observed with a huff of frustration at their need to deal with the woman again.

"I agree," Georgiana giggled. "William and I have given her many not-so-subtle hints, yet she has never taken them."

"It seems," Jane stated as she re-joined the rest, "money cannot buy intelligence."

"That, dearest niece," Lady Marie said with a brilliant smile, "is the most unforgiving speech I have heard you make. *Brava*! And a most fitting notation for that social climber. Are we ready to make an end of this?" Everyone in the party nodded.

~~~~~~~/~~~~~~~

"Miss Bingley, if I may, it seems like the shopping party means to board their coaches and depart. You may upset them by trying to detain them," Mrs. Younge said, trying to avoid being in close proximity to Miss Darcy.

She had always liked the girl who was such an easy charge, but when George had offered her five thousand of the dowry for her help, she had made the wrong decision. It was something Mrs. Younge regretted every day, and more often when she considered how she had been used. If the Darcys would allow it, she would give anything to make amends.

"Be quiet unless you want to be dismissed," Miss Bingley snapped at her as she saw the shop's door open. It was the *perfect* setting, as several influential members of the *Ton* were present to see her triumph, trying to hide that they too were hoping to see those who had arrived in the coaches which now waited for those in the shop few could enter. She was expressly pleased to see that one or two were her erstwhile friends who had not responded to her overtures. She was convinced they would soon be eating humble pie.

Ladies Jane and Eliza followed the Marchioness and Viscountess out of the modiste's shop. One of the huge footmen was close to them while another brought up the rear behind the three younger girls. "Why Lady Jane, what a providence of chance to run into my friend here," Miss Bingley spoke loudly as she gave a perfunctory curtsy.

"Miss Bingley, what in our past, what in the tone of my voice, address, or expressions would ever give you reason to think you are counted as my friend?" Jane demanded; her eyes fixed on the now shocked woman as watching members of the *Ton* tittered behind their hands. Jane had never intended to do more than cut the shrew, but as soon as the woman had spoken, she knew she needed to leave no doubt about the esteem, or lack thereof, in which Miss Bingley was held. "As to your letter, my sister," Jane inclined her head to a smirking Elizabeth, "and I consigned it to the fire. Since when is the daughter of a tradesman qualified to guide the daughter of a Duke? Are you so delusional? It is no wonder your siblings left the country to get away from you!"

With a nod of her head, all seven woman turned their backs on Miss Bingley and gave her the cut direct. The members of the *Ton* who were privileged to watch the set down, clearly understood it was folly to anger Lady Jane Bennet. The seven ladies, after Lady Marie and her sister-in-law greeted some of their friends, climbed back into the same coaches in which they arrived and were soon away, leaving a gobsmacked Miss Bingley sputtering on the pavement, her torn reputation now completely in tatters.

Mrs. Younge could not forget the look of anger on Miss Darcy's face. She had said not a word, just stared at her, turned, and left. Miss Bingley said nothing on the ride back to their lodgings, but the furious woman had obviously turned to vengeance, and she was wearing a look Mrs. Younge had often seen when George Wickham had spoken of Mr. Darcy. She had no

doubt that Miss Bingley intended to get even! Her reputation
was destroyed, so what else did she have to lose?

VOL 2, CHAPTER 10

Longbourn was a sight for sore eyes to the four Bennet ladies and the younger Bennet lad. If someone had told them how their lives would change when they were last at the estate, they would have had that person consigned to Bedlam. Yet even here in Hertfordshire only the house they were approaching was the same.

In a little more than ten days, Jane would be married and leave them for her own home as Viscountess Hilldale. And there were the massive changes that had occurred to the Bennets as a whole. The three large coaches, all with the Bedford arms on the doors, came to a halt in the drive with fourteen outriders as escorts, not to mention the footmen-guards with each carriage.

None of the occupants had missed the deferential looks they had received as they had rolled through Meryton. No matter how they tried to tell themselves all would be the same once they were at Longbourn, the reality was nothing would ever be the same again.

"Welcome home, your Grace, my Ladies, and Lord Meryton," Hill bowed low as his wife gave a deep curtsy.

"Thank you, Hill, Mrs. Hill," Lady Priscilla smiled warmly at the couple. "We will discuss the wedding preparations as soon as I return from changing, Mrs. Hill."

"Yes, your Grace," Mrs. Hill replied.

A half hour later the family met in the drawing room. "I know everything feels strange, and, in some ways, we wish things were the same as they were before we departed the estate months ago. We cannot go back and you, we, will have to get used to the way those who have been our friends and servants for these long years address us and relate to us differently than they did before. It will not be due to a *lack* of affection, but it is not every day someone in this little part of the kingdom is confronted by a duke, duchess, and the plethora of titles we now claim.

"The difference in the way the Hills were with us is only the beginning, and I ask all of you to try and make it as easy for our friends as can be. Once they see we are as we ever were, they will relax, but we cannot force them to that point. They will need to get there on their own, so it is as I said, the way we behave with them will go a long way towards putting them at ease," Lady Priscilla explained when she saw that her children had been frustrated at the stilted conversation from the Longbourn servants.

She had no doubt of her family's behaviour, but she felt she would be remiss in not preparing them for the reactions she believed would be forthcoming from the populace of the neighbourhood. "I can see you girls want to ask my permission for something! Out with it," she encouraged.

"It has been a while since we rode Mama, may we ride and then stop at Lucas Lodge on our return home?" Elizabeth asked pleadingly.

"I see no reason why not. Do not be too long though; you know the new rules when you are out of our home, do you not?" their mother reminded them.

"Yes, Mama," the three chorused.

"May I join my sisters Mama?" Mark asked hopefully.

"Sorry Scamp, but no." Priscilla almost laughed as her son's face fell and he affected a pout. He was an earl, but he was still a boy of eleven, for another three weeks anyway. "For obvious reasons, we have not insisted on you taking your lessons recently, Mark, but we are home now so you have a lot of catching up to do." Seeing her son was about to plead his case, Priscilla shook her head and stopped his planned bargain. "Work hard today, and in the morning, you will be able to ride with your sisters."

"Thank you, Mama," Mark reluctantly accepted her decision and took himself up the schoolroom to his waiting tutor.

While her daughters changed into riding habits, the Duchess asked Hill to let Biggs and Johns know her daughters wanted to go riding. Hill had not met the arriving men yet. However, once she mentioned that they were the two biggest men of the new servants, Hill nodded that he knew who the Mistress meant.

~~~~~~~/~~~~~~~~

By the time the three sisters walked outside, their horses were saddled and waiting for them with two grooms and four of the new footmen, including the two aforementioned giant-sized men. As they rode past some of their long-time tenants, it was not hard to see what their mother had warned them about. The reactions were much more formal, but the three sisters followed their mother's sage advice and behaved no differently than they always had, greeting them warmly in return to their guarded bows and curtsies with averted eyes. And there was understandable intimidation when Mrs. Black and her daughters beheld the men escorting the Bennet sisters.

The fact that they behaved without airs, or a feeling of superiority was noted by the Blacks, who shared such unexpected news with their neighbours, which led to the tenants feeling more relaxed around the Bennets over the coming days.

After a long-awaited gallop over the fields, the same ones bordering Netherfield which Darcy had seen the Bennets ride several times, the sisters turned their mounts towards Lucas Lodge. There was a long history of friendship between the two families going back manyy years before Sir William had been knighted and purchased the small estate. The grooms led the sisters' horses to the Lodge's stables, while Biggs and one other footman stationed themselves in the front of the house, and Johns with the other man were in the area at the back of the building.

"Welcome Ladies Jane, Elizabeth, and Esther," Lady Lucas welcomed them formally as she and her daughters curtsied deeply, and the oldest Lucas son bowed low to them.

"It is good to see all our friends in the neighbourhood again," Jane said as she and her sisters sat. "We do have a request. We understand the need for formality in public, but in private we are Jane, Lizzy or Eliza to the Lucas family, and Esther; there is no need for the honorific."

The request had the desired effect, and soon they were chatting as one would expect friends who had not seen one another for a while to do. It did not take long for Esther and Maria to excuse themselves and make for the latter's bedchamber, and Franklin Lucas excused himself not long after the younger girls' exit from the parlour.

After informing Jane of the status and progress of the upcoming wedding preparations her mother had asked them to help with and informing the Bennets that her husband was away from the estate in the town, Lady Lucas left the parlour, allowing the three long-time friends alone. She smiled to herself at Charlotte having such true affection with the elder Bennet daughters who had always been her truest confidants.

"Charlotte, you have not told your parents of the intelligence you tricked my father into confirming at Rosings Park, have you?" Jane asked.

"I will not lie to my parents if either ask me a direct question, but no, I have not volunteered the information. My father has his pride, he would not be easy if he knew what your family has done for ours," Charlotte opined. "How was Richard...and Andrew," Charlotte added quickly, "when you saw them last?" she asked hoping to hear some news of the man she loved.

"*Both* brothers were well. Would you like to hear all about what Andrew has been up to lately?" Jane teased.

"Richard is very well and specifically asked that we convey his deepest regards to you, Charlotte," Elizabeth relayed, as she swatted her older sister's arm playfully.

"Charlotte, you may also be interested to know Andrew... and the *rest* of his family arrive on Thursday. They will be hosted at Netherfield Park. The rest of our family arrive on

Friday with Papa," Jane smiled playfully at Charlotte who was looking well pleased that Richard would be in the area in but a few days - mere hours really!

"When we were at Rosings Park, it looked to me like our Eliza did not object to Mr. Darcy's company any longer," Charlotte smiled, as she moved the attention off herself.

"You know we decided to start again, Charlotte." Elizabeth rolled her eyes, fully aware of the tactics her friend was employing.

"Methinks at this point you more than just *tolerate* William, Lizzy," Jane stated slyly, and neither she nor Charlotte missed the deep blush evoked at Jane's intimation.

"Yes, fine, I will freely admit the more I get to know him, the more I like him," Elizabeth revealed. "Seeing him at Pemberley..." Elizabeth related their two-day break at Pemberley.

Jane filled Charlotte in on Miss Bingley's attempt to intrude on their lives, and the set down and cuts direct the harpy earned for her troubles. Just before the three sisters departed to return to Longbourn, Sir William returned home and greeted his friends' daughters as jovially as he always had. They appreciated the fact their change in rank and wealth seemed not to influence how he related to them, at least, and knew their father would appreciate it even more than they.

~~~~~~~~/~~~~~~~~

Mrs. Younge was afraid that her mistress would have an apoplexy, or worse, was completely insane. For two days straight the unhinged woman had railed against all things Bennet, but on the third day she had been strangely calm.

"Mrs. Younge, sit," Miss Bingley commanded, and the companion complied.

"Do you know any unsavoury people?" Miss Bingley asked as if it were an everyday question.

"I have known some in the past, Miss Bingley, why do you ask?" Mrs. Younge replied nervously.

"I want you to find some men for me. I will pay them more money than they could earn in many years," Miss Bingley stated, her placid tone of voice more eerie than any screech.

"Do you mind my asking why you need such men, Miss Bingley?" Mrs. Younge asked as calmly as she could.

"You saw how those Bennets responded to my gesture of friendship. They ruined me in society without cause, so I *will* have my revenge! I want men who will do whatever is needed to be done," Miss Bingley explained, her voice as calm as it was when she ordered a fresh pot of tea.

Mrs. Younge then searched the woman's eyes and saw the vacant detachment within. She was no expert, but she surmised something had snapped in the lady's head, and she would have to seek help from the very last man in the world who would want to see her. "I do know where some such men are to be found, Miss Bingley. I will leave now and be back this afternoon or early this evening, depending on where I find them," Mrs. Younge spoke as her very mind raced. Miss Bingley waved her away with an imperious flick of her wrist, needing this next part of her plan to begin so she could have her justifiable revenge.

~~~~~~~/~~~~~~~

Mrs. Younge was scared, as scared as she had ever been, when the hackney dropped her off outside Darcy House on Grosvenor square. It was the only option; and seeing Miss Darcy in the carriage proved there was some connection between the objects of her mistress' madness and the young lady. If nothing else, Mr. Darcy would at least be able to direct her to the Bennets' house. She took a deep breath and knocked on the front door, which was opened by the butler, Killion.

"Yes, *madam*," Killion words dripped with disdain when he recognised their little miss's former companion.

"Mr. Killion, I know I am the last person in the world Mr. Darcy wishes to see, but I swear to you it is a matter of life and death, and not my own," Mrs. Younge pleaded.

"*You* are not welcome here; please leave before I have the runners summoned," Killion started to close the door.

"**MR. DARCY!**" Mrs. Younge screamed as hard as her lungs

would allow.

"Killion! What the ▇▇▇ is going..." Darcy stopped mid-sentence as he recognised Mrs. Younge. "Why are you here?" He demanded hotly.

"Please, Mr. Darcy, I swear it is a matter of life or death. Just hear me out. If you do not believe me, then you will not have to throw me out. I will go willingly, or you may even have me arrested, whichever you choose, but please *listen*!" she beseeched.

His first inclination was to throw the woman out, but something in her tone told him it would be a critical error. "Follow me." Darcy ordered briskly.

Once in his study, he offered no refreshment. He raised his eyebrows, only waved an indication that Mrs. Younge should talk. "Did your sister tell you I saw her the other day?" Darcy nodded. "Did she inform you who my employer is?" He allowed it was so. "After I finally realised I was never anything but a pawn in Wickham's schemes, to be used and discarded as he needed, I sought honest employment. Before you say it, yes, I used false characters, but I was determined to do it right, to live an honest life and never return to the person I was."

"What you say sounds all well and good, but how is one to know when you are prevaricating or telling the truth," Darcy asked sceptically.

"Ask yourself, Mr. Darcy, why I would come here of all places to see you. Who would believe me less than any other in the world?" She challenged, and Darcy had to allow it was so. "The *only* reason I came here is that I know after seeing Miss Darcy with her friends that you have some connection to the Bennets," Mrs. Younge relayed.

Darcy sat up straight all of his senses wide awake at the mention of the Bennets. "What has this to do with the Bennets?"

"Your sister told you how Lady Jane, I believe that is name of the older sister, dealt with Miss Bingley?" Mrs. Younge asked.

"She did, what has this to do with why you are here?" He

pressed, needing to understand what she was trying to say.

Mrs. Younge detailed the whole tale of how Miss Bingley had acted for two days after the set down, finishing with the demands of herself that very morning which had, in the lady's opinion, left her no choice but to try and seek him, as she would not be party to whatever the insane woman was planning.

"Killion," Darcy barked out. "Mrs. Younge will scribe an address for you. Send four of my biggest footmen to watch that house. If Miss Bingley attempts to exit, they are to detain her and bring her here, both bound and gagged," Darcy instructed. Mrs. Younge wrote the address and handed it over to Mr. Killion, though she knew there was little to no chance of Miss Bingley exposing herself to ridicule by going out. "Killion, have my carriage made ready! You are coming with me, Mrs. Younge." It was not a request.

~~~~~~~/~~~~~~~

Having been inducted into the House of Lords the day before, Bennet was completing the last of the business he needed to address before his departure, scheduled for the early hours on the morrow, when the Bedford House butler announced Mr. Darcy and a Mrs. Younge.

The Duke remembered the name from the Ramsgate affair, but he could not believe Darcy would bring to his house the very woman who had conspired against his sister. "Darcy," Bennet inclined his head as he sat behind his desk. "Please introduce your companion," he requested as he stood.

Darcy introduced Mrs. Younge. When the Duke looked at the younger man questioningly, Darcy nodded, sending the older man's eyebrows up as far as they would go in surprise, and Mrs. Younge saw the interplay between the men.

"You know of my despicable actions at Ramsgate, your Grace?" she asked evenly.

"I do. Why is this *lady* here with you, Darcy?" Bennet frowned, unable to fathom a reason, no matter how good his imagination was.

"Mrs. Younge was recently employed by one Miss Caroline Bingley," Darcy began. "She was present when Jane took the shrew to task and then cut her."

"I am aware," Bennet stated, still not clear what the woman was doing with Darcy in his study, or how the younger man could even tolerate being in her company.

"Mrs. Younge, please tell the Duke *everything* you told me," Darcy instructed. And Mrs. Younge did so. As she told her story, the Duke's look went from disbelief to murderous.

"What do you hope to gain by telling us this, Mrs. Younge? A reward?" the Duke bit out when she was done.

"Nothing, your Grace. I could not be party to anything illegal again. As it is, I regret ever helping Mr. Wickham, the guilt of it my constant companion. I could not sit by and allow an insane woman try to harm others," Mrs. Younge said evenly. She understood, given her past, the men in the study would be sceptical of her motives, but she hoped they would act despite the quarter from which the information was attained.

"What do you suggest, Darcy?" Bennet asked.

"We should have Mrs. Younge return with a doctor and some footmen dressed like brigands. Once the doctor hears what it is Miss Bingley is ordering, he will be able to commit her to Bedlam," Darcy suggested.

Bennet cogitated for a minute. "That is a sound plan, Darcy. You are willing to assist, and you expect nothing in return?" Bennet looked at Mrs. Younge and saw the deep relief and sincerity of her willingness in her mien.

"Yes, your Grace, I am," Mrs. Younge responded succinctly. "There is one thing I would ask of Mr. Darcy, but my help is not contingent on his granting my request."

"Ask," Darcy allowed.

"If your sister will hear it from me, I would like to apologise to her for my reprehensible actions against her. If you and any others wish to be present, I will understand, but I cannot but despise my own actions, more so when I saw the truth of the man I was being used by, but even before that I was

371

ashamed of myself." Mrs. Younge asked quietly.

"I will speak to my sister. If she allows it, I will agree," Darcy stated.

The Duke summoned the butler and asked him to request Dr. Bartholomew and three of the new footmen-guards join them. It was an unexpected luxury that Bedford House had a resident physician who cared for everyone in the household from the lowest scullery maid on up.

"Your Grace," the doctor bowed as he was followed in by three large men. Between the Duke and Darcy the task was explained to the men who departed with Mrs. Younge, after changing into old street clothes.

~~~~~~~/~~~~~~~

"You have done very well, Mrs. Younge," Miss Bingley cackled.

"Thank you, Miss Bingley. Explain exactly what you require to these men, and they will make sure you receive what you deserve," Mrs. Younge stated, the double meaning missed by Miss Bingley who had lost all ability to reason—not that she ever had any.

"You know the new Duke of Bedford," she spat out, and the doctor nodded without comment. "On the first of May, the one that ruined my life is to be married in the church at their former, insignificant estate of Longbourn, near the nowhere town of Meryton in Hertfordshire."

"What of it?" Bartholomew prodded.

"Once the bride is inside, I want all doors barred so no one may escape, then I want you to set fire to the church. After, I also want you to burn down their manor houses of Longbourn and Netherfield," Miss Bingley instructed, her blissfully maniacal look truly alarming the doctor.

"What of all of the other people who will die?" the doctor asked.

"I do not care. They all deserve to die for they stole what is mine!" she shrieked.

The doctor stood up. "I have heard more than enough,

Miss Bingley. I am Dr. Bartholomew, and I find you insane and hereby consign you to Bedlam." He nodded to two of the men, the third produced a straitjacket.

Before Miss Bingley realised it, she was secured and no amount of invectives or attempts to shake herself free made a difference. The doctor nodded to the third man who gagged the woman, and then the men carried her down to the waiting cart in front of the widow's house. "Miss Bingley is ill, hysterics it seems." Mrs. Younge informed the landlady. "She will not be renewing her rental after the two months are completed."

~~~~~~~/~~~~~~~

The doctor and Mrs. Younge returned to Bedford House to report the threat had been eliminated. After the doctor made his report, he vacated the office. "I understand there was close to ten thousand pounds of the woman's fortune remaining in the apartments. As you could have taken the money and simply disappeared, it shows your determination to change. Miss Bingley's money will be sent to her aunt in Scarborough. I understand she purchased a carriage; the cash value will be sent to her aunt as well. In recognition of the good deeds you have done without the expectation of reward I am gifting you ten thousand pounds and the carriage. After you speak to Miss Darcy, if she allows it, take the money and the carriage, and live a good life Mrs. Younge," the Duke granted. Mrs. Younge was rendered speechless! Once she regained her ability to speak, she thanked the Duke profusely and swore she would live an honest life.

The next day, before they departed for Hertfordshire, Georgiana Darcy, with William and the Duke of Bedford at her side, listened to Mrs. Younge apology, which was judged to be sincere, and forgiveness was granted. Mrs. Younge travelled from London to Fowey in Cornwall where her brother was a fisherman.

She used part of her windfall to buy a small structure she turned into a school for young ladies, regardless of social standing.

~~~~~~~/~~~~~~~

Some six weeks later, in New York, Bingley received a letter from his solicitor in Scarborough telling him of his sister's confinement to Bedlam. Neither Charles Bingley nor Louisa Hurst was overly surprised by the news.

VOL 2, CHAPTER 11

Darcy and Georgiana shared a coach with Bennet as the Darcy carriage followed behind. Their first stop was Netherfield Park, and the Darcys arrived just in time to be caught up in the whirlwind of preparation for the betrothal ball that would be held on the coming Monday, which was two days before the wedding.

The bride's grandmother was acting as hostess at Netherfield and was the driving force behind the organization of the ball, Lady Elaine, her daughter-in-law Jacqui, Lady Marie and Madeline Gardiner were her able and willing assistants. With the whirlwind of activity, Darcy was happy to join the men who were planning to fill their days with things that would ensure they were as far from the mayhem as they could reasonably escape.

Andrew was absent when Darcy sought him out to tell him about Miss Bingley's insane plan that had been thwarted. The gentlemen present informed Darcy that Andrew had ridden over to Longbourn to deliver the final copy of the marriage settlement.

Despite his absence, Darcy relayed the drama that had played out the previous day in London. "Even I did not imagine her quite so bad," Richard shook his head. "And Mrs. Younge was the one who informed you? Wonders never cease."

"Miss Bingley is where she belongs and will never be able to hurt anyone, other than herself, again," Lord Matlock opined.

"What Miss Bingley wanted done is beyond insane!" Lord Jersey stated.

"From what Mrs. Younge told me, when Jane destroyed

the harpy's delusions so publicly, and having it end with multiple cuts direct, it pushed Miss Bingley over the edge of reason which led to her form such a maniacal plan," Darcy related.

"With all of the guards my brother had hired, even had she found someone willing to commit mass murder for her, they would not have succeeded," Viscount Westmore surmised. "However, it is preferable to have nipped it in the bud before that theory was tested."

"William, you are in time for a hunt this afternoon. I warn you, if you stand around looking as if you are in want of an occupation, you will be ordered into the line and find yourself helping with the ball preparations. If we had generals as effective as Aunt Sarah, the war with the little tyrant would have been won years ago," Richard quipped, his warning absolutely serious, as proven in the tone with which it was said.

"It is the hunt for me then," Darcy decided.

"Good decision, Nephew," Lord Matlock slapped him on the back. "What of Gigi?

"She was invited to join Elizabeth and Esther at Longbourn. When she is ready, I will escort her thither," Darcy replied.

"As she is my ward too, I will join you on your mission to escort Gigi," Richard volunteered. None doubted his ulterior motive for wanting to accompany his cousins, and Darcy only shot his cousin a wry look then beckoned him to come with, so they excused themselves to find Georgiana.

~~~~~~~/~~~~~~~

Once he had washed off the dirt from travelling almost twenty miles that morning, the first thing Bennet did was address the family, including Andrew and Charlotte, about Miss Bingley's insanity. "I knew she was bad, but I had not imagined her to be an insane criminal," Jane shook her head.

"It was not a case of good or bad, Jane, it was insanity, pure and simple," Bennet opined. "By the time she decided on this course of action, I do not believe she had the capacity to distinguish right from wrong any longer. Doctor Bartholomew opined she had been living in a delusional world of her own making for so long that when she was confronted with a reality that did not match her delusions, something inside of her broke and she fully descended into her insanity."

"At least she will be unable to cause any more mischief," Tom stated. He had arrived home from Oxford a few days after the end of the school year.

"She will *never* see the outside of that institution again, at least not while still living," Bennet stated categorically.

"William aided you in all of this?" Elizabeth asked softly.

"He accompanied Miss Bingley's companion and had the idea of having her disclose her plan to a doctor. Now, unless there are more questions, Andrew, shall we?" Bennet stood.

"If this is about the settlement, then I would like to be party to the meeting, Papa," Jane requested.

"I have no objection, do you Andrew?" Bennet asked.

"None, sir," Andrew replied emphatically, his arm out for Jane so he could escort her to her father's study.

As she watched them go, Elizabeth looked around again for Mr. Darcy and realized she missed seeing William. Not just seeing him, but also being in his particular company, their conversations, his eyes speaking to her alone, their debates, all of it. *'Oh my, am I falling in love with William?'* she asked herself. As if the question had conjured the man, he, Gigi, and Richard were announced.

"You are all most welcome," Priscilla intoned warmly. "Where is Ally?"

"She was tasked by her grandmother to help with decorating the ballroom before we departed," Richard informed the Duchess. His eyes had sought out Charlotte's as soon as he entered the drawing room, and as he spoke their eyes locked on one another. "She made the fatal error of making a comment about the decorations, and your mother happened to be within hearing when she did."

"Yes, my mother can be quite focused when she takes on a task like this. You can be thankful she will not be weighing each attendant to decide whether or not to issue a voucher," Priscilla quipped. When one's mother was a patroness of Almack's, she liked things just so.

"We must return to Netherfield in a little while," Darcy announced, "as the men are having a hunting party this afternoon. I understand my uncle invited gentlemen from the neighbourhood to join us."

"So this is how you men are escaping my mother's pressing you into service to assist with preparing for the ball," Priscilla laughed.

"I can neither confirm nor deny that conjecture," Richard grinned.

"Elizabeth, you look well," Darcy offered quietly as he sat down next to her.

"Thank you, William, you look well too," Elizabeth smiled coyly.

"Will you dance at the ball?" William asked.

"I will. When Grandmama suggested a ball, at first Mama said no. Lady Rose opined that as it will be a month to the day since Uncle Sed passed, and he wanted us to celebrate life rather than to mourn death, she said he would have wholeheartedly approved of it, so it is as you see now," Elizabeth explained.

"In that case, may I have the first set, if it is not already taken?" Darcy asked hopefully.

"It is yours, William," Elizabeth blushed with pleasure.

"Is the supper set open?" He asked, his voice thick with emotion. His heart thudded when Elizabeth nodded. "Then I request that one as well."

"I am happy to grant you the supper set, William," Elizabeth responded softly.

Darcy decided not to push his luck with a third request for the final set. The last thing he wanted to do was pressure her before she was ready to make what was tantamount to a public declaration. For her part, Elizabeth was hoping he would ask for the final set, almost hinted her final too was still open, but understood why he did not.

"It pleases me to see you in half mourning, Charlotte," Richard leaned in towards the lady he loved.

"No more than I am to be out of full mourning. Less than three weeks, and I will be done with the show of mourning him completely," Charlotte said boldly, as she looked into Richard's eyes.

Richard received her message with pleasure. "Am I correct that you will not attend the ball?" he asked, hoping he was wrong.

"I will attend," Charlotte promised. "However, I will not be dancing."

"It is better than I had originally hoped, so if you intend to be present for supper, may I claim a seat next to you for the meal?" Richard asked, his eyes locked on hers as it would show her friends and family she was choosing him to move on with.

"You may," Charlotte responded with pleasure.

~~~~~~~/~~~~~~~

"This is far too generous, Andrew. And you are also leaving my dowry under my control," Jane remonstrated after she read the settlement, astonished he was settling one hundred thousand pounds on her.

"I suggest a compromise," Bennet interjected between the two. "The interest and dividends from the dowry will be between ten and twelve thousand pounds per annum. Jane's pin money can be drawn from that amount, the rest can be used in any way you both see fit. If Jane wants to add fifty thousand from her dowry to each of your daughters, and, or a second and third son's legacy, I would not fight her on it if I were you. Surely by now you know there is no winning against a determined Bennet woman?" Bennet asked sardonically.

"It shall be as you say, as long as Jane agrees and understands I will not change the amount I am settling on her," Andrew capitulated.

"Then I too agree," Jane said with a sweet smile as she had gotten exactly what she had wanted. How Andrew loved this pillar of strength he was marrying in but a few days.

"Bennet, will you join us for the hunt?" Andrew verified.

"I think I will; we will leave the ladies to speak of fashion and lace," Bennet grinned.

"Papa!" Jane admonished playfully.

"Let us go collect that wayward brother and cousin of mine," Andrew stood.

"Give me half an hour to change," Bennet requested.

"We will wait for you in the study," Andrew suggested hopefully. He and Jane had managed to steal a rare moment of privacy since their betrothal, but far fewer than either wanted.

"Not a chance," Bennet replied with a guffaw. "Good try though. I will join you, William, and Richard in the *drawing room* where you are going now." Bennet shooed the couple out of his study before pulling the door shut.

~~~~~~~/~~~~~~~

The night of the betrothal ball at Netherfield was a warm, clear night. It was the first time most in the neighbourhood would be able to see the new Duke since his return the day before. It was no surprise to the hosts that the receiving line moved slowly, as each of his neighbours who had known him for many years wanted a welcoming word with his and her Grace before they moved into the ball room. The line had eight people in it. The soon-to-be married couple and their parents made six, and Lord and Lady Jersey rounded out the number as the hosts of the event.

Darcy had decided, as Esther and her cousin Ally were considered *out* locally, he would apply same rules to his sister. The three were to dance with family, soon-to-be family, and pre-approved friends only. Darcy smiled as he remembered how pleased Gigi had been at the news. He then remembered her shy pleasure as Tom Bennet had requested and been granted the supper set with her. After learning that her first set had been claimed by Richard, no one could really blame him. The three younger ladies were allowed to stay until the end of the ball unless they felt too tired and decided to withdraw earlier.

While he was waiting for the orchestra to signal the start of the dancing Darcy also remembered with pleasure when the Bennets had arrived earlier to join those residing at Netherfield in an aperitif and to toast the soon-to-be wed couple.

He had never seen Elizabeth looking more beautiful than she did when she walked into the drawing room. Her wavy, chestnut curls were piled high on her head, though a few shorter, teasing curls fell along her neck and cheek. Her gown was hunter-green, and she had a diamond necklace with a large emerald centrepiece which rested over the swell of her breasts. Earbobs of two emeralds and two diamonds, each one dangling lower than the one before it, completed her ensemble. The total effect made her eyes all the more green, and oh so beautiful. He very much desired to get lost in those fine eyes for the rest of his life.

Then she smiled at him—a smile only for him—and he had felt his heart accelerate in his chest until he was sure that every-one in the room could hear the deafening pounding he heard in his ears.

"You are so much more than tolerable enough to tempt me," *he whispered down at her when he finally was close enough to be able to, hoping she appreciated that she was the one teaching him how to laugh at himself.*

"You look far more than tolerable yourself, William," *she had answered with arched eyebrow.*

His blood raced as he remembered how warm Elizabeth had been toward him since his arrival in the neighbourhood. Darcy greeted his Aunt Catherine and Cousin Anne as he made a circuit of the room to expend some nervous energy while waiting for the first set.

Now that there was no more illusion to the non-existent betrothal between him and Anne, coupled with her general improvement in the way she behaved around others, it was pleasant to spend time with his mother's only sister. Even better was that Darcy and Anne could enjoy their natural cousinly affection without Lady Catherine's presumptions. He had asked Anne for a dance, and was saddened when she had demurred, telling him dancing would be too fatiguing for her.

As soon as Darcy noted the members of the receiving line entering the ballroom, he made a beeline for Elizabeth to claim her for the first dance. "William," she greeted him with a curtsey to his bow.

"It is time to line up," William offered Elizabeth his arm which she gladly accepted. As they walked toward the forming line, both noticed the moment that Tom offered Gigi his arm and her allowing him to lead her to the line. Richard had claimed a *conflict* in his requests to dance and so he had asked Tom to take his place for the first. Richard instead danced the first with Maria Lucas, hoping to get to know the young woman better as she would be his younger sister as well, if his most important goal in life was realised.

Darcy and Elizabeth were four or five couples from the head of the line. Jane and Andrew were the first couple, the Duke and his Duchess second, the Earl and his Countess third. "Does not my sister look like an angel?" Elizabeth inclined her head towards her older sister.

"She is a pretty woman, Elizabeth, but in my eyes, she is nothing compared to you," he answered sincerely. He was not unhappy at the blush his response caused. He was not sure of her feelings for him—yet, but he was sure they had progressed beyond friendship.

"Our dance in this ballroom was not nearly as pleasurable last time as it is now," Elizabeth admitted.

"Yes, I must admit not talking about any *unpleasant* subjects while we dance improves the atmosphere significantly," Darcy teased.

"Do not remind me of how I tried to provoke you when we last danced here," she beseeched. "Hopefully, the misunderstandings are behind us permanently."

There were several members of the *Ton* present, a necessary evil. As much as Bennet would have preferred, his mother-in-law pointed out the impossibility of not including any others from London. Those who had designs on Lady Elizabeth or Lord Birchington for one of their sons or daughters, were not happy to see the intimacy between the Bennet and Darcy siblings. Though even they had to admit it was reasonable with Lady Jane marrying the Matlock heir it was inevitable the Darcys would be in the Bennets' company quite often.

"Tom and Gigi dance well together," Elizabeth noted. "As do your younger sister and her cousin Robert Jamison," Darcy returned. Elizabeth pointed out Robert's parents to Darcy, William and Yvette Jamison, and introduced them after she explained the connection before the dancing commenced.

The two lapsed into companionable silence, not needing to say more than they were wordlessly communicating with every touch. At the end of the first set, Darcy returned Elizabeth to her grandparents as her parents had been waylaid on their way back from their dance. Darcy felt bereft of her company, but he had, unlike the first two dances he attended in Meryton, a partner for almost every set, though he had resolutely asked no one to dance the final set with him. He hoped that in the future he would only dance the final set with Elizabeth.

~~~~~~~/~~~~~~~

After the enjoyable supper set, Darcy and Elizabeth sat at a table with Jane and Andrew, Gigi and Tom, Charlotte and Richard, and Robert and Esther. "Just two more days," Jane said to no one in particular.

"I am counting the hours as well, my love," Andrew replied quietly to his betrothed. "Once we are married, I will be able to receive your sweet kisses whenever we desire them."

Charlotte gave Elizabeth a knowing look when she saw Jane turn crimson. "Hmmm, I wonder what Andrew said to produce that reaction In Jane," Richard asked Charlotte quietly.

"Richard Fitzwilliam!" Charlotte exclaimed softly to Richard. "You will not embarrass my friend!"

"You are killing me, woman. I surrender." He groaned under his breath, she smiled to herself at the hearing if it.

"You will be at Longfield Meadows with the Bennets when your mourning period ends, will you not?" Richard verified.

"I will be with the Bennets, Richard, as will my sister Maria," Charlotte confirmed. His relief gave her hope her time of waiting to make a love match was not far in the future. Charlotte had told her mother her opinion, that her teachings on what to look for in matrimony were not correct, and she had further told her mother she would do whatever she could to make sure Maria knew that as well.

"I look forward to seeing you there—and out of mourning," Richard murmured, his knee casually resting against hers for the duration of the meal. Every now and again, just to keep him attuned with her preferences, she pressed hers against his, and was deeply relieved his did not give way but stayed steady for her to take strength from.

The second ball held at Netherfield Park in recent history was deemed the most enjoyable any had ever attended in the area.

~~~~~~~/~~~~~~~

The night before her daughter's wedding, Priscilla Bennet gave Jane *the talk*. Like her mother had with her, Priscilla explained what Jane could expect, and made sure her daughter understood it was not only her task to please her husband, but equally his to please her in the marital bed. She explained there would be some pain as her husband breeched her maidenly barrier and possibly some blood.

Jane, having lived on a working farm the whole of her life, had a good idea about the mechanics of the act, but found her mother's words comforting and pleasantly surprising as it went a little against doctrine. She never doubted it to be true, but her mother's confirmation the marital act was much enhanced when the couple was in love chased away her lingering anxiety all brides of a certain age are required to have.

"Do you have any more questions, my dearest Jane?" Priscilla asked when her talk was complete.

"No Mama, I do not, but I do want to thank you. For the

whole of my life you have treated me as a beloved daughter, not a stepdaughter. You could have treated me like the little cinder girl in *Cendrillon ou la petite pantoufle de verre* and been an evil stepmother of the ilk in the story. Yet you never, not for one instant, ever made me feel less than a child of your body, Mama." Tears of gratitude and happiness pooled as she looked up at her mother.

"The minute I married your father, you were my daughter. Perhaps, as I met you the day I met him, it may be it was you I loved first, though we will not exactly tell him that. I had to keep him to have you." She teased. "You were, and always will be, my first child. I am so proud of you, Jane. I know you will be happy with Andrew; and the love you two share would make it impossible to be otherwise!" Priscilla hugged her daughter tightly as she kissed her forehead.

They hugged for a long while and then Priscilla kissed her daughter again and left her chambers. Her firstborn was leaving the house in but a matter of hours.

<center>~~~~~~~/~~~~~~~</center>

Jane was extremely close to Elizabeth, but as she was also close to Esther and did not want her to feel left out, after asking Elizabeth who thought it was a capital idea, she had requested her younger sister also stand up with her. Esther never would have felt slighted and would have understood but being so close to Jane for her wedding was a request she was grateful to have the chance to accept.

Little May Gardiner was first up the aisle at the Longbourn church, dropping her rose petals as she had been told to do and rehearsed not a few times. She was followed by her brother Peter, who had a satin pillow with two rings on it. The real ones were secure in Richard's inside jacket pocket as he waited next to the altar with his brother.

Esther walked up the aisle next followed by Elizabeth. The vestibule doors closed, and the clergyman lifted his hands to signal the congregation to stand. The doors opened again, and Jane entered on her father's arm. Her gown was simple, there was hardly any lace, but oh so elegant and perfect for Jane. Near the altar, Bennet halted and lifted his daughter's fine gossamer veil and kissed her cheek. "You will be a very happy woman, Jane," he told her, his voice thick with emotion.

Bennet placed his firstborn's hand on Andrew's arm and joined his family in their pew as Andrew led his bride up to the altar until they were kneeling before the rector. "Dearly beloved..." the clergyman intoned the rituals of the Church of England from the Book of Common Prayer.

When he asked if anyone objected, there was silence and then each repeated the vows to one another. Andrew placed a gold wedding band on Jane's ring finger and then, bucking tradition, Jane did the same for Andrew.

Once the final benedictions were made, Andrew and Lady Jane Fitzwilliam, Viscount and Viscountess Hilldale, were presented to the congregation amidst raucous cheers. Jane and her husband accompanied by her two sisters and his brother signed the register in the vestry where Jane signed Bennet as her family name for the last time.

After hugs and kisses, Jane's sisters and Andrew's brother left and closed the door. For a few minutes, the couple took advantage of the chance to share kisses which were not forbidden, nor of too short a duration to be satisfying as all had been during their betrothal.

~~~~~~~/~~~~~~~

"Viscount and Viscountess Hilldale," Hill announced, causing a round of applause and calls of congratulations as the couple entered Longbourn's ball room where the wedding breakfast was being held. Jane and Andrew made the rounds, making sure to stop and accept wishes from each guest, saying a few words of thanks for joining them in witness of their special day.

Between Elizabeth, Georgiana, Darcy, and Richard, they made sure the newlyweds sat down from time to time and actually had something to eat and drink. For good measure, Lady Elaine had them sit with her and her husband and also plied them with food and drink. After about three hours, and with Elizabeth at her side, Jane made her way to her former bedchamber.

"I am going to miss you so much Jane. It is easier for me as my new brother is such a good man. He really deserves you, sister," Elizabeth hugged her sister with all of her might.

"Lizzy, I love you, but you have to allow me to breathe," Jane teased. "Hilldale is not far from Longfield Meadows, and besides, I suspect it will be sooner rather than later that you will be living even closer to me," Jane intimated slyly as she changed.

"I think I am falling in love with him, Jane. How did you know Andrew was the only man for you?" Elizabeth asked.

"When I thought of the future, I tried to see mine without Andrew in it, and I was not happy with *any* version in which he was not the most integral part. It was then I knew beyond all doubt. If you can see yourself being happy without William in your future, then he is not the man for you," Jane imparted the wisdom she had gained and how she had known she had truly fallen in love with the man she wanted to share her future with.

"You have given me much to think on, oh wise one!" Elizabeth gave her sister a playful bow.

Not long after, the family was standing in the drive waving at the retreating form of the large comfortable coach and six horses the bride's parents had gifted the newlyweds. When the conveyance and outriders were out of sight, the family drifted back into the house to re-join the revellers.

VOL 2, CHAPTER 12

"This is your new home?" Maria almost squeaked. "It looks like a palace! How am I ever to find my way around this gigantic mansion?" Not only had Maria Lucas never seen a house the size of the one they were approaching, but she had never before imagined one close to this size.

"When we were first here, it took us a few days to find our way around Maria," Elizabeth laughed. She was in one of the coaches with Charlotte, Esther, Maria, and Georgiana. Much to her delight, William had accepted an invitation to join the Bennets on this second trip to their new home. He was riding in the front coach with her parents, Lady Rose, and her brothers. "But it is only a house, Maria. A large one to be sure, but a house nonetheless."

"I thought I would get lost when we were here for the late Duke's funeral," Georgiana shared, "but there are footmen on duty in each hall, and the maids are often about so at worst is you would have to ask one of them for direction."

"Besides, you are sharing a suite with me," Esther informed her friend.

"I am used to sharing a chamber with Charlotte before she married, so it will not be a hardship," Maria misunderstood.

"Maria, Esther said a *suite* not a bedchamber," Charlotte explained. "If it is anything like Rosings Park, then there are two bedchambers with a shared sitting room."

"Charlotte is correct," Elizabeth confirmed. "My suitemate will be Gigi, and Charlotte will have a single suite across the hall from us."

These explanations did little to quell Maria's feeling of

awe as the coaches came to a halt under the massive portico. She believed it enough when there was a cadre of outriders with them, but as soon as the carriage came to a stop, a swarm of footmen all wearing the same green and gold livery seemed to materialise from nowhere.

"It is a *little* larger than Longbourn," Charlotte noted quietly to Elizabeth.

"The *ballroom* has more space than Longbourn," Elizabeth whispered back, enjoying that her friend's mouth fell open from the shock. "I, all of us, were as much in awe the first time we arrived here so you are not alone in your feelings, Charlotte."

Mrs. Sherman and Mr. Beckman had the servants lined up neatly when the Duke and Duchess led the way into the entrance hall. After a brief word of thanks from the mistress, the servants were dismissed to return to their duties. The Bennets led their guests up to the family floor where all would find their chambers as well as warm water in order to wash the dust of the road off and change.

Elizabeth indicated a door opposite her suite. "That is your suite, Charlotte." She smiled at her friend, knowing she would love it.

Charlotte entered and was struck dumb. The *sitting room* was two to three times what her bedchamber had been in Hunsford! She walked through a door that led to the bedchamber to discover a bathing room to one side. Additionally, there was a dressing room and a walk-in closet that was about the size of her and Maria's shared bedchamber at Lucas Lodge. Her suite was as large as *all* of the combined bedchambers at Lucas Lodge alone. She fully understood why the Bennets had been awed the first time they visited their new estate.

Until the moment she saw the manor house at the Bennets' new estate, and now her suite, she thought she understood how much wealth her friends had. What Charlotte had seen convinced her that her estimate was but a drop in the ocean.

~~~~~~~/~~~~~~~

After the midday meal, the younger residents chose to take a walk in the expansive rose garden. Mark, to his chagrin, was sent to the school room. The walking party consisted of five ladies plus Mr. Darcy and Mrs. Ponsonby trailing behind.

The security was somewhat relaxed at Longfield Meadows, at least from the residents' standpoint. Mr. Burnett had met with the two former lieutenants, Biggs and Johns, to set up a schedule of patrols. The latter two were in charge of the Bennet children's personal security, so they had the latitude to decide how many men would accompany them when they walked or rode. On this occasion, Biggs followed behind the companion with two other footmen-guards, one either side of the group of walkers.

Charlotte had been walking next to Elizabeth while the three younger girls walked ahead of them. When she saw Mr. Darcy approach, Charlotte winked at Elizabeth then sped up to join the group of girls. "I did not mean to disturb your friend," Darcy started to apologise.

"You did nothing, William. Charlotte chose to join the others on her own volition," Elizabeth absolved him. "Believe me when I tell you my friend is not one to be cowed into doing anything she does not desire."

"It pleases me to know that." Darcy responded. "When we were at Pemberley, I told you about the place I go to for deep contemplation."

"You did, and I enjoyed learning more about you," Elizabeth stated shyly.

"May I ask you the same?" He asked expectantly and she nodded. "Do you have a special spot?"

"Oakham Mount," Elizabeth related simply.

"I heard of it when in Hertfordshire the first time, when I...well yes, we have agreed to leave the past where it belongs. I never had the occasion to go to the summit of the hill, but I did see it on occasion when I was riding," Darcy related.

"It was my place of solitude. I suppose it will be still when we are in residence at Longbourn, which will be far less now we have all this," Elizabeth sighed as she made a wide sweep of her hand.

"You will miss Longbourn, I think," Darcy empathised as he changed the subject slightly.

"I will. It was my home, a home I have loved, for over twenty years. It is a fundamental truth that a lady's lot in life is to leave the home of her childhood and follow her husband to his home. I never expected to be leaving the old neighbourhood before that point," Elizabeth shared wistfully.

The last thing Darcy wanted was to make Elizabeth sad. "Tell me what Oakham Mount was to you." He deftly redirected her to the original question.

"It was the one place where I found true solitude. As you know, even before all of this, my father and mother would not allow us to venture out of the house unaccompanied." Darcy nodded. "Whoever my escort was when I walked to Oakham mount waited on a bench about halfway up, allowing me to gain the summit on my own. I had my father's permission for that compromise," Elizabeth remembered. "Many a day in the warmer months, and sometimes even in the wintertime, I would watch the sun rise. When it peaks over the horizon, it reaffirms for me that, no matter how dark things may get, the sun will always rise in the east again."

"It has been many a time that I ride up the bridle path to watch the sun rise over the hill behind the house and then the magnificence as the fingers of light hit the Peaks. On a clear day, there is nothing more beautiful—in nature," Darcy clarified quietly, his gaze focused on her profile as he said the last, leaving her in no doubt of his meaning. "Wait until you see the sun set over the Peaks, that is a sight to behold."

"The sunrises and sunsets were beautiful, but it was also the place I found I could contemplate in peace and quiet aside from an occasional birds' song, which never disturbed my reverie. When I was younger, well, not so *very* much younger, I would climb the old oak on the summit and sit in its welcoming branches. If I am not using the time to think, I have been known to read and rest in the welcoming branches on occasion."

"Does your mother approve of your penchant to climb trees?" he chuckled.

"She did when I was younger but assumes I grew out of the habit. I just never disabused her of the notion," Elizabeth smiled slyly. "If she ever specifically asked, I would be forthcoming."

Both revelled in the fact things had become so easy between themselves.

"Knowing your mother's perspicacity, do you honestly believe she is not aware of her daughter's penchants?" Darcy countered.

"I suppose you have the right of it, little gets by my mother's notice!" Elizabeth owned.

"To me it seems like strong women are the rule rather than the exception in your family," Darcy observed.

"That does not frighten you, William?" Elizabeth asked directly.

"Not at all. Like Andrew, I want a women who has her own opinions and is willing to defend them, regardless of my own. I am looking for a partner, not a wilting flower or a puppet with no mind of her own," Darcy stated firmly. "And if she happens to improve her mind by extensive reading, so much the better."

Elizabeth laughed, in no doubt of who that comment was aimed at and appreciated the multiple insinuations during their walk. Her conversation with Jane had caused her to do much soul searching. The more she asked herself about the future and if she could see one without William in it, the more resounding the answer 'no' echoed in her heart. Did this mean she was in love with William? It was not a question she was quite willing to answer just yet.

All too soon, the walkers turned back toward the manor house, as for the last pair, they would have been happy if the walk had been hours longer.

~~~~~~~/~~~~~~~

Jane and Andrew were aboard *The Rose,* the personal vessel which had been inherited along with the Dennington Lines. She was as large as a frigate and sailed with two escort ships, both the equivalent of fully armed frigates.

They were sailing from London to Dublin, Ireland where they would stay for ten days before sailing to Liverpool. Their next destination was the Lake District and Lake Vista House that belonged to the Fitzwilliams. After another ten days there, they would first visit Longfield Meadows and then Snowhaven on their way to Hilldale.

If he had his way, Andrew would have taken Jane to the Continent to see Paris and Florence, mayhap even Venice. Unfortunately, the little problem, otherwise known as the dictator Napoleon Bonaparte, had forced him to wait on that intention. Andrew was sure it was only a matter of time before Wellington brought the Corsican to heel, and then he would be able to show his wife the delights of Europe.

As the newlyweds stood on the quarterdeck looking to the west, they watched as the setting sun seemed to turn the sea a blood red and gave the optical illusion that the water was boiling at the point where the sun was sinking below the horizon. They could almost hear the sound of boiling water as the blood red sun disappeared below the horizon.

Jane was a most contented woman. Their first night as married man and woman had been at Hilldale House in London. The house was located in Hanover Square, at walking distance from St. George's Church. It had been everything Jane imagined and more, a lot more.

Andrew was a most attentive and generous lover who would do *anything* to give his wife pleasure before he took any, even if he did not succeed all of the time. It had not taken them long to find a rhythm where sometimes they would both reach their releases simultaneously. Once their passion for one another had been released, it was a genie neither wanted put back into its lamp.

That night at Hilldale House, Jane had screamed out in ecstasy as they joined multiple times. There had been a little pain as her mother told her there would be, but not enough to bother Jane and certainly nothing that would halt their activities. Andrew had wanted to stop in deference to his wife, but she had urged him to continue his thrusts.

Since the first night, that activity had been repeated multiple times, day and night, in their spacious owner's cabin. Jane's courses had begun a few days previously making them hunger for more of what only their loving could give, so even that did not stop them, with the exception of joining. They found other ways to pleasure one another, it was enjoyable in the extreme. Both were impatient for her indisposition to end so they could commence joining once again. For his part, Andrew had suspected his Jane had hidden depths of passion waiting to be released. To his everlasting joy, he had been proven correct! And to his pleasure alone, her passion had not simply been released, it was like the eruption of a long dormant volcano. Since their wedding night, neither had slept very much when they were alone, and neither repined their lack of sleep.

At dinner that night, the Captain informed them they would be arriving in Dublin with the tide in the morrow. When they retired, they vaguely considered just how much time they would spend actually exploring the city, promising each other and themselves they would see the city and all its splendour. If it did not happen to have occurred on this trip, that did not mean they did not eventually fulfil them.

~~~~~~~/~~~~~~~

Elizabeth was feeling bereft of William's company. He had been called to Pemberley to work with his steward on some issues two days previously, and it had not taken much convincing for his sister to remain with the Bennets.

Once Maria Lucas had calmed herself about the size and opulence of the Bennet's estate in general, and her bedchamber in particular, she had relaxed. And once she had, Maria grew closer to Georgiana. By the time Darcy needed to depart, the three younger girls were nearly inseparable.

They had pleaded their case to the Duchess, who had happily extended an invitation for Georgiana to remain at Longfield Meadows, and Darcy had nodded his approval as his excited sister had accepted the invitation with alacrity.

It was not just the blossoming friendship with the two younger girls that Darcy saw helping Gigi further come into her own, but the close relationship between his sister and Elizabeth which in itself was becoming more sisterly by the day. In a little more than a month, the three-month period of mourning would be complete, and Darcy would begin to try and gift his sister with having Elizabeth as a sister not just of the heart but indeed.

A sennight earlier, the Jamisons had arrived to visit for a month; the parents spent most of their time with the Bennet parents. The friendship between the Jamisons and the Bennets was more than a century in duration and had begun when Karen Jamison wed the first Tom Bennet all those years ago. The Jamison's daughter, Karen, had arrived eleven years after Robert when Will and Yvette had been convinced there would be no more children. At eight, Karen was too young for the older girls, so she spent a lot of time with Mark. They would soon have company as the Gardiners and their four children were scheduled to arrive within days, and as Karen was in between Lilly and May Gardiner in age, the nursery would be a lively place.

In order to give Tom some company, in addition to the Jamisons, the Bennets extended an invitation to the Lucases so that the three Lucas brothers would be present, also making a nice group of young men. Sir William and Lady Lucas and sons would arrive in three days.

Charlotte was happy to see the rest of her family again, but the date *she* was eyeing was five days away: the one and twentieth. It was the day her mourning period ended, and, she hoped, was the very day Richard Fitzwilliam was to arrive.

~~~~~~~/~~~~~~~

Mr. Chalmers, Pemberley's steward, was amused. He had never before seen his master so distracted. There was one-time last summer after the little miss returned from Ramsgate, but that had been driven by sadness. What he was seeing in Mr. Darcy now was quite the opposite.

Neither he nor any of the servants employed on the estate had ever seen Mr. Darcy so happy; he was downright ebullient! For the fourth or fifth time so far that morning, the steward heard: "Sorry, Chalmers, please repeat what you said, my mind was elsewhere." The steward was sure it had something to do with that Duke's daughter the master had been trying to impress when her family visited in April. He suspected Pemberley would not be without a mistress for too much longer.

Darcy knew his mind was fifty miles away in Yorkshire, but he was doing his best to complete the work that needed his attention. No matter how he tried, his mind kept returning to his conversation with Elizabeth the night before his departure.

"I will be sorry to see you go, William," she had said.

"Not as sorry as I am to need to go," he had returned.

"William, you know you are much more than just a friend to me do you not?" Elizabeth had asked boldly.

"That was my hope, Elizabeth, as you know how I feel about you, do you not?" he had asked.

"I have an idea that you hold me in tender regard," Elizabeth teased him by understating the obvious.

"It has been some time that I have loved you most ardently. I passed tender feelings some time ago," he said, trying to lighten the moment some in case it was needed.

"Oh! I will be honest, William; your feelings are NOT unwelcome. I will tell you I most definitely have tender feelings for you, but I am not ready to say more—yet. When you ask me the question I believe you want to, I will have an answer ready for you, one I dare say you will like." She had looked at him with meaning and Darcy's heart had taken wings, soaring high above the highest cloud.

As he sat atop Zeus surveying the crops that would be harvested in the autumn, Darcy knew Elizabeth had been telling him that when he asked for a courtship she would agree; mayhap she would not demure if he requested a betrothal!

~~~~~~~/~~~~~~~

When the Lucases arrived at the Bennet's new primary estate in a Bennet travelling coach, the reaction of the five was quite similar to what Maria's and the Bennets themselves had been. The normally ebullient Sir William had been silent as he, his wife, and sons were shown to their chambers on a guest floor. They met in the parent's suite's sitting room before joining the rest of those in residence in one of the many drawing rooms.

"Good Lord, William, I have never, in my wildest imaginings, conjured such a house!" Lady Lucas began.

"Nick and I are sharing a suite, not a bedchamber, but a suite! We each have our own bedchamber. There was a man waiting in mine. He is to be my valet while I am here!" John Lucas added with awe.

"I have a lady's maid, John; I believe each of you have a man working with you. I know your father has," Lady Lucas shared, "Do you realise that we could place all of Lucas Lodge in two or three of these suites?"

Just as the changes to their life had been realised by the Bennets, and brought home to Charlotte, the realisation fully hit the Lucases at that moment. With the help of two different footmen, the Lucases found their way to the drawing room. In addition to the Bennets, the Lucases were happy to see the Gardiners and the Jamisons were also present, all of whom they were already acquainted with. They also recognised Miss Darcy who they had met at Jane's wedding.

Just as Sir William was casting about to see if Mr. Darcy was present, Elizabeth stood. "William," She was looking past the Lucases with the biggest smile, her eyes shining with pleasure, "you have returned."

The Duke and Duchess shared knowing looks. It seemed

that their middle daughter's feelings for Mr. Darcy were quite the opposite of what they had been some months ago!

VOL 2, CHAPTER 13

Richard's senses were heightened, almost like they were when he went into battle, as his horse approached Longfield Meadows. Charlotte's mourning period was over. He knew she had made an imprudent choice in her first husband, but all he cared about was whether or not she loved him as much as he loved her. He would not, could not, rejoice the death of another, but neither would he find remorse in this part of the Almighty's plan.

If his suit were successful, he knew she would not be a maid as she had been married before and was now a widow. He had always found this somewhat hypocritical: a man was lauded for his *prowess* regardless of his marital state, but if a woman did anything before she was married, she was ruined, to be shunned! It was one of the patriarchal society's arbitrary rules for which he cared not a wit.

Richard was enjoying running his estate, Brookfield, and he especially enjoyed working with the horses in the horse breeding program. In the space of six months he had gone from *poor* soldier to estate owner. If that were not enough, Anne had named him the heir of Rosings Park!

Richard handed the care of his horse to a groom while a footman took his valise with a change of clothing to his chambers. His carriage with his man and trunk were about an hour or two behind him. His first stop was to greet Bennet in his study, where he informed his host that his parents would arrive a day later, as they wanted to be present to welcome Jane and Andrew when they arrived at Longfield Meadows.

Richard made his way to his suite, the same one he occupied last time he was at the estate, if for a much more sombre reason. When he looked at his pillow, he saw a handkerchief he thought he lost at Broadhurst decorated neatly with his initials in embroidery. He was sure there was only one person who would place it there for him.

"Welcome, Richard," the Duchess welcomed her daughter's new brother with a kiss on the cheek. "I trust that you are well, as is everything at Brookfield?"

"Yes, thank you, all is well Aunt Priscilla," Richard answered in an absent-minded fashion, his eyes locked to Charlotte's. After greeting everyone else, Richard sat himself down in an armchair right next to the corner of the settee where Charlotte was sitting.

"You are looking well, Richard," Charlotte opened softly, aware her mother was watching intently. "I especially like your *new* handkerchief sticking out of your pocket!"

"As are you, Charlotte. I am pleased to see you are no longer wearing mourning garb," Richard stated. "Oh, enough! We have waited far too long as it is!" Richard exclaimed. "We are neither of us children, I request a private audience with you. I assume as you are a widow who places token in men's bedchambers I need no one's permission but yours?"

"That is a safe assumption, Richard, and I would very much like to hear what you have to say. Allow me a short while, for I would like to at least inform my parents." Charlotte stood and crossed the drawing room to where her parents were sitting near Bennet and Priscilla.

Richard watched her talk to Sir William and Lady Lucas but could not hear what was being said. Both her parents nodded, and Charlotte returned to Richard. "I assume since they are not having me run off, that means we may talk?" Richard asked.

"Indeed. Follow me, sir." Richard complied, relieved he would soon have this cycle of waiting broken as he was a man of action, and he needed *her* as parched man needed water.

Charlotte led Richard across the hall to what was considered a *small* drawing room but was far larger than the one at Longbourn. "Richard, I request you sit. There is something I must tell you before you speak. Will you allow me to say what I need to first?" Charlotte requested firmly.

"If that is what you desire, of course I will. Please, Charlotte, proceed." Richard sat, the initial wave of panic having settled, for she still called him Richard rather than reverted back to the distance of formality.

"Richard, you are the first and only man I have loved. Until I tell you what I need to now, and if you are still willing to have me after, I would feel like a fraud if we started our life together without your knowing all." With some trepidation Richard nodded for Charlotte to proceed. "My first husband never proposed to me, I, for all intents and purposes, proposed to him." Charlotte winced at his obvious shock and disbelief.

"Surely not!" Richard blurted out and then stopped himself. "I apologise, Charlotte, please."

"That you had a reaction was not unexpected; I only expected a louder and longer outburst," Charlotte smiled. "My mother is not a romantic, and for years she indoctrinated both of her daughters, especially me as I am almost twelve years Maria's senior, with her jaded view of matrimony." Charlotte proceeded to explain their shared former views on selecting a life partner. "By the time I met my late husband, I had heard for more years than I care to remember that I was on the shelf and how I was a burden to my father and would be one to my brother when my father was no longer with us," Charlotte explained. "When Collins articulated his need, by his patroness's order, to return to Hunsford married or at the very least betrothed, I offered myself as a solution for his problem and he as one to mine." Richard could not help scoffing at the fool Collins was and how ridiculous his aunt used to be.

"I had resigned myself to living with a man of mean understanding who thought anything his patroness said was gospel. Then I met you at Broadhurst, and no matter how I fought against it, I fell in love with you, and I hoped they were not, but suspected my feelings were returned. If there was to be suffering, I prayed it would all be on my side. It was then I learnt what I had been taught about matrimony was all wrong, and what I used to consider *silly romantic* ideals Jane and Eliza espoused were correct. No matter how my heart yearned to be with you, without dishonouring my family, myself, and causing a scandal, I could do nothing but marry him as planned." Charlotte paused. "In addition, I am worried that if I were to become with child early in our marriage those who know of my first marriage, granted that is the small society of Meryton, will question whether it is your child or his. Lastly, I am concerned there will be talk that will hurt your family even with me being an unknown within the *Ton*." Charlotte hung her head, sure after what she shared Richard would want nothing to do with her.

Richard placed a finger under her chin and gently lifted her head so he could look into her eyes as he spoke. "Firstly I do not give a damn, excuse me Charlotte, what anyone else thinks or says. I discussed my intention with my parents, and they know all regarding you and me, and I, we, have their unreserved support. In our world, what is open to most women is to marry and usually for a home and security. It is a rare case that ladies are as wealthy as the Bennets or my cousins Gigi and Anne in order to afford not to marry if they choose, or only for love. I did fall in love with you at Broadhurst, Charlotte. I knew you were betrothed to another, but my heart overruled my head. The night before your wedding, I got foxed to try to dull the pain of knowing you would be another's wife, that he would be the father of your children." Richard stopped and realised he had omitted an important question. "You are not with child, are you? It will not change anything for me, but I would like to know."

"As far as I know, I am still a maid, so it would be a highly impossible," Charlotte admitted begrudgingly as she burned scarlet from the embarrassment of the disclosure. She decided as she had told him that much and seeing his incredulous look, she should explain that Mr. Collins had not only been lacking in mental acuity. She also informed him she had suffered her monthly indisposition every month since her late husband's death.

"In cases such as this, a good memory is unpardonable, let us only look forward," Richard stated firmly, then dropped to one knee. He was aware and appreciated she did not want to be called by the name Collins which reminded her of her great folly. "Charlotte, I am a simple ex-soldier and have never been good at making flowery speeches, so I tell you simply that I love you with all I am and will until I draw my final breath. Please grant me your hand and become my wife. Charlotte, please, marry *me*."

"Of course I will marry you, Richard. You have made me the happiest of women. My heart has been crying out for yours and yours heard and answered." Whatever else Charlotte was about to say was left unsaid as Richard captured her lips with his own.

Some ten minutes later there was a knock on the door, and after the third time which resulted in no response, Elizabeth opened the door slowly. It was only then the betrothed couple stepped back from one another. "This had better mean you are gifting me Charlotte as a sister, Brother dearest!" Elizabeth arched her eyebrow.

"Yes, Eliza, we are to be sisters! Richard proposed and I accepted him," Charlotte beamed.

"*You* allowed *him* to propose? That *is* progress Charlotte," Elizabeth teased as she hugged her brother-in-law and soon-to-be sister-in-law. "Have you two decided on a date yet?"

"We had not discussed it, but what think you, Charlotte? Your parents are here, the Bennets and the Darcys too. My parents arrive on the morrow, and Jane and Andrew a day or two after. We could apply for a common license and marry after my brother and Jane arrive," Richard suggested.

"I think that a fine idea, for the sooner I marry you the happier I will be. You are the *only* man I would agree to marry Richard. The added benefit is no one will ever have to use my first married name again," Charlotte agreed.

"Only one more time my love, when you sign the register," Richard stated as he kissed Charlotte's hand softly.

"My suggestion is we go break the news to Mama. She is the one that will have to plan for a wedding at the estate in a matter of days!" Elizabeth was amused at the wince both Charlotte and Richard had at the prospect of breaking the news to the Duchess.

~~~~~~~/~~~~~~~

Since his return from Pemberley, besides spending as much time as he could in Elizabeth's company and their on-going conversations, it had not escaped Darcy's notice Gigi and Tom seemed to gravitate toward one another. They would sit and talk for periods of time when his sister was not engaged in an activity with the other young ladies and Tom was not busy with his friends.

Two days previously, Darcy had knocked on Gigi's bed-chamber door in the morning before breaking their fasts.

"Gigi, I have noted that you and Tom seem to get along very well," Darcy had opened. *His sister blushed at the mention of their new cousin.*

"We only talk, William, and never without many others around us," Georgiana said defensively.

"Gigi, please do not misunderstand me. This is in no way censure, quite the opposite. I think Tom to be an exceptionally fine and honourable young man. You know he still has another year at Oxford, do you not?" Darcy had asked.

"Yes, I am well aware of that, William. We have discussed his time at university, and, yes, I am fully aware I am only sixteen and not out yet. If anything progresses between us, it will not be for some years. Tom plans to take a grand tour after Oxford. It is one of the subjects we have canvassed, as is where he would travel with the war precluding the Continent as a destination," Georgiana replied evenly.

"When did my baby sister grow up so much? It seems what I wanted to say is superfluous. I just did not want you to get your

hopes up and then have your heart broken," Darcy explained, relieved when she smiled at him.

"Your concern is heart-warming William, but remember, try as you may, you will not be able to protect me from every hurt, especially of the heart. I heard Uncle Thomas jest once that it is good for a young lady to be crossed in love at least once. It is not what I desire for myself, but there is always the possibility of unrequited love for any of us. Before you ask, I am not in love with Tom at this point, I simply enjoy his company and find him interesting to talk to. He never talks down to me and is respectful of my points of view, even when they disagree with his." Georgiana, it seemed, was far more mature and stronger than Darcy had given her the credit of being.

"In that case, Gigi, there is no more for me to say on this subject. Just know you may come to talk to me about anything, and you have Elizabeth to talk to for anything you feel uncomfortable addressing with your old, sometimes unwise, brother." Darcy had kissed his sister on the forehead.

"When will I have Elizabeth as a sister?" Georgiana asked teasingly.

"All in good time, Gigi, all in good time."

As Darcy remembered the conversation, he knew he would need to share with Richard their ward no longer needed as much protection as she had in the past, and the days of them trying to coddle her were over.

~~~~~~~/~~~~~~~

Although he knew it was not technically needed to request Charlotte's father's consent, Richard asked Elizabeth to ask Sir William and Lady Lucas to join them in the *small* drawing room so he could do just that. A happy consent and an effusive blessing for the union was granted by the beaming father. He was not blind, and no one could miss the happiness his daughter had displayed the instant Richard Fitzwilliam had walked into the drawing room earlier.

"I must apologise to both of you," Lady Lucas stated before the group returned to the other drawing room. "If it were not for my misguided advice, Charlotte would never have felt the need to marry her late husband."

"Mother, as I will be incandescently happy for the rest of my days, there is nothing to forgive, as long as you correct the advice you have given Maria," Charlotte's arched eyebrows proved her expectation, and her mother raised her hands in surrender. "I suggest we adopt some of the Bennet's philosophy to only remember the past…"

"As that remembrance gives you pleasure," Lady Lucas completed and hugged her daughter and soon to be son.

When the newly betrothed couple announced the news that surprised no one, there was a round of hearty congratulations and well wishes for their future felicity. "Have you decided on a date for your wedding yet?" Priscilla asked, a stifled noise causing her to glance at her second daughter, finding her trying to hide her amusement behind her hand. "Out with it, you two. How soon will you marry?" Pricilla asked, her arched eyebrow as powerful an expectation as Charlotte's.

"We were hoping a few days after Andrew and Jane arrive," Richard informed the Duchess sheepishly.

Priscilla turned to Lady Rose as they were still within the three-month mourning period for her late husband. "As the last event here was a sad one, I think a wedding is perfect. As it will only be us who are present with the rest of Richard's family, I see no reason to delay," Lady Rose granted.

"If that is the case, then I suppose we have less than a sennight to plan. What day are you thinking?" Priscilla asked the betrothed couple.

"Andrew and Jane should arrive no later than Tuesday, what say you to Thursday, the three and twentieth day of May?" Richard asked hopefully.

"You will hear no argument from me against any date to marry you, Richard," Charlotte smiled at him when she saw he was more directing the question toward herself.

"In that case, Sarah, I am able to return the favour you did for me in helping organise Jane's wedding while I was away from Longbourn," Priscilla told her friend. "Let us begin to plan." With that, the ladies followed the Duchess out of the drawing room to the mistress's study.

After they had departed, Richard leaned over to his cousin Darcy. "Your turn!" was all he whispered.

The balance of a month and few days until mourning for the late Duke was complete could not pass fast enough for Darcy.

~~~~~~~/~~~~~~~~

Richard's parents were effusive in their joy when they were informed that their second son had decided to marry. Lady Elaine was well aware her son had fallen in love with the then Miss Charlotte Lucas at Broadhurst, and like the principals, at the time, she believed it would be a case of unrequited love.

She had noticed something had changed between the two at Rosings Park after the corpulent rector had shuffled off the mortal coil, but she had not commented about it to any besides her husband, who until then had been blissfully unaware of his son's feelings for the late rector's wife. When Richard had canvassed the subject with them at Snowhaven, there had been no wavering in their support for Richard's decision.

They welcomed Charlotte as a daughter, and soon had gotten their way with her calling them Mother Elaine and Father Reggie. Lady Elaine was more than happy to be co-opted into the planning for the wedding. The younger group, however, found much to do outdoors so they would not be volunteered to assist with the preparations for the wedding.

Jane and Andrew arrived at Longfield Meadows the Monday before the wedding, neither overly surprised by the news about Charlotte and Richard. The only question the two had before their arrival was not if, but when. Jane had suggested Saturday, and he Monday. They had both slightly overshot.

The evening of their arrival after dinner, the newlyweds were plied with questions about their wedding trip and how they enjoyed their time on board *The Rose*. No one pushed them too much when they were short on details about the places they had visited.

"Jane, I have never seen you look happier," Elizabeth stated as she sat with her sister on a loveseat.

"How could I not feel overjoyed being married to my soul-mate?" Jane asked softly, looking across the room at her husband then again turned to her younger sister. "Did you answer the questions I gave you to ask of yourself, Lizzy?"

"Which questions…Oh," Elizabeth realised what Jane was asking. "Yes, Jane, I was able to ascertain the answers to the questions you advised me to ask myself."

"Well?" Jane pushed.

"I love him, Jane!" Elizabeth declared softly. "There is no version of my future I can imagine that does not include William in it. I was so blind in the beginning. Yes, his behaviour was atrocious, but now I know he is the best man for me. The *only* man for me!" Elizabeth informed her sister.

"Have you told William yet?" Jane asked.

"William told me he loves me before he returned to Pemberley for business some weeks ago. At that point I was not quite in love with him yet, but I shared I had tender feelings for him. While he was away, it struck me how much I missed seeing him and was finally able to acknowledge my true feelings for him to myself," Elizabeth shared softly so no other would be able to hear her declaration.

"Do you plan to tell William?" Jane asked as she held her younger sister's hands.

"If he raises the issue again. If he does not do so before the end of the mourning period for Uncle Sed, I will prod him a little after it passes," Elizabeth told Jane shyly.

"You will not propose to him like Charlotte did to her late husband, will you?" Jane teased.

"One never knows, Jane, one never knows. However, as William is not as obtuse as that man was, I have no doubt that he will not need any prompting to declare himself in July," Elizabeth assured her sister.

~~~~~~~/~~~~~~~

The rector in the adjacent town of Bedford, who held the Longfield Meadows living as well, issued the common licence on the Tuesday before the wedding. It was with little surprise to Lady Priscilla and others that it was Lady Lucas who cried the most at the happiness she gained as she witnessed her oldest daughter marry for love after said rector intoned the final benediction.

After signing the register and the short ride from the church to the manor house, the Honourable Mr. and Mrs. Fitzwilliam were announced by the butler as they joined those present in the cavernous ballroom were one corner had been set up for the wedding breakfast.

Elizabeth hugged her newest sister tightly. "At last we are sisters in deed and not just of the heart. You and Richard could not look happier, Charlotte," Elizabeth gushed.

"As I have thought of you as my sister for so long it is not new, you will understand when I say I am *far* happier to be Richard's wife than your sister," Charlotte quipped.

"One would have to be blind not to be able to see how happy my *little* brother is with you as his wife, Charlotte," Andrew stated as he kissed his new sister on her cheek. "I thank you for adding three younger brothers and a little sister to the family."

"Now that we are related in truth, I assume you will not object if I help a little would you, Lucas?" Bennet asked his long-time friend.

"What do you mean, your G…Bennet?" Sir William asked suspiciously.

"We cannot have a duke's cousin enter society with five hundred pounds as a dowry, can we?" Bennet ribbed.

"Bennet what are you about to do?" Sir William looked at his long-time friend, who was now also family.

"Unless you object, I have set up funds with Gardiner for Maria and your two younger sons of twenty thousand pounds each," Bennet stated matter-of-factually.

"You know I could never allow you to do that, Bennet," Sir William insisted.

"Will you allow your pride to sink your children's prospects?" Bennet challenged.

"I suppose when your put it like that," Sir William responded, the fight leaving him as quickly as it had gathered.

"Lucas, we have more wealth than Croesus. I know you do not expect anything but friendship, but Priscilla and I feel it is something we want to do to make sure all of your offspring have a good start in life," Bennet explained. "Charlotte too will receive the same. And for her I give you no choice as she is now, after all, my children's sister by marriage, but a daughter of the heart, which you always have known."

Sir William could not believe the generosity of his friend and relative. He started to suspect from where the scholarship funds that sent his three boys to Oxford came, but he decided not to ask and left well enough alone, thanking his friend with a long handshake, chuckling when Bennet winked at him as he disconnected. He was gratified that, in this moment, he saw the very Bennet he knew looking back at him.

Not long after the conversation between Sir William and the Duke, the new Mr. and Mrs. Fitzwilliam departed for the Brighton area for three weeks at Darcy's Seaview Cottage. That night, Charlotte's time of being a maiden came to a pleasurable end as she felt what it was to be loved by a true man and was loathe to let him out of her bed for the duration of the visit.

VOL 2, CHAPTER 14

July 1811

T he previous month plus had confirmed Elizabeth's love for Darcy a number of times over. As would be expected, he returned to Pemberley now and again to take care of issues that needed his attention, and to complete the plans for the autumn harvest with his steward. Whenever he was not present, Elizabeth felt as if a piece of her heart were missing.

Each time Darcy went to Pemberley, Georgiana remained at Longfield Meadows. Maria Lucas had departed with her family, but there were still three young ladies in residence as the Carringtons had arrived, bringing Ally with them. Not long after the Marquess and Marchioness arrived, the Earl and Countess of Jersey too joined the family in Yorkshire, though the Gardiners returned to Town days after the Lucas's departure.

The three-month mourning period for the late Duke had ended on the first day of July for all except his widow, who would only go into half mourning after a full year. With the younger generation out riding and the men on a bird shooting outing, Priscilla was in a family sitting room with her mother, Lady Rose, her sister, and Yvette Jamison.

"I would have to be blind to have missed the looks that pass between young William Darcy and our Lizzy," Lady Sarah observed. "Given their less than auspicious beginning, I would not have imagined such a thing."

"Once they got out of their own way, they started to get closer and closer, Mama. I believe it started when Lizzy was visiting at Hunsford and William apologised before he was aware of anything about us beyond what he knew in Hertford-shire," Priscilla stated.

"Do we know the state of my niece's feelings, Cilla?" Lady Marie enquired.

"That we do. She has confided in both Jane and me that she is very much in love with William," Priscilla replied.

"When will Mr. Darcy return to Longfield Meadows?" Yvette asked.

"Elizabeth informed me that Gigi was steadfast in her mission to let her know that William will arrive later today," Lady Rose reported with a smile.

"What news is there from Hilldale, Priscilla?" Lady Sarah changed the topic to her older granddaughter.

"In the one letter I received from Jane since her wedding, she seemed most contented," Lady Marie related.

"*That*, sister dearest, is an understatement. My eldest could not be happier if she tried to be. When they arrived here before Charlotte's and Richard's wedding, it was almost impossible to separate them one from the other. In each other they have found the perfect match," Priscilla opined.

"Speaking of Charlotte and Richard, how are they?" Lady Sarah asked, unable to help but do so at their very own love triumphing over all story which would be shared for many generations to come, she was certain.

"Lizzy told me they too sound deliriously happy based on the last letter she received from Brookfield." Priscilla considered her next words carefully. "I love my friend Sarah, Lady Lucas, but the ideas about matrimony and selecting one's life partner she imparted to Charlotte could have sentenced her daughter to a lifetime of misery."

"I do not want to sound too critical, but should she have not spent more time in mourning before marrying Richard in case she was with child?" Yvette asked carefully.

"Had her marriage been consummated, she would have," Priscilla stated blandly, if effectively closing that line of discussion. More than one in the family sitting room stared at her in surprise. Lady Pricilla smiled when Yvette's amazement grew as Lady Sarah expressed her pleasure of such a happy outcome for a most deserving couple.

~~~~~~~/~~~~~~~

The six in the riding party were allowing their mounts to trot after a lengthy gallop across some fields. The grooms, companions, and footmen-guards, while being vigilant, gave the six space, the riders themselves in sets of twos. The leading pair were Esther and Ally, followed by Tom and Georgiana, then were Lizzy and Robert.

"It seems I have been replaced as a favourite cousin," Robert quipped as he inclined his head toward the pair of riders ahead.

"And I thought I was Gigi's favourite Bennet. Tom has usurped my position," Elizabeth sighed dramatically as she placed the back of one hand on her forehead in playful exaggeration.

"I have never seen any of the fairer sex garner so much of Tom's attention," Robert observed.

"*If* anything serious develops, it will be in a number of years," Elizabeth remarked, and Robert could only agree. "Besides, I see Ally took your place next to Esther!" Robert had the decency to blush.

Just then the riders all halted and looked behind them as they heard the sound of galloping hooves. Elizabeth watched both Biggs and Johns for their direction, relieved when they relaxed as they identified the horse and rider. Elizabeth's heart quickened considerably when she too saw Zeus galloping toward them, his master the only man who could make it do so.

Robert gave his horse's flanks a kick and surged ahead to join Esther and Ally as Darcy slowed his horse and took up station next to Mercury and Elizabeth. "William!" Elizabeth exclaimed with obvious pleasure.

"Hello, Elizabeth, I trust you are well," Darcy returned. The pleasure of seeing the way her green eyes were locked onto his made his heart race.

"I am well, and all the better for seeing you, William," Elizabeth stated meaningfully. "How did you know where to find us?" she asked before he could react to her forward statement.

"When I arrived at the stables, I noticed Mercury and other horses were not in their stalls, so I asked the stable master who informed me you and others were out riding. He was able to point me in the right direction," Darcy explained.

"Did you accomplish all you hoped to at Pemberley, or will you need to return again before we depart for the little season?" Elizabeth asked.

"Unless there is some sort of emergency that demands my attention, I see no reason why I will have to leave your estate again before we are to London," Darcy informed his riding partner.

"That news pleases me greatly," Elizabeth owned as she blushed.

"Elizabeth, do I have your permission to request a private audience with you from your father?" Darcy asked hopefully.

"William, are you asking my permission to ask my father's permission to talk to me?" Elizabeth arched her eyebrow as high as she was able.

"Yes, I suppose I am. I want there to be no misunderstandings between us, Elizabeth, and I do not want to seem officious," Darcy clarified.

"In that case, yes William, you have my consent to make that request of my father," Elizabeth gifted him with the tinkling laugh he loved and Darcy smiled, both of his dimples on full display.

~~~~~~~/~~~~~~~

"Enter!" Bennet called, responding to the knock on his study door. "What may I do for you, William?" he asked, although he was sure he knew the purpose of the younger man's presence in his study.

"I am seeking your permission to have a private audience

with your second daughter, Elizabeth," Darcy stated plainly.

"What is it you would like to discuss with Lizzy, William?" Bennet asked, knowing full well Darcy's aim.

"To ask for Elizabeth's hand in marriage and failing that a courtship; I will leave it up to her to decide which," Darcy informed the man he hoped would be his father-in-law sooner rather than later.

"If we were still the Bennets of Longbourn," Bennet started to reply, and Darcy almost panicked. Was he being refused as not being good enough for a Duke's daughter? "Then I would not have stood in the way of Elizabeth choosing between a courtship or a betrothal. We are, however, no longer just the Bennets of Longbourn. I grant you permission to request a courtship." Darcy visibly relaxed as he was not being refused permission to address his beloved Elizabeth. "*If* she accepts, and if you both desire to move forward, you may request her hand in no less than three weeks. At that point, should she accept you, there will be a minimum of a two-month betrothal period."

"I thank you, Bennet. I was concerned you were about to refuse permission for me to pay my addresses to Elizabeth at all," Darcy admitted.

"No, Son, notwithstanding your past behaviour, I know you to be a good and honourable man. If you are Lizzy's choice, then I will be the first to welcome you to the family," Bennet stood and held out his hand which Darcy shook vigorously.

"Slow down there," Bennet ribbed, "I am not as young as I once was." Bennet grinned widely. "I will summon Lizzy." Bennet looked at the door and back at Darcy.

"Yes, I know, door is to remain partially open," Darcy preempted Bennet.

"And a companion will be seated outside in the hallway," Bennet grinned. It was good to see that William Darcy had a sense of humour.

"My father informed me you would like to talk to me, William; it came as *such* a surprise," Elizabeth teased as she entered the study ahead of her father.

"I will leave you to it. You have ten minutes, Darcy." With that, Bennet turned and left the door half open on his way out.

"The last time I was granted a private interview with you, I requested permission to call on you," Darcy began.

"I do remember the request," Elizabeth smiled at the memory.

"As I told you before one of my trips to Pemberley, I have come to love you most ardently. You are my other half and complete me in every way. As much as I would like to ask for your hand today, I am requesting a formal courtship so you may discover if I am your perfect match, and you, at least in some small measure, feel the way about me as I feel about you," Darcy requested as he took her hands in his.

"Before Jane and Andrew wed, I asked Jane how she knew she was in love with Andrew. I knew I already held you in tender regard, but I did not think, or know, that I was in love with you—yet. Jane told me to think of my future, and if you were not part of any version of it, I imagined, then I was not in love with you.

"I have done much soul searching, and when you declared your love for me, I had answered most of my questions, but that separation clearly highlighted for me how empty by life would be without you in it. I was able to unequivocally answer for myself there was no future for myself I could see or wanted to see that does not include you by my side, so yes, William, I will accept a courtship with you as I also love you, and most ardently," Elizabeth concluded.

Throughout her speech, William's expression grew happier and happier. By the time she reached the end and declared her love for him, he felt as if, were he not holding her hands, he would be floating among the clouds. Without thinking, Darcy leaned forward and brushed Elizabeth's upturned lips with his own for their first, chaste kiss. Both felt a fission of tingles when their lips met, and they gasped, allowing also for this first instance of breathing one another in. There was no question that they both would have preferred more, but they instead rested into one another so their foreheads connected, and they could continue to share the same breath.

"I have long dreamed of hearing those very words from you, Elizabeth. Yes, they are three small words in syllables, but they are the most powerful words in the world when spoken to one another by two who are genuinely in love," Darcy murmured.

"If you are looking for a debate, you will get none from me on *this* subject, William. I find I am completely in accord with you," Elizabeth smiled widely.

"Ahem," Bennet cleared his throat as the couple stepped back. Each one felt the deprivation of the warmth of the other's hand as the physical contact between them was broken. "Am I to assume you accepted William's offer of a courtship, Lizzy?"

"Yes, Papa, I did. Can I assume asking for a courtship was a restriction imposed by you?" Elizabeth countered.

"It was." Bennet walked to his desk and rested against it as he explained the reasoning he had given to Darcy to his daughter.

"Three weeks is such a small amount of time in the context of our lives, Papa. I understand your reasons and look forward to our relationship growing to the next level." Looking at Darcy as she said the last, he could not have been happier at her statement.

"I suppose we should inform the family," Bennet stated as he led the courting couple out of his study.

Everyone in the drawing room had been anticipating such an announcement, but the expectation did nothing to reduce the warm reactions to the news after Bennet informed them of Lizzy's accepting a formal courtship with William.

Georgiana hugged Elizabeth tightly. "I knew how it would be! You two could not be so in love for no reason. I will have a sister, *many* sisters!" Georgiana enthused.

"I suppose we were more transparent than we thought we were," Elizabeth admitted as she returned the younger girl's hug. Georgiana was not the only one in the room to nod their agreement with her rhetorical observation.

Bennet was standing next to his own beloved wife as he watched the couple receive wishes for their future from the rest of the family. "Was I wrong to impose a courtship before a betrothal, Cilla?" he asked quietly.

"No, Thomas, I think it a wise decision on your part. Forget about the *Ton* and what they may or may not say but given the beginning of their relationship this additional time will not hurt them as they grow to know one another better," Priscilla agreed.

"I thank you for you continued and unstinting support, my love," Bennet kissed his wife's cheek.

~~~~~~~/~~~~~~~

"Andrew, Lizzy and William are courting!" Jane enthused after reading the happy missive from her sister the following day.

"Only a courtship? After we saw them in May and June, I was sure when the time came, William would ask for her hand," Andrew frowned, wondering how he had read them so wrong.

"He wanted to, but Papa had other ideas. He told them he wanted a three-week formal courtship followed by at least a two-month betrothal," Jane laughed as she re-scanned the missive for the facts as written by her younger sister. "It seems we will be gaining William and Gigi as brother and sister."

"So it does, my Jane. Now if we can go look at that issue in the bedchamber I mentioned to you this morning," Andrew stated with a deadpan expression.

"What issue—Andrew Fitzwilliam you are insatiable!" Jane gave her husband a playful slap on the arm.

"Only when it comes to you, Jane, I can never have too much of you," he growled, and in hearing it Jane decided a trip to view the *issue* in their bedchamber was, in fact, most necessary.

~~~~~~~/~~~~~~~

Charlotte Fitzwilliam joined her husband in his study as he was going over information from the horse breeding programme. "There is news from Lizzy, Rich," Charlotte informed her husband after first kissing him until he sighed in contentment.

"Did my cousin finally work up the gumption to propose?" Richard asked with a grin.

"They are formally courting," Charlotte clarified. Seeing her husband's questioning look she explained the restrictions that Bennet had placed. "In my opinion, it is part the change in their situation, and the other part of it is he recently lost his firstborn to our brother. I think he is trying to make sure that Eliza does not leave their house too soon."

"There may be some truth to your conjecture," Richard allowed, then pulled his wife onto his lap and showed her how much he loved her again, and again.

~~~~~~~/~~~~~~~

Two days later, Anne de Bourgh informed her mother that William was officially courting Elizabeth. Even knowing that was inevitable, Lady Catherine felt a pang of regret of opportunities lost. She had settled into her new role as mother of the mistress of Rosings well enough, but that did not mean from time to time she did not have maudlin thoughts about what might have been.

Anne was extremely happy for her cousins finally moving forward together. She looked around her home and was even more pleased by the way it looked now all of the uncomfortable furniture had been replaced by the elegant and comfortable pieces that had been delivered.

Even more pleasing was Mr. Gardiner's company's success in selling all of the gaudy pieces and ostentatious furniture. They had sold every last piece so, in the end the redecoration of her home had cost no additional funds, not even with the commission which had been paid to Gardiner and Associates.

Lady Catherine had long acknowledged that Anne had done a remarkable job with the changes to the manor house.

Privately, the former mistress also admitted the servants performed far better when treated fairly and with respect than they had under her stingy, iron fist.

<div align="center">~~~~~~~/~~~~~~~</div>

On many estates owned by members of the *Ton*, plans were being made for October when the little season would commence. The object of their machinations was Lady Elizabeth Bennet. With the younger sister not out yet and the brother at university, she was considered the catch of the season.

VOL 2, CHAPTER 15

The three-week courtship seemed to fly by for the couple involved, for they spent as much time as they were able in one another's company. As the month of July waned, both were looking forward to the promise of August.

Darcy found he enjoyed spending time with Mark, who had turned twelve in May. The boy did not care about his rank or the family's wealth, all he cared about was he was out of the nursery and had been placed in a suite near his parents. His tutor was also given leave to use the second bedchamber of the suite so Mark would have someone nearby if and when needed. The boy was intelligent, and like his father, Elizabeth, and older brother, he was a bibliophile.

Elizabeth found the attention Darcy paid to her little brother endearing. She glowed with pleasure as she considered how well it boded for the days when they had their own children. Not for the first time, Elizabeth reaffirmed her decision; William was the *only* man in the world that she would agree to marry.

Darcy, knowing all too well what it was like to be hunted by fortune hunters, was thankful by the time they departed for Longbourn, he would be betrothed to his beloved Elizabeth. When the party decamped for London, the *Ton* would have had almost two months to assimilate the fact Lady Elizabeth Bennet was not available for any who were vying for the opportunity to get their hands on her enormous fortune.

He chuckled because he knew when word of Bennet's decision regarding the Dennington Lines reached the ears of the *Ton,* there would be much gnashing of teeth that another

Bennet had slipped through their fingers. Darcy ruminated on the evening the Duke had asked all the family to gather in the family sitting room a fortnight earlier. Darcy had felt the compliment that he and Gigi were routinely included in family meetings like the one that had occurred.

"Priscilla and I thank you all for attending without knowing what we wanted to address," Bennet had stated. "It is my intention to inform you of a decision we, my wife and I, in consultation with Aunt Rose," Bennet had inclined his head to the dowager duchess, "have taken regarding the ownership if the Dennington Shipping Lines and related shipyards."

"When can we sail on The Rose *like Jane and Andrew did?" Mark asked his youthful exuberance coming to the fore.*

"Soon, Son, but that is not what I am discussing today. We have decided ownership of all of the shipping related concerns is to be split between the five of our children," Bennet related quite nonchalantly, considering the enormity of the news, even a little amused at the stunned silence.

"Papa, no! That is far too much! After the massive dowries you and Mama have given us, what do we need with more?" Elizabeth asked, three of her siblings nodding their agreement while Mark was flummoxed as to the meaning.

"The family is rich beyond all reason, Lizzy. Even without the income from the shipping line our income exceeds one hundred thousand pounds per annum. What could we do with even that amount in multiple lifetimes? The profits from the yards and the line are a little more than one hundred thousand pounds per annum, and, as such, each of you will receive a distribution of around twenty thousand pounds a year. Spend it, give it to charity, invest it, or keep it for your future children's benefit. It is yours to do with as you wish," Bennet laid out the possibilities in hopes they could quickly see the benefits.

"Would you deny your father and me the pleasure of gifting this to our children?" Priscilla asked. "You will see once you have your own children that you will want to do as much as you can for them."

"You should know there will be an entail, of sorts," Bennet stated. *"You will not be allowed to sell your stake in the company to anyone not a relation by blood to us. Like Longbourn and Nether-field Park were protected, the same is being put in place here."*

"Do any of you have any questions?" Priscilla asked.

"So I am part owner of The Rose?*"* Mark asked carefully.

"Yes, Son you are," Bennet chuckled.

"Then may I not sail with her any time I like?" Mark pressed.

"While technically true, Scamp," his mother smiled at her youngest, *"it is not that simple. You have your lessons and we our duties, but your father and I promise when we leave for Long-bourn, rather than go by carriage, we will leave a little sooner, travel to Liverpool, and sail to London. How does that sound?"* Priscilla asked. The youngest Bennet had lit up with pleasure.

The meeting had ended soon after. If Darcy was not a more secure man, he may have felt emasculated by the fact his wife's income from the shipping line exceeded all of his income from the three estates the Darcys owned, which had once made him the catch of the *ton*.

Darcy had requested a copy of the settlement Andrew used and had already asked his solicitor to prepare a copy along the same lines as his cousin's to present to both the Duke and, he hoped, his soon-to-be wife's review. After the meeting, he had also sent instructions to account for her added income from the shipping concerns, so any wealth she brought to the union would remain under her control.

~~~~~~~/~~~~~~~

As he had three weeks earlier, Darcy was in the Duke's study requesting a private interview with his second daughter. "This seems awfully familiar to me Darcy. Has it been a *full* three weeks since I granted your request to court my Lizzy?" Bennet asked sardonically.

"It is a few days past the time limit you set, and now I seek permission to propose to your daughter—Elizabeth." Darcy was familiar with the Duke's wit and did not want to give him an easy opening to make sport.

"I have no doubt you are my Lizzy's choice, Son. Please make sure you always make her happy," Bennet said with resignation as he saw his second daughter leaving his homes sooner rather than later. At least Pemberley was but a few hours from Longfield Meadows as Yorkshire and Derbyshire shared a border. And it did not hurt that Darcy's library rivalled his own in the quality of its contents. "I will summon her; you know the requirements for meeting with her do you not?" Darcy nodded.

Elizabeth entered on her own without her father. "Elizabeth, you have known of my love for you for some time now," Darcy said as he dropped to one knee her hands in his. "I know of your love for me, so rather than waste time on speeches, if your feelings are what they were the last time we met in this room tell me now, for my wishes and affections are unchanged, or if they are, it is that they are stronger!"

"William, my love for you also deepens by the day, you are the *only* man I would *ever* agree to marry, so if that is what the next question is to be, then let me help you save your breath to cool your porridge. Yes William, I will marry you, yes, yes, YES!" Elizabeth promised, with the love she felt for the man kneeling before her fully evidenced in her gaze.

Darcy rose, and from his inside pocket he produced a ring with a large emerald in the centre surrounded by a ring of small diamonds and emeralds alternating one after the other. "When I saw this among the Darcy jewels, I knew that it was the perfect ring for you, my dearest, loveliest Elizabeth," he said as he slid the ring onto her ring finger.

"William, I love you with all that I am," Elizabeth said as he stood in front of her and gently tilted her head up.

"You own my heart, Elizabeth," he murmured just before their lips met. This was no brush of the lips as their first kiss had been. Darcy captured her lips with his own and in a demonstration of how a kiss between lovers should feel. The kisses became sensual, deeper, slower, softer, and awoke the passion of both. Elizabeth felt the passion rush through her, all the way to the pit of her stomach then all the way to the tips of her toes.

She returned the kisses with a sensuality which made Darcy ache for more of her. They tasted each other for the first time when William slowly applied some pressure to Elizabeth's lips with his tongue and she opened her mouth to allow him access as her heart raced.

If Darcy had not been supporting her with his arms around her, and her arms were not so tightly wound around his neck, Elizabeth was sure her legs would not have held her up as she went weak at the knees. She could not get enough of him so constrained as this, and it was obvious by the way he pulled her in tighter he too needed more of her, each frustrated and revelling at the promises of how happily matched they would be.

Knowing they were closing in on their limits, time and others, and despite neither wanting to, they pulled back from each other. Neither spoke, but their eyes were locked as they took short, quick breaths to slow their racing hearts, the beating of which could be heard anywhere in the house, they were certain.

There was a knock at the door, and, after a pause, Elizabeth's parents entered. "Elizabeth, you accepted, William!" Priscilla exclaimed as soon as she saw the magnificent ring on a finger of her daughter's left hand. "You will be very happy together, I am sure."

"It seems I have no choice but to bestow my consent and blessing, as my wife has already done so," Bennet stated with mock exasperation.

"Your father told me he has asked for a two-month betrothal, which I agree is reasonable. Will you call me Mother Priscilla now, William?" Priscilla requested hopefully. "And as I have no doubt you will treat our Lizzy with the love and respect she deserves, I shall only ask you to allow me to be as much a mother to you as I am to Lizzy. And if our Gigi will allow it, I will have gained a son and a daughter."

"Neither do I doubt that Mama, he is the best man for me," Elizabeth stated as she smiled up at her betrothed.

"Do you two have a preference on a location where you would like to marry?" Bennet asked. "I am sure once the two months have passed neither of you will want to wait too long before you do."

"Unless William objects, I think I would like to marry from Longbourn, as Jane and Andrew did," Elizabeth stated.

"I have no objection at all," Darcy returned.

"That would work, as we will be in Hertfordshire for the month of September," Priscilla added.

"How about the first day of October, Mama? William and I will go on our wedding trip and leave the *delights* of the little season to you," Elizabeth teased. None of them were overjoyed at having to partake in the London social goings on, but with their new rank and station there was no real choice.

"Unless I deny permission for you to marry until the end of the little season," Bennet threatened in jest.

"The first day of October will be perfect, Lizzy," Priscilla responded, smiling sweetly as she defied her husband's intent to make sport.

"Should we go announce your betrothal to the family? Though I daresay it will surprise no one." Bennet sadly looked at his incandescently happy daughter. He was happy for her; she had found her love match, but all too soon she would no longer be his to protect.

~~~~~~~/~~~~~~~

Three days after the betrothal of Lady Elizabeth Bennet and Mr. Fitzwilliam Darcy of Pemberley, it was announced in the London papers. There were congratulatory notices from the De Melvilles, Carringtons, Fitzwilliams, and one from the Queen wishing her *cousin* well on her betrothal.

There was much wailing and despair as the notice was read first by those members of the *Ton* still in London, and then by those at their country estates as the papers reached them from Town in the subsequent days. Many mothers of first and second sons bemoaned their misfortune at the anticipated jewel of the upcoming season being snapped up before they had a chance to put their plans into practice.

Not a few men whose estates were in financial distress due to their mismanagement, gambling, or a combination of both, were angry they had missed the chance to acquire the reputed massive dowry of the second Bennet daughter.

And word the Bennet children were always guarded, and guarded well, nipped not a few plans for compromising the Marquess or the remaining unattached daughter in the bud. The only man who would have made an attempt regardless of the security surrounding the Duke's daughters was safely locked away in Marshalsea.

~~~~~~~/~~~~~~~

The departure from Longfield Meadows was advanced by a week. The first stop, rather than Liverpool, was at Pemberley to allow Darcy to have Mrs. Reynolds give his betrothed a formal tour of the house to find out what, if anything, Elizabeth desired to have changed before their wedding.

Besides some minor updating of a few guest chambers, there was nothing that Elizabeth, with the full agreement of her mother, found wanting or in need of change. The only place Elizabeth asked to be completely redone were her future chambers.

Darcy's mother had updated them to her style over thirty years previously, a style while elegant, did not fit Elizabeth's preferences, and Mrs. Reynolds made notes of her soon-to-be mistress's choices for the chambers. Pemberley's housekeeper had almost been a surrogate mother to the two Darcys after Lady Anne had passed away, and the first time the Bennets visited, she had been impressed with all of them. She had particularly watched Lady Elizabeth, as she had noted Master William's preference for the lady without too much difficulty. As she led the future mistress and the Duchess on the tour, Mrs. Reynolds only became firmer in her good opinions of the Bennets in general, and Lady Elizabeth specifically.

After the tour, Mrs. Reynolds returned the two Bennet ladies to the drawing room where all except Tom, Mark, and their friend Robert, who had remained with Tom when his parents departed, had gone to the stables to look over Pemberley's horseflesh.

Darcy drew his betrothed to a settee and sat next to her. "Is there much work to be done, my love? I am sure whatever it is will be completed by the time we return to Pemberley after our wedding trip and the season," Darcy enquired.

"There was very little that needs changing, William, with the exception of my future chambers," Elizabeth replied.

"It is my hope we will share a bed every night after we are wed, unless you prefer to sleep in your own chambers?" William looked at his betrothed hopefully.

"I agree with you. I could not help but notice the bed in your bedchamber is huge. I suppose there *may be* enough room for both of us if we squeeze tightly together as I too would prefer not to sleep separately," Elizabeth informed him with arched eyebrow.

"You two do remember you are not alone in the drawing room, do you not?" Richard snapped them out of their private world.

"That is the pot calling the kettle black," Andrew pointed out to his brother.

"That is brown from both of you," Darcy shot back at his cousins, soon to also be his brothers. "You two are *almost* as besotted with your wives as I am with my betrothed," William teased.

Elizabeth loved catching glimpses of this playful side of William. When he was comfortable around people, as he was with all currently in the drawing room, he did not hold back displaying his wit. "There is no need to complete over who loves his lady most boys," Elizabeth headed off the retorts that were ready to be unleashed. "Let us agree all three of you are lucky to have been accepted by such exceptional women," Elizabeth teased them in turn.

With the plans made for the Liverpool to London voyage, Andrew and Jane, who had many pleasant memories from their time on *The Rose*, and Richard and Charlotte jumped at the offer when the Duke invited them to join the family on board the ship.

"Is it time to leave yet?" Mark asked as he returned to the drawing room after his expedition to Pemberley's stables.

"And I thought you enjoyed spending time with us," Georgiana said with mock hurt as she placed her hand over her heart dramatically.

"Gigi, you know what I mean!" Mark huffed.

"Yes, we all know Scamp," his father chuckled. "We depart the day after the morrow, early in the morning. As I promised you will be boarding *The Rose* soon, son."

Mark was grinning at his father's words. And while he may have been the most voluble about his desire to reach the ship, he was certainly not alone in his desire.

~~~~~~~~/~~~~~~~~

The family were all on deck as *The Rose* approached the quay on the Thames where the Dennington Lines had a private docking area. Much to Mark's chagrin, the family spent one night in Liverpool so that the new owners of the shipping line could meet the senior staff in the offices. Once Mark understood the purpose of the visit he put his disappointment aside, especially when he had been informed the younger, unmarried men would be allowed to sleep onboard the ship that night.

The voyage had taken a sennight plus, and luckily for the passengers, the seas were relatively calm. Mark had spent as much time as he could on the quarterdeck quizzing the Captain, his officers, and the men about what they were doing. Even without knowing he was one of their new employers, he was indulged by all with good cheer. He was amazed as he watched the sailors climb up and down the rigging to reach sails. The only negative for him was that his father flatly refused permission for Mark to climb up to the crow's nest.

The two escorts had fascinated Mark as well. Sometimes one would be on station forward of them, one aft, and other times one or both of them would be sailing a few hundred yards to the port or starboard side of *The Rose*.

With more than enough sailors on board, only Biggs, Johns, Mr. Burnett, and his two commanders sailed with the family. The rest had been sent ahead so they would be waiting with the carriages in London. The only point of contention, if one could call it such, was when Bennet and Priscilla insisted that Aunt Rose take the owner's cabin and she refused. In the end, her argument won out and she took one of the ten large, comfortable cabins available for family and friends.

The family watched as the coxswain steered the ship under the captain's watchful eye and docked expertly as they hardly felt anything as the quay and the ships hulls met softly. The family had been warned when they were first back on dry-land it would feel as if the ship were still moving under their feet. Mark was highly amused, as it felt like the land was going to rise up and meet his foot like the deck tended to do.

From the dock, the carriages bore them to Darcy and Matlock Houses. Elizabeth and her mother accompanied Mrs. Killion on a tour of the house, and after Elizabeth reported it was much the same as at Pemberley, a few minor repairs where paper was coming loose in a guest chamber or two had been noted, and the redecoration of the mistress's chambers.

Rather than stay at Bedford House and have the servants open the house for one night, the Bennets accepted an invitation to be hosted at Matlock House for the night they would be in London, while the rest of the party remained at Darcy House. The next morning just after sunrise, the Bennets departed for Hertfordshire.

VOL 2, CHAPTER 16

No matter how much wealth and opulence the manor house at Longfield Meadows represented, the Bennets felt they were home when they arrived at Longbourn. On their first visit after their elevation, after at first being nervous, their friends, neighbours, and tenants were pleased to see other than the titles, the Bennets were as they always had been.

Darcy intended to follow them to Hertfordshire in a few days after his solicitors delivered the final draft of the settlement. He would arrive by the coming Saturday to join the family and his sister for Sunday services so he would have the pleasure, along with his betrothed, to hear the first banns read. They would also be read in both Kympton and the church at Pemberley starting the same day.

As much as Elizabeth would have preferred that when he arrived, he would not be sleeping three miles distant, she knew come the first day of October they would never be required to sleep in separate bedchambers again, let alone separate houses! As much as Elizabeth had grown to love her soon-to-be sister, Gigi, it was poor consolation that only one Darcy was living with them at Longbourn until their wedding.

Plans had been put in place for Gigi to be with Esther in Town after the wedding until the Darcys returned from their month-long wedding trip. Their wedding night was planned to be spent at Darcy House before taking *The Rose* to the Kingdom of Portugal, the only country in the southern part of the continent not controlled by the little tyrant.

Elizabeth felt like a big piece of her heart was missing, and the hours of the day seemed interminable to her as she waited for her William to arrive and bring the part of her heart that resided with him back to her.

In order to keep as low a profile as possible, the Bennets had decided rather than the spectacle of shopping in London, they would do so from Meryton. To achieve that aim, Madam Chambourg herself would be arriving the next day with two of her seamstresses. In addition, one of Uncle Gardiner's men had delivered every catalogue he could. Gardiner would acquire anything Elizabeth chose after she had been measured by the modiste's seamstresses.

The family wanted to purchase as much as possible from the merchants in Meryton so it would provide a boon to the local economy, which, if it were possible, would have the un-intended consequence of increase the admiration of Bennets for the local populace. If, after all of this, there were still items that Elizabeth required, she would be able to shop to her heart's content in London once she returned after the wedding trip.

~~~~~~~/~~~~~~~

"Bennet, you asked to see us," Sir William said as he entered his friend's study accompanied by his two eldest sons, Franklin and John. "Bennington," he greeted his neighbour who was also present.

"Sir William," Bennington inclined his head.

Once everyone was seated, Bennet looked at his friend and his sons. "You know, even though your son-in-law would dispute this, I believe the breeding programme at Bennington Fields is one of the finest in the land, do you not?" All three Lucas men nodded. Bennet had always admired the horseflesh from the programme, and it was the only place he purchased his horses. "Bennington here wants to retire and has no heir and as there is no entail on the Fields, he may do with it what he will."

"Bennet, please tell me you have not purchased it to add to Lucas Lodge! That is far too much, and I could never accept it from you no matter your argument," Sir William stated firmly.

"Yes, I am the new owner, and no, I am not gifting it to

you, so you may relax Lucas. The reason you are here is I have a business proposition for you." Sir William visibly relaxed. "Mr. Bennington has kindly agreed to remain for up to six months, if needed. What I propose is *your* sons take over the management of the Fields. They will learn all there is to learn from Bennington here, and in return for watching over my investment, and as incentive to see the place continues to thrive, you will receive half of the annual profit of the estate," Bennet proposed.

Sir William looked at his two sons who both nodded. "This is a business arrangement for which we should be committed to Bedlam if we refused this opportunity."

With that, Bennington stood. "I assume, your Grace, our business is concluded?" The Duke nodded and rose as he shook the man's hand. Bennington farewelled the three Lucas men and then departed.

"You know adding four thousand pounds per annum will increase our income by a factor of three," Sir William shook his head slowly in amazement. It seemed his friend was determined to help the Lucas family and was doing so in a way that could not be refused.

"I do know that," Bennet returned. "In fairness to Franklin, as his sisters and brothers have each received an amount from us, I have purchased land adjacent to Lucas Lodge to be gifted to your son. Before you protest, Lucas, after the purchase, it leaves a little more than six thousand pounds. If I were the future master of Lucas Lodge, I might use that money to add some space to my family's home, but that is just me," Bennet grinned slyly. When Bennet explained what tract of land he had gifted Franklin, it was rather obvious Lucas Lodge had just doubled in size.

"As I accepted your gifts to my other children, you knew full well I could not refuse this on Franklin's behalf as it would be unfair to him. You do too much for us, my friend, but on behalf of my eldest son, I accept with much gratitude and an entreaty. It is enough, old friend. Like your life has been irrevocably changed, you have done the same for us," Sir William stated, his voice gruff with emotion as he saw a future for his children he could never have imagined but a few short months previously.

"Your Grace," Franklin Lucas stood and offered his hand which Bennet took without delay. "I thank you for my family and myself. I am sure you know horses are a passion for both John and me, even though we have not been able to afford the quality of horse raised at the Fields."

"Why do you think the two of you were asked to join your father for this meeting?" Bennet asked easily. "As far as affording the horses, one of the perks of managing the estate is you will only pay ten percent of the price of any animals you would like to acquire for yourselves." Both Lucas sons had a look of unadulterated joy at the prospect of owning some of the horses that had once only seemed a dream. "As long as you leave enough horses for sale," Bennet ribbed.

Bennet produced a document that Phillips had drawn up to formalise the management agreement, which Bennet and all three Lucases signed. It was no oversight that Nick had been excluded. He loved the law and was determined to have a career as a solicitor or perhaps even a barrister one day.

After the two Lucas sons' profuse and repeated thanks, they departed, leaving the old friends to a game of chess and some of Bennets fine port.

~~~~~~~/~~~~~~~

As Charlotte's and Richard's carriage traversed Meryton on the way to her parent's estate, Charlotte was a little nervous. This was the first time she had returned to the neighbourhood since her earlier departure and subsequent marriage.

Lady Lucas had told her daughter there had been little or no talk, especially as the knowledge Charlotte had the full support of the Duke and Duchess and their extended family, which now included several peers of the realm. If that was not enough, the denizens of the areas were informed of the full support of Charlotte's husband's family, there inevitably were one or two comments made about the possibility of Charlotte being with child. As she had just had her courses some days before they departed Town, and as much as she would have liked to attain the state of being with child already, Charlotte was as slender as she was the day she married he first husband.

Richard used his cane to strike the ceiling bringing their carriage to a halt. "I find I would like to take my wife shopping in Meryton *before* we arrive at Lucas Lodge." Richard knew Charlotte was concerned about the one or two biddies who had nothing better to do than speculate about her being with child from her previous marriage. His strategic mind came up with the plan to be seen as soon as they arrived, so no one would think they were hiding. As it was a fortnight or so from six months since Collins's death, one look at his wife would kill any thought she had been with child when her late husband met his end.

"We do not need to, Richard; let them talk if they have nothing better to do," Charlotte stated, forcing a brave smile for him.

"I desire some exercise, Wife; will you not join me? We do not want people to assume we are unhappy if I walk out on my own now, do we?" Richard waggled his eyebrows at his wife.

"When you put it like that, you silly man, then yes I will join you," Charlotte beamed at her husband, her love of him having grown as only intimacy and happiness would allow.

Richard nodded once for the footman to place the step and open the door. Richard stepped out, turned, and handed Charlotte out, and in full view of many in the Meryton main street, Richard kissed his wife's hands languidly and then offered her his arm. Charlotte wound her arm around her husband's as they walked down the street, stopping in most stores, and making the odd purchase here and there.

Within an hour of their promenade in the middle of Meryton, word spread throughout the neighbourhood that Charlotte Fitzwilliam was not with child—well not as one would expect at six or seven months, forever putting any talk to bed that she had been in that state when her late husband perished. A secondary result, which soon became the news of most import, was how felicitous the couple looked as they walked around the town.

By the time the Fitzwilliams arrived at Lucas Lodge a little over an hour later, word had reached Lady Lucas already, who could not have been prouder of her daughter and son-in-law for the effective way they had silenced the few remaining critics of their union in Meryton.

~~~~~~~/~~~~~~~

Darcy arrived at Netherfield Park and found his betrothed's grandparents, aunts, and uncles already in residence. Lady Sarah was once again organizing a betrothal ball, this one to be held the Friday before the wedding, giving the family three full days to recover before the wedding. Ally had learnt her lesson, and with her parent's permission had accepted an invitation to reside at Longbourn with Esther and Gigi. If added incentive was needed, Maria Lucas had also accepted an invitation to stay at Longbourn with her friends.

Jane and Andrew and Charlotte and Richard were at Longbourn and Lucas Lodge respectively with the intention of returning later that evening. After quickly greeting the De Melvilles and Carringtons, Darcy took the stairs three at a time to reach his bedchamber. After Carstens made quick work of a wash and change of clothing for his master, Darcy vaulted into Zeus's saddle and made a mad dash to Longbourn over the fields, taking the shortest route between him and his Lizzy.

As Zeus made the effortless jump over the fence, Darcy thought he was dreaming as galloping across the field on the Longbourn side of the fence was Mercury bearing his betrothed to him. Darcy's heart sped up with the anticipation of seeing his beloved again, the pounding of which reverberated through his body like a drum.

"William!" Elizabeth exclaimed as she brought Mercury to a halt. There were mere inches of space between the two mounts who stood head to tail alongside one another. "I missed you so very much," Elizabeth told him her heart racing, and not from the exercise.

Darcy's first inclination was to kiss his betrothed with all of the pent-up passion he felt, but the proximity of Biggs, another footman-guard, and a groom put paid to that inclination. Darcy was in no mood to test the catlike reflexes of Biggs that Richard had told him about. Rather, he leaned in to kiss her forehead then took her free hand and bestowed a kiss on the inside of her wrist.

"I too missed you, Elizabeth," he told his betrothed. "When we are separated it feels like half of my heart is missing."

"Oh, William, I feel the same. Should we ride back to the house?" Elizabeth asked and her betrothed nodded. "Catch me if you can," Elizabeth called over her shoulder as she dug her heels into her horse's flanks who took off like a shot fired out of a pistol.

After a few seconds as he watched her magnificently tearing across the field, Darcy spurred Zeus into action confident that his larger, and he assumed stronger, horse would catch Mercury. He was wrong, yet again. He never got closer than to eat some of Mercury's dust trail while hearing the tinkling laugh he loved so much mingled in with the wind rushing past his ears.

Elizabeth had Mercury next to the mounting block by the time Darcy reached her. He looked with wonder at the smaller horse's still twitching muscles and realised that once again an assumption he made had been proven quite incorrect and he did not miss Elizabeth's triumphant look. "There is a reason I named him Mercury, and it had nothing to do with a celestial body," Elizabeth smiled widely.

"He does run like the wind, Elizabeth. No matter how hard I pushed this old man here," Darcy rubbed his horse's neck affectionately after he dismounted, "he never came close to you and Mercury," Darcy owned.

The couple was still laughing when they were admitted to the master's study. Darcy had modelled the settlement after Andrew's, except he settled one hundred fifty thousand pounds on Elizabeth. With the quarterly interest from Elizabeth's dowry and the shipping concerns, his income as a married man would be about triple what it was currently.

Elizabeth had no objection other than telling Darcy that she did not need so much, so it was soon after that the settlement was signed by both parties.

~~~~~~~/~~~~~~~

"Did I hear my brothers are about to start managing a breeding programme *almost* as good as mine," Richard ribbed his brother-in-law.

"We are Richard," Franklin replied for himself and his brother. "Although yours is *almost* as good as ours."

"Enough boys," Sir William interjected. "The rest of us are moving to Bennington Fields, and Franklin will effect a refurbishment of the Lodge before he moves into the enlarged manor house." Sir William explained what Bennet had done for them in a way that made it impossible to be refused.

"All I heard at Longbourn was you are managing the programme," Richard let out a low whistle. "It pleases me your lives will be so much easier going forward. We will have to see if we can collaborate, breed some of my best with Bennington Fields's best and create some new, possibly even better bloodlines," Richard proposed.

"You pre-empted my making the same suggestion, Brother," John Lucas responded.

"How do you like your new stallions?" Richard asked his brothers-in-law. One of the tangible benefits was the fact both Franklin and John had each acquired a new horse the day after the Duke had appointed their family to the management of the programme.

"We could not be more satisfied with our horses," Frnaklin answered for both Lucas brothers.

In the drawing room, Lady Lucas was talking to her eldest

daughter, again marvelling at how contented Charlotte looked. "Can you believe all the Bennets have done for us, Charlotte? Rather than leave their old contacts behind, they are sharing their good fortune with those they have long been friends. Did you hear what they did for the tenants of both Longbourn and Netherfield Park?" Lady Lucas asked.

"If you mean they have given all of their tenants at the two estates a year of free rent so they may build up some savings and better their positions, then yes, Mama, I have. But it is what I would have guessed from the Bennets. Even before their elevation, they helped where they could, whether or few of those receiving help knew to whom they were indebted. Nothing was ever done for accolades, but for the purest reasons there are—helping one's fellow man," Charlotte stated quietly. She believed her father had an idea that his son's *scholarships* had come from the Bennets, but had said nothing himself, and unless her mother asked her a direct question, Charlotte would not betray the secret she had learned.

"We need to get ready for the family dinner at Longbourn tonight," Lady Lucas stated. Not only were the Bennets friends now, but thanks to Charlotte's marriage, they were related.

"I will have to forcibly extract Richard from my brothers' company to return to Netherfield, as I am sure they will talk of horseflesh for days otherwise," Charlotte smiled as she stood then kissed her mother on both cheeks then went in search of her husband.

~~~~~~~/~~~~~~~

The morning of their betrothal ball, Darcy met his soon-to-be wife before sunrise and the two, with their escorts, made for Oakham Mount. After posting one guard on each side of the hill, Biggs took up station a little before the summit.

"Come, William," Elizabeth led him to the big rock below the lone oak tree on the eastern side of the summit which offered a clear view of the eastern horizon as the dawn started to lighten the sky in preparation for the sun to peek above it.

They sat in companionable silence as the sun's first rays

broke over the horizon. Their bodies were as close to one another as possible for added warmth; steam showing each time one of them breathed out in the cold of the late September morning. The few clouds in the sky lit up in golds and silvers as the sun's rays kissed them.

Elizabeth turned her betrothed's head with her hands and placed her lips on his to claim a kiss as the first rays of the morning sun caressed them. The couple drew back one from the other and sat for a while longer, fingers interlaced with their heads leaning against each other as they watched the birth of the new day. Knowing that Biggs would come and make sure all was well if too much time passed, they stood and made their way to the head of the path and found the big man waiting for them where they left him.

When they reached the fork Darcy took to return to Netherfield, each felt bereft of the other's company, but they were fortified knowing that in four days they would be married.

~~~~~~~/~~~~~~~

The second Bennet daughter's betrothal ball at Netherfield was no less enjoyable than the ball for the first. The main difference was at this ball Darcy claimed the first, supper, and final sets, and as the last set was a waltz, they both looked forward to that dance with much pleasure.

As he had at Jane's and Andrew's ball, Tom opened the ball with Georgiana and, with both guardian's permission to request a second set, claimed her for the supper set as well. Unsurprisingly, Robert Jamison danced the same two sets with Lady Esther Bennet.

Charlotte Fitzwilliam had never enjoyed a ball or assembly as much as she did this one. She also danced the three significant sets with her husband, who had planned to dance every set with her until the Countess of Jersey got wind of his plans and told him, in no uncertain terms, no more than three sets would be allowed with one's spouse or betrothed.

When it came time for the final set, Elizabeth and Darcy

relished the contact the formerly scandalous dance allowed them, grateful it was now widely accepted in London's polite society. To Elizabeth, it felt like she was floating on air as William twirled her around the ballroom. And in but a few short days she would attain her heart's desire, marriage to William.

~~~~~~~/~~~~~~~

There had been a few scheming fortune hunters who had hoped to try to convince Lady Elizabeth away from the prig Darcy before they wed. When it became clear the lady would not be seen in London before she returned a married woman, the final and desperate plans to try and capture the lady died on the vine. But those involved in machinations to win the hand of the jewel of the upcoming season consoled themselves that at least there was one more Bennet daughter who would come out next year, and two Bennet sons would soon be available for them to pin their hopes on.

VOL 2, CHAPTER 17

As she had with Jane the night before her wedding, Priscilla joined Elizabeth in the chambers of her childhood on this final night she would sleep at Longbourn as a single woman. To open the conversation, she asked, "Are you nervous about the morrow, Lizzy?"

"At some level, I am nervous about the unknown, Mama, but about marrying William, not at all," Elizabeth said with a sigh. "If I am not mistaken, you are here to talk about the unknown, are you not?"

"Yes, Lizzy, I am. You have an advantage of being able to talk to Jane after we part company, and thus the added benefit of hearing how effective my advice was from the only person I have ever given it to," Priscilla smiled wistfully as she remembered the impertinent little girl who had grown into the accomplished woman sitting on the bed with her.

"Both from living on a farm and the fact that I am sure that you peaked into some of the books your father told you were off limits, it is safe to assume you are aware of the mechanics of the act." Elizabeth blushed as she nodded. Her mother had the right of it, for she had, on more than one occasion, read a little of the *forbidden* books. "In that case, I will tell you about things no books can truly explain.

"Do not allow anyone in society to *ever* tell you there is a time and place for you and your husband to be intimate. As long as you are in private and *both* desire the same, it is never wrong or, as some claim, wanton. On one hand, society tries to dictate what is proper between a man and his wife as on the other it is turning a blind eye to debaucheries and decadent behaviour by both genders."

"That kind of behaviour was one of the reasons that Papa eschewed Town, was it not?" Elizabeth asked.

"Yes, it was, Lizzy. When you have a love match like your father and I, or Jane and Andrew, and the rest of the examples you see in our extended family, there is no need to seek succour outside of the marriage. As long as unions among the majority of polite society are business arrangements between wholly incompatible couples, the kind of despicable actions of infidelity will continue unabated." Priscilla paused as she gathered her thoughts to return to the topic at hand. "What I was intending to say before we got side-tracked is that what happens between you and William, as long as it is what you both want, will never be wrong.

"There are some who would tell you to 'lie back and close your eyes and hope your husband is done quickly' but they could not be further from the truth. The giving *and* receiving of pleasure are the joy which is found in the marital act. The more you love one another, the more you will want to give pleasure to your mate."

"How will I know what is pleasurable to William, or for me?" Elizabeth blushed as she enquired because she did understand a little bit of that pleasure.

"If it is something you enjoy, you will know by the way your body reacts, as will William. And soon you will know how to read one another well enough to know you are giving them pleasure. But more importantly, it is the communication you share. Ask him what gives him pleasure, and do not be shy to tell him the same for yourself. Have you two discussed sleeping arrangements?" Priscilla asked her daughter.

"We have, Mama. We want to share a bed, although it is not something *done* by most in society," Elizabeth stated, her chin up and ready to be chastised, knowing even if she were, she would not forego the wish she and her William shared.

"As we have discussed, the mores of the *Ton* are usually an indicator of what *not* to do more than the other way round. That is a sensible decision, yes, but it is also a good decision. It will increase the intimacy between you, and there is nothing better than cuddling with a beloved partner on a cold winter's night," Priscilla smiled. "Unless you inform people in society, who will know? I am sure William's servants are as discreet as the rest of ours. If you canvassed the married couples in our extended family, I think you will find that few, if any, sleep in separate beds."

"I love him so much, Mama, that the idea of another night without him after tonight is unthinkable," Elizabeth stated quietly.

"Then you love him as much as I hoped you did." Lady Priscilla smiled sweetly at her Lizzy. "Always talk to one another, and never allow the misunderstandings that you and William had in the beginning to curdle relations between you. And the piece of advice my mother gave me, which I am grateful for even now, is never go to bed angry with one another. You are both strong, intelligent, and sometimes stubborn individuals. There will be times when there are disagreements, and that is normal; no couple, no matter how much in love they are, are without quarrels. It is *how* you conduct yourselves in a disagreement and afterward that helps strengthen the bonds of love. It is possible to disagree without acrimony."

"We have promised to do whatever we can to resolve any misunderstandings between us on the spot, so they do not fester and become something that they are not," Elizabeth relayed. "We have both seen what that can do and want a relationship without those regrets. Lady Catherine has many regrets, and of them all, she most often regrets not listening to her daughter. It is what led us to have the conversation."

"If that be the case, then there is nothing more I can impart to you, Lizzy. Do you have any questions of me?" Priscilla asked.

"When I am with child, are we still able to have marital relations?" Elizabeth blushed as she asked.

"When you are with child, there is no reason to stop having relations with your husband until you feel it is too hard or uncomfortable for you as you near your confinement. Remember, it will be a partnership, and like any good and equal partnership, the shared experience of love, passion, and pleasure will be very fulfilling even when you are with child." Priscilla asked again if there was anything else, and Elizabeth shook her head.

"In that case, I will take my leave of you. You are perfectly matched, Lizzy. I will miss seeing you with us every day, but I know you will be an incredibly happy and well-respected woman." Priscilla kissed both of Elizabeth's cheeks and her forehead. She squeezed her daughter's hand, stood up, and with a nod as she readied the door, exited.

Jane replaced her mother in Elizabeth's bedchamber. "Is there anything you want to ask that you did not feel you could ask, Mama?" Jane enquired.

"I do not think so Jane. Mama did say you could tell me how effective her advice was."

"Without going into details of what transpires between Andrew and me, I can tell you without any equivocation that Mama was spot on with her advice."

"Thank you, Jane. I wish tomorrow was over and I was William's wife already. Am I wanton that I lust after him before we are married Jane?"

"No, Lizzy! You are a woman in love with a man who loves her back with equal measure. You never crossed any lines as I am sure that neither you nor William would have done so." Elizabeth allowed that it was so. "I would be worried if you did not have feelings of that nature for William." Jane hugged her sister.

"Jane, there is something about you that I cannot place," Elizabeth stated suspiciously as she looked her sister up and down.

"I will share a secret with you Lizzy, but I entreat you to tell no one other than your husband," Jane stated seriously.

"You have my word, other than William I will not breathe a word," Elizabeth swore.

"I am with child, Lizzy!" Jane beamed as she shared her news.

"Jane, I am so happy for you and Andrew. My brother knows does he not?"

"Lizzy, he practically knew before me! He is so observant when it comes to me, my moods, and my body, that as soon as I missed my first courses, he noted it. During our voyage to London I missed my third monthly courses. We saw an accoucheur in London who confirmed my state," Jane gushed, a wave of joy emanating from her. "I should feel the quickening in the next month or so, and as soon as I do, we will inform the family. Mama has been looking at me in a knowing way, so I am sure she suspects, but seems to be waiting for me to broach the subject."

"That is the best news, Jane! I am so happy for you and my brother! Do you know when you will enter your confinement?" the aunt-to-be asked with a huge smile.

"Next year in April or May, according to the doctor," Jane revealed. "If you were not about to leave for a month, I would have waited to tell you, Sister dearest, but I suspect I will feel the quickening while you are on your wedding trip."

The sisters spoke for another hour; and it was after midnight when Elizabeth finally slipped into the arms of Morpheus and dreamt of her William.

~~~~~~~/~~~~~~~

Darcy spent the night before his wedding surrounded by his soon-to-be family. He was about to go from two aunts, an uncle, and three cousins, not counting the Bennets who were cousins by marriage, to a slew of in-laws that included parents, grandparents, aunts, uncles, brothers, sisters, and a good number of cousins. The day of the Darcys and Fitzwilliams being members of a small family were over all because he had the good sense to fall in love with his Elizabeth.

He endured good natured ribbing by Lord Jersey, his son, and son-in-law, as well as Uncle Reggie about how to treat a woman properly. Both Andrew and Richard with their *vast* matrimonial experience had asked him if he needed any pointers. He had scowled at the brothers who had backed off with grins.

Darcy was the furthest thing from a rake or, heaven forbid, a dandy you could find, but that is not to say he was inexperienced in the ways of the flesh. When he came of age, his father had gifted him a night at the house of the most exclusive courtesans in London. On his grand tour, he had partaken of carnal pleasure once or twice, but since then nothing.

Like the rest of the married couples in the extended, or soon-to-be extended family, the vows he would recite on the morrow were sacrosanct, and he would no sooner be unfaithful to the woman of his dreams than he would cut off his legs and arms.

After his uncle, soon-to-be grandfather and uncles retired, Darcy was left in Netherfield's library with Andrew and Richard. Each had a snifter with two fingers of brandy that he was nursing. At the worst of times, Darcy hated to over imbibe and tonight there was no chance. He did not want his senses dulled or to be dealing with the aftereffects of being in his cups when Elizabeth walked up the aisle toward him.

"As you are to stand up with me in the morning, Richard, it would not do to overindulge tonight," Darcy stated distractedly.

"When have you ever known me to be in my cups, William...besides at Cambridge, and before I left for the continent to chase after Bony, and the night before Charlotte married that dimwit, I mean?" Richard asked with a grin.

"True, Richard, and besides, and I do not think Charlotte will appreciate a sloppy drunk crawling into bed tonight," Andrew ribbed his brother.

"No more than Jane would appreciate you in that state, Brother!" Richard shot back in jest.

"Are you two intending to keep me company or fight like little boys?" Darcy asked with a grin, for they had never ceased to help him relax when he needed it most.

"It is a great thing that we will all be brothers on the morrow," Richard stated as he raised his glass in salute to the other two.

"To brothers," Darcy proposed as the three clinked their snifters and downed the rest of the rich, brown coloured spirit. Not long after, the three joined the rest of the estate's residents in going to sleep. The last one to succumb was Darcy, wishing Elizabeth was already next to him in his bed.

~~~~~~~/~~~~~~~

Elizabeth was tempted to ask for Mercury to be saddled and to go for a ride the morning of her wedding, but good sense won out. The ceremony was to start at nine, so she would need to be dressed and ready in two hours. She was grateful for her decision when not ten minutes later there was a knock on the door and her mother entered the chamber, followed by Elizabeth's maid.

"Your bath is ready for you, Lizzy, nice and hot just the way you prefer it," Priscilla informed her second daughter after giving her a warm hug.

"Today is the day I have been dreaming of Mama. I will marry William in a few short hours, but I will miss you all, you know!" Elizabeth said as a momentary tinge of melancholy at leaving her parents' home struck her. Then she reminded herself who would be waiting next to the altar when she entered the church; and her maudlin thoughts were displaced by excitement.

"Yes, my dearest daughter, in a few hours you will be a Darcy," Priscilla hugged her daughter tightly to herself once again before releasing her to the maid to assist with washing her daughter's long, chestnut curls.

A few minutes later, Elizabeth was luxuriating in her hot bath infused with lavender water. A half hour later, with the water already tepid at best, Elizabeth emerged from the bath to be wrapped in the toasty-warm towel by her maid. After she was dry, she wore a robe and sat with her back to the fire as the maid brushed out her hair to dry it fully.

Once she had her chemise, stays, and small clothing on, Jane joined her mother to help her into the gown that had been created for her wedding. Albeit having unlimited funds, like Jane before her, Elizabeth chose a simple design with little adornment. There were a few teardrop pearls attached to the gossamer overlay of the cream gown. The gown itself had no lace on it and made a stunning contrast against Elizabeth's darker colouring. Jane held the gossamer veil for the maid to attach to the bride's hair. Other than three or four emerald chips, it too was unadorned.

Just after half after eight, Elizabeth descended the stairs to her waiting family. After giving the bride light pecks on the cheek, Ally, Gigi, and Maria, left the house with Tom and Mark. Bennet had to regulate his emotions before he was able to articulate his thoughts.

"I have never seen you look more beautiful than you do right now, my Lizzy," Bennet's voice was gruff with emotion.

Elizabeth looked at both of her parents, "I could not have wished for better parents than I, all of us, have. I know it is the way of things that daughters eventually leave their parents' house, but no matter how much I love William, it is still hard to fathom that in a short time, I will no longer be a Bennet," Elizabeth kissed both of her parents.

"You may not bear the name any longer after today, but you will *always* be a Bennet, Lizzy," her mother told her as she fought to keep the tears from spilling down her cheeks.

"I think it is time. Cilla, Jane, Lizzy, are you ready?" All three nodded, none daring to speak at that moment as they knew they would not be able to hold back the threatening tears.

~~~~~~~/~~~~~~~

The church was filled to overflowing. Only two seats were open in the front row, those to be occupied by the Duke and his Duchess. The congregation was made up of peers, lesser nobility, local landowners, merchants, and tenants.

The only person who felt somewhat uncomfortable with

the eclectic mix of classes and ranks was Lady Catherine de Bourgh. Some old habits took longer than others to die. However, she schooled her features as there were too many powerful members of society present for her to make herself standout.

Hearing about the Bennets' connections was one thing, seeing the extended family arrayed in front of her reminded her how close she could have come to ruining herself if she had not been woken up by Anne's words. She looked at her daughter sitting next to her and saw how happy she was being among her family. There were advantages. After Darcy married, she would be aunt to two daughters of a duke. As it was, when her nephew Andrew had married Lady Jane, she gained connections to the De Melvilles and Carringtons.

The vestibule door opened, and the mother of the bride made her way up the aisle to her seat, nodding to the rector to let him know all was ready. The door opened again, and May and Peter Gardiner proceeded up the aisle. May was sprinkling rose petals while Peter followed looking as serious as he could with his pillow in his hands bearing the two substitute rings.

When the door opened again, Lady Jane Fitzwilliam glided up the aisle and took her place opposite her brother Richard across the altar from where he was standing with Darcy. She looked at Andrew sitting with his parents and gave him one of her beatific smiles.

~~~~~~~/~~~~~~~

"Are you ready, Lizzy?" Bennet asked his second daughter.

"I am, Papa," Elizabeth responded softly.

"You will be missed, my Lizzy," Bennet said gruffly.

"As will you, Mama, and my siblings be missed," Elizabeth returned, squeezing her father's arm as both vestibule doors opened, and they heard the congregation come to its feet.

The Duke led his daughter through the open doors, and they began their walk up the aisle. Elizabeth marvelled at just how handsome her groom was as he stood tall and waiting for her to approach, his eyes locked onto hers. While everyone was commenting on her beauty, she basked in the love shining from his eyes directed only at her.

For his part, Darcy thought it was a vision. He had never seen Elizabeth look prettier, and he was mesmerised by her green eyes that seemed to be seeing into the depths of his soul. As she approached him, he descended the steps from the altar to wait for her at the top of the aisle.

The Duke lifted his daughter's veil gently and bestowed a kiss on her cheek, and after it was lowered, he placed her hand on her groom's arm and made his way to his seat next to his wife.

Darcy led her up to the point in front of the clergyman who gave the congregants a signal to be seated. Longbourn's vicar opened his copy of *The Book of Common Prayer* to the relevant page.

"Dearly beloved, we are gathered together here in the sight of God, and in the face of this congregation, to join together this Man and this Woman in holy Matrimony, which is an honourable estate, instituted of God in the time of man's innocency..."

After no one objected when the vicar reached that part of the service, the vows followed:

"I, Fitzwilliam Alexander Darcy, take thee, Elizabeth Sarah Bennet, to be my wedded Wife, to have and to hold from this day forward, for better for worse, for richer or for poorer, in sickness and in health, to love, *obey*, and to cherish, till death us do part, according to God's holy ordinance; and thereto I plight thee my troth."

The clergyman raised his eyebrows as Darcy added the one word to his vows but said nothing and nodded for Elizabeth to continue:

"I, Elizabeth Sarah Bennet, take thee, Fitzwilliam Alexander Darcy to be my wedded Husband, to have and to hold from this day forward, for better for worse, for richer or for poorer, in sickness and in health, to love, cherish, and to *obey*," Lizzy paused, gave Darcy an appreciative look as he added the same

451

word to his vows and continued, "till death us do part, according to God's holy ordinance; and thereto I give thee my troth."

The couple released each other's hands and Richard placed the rings on the pages of the vicar's open bible. He handed Lizzy's ring to Darcy who took it and then placed it on the fourth finger of Lizzy's left hand saying:

"With this Ring I thee wed, with my Body I thee worship, and with all my worldly Goods I thee endow: In the Name of the Father, and of the Son, and of the Holy Ghost. Amen."

Although not normally done, the process was repeated as it was with Jane and Andrew when Lizzy placed a ring on the fourth finger of Darcy's left hand and repeated the same vow.

After the giving and receiving of rings, they knelt as the vicar intoned a prayer of blessing. Once the prayer was complete, he joined their right hands together and said:

"Those whom God hath joined together let no man put asunder. Forasmuch as Fitzwilliam Alexander and Elizabeth Sarah have consented together in holy Wedlock and have witnessed the same before God and this company, and thereto have given and pledged their troth either to other and have declared the same by giving and receiving of a ring, and by joining of hands; I pronounce that they be Man and Wife together, In the Name of the Father, and of the Son, and of the Holy Ghost. Amen.

"God the Father, God the Son, God the Holy Ghost, bless, preserve, and keep you; the Lord mercifully with his favour look upon you; and so, fill you with all spiritual benediction and grace, that ye may so live together in this life, that in the world to come ye may have life everlasting. Amen."

It was done, they were married! As their family and friends called out their good wishes, the newlyweds felt a surge of joy like they had never felt before. Jane and Richard followed them into the vestry where they signed their names just three spaces under where Jane and Andrew had written their names in May. After witnessing the signatures, Jane and Richard wished the couple well again and followed the vicar out of the vestry.

"Wife!" Darcy exclaimed.

"Husband!" Elizabeth returned. "Kiss me, William, I have never been kissed as a married woman," She gave her husband a saucy look.

As he had just vowed to obey her, he kissed his wife thoroughly.

~~~~~~~/~~~~~~~

"Mr. Fitzwilliam and Lady Elizabeth Darcy," Hill announced proudly as the couple entered Longbourn's ballroom to join the revellers celebrating their wedding with the celebratory meal. Gigi reached her new sister ahead of Esther, Tom, and Mark.

"You are my sister, Lizzy!" Georgiana gushed.

"As am I," Esther added as she curled her arm around Gigi's.

"And Tom and I are your brother's now, Gigi," Mark pointed out.

"And William is brother to all of you," Elizabeth reminded them.

After a few minutes with their siblings, Elizabeth and Darcy started to make the rounds. Almost an hour later, Darcy noticed that his wife looked a little wan, which was out of character for her. "Have you eaten or had something to drink today, my love?" Darcy asked with concern.

"With all of the excitement this morning, I own I did not," Elizabeth confessed. Darcy led his wife to where her parents, grandparents, and some of her aunts and uncles were seated. He helped her into a chair and then proceeded to bring her a little repast, and both water and lemonade.

"I have not eaten today, Mama," Elizabeth informed her mother when she received a questioning look. "And I did not drink either," Elizabeth admitted sheepishly.

"Thank goodness William is so solicitous of your needs, Lizzy," Priscilla teased as she rolled her eyes at the unnecessary sufferings of young love.

After eating a little and more importantly, drinking, it did not take too long before Elizabeth looked and felt somewhat better. She was still hungry, but at least she had something to tide herself over. For the next hour, the newlyweds made the rounds of the ballroom, making sure they spoke with each of their guests. Before they knew it, Elizabeth was changed into her travel attire, and she and Darcy were being wished safe travels by the family who gathered in front of the house to farewell them.

Once the couple was situated in the comfortable Darcy coach and the door had been closed by a footman, Darcy struck the ceiling with his cane and the driver urged his team of six to walk on.

VOL 2, CHAPTER 18

The newlyweds blessed Mrs. Hill as their carriage rolled on towards London. On the floor was a basket full of comestibles and various flagons of both cold and warm drinks. Even with her husband's insistence she eat and drink some at the wedding breakfast, Elizabeth's stomach growled, letting her and, to her embarrassment, her husband know she needed to eat.

Darcy too was ready to eat as all he had had for breakfast was two small mince pies and a glass of lemonade, and it was not long before the blissful couple were sated after having enjoyed some of their favourites which Mrs. Hill had made sure to pack, though they did laugh at the amount she had managed to stuff into the basket. The footmen, led by Johns who was now a Darcy employee, outriders, and driver were gifted the rest of the almost full basket when they stopped to rest the horses about halfway to London, and they smiled at one another as they heard many others extolling Mrs. Hill that morning.

After the break, the couple sat next to one other on the forward-facing bench. As much as they wanted to slake their passion, both were tired and not many minutes after the departure from the coaching inn, they were asleep. Elizabeth was secure in the cocoon of her husband's arms with her head resting on one of his broad shoulders.

Some two hours later, Darcy woke before his wife as the conveyance bumped over the cobblestones telling him they were in London. "It is time to wake up, my love," he said softly as he kissed Elizabeth on the forehead.

"Where are we?" She asked as her eyes blinked several times before remaining open.

"About to pull up to our house in Town, my beautiful wife," Darcy informed his Elizabeth.

"Oh, I must look a fright," Elizabeth gasped as she sat upright and attempted to put herself to rights.

"You look as you always do to me, love, the most handsome woman of my acquaintance," Darcy soothed, understanding she wanted to make a good impression on the Darcy House servants. "You have nothing to worry about, Elizabeth. The servants already love you."

By the time the footman placed the steps and opened the door, Elizabeth felt she had done a creditable job of repairing her appearance. Darcy stepped down and then turned and handed his wife down. Mr. and Mrs. Killion were waiting for the couple on the top step, in front of the open heavy oak door.

Before she knew what was happening, and not caring who would see them, Darcy scooped his bride up into his arms effortlessly and proceeded up the stairs. Even his stoic butler could not help but have the edges of his mouth turn up at the master's antics. "William!" Elizabeth objected half-heartedly. "What will people say?"

"I care not, but if they have any sense, they will recognise I am a man who is besotted with his wife," Darcy announced as he carried his smiling wife over the threshold and then put her down, neither missing the smiles and grins from the servants lined up to welcome them home.

None had ever seen the master so happy and playful before, and correctly ascribed the change they noted in the master to the petite woman he had just married. "I thank you all for welcoming us home on our wedding day," Elizabeth addressed the waiting servants. "Those I did not have the pleasure of meeting on my tour, I will do so as soon as possible. Please carry on with your duties."

The couple retired to their suite to change and rest before dinner. "How much time do you need Elizabeth?" Darcy asked gruffly, his eyes dark with desire.

"A half hour should be more than enough time, William,"

Elizabeth returned, her heart racing with anticipation.

They entered their shared sitting room and parted with a long, languid kiss. Elizabeth's maid was waiting for her and helped her undress. Once her stays were off and she was only in a light, almost transparent chemise, Elizabeth excused her maid, telling her that she would ring for her bath when needed.

Just on half an hour there was a knock on Darcy's bed-chamber door. He had dismissed Carstens already leaving him alone in his chambers as he counted the minutes before making his way to his wife's chambers. He was dressed in a lawn shirt and breeches. When he opened the door, the sight that met his eyes took his breath away.

For many months he had dreamt about seeing Elizabeth's thusly, but the dreams were nothing to the reality. She was not a tall woman, but she had a curvaceous, womanly body. Her breasts were on the large side and his eyes locked onto the purple circle surrounding her pert, pink nipples.

The chemise ended just above her knees but being transparent giving him an almost unobstructed view of the triangle of dark hair between her legs. Darcy felt like his manhood was about to burst through his breeches on its own accord.

As she gave him a come-hither look, Elizabeth slowly lifted the chemise over her head and allowed it to fall at her feet. "William, you are far too dressed for the occasion," Elizabeth told her husband saucily.

The lawn shirt was quickly pulled over his head and tossed aside. Elizabeth stood in awe of the unimpeded view of her husband's muscular chest. As she watched, licking her lips in anticipation, he opened and dropped his breeches to the floor, kicking them away and not caring a whit in which direction.

Elizabeth sucked in a deep breath as her eyes took in his rather large appendage. Without a word, Darcy drew his wife into his chest and captured her lips with his own as he revelled in the feel of her against his chest, while she marvelled at the heat emanating off his manhood pressing against her stomach.

He lowered his head and took a nipple in his mouth to suckle and lick, and her hand circled his shaft, which throbbed in appreciation. When she instinctively began to stroke it, Darcy growled and picked his wife up, dropping her onto the bed joining her on it with speed as he kissed that sensitive area behind her ears.

He started a journey with his mouth that found first the one then the other breast, before he started feathering kisses down her body, feeling her tense when his mouth reached the top of the triangle of hair.

"Trust me, my love!" he beseeched as he lifted his head to lock their eyes.

Elizabeth relaxed and then she felt his fingers gently coaxing her legs open. She gasped, loving the sensations he caused as he started to stroke her in ways that caused her body to soak his fingers as they stroked her. As his mouth replaced his fingers, her body arched into him, and she gasped in pleasure and an explosion of passion as he lapped her while a finger slipped inside of her.

On a few occasions in the past, Elizabeth had given herself a release, but the sensations that came from her husband's ministrations made this one infinitely more powerful. The waves of pleasure seemed to come one after the other, and before they ceased, William was above her, supporting himself on his strong arms. Controlled movement of his hips caused the head of his appendage to traverse back and forth a few times, groaning when she coated him in wet heat and positioned the tip at the entrance to her core. He was shaking with need as he slowly inserted it inside of her, himself gasping when she thrust her hips upwards to meet him.

Elizabeth's unexpected movement had caused him to bury his member all the way inside of her, bursting through her maidenly barrier without pause as he had intended to do. She had whimpered softly when the barrier was destroyed, but urged him not to stop, and Darcy, being a gentleman, could not but accede to his wife's demands. Each time he thrust back into her; she raised her hips to meet him, revelling in the feel of him and helping him reach as deep in her as was possible.

Never before had Elizabeth experienced more than one release in a night, but was soon moaning, writhing, and digging her nails into his back as she attained her second release and her reaction drove Darcy over the edge and his seed pulsed even deeper within his wife.

He rolled onto his back, bringing her with him. Neither knew for how long they lay in that position, still connected in the most intimate way, until both of them were once again breathing normally and their hearts had slowed down to a normal pace. Both experienced a sense of loss when they were no longer so intimately connected.

"Oh, William! Tell me you enjoyed that as much as I, for I felt like I was flying!" Elizabeth gushed in the afterglow of their lovemaking.

"I have *never* experienced so much pleasure and passion combined, my love," Darcy agreed, guiding her down to him to kiss her. As he deepened the kisses, both felt his manhood swelling, and he reached down to her bottom to press her against it, groaning when she undulated and smiled when she saw he desired her as much as she did him.

An hour later, they rang for their baths and informed the housekeeper, through Elizabeth's maid, they would take their dinner on trays in their sitting room in an hour. After each soaked in a relaxing, steamy bath, they enjoyed some of the tasty repast their cook had created for them, then they returned to the enormous bed in the master's suite and were not heard from until they rang for their personal servants in the early morning.

~~~~~~~/~~~~~~~

The day after *The Rose* sailed bearing the happy newly-weds towards the Kingdom of Portugal, the extended family arrived in London. The notice of the wedding of Fitzwilliam

Darcy and Lady Elizabeth Bennet had appeared in *The Times* the previous day, killing the last shred of hope any may have had at turning Lady Elizabeth's head before she married Darcy.

Not needing the funds from leasing the two townhouses on Grosvenor Square any longer, the Duke had not renewed either lease. As Hilldale House in Hanover Square was smaller but still a nice size, the Duke and Duchess gifted one of the homes to Jane and Andrew, who renamed it Hilldale House. The original townhouse was presented to Charlotte and Richard, who named it Fitzwilliam House.

The second townhouse was renamed Meryton House and made part of the Earldom of Meryton. The last thing the Bennets needed were more townhouses. As the Rhys-Davies had begun to develop the area that would become Russell Square in 1761, they had reserved four enormous townhouses for themselves, which did not include the one on St. James Square or the one on Portman square.

Of the four homes on Russell Square, one was Bedford House, Tom's Birchington House, was to the left of the Duke's and Duchess's house. One of the remaining two was designated for Esther, and the last on Russell Square was unassigned. It would be held for the first grandchild that did not have his or her own.

While the Darcy's travelled for their honeymoon, Gigi was staying at Bedford House with Esther, quietly sad that Tom had returned to Oxford for his final year. Esther was also feeling a sense of loss, as Robert Jamison too had departed for university. The consolation for the two young ladies was that both Maria Lucas and Ally Carrington resided at Bedford House with them.

Now part of an extremely influential group of peers which included Lords Jersey and Matlock, the Duke attended sessions in the House of Lords each day. Among other things, the three took up the push for the abolition slavery in all British colonies. Mr. William Wilberforce, a member of the House of Commons, was the driving force behind this effort.

Notwithstanding their antipathy towards the mores of the *Ton*, the Duke and Duchess of Bedford, surrounded by their extended family, attended a fair number of the events of the little season. They even held a ball at Bedford House, and members of polite society waited with bated breath for this most desired invitation to arrive. Those who received them salivated over them, and those who did not cursed the Bennets for excluding them.

With Lady Sarah De Melville assisting her youngest daughter in the planning of the Bedford Ball, it was by anyone's standards a roaring success, unintentionally deepening the feelings of ill use by those who did not receive an invitation. As was always the case for much coveted occasions, it was easy to forget that as large as Bedford House was, it did not have the space for every member of the *Ton* to be accommodated.

Charlotte and Richard stayed at Fitzwilliam House for the first time and found the house more than fit their needs. It would be a squeeze with her family and guests visiting, but Charlotte already knew what her father soon would, which was that the Duke had slipped a clause into the management contract of Bennington Fields that the townhouse on Portman Square was the Lucas's for as long as the Fields was managed by a Lucas for the princely sum of one pound per annum. Sir William had always dreamed of a house in Town but had always been reasonable enough to know it was beyond his reach. He would find out soon enough his long-time friend had made another of his long-held dreams a reality.

As the month anniversary since the wedding approached, the family was in anticipation of Elizabeth's and William's return from their adventure on the Iberian Peninsula.

~~~~~~~/~~~~~~~

Darcy was standing behind his wife, his arms wrapped around her as *The Rose* approached her dock on the Thames. If the two had been felicitous before they departed on their wedding trip, then they were in utopia on the return. During their two and a half weeks in the Kingdom of Portugal, they

461

had seen much and had trunks full of gifts safely stowed in the hold.

Once the ship was made secure, Elizabeth and Darcy thanked the captain, officers, and crew for taking such good care of them, then they walked down the gangplank to the quay. As they had on the first trip to London, and the one from London a month earlier, they felt the sensation of the rise and fall of the ship once they were back on dry land.

"That was the most enjoyable trip, husband dearest, but I am not unhappy to be back on English soil once again," Elizabeth said as they seated themselves in the Darcy coach.

"It was, my love, and when the little tyrant is finally defeated, you will see the rest of the continent, that I swear to you," Darcy told his wife as he leaned over and captured her lips.

"I can never get enough of you, William," Elizabeth whispered breathlessly when he pulled away.

"It is no different for me," Darcy vowed quietly, capturing her face in his hands, and kissing her slowly to reinforce his promise with proof.

On their arrival at Darcy House, they were met by Charlotte and Richard who had come to make sure the house was opened for them. Charlotte was beaming as she had just missed her first month's courses but would not mention a word to anyone outside of Richard for another two months at least.

Georgiana was conspicuous by her absence, but her brother and new sister laughed when informed she was shopping at the Harding, Howell, and Company department store with the ladies of the extended family as they would see everyone at a family dinner to be held at Bedford House that evening.

A sennight after returning, Elizabeth, Jane, and Esther received their invitation from Queen Charlotte, and delighted the Queen and her daughters who were in attendance with their musical prowess. As was usually the case, Elizabeth closed the performance. She sang a German folk song she learnt especially for the Queen. At the end of the performance, there was an almost unheard of occurrence in the Queen's drawing room; she and her daughters gave a standing ovation.

~~~~~~~/~~~~~~~~

Priscilla was sitting alone with her husband in the study at Bedford House the day after the dinner. The younger members of the family were visiting with Elizabeth and William at Darcy House, leaving the Duke, Duchess, and Dowager Duchess to their own devices.

"Can you believe how our life has changed, Cilla? We have two daughters married, and if young Robert has any say in the matter, it will not be too many years until he carries Esther away," Bennet stated wistfully. "And to all this we must include the fact that we also gained the most wonderful relation in Aunt Rose."

"Without her help and support, the transition would have been much harder for me." Priscilla agreed thoughtfully. "Do you know, I often imagine that Lizzy or Jane will walk through the door at any minute to join us when we are in the drawing room like they used to at Longbourn, Thomas. I know how happy both of our older girls are with their husbands, but I do miss seeing them daily. Does that make me selfish?"

"No, it makes you a mother, and one who loves all of her children. It is natural to miss one's children when they are taken from their parent's home in matrimony. I too miss them. Neither you nor I would ever have stood in the way of their happiness, that indeed would have made us selfish, but it does not mean that we do not miss them," Bennet stated as he pulled his wife close and kissed her soundly causing her toes to curl.

"All of this," Priscilla swept her arm in a circle pointing towards the house beyond the walls of the study, "came to us all because an evil man's machinations failed in spectacular fashion one hundred and fifty years after his death. I have a feeling that were he alive to see the results of his actions that his heart would seize, and he would die again!" Priscilla smiled at the thought.

"And all of these connections were unknown to us. But now it is our family's duty to continue the Bedford line, and I make a solemn promise, that this is the last time that any of us mention the third Duke!" Bennet kissed his wife again and then led her from the study towards their suite.

The End of Volume 2

EPILOGUE

Longfield Meadows, Summer 1832

Since you probably wonder what happened to Bingley and the Hursts who escaped to the Americas? They lived quietly in New York and never set foot in the Kingdom again. Bingley opened a department store with Hurst. He eventually married an Angel as opposite in looks of Miss Bennet as he could find, and they had three children. The Hursts had a son and daughter.

Miss Mathilda Bingley used some of the money that she received from the balance of Caroline's dowry to have her niece transferred to a facility just outside of Scarborough weeks after her commitment to Bedlam. It was a humane place that treated the patients with respect and kindness. Miss Caroline Bingley lived there for close to fifteen years until she suffered an apoplexy and passed on. It was not the life she had wanted for herself, but she was always well cared for, and her aunt visited her no less than once a week.

~~~~~~~/~~~~~~~

The Duke and Duchess of Bedford would start to welcome the extended family later this afternoon, the first to arrive would be the Darcy brood from Pemberley in an hour. These days, thanks to the railway line that connected Bedford to London which went through Lambton, it took the Darcys less than two hours to make the journey. With nine of them, having a private car on the train belonging to the family, travel was far more palatable.

The Darcys' firstborn was Cilla Anne Elizabeth, who just turned nineteen and was being courted by the Marquess of

Holder, the grandson of Elizabeth's Uncle Stan. She had been followed by the twins two years later, Bennet Alexander Fitzwilliam and his identical twin brother, George Thomas Fitzwilliam. At seventeen, the boys had just completed their studies at Eton and would be going on to Cambridge.

There had been much negotiation not long after the boys were born between their grandfather and father about their schools. In the end Bennet, had acceded and agreed it was his son-in-law's prerogative to send his sons to the schools of his choice.

A year and a half after the twins, Sarah-Beth, fifteen, was born, followed two years later by Rosemarie, called Rose by all, who was thirteen. Four years later, when Elizabeth suspected their family was finished growing, she became with child again, and Jane Priscilla was born. She was nine, and in looks and character, to her father's delight, was an exact copy of her mother. To their further amazement, almost to the day two years later, the baby of the family, Richard Andrew, who had just turned seven, arrived.

To say that the Darcys were a happy family would have been a vast understatement. Elizabeth and William were even more in love now than they had been when they married. Given both of their natures, there had been numerous arguments and disagreements over the years, but never in the presence of their children, and they had always resolved their disagreements before joining one another in bed so they never went to bed angry with each other. A year after Waterloo, Darcy had fulfilled his promise to his wife and taken her for a three-month tour of the continent while the grandchildren were spoilt by their grandparents, great-grandparents, aunts, and uncles.

The next to arrive would be the five Fitzwilliams from Brookfield. Lucas Reggie, their firstborn who, at eighteen, was going into his second year at Cambridge, and three years after Lucas, Rich William, who was fifteen and at Eton, had been born. Rich would inherit Rosings Park when he came of age, as

Anne had passed some seven years previously and Lady Catherine a year after her daughter. Charlotte had thought she was done when five years later they were gifted with Elaine Sarah, who was called Ellie. At ten she thought herself very grown up, but, like her brothers, had a sweet disposition.

Charlotte and Richard were as happy as they ever were. Her folly of a first marriage was but a distant memory, one that was never mentioned. The couple had been honest with their children, who knew that their mother had been married for two months at some point before their parents married. Lady Lucas lived with them at Brookfield, having lost her husband some four years previously. As had been predicted, after Sir William got over the townhouse being slipped into the management agreement, he had enjoyed spending time in Town with his family over the years, and had been especially proud when Maria joined Georgiana, Esther, and Ally in being presented to the Queen and coming out together.

Franklin and his wife and four children lived at Lucas Lodge, while John and his family, a wife and three children, lived at the Fields. John was the primary manager of the estate, but Franklin still assisted him. With the improvements they had made, the profits had climbed to twelve thousand per annum and they were helping the town of Meryton flourish. The competition between them and Richard as to who had the better programme still raged, but they had done as planned and created some lines merging breeding stock from both programmes. The result was the most in demand horses in the country.

Maria married a young man with a medium sized estate in Essex, and they so far had three children and Maria was expecting her fourth before the end of the year. Even though her three best friends were all married and living in different parts of the country, they always found time to see each other several times a year, for the four had an unbreakable bond of friendship, much as their sisters Elizabeth, Jane, and Charlotte shared.

Jane and Andrew and their five children would arrive on the morrow in the morning. Some six years previously, when Lord Reginald Fitzwilliam had passed peacefully in his sleep, Andrew and Jane had become the Earl and Countess of Matlock. Their first born, Reggie Thomas, Viscount Hilldale, who had been born on the final day of April 1812, was the oldest of his generation. He had one more year at Cambridge before he took his grand tour around Europe. The next three had been girls. Lady Elizabeth Elaine was seventeen, Lady Priscilla Sarah fifteen and Lady Jacqui Rose, eleven. The baby, who was eight, Sed Tom had surprised and delighted his parents, who suspected there would be no more after Jacqui.

Jane and Andrew did not allow the Dowager Countess to move to the dower house. She happily shared time between her sons' houses, spending time with them, her daughters, and grandchildren. Lady Elaine missed her beloved Reggie every day, but she had so much for which to live, and they had promised one another to do so some years before he had left her.

As would be expected, Jane and Elizabeth were as close as two sisters could be and saw one another at least once a week given the relatively short distance between their estates. They saw Charlotte almost as much, and occasionally planned an outing the three of them enjoyed while their husbands entertained the children together.

Esther, to no one's surprise, had accepted and married Robert Jamison in 1816. As a wedding present, the Duke and Duchess purchased two estates bordering Ashford Dale in Bedfordshire. It quadrupled the size of the estate, and with a little money from Esther's amassed dowry, a new manor house was built, leaving the old manor house to become a dower house.

Will and Yvette had insisted on staying in their original home, and so Robert and Esther had taken up residence in the new house. They had four children, Robert Junior, thirteen, who would go to Harrow and Oxford, Sarah Yvette, eleven, Jane Karen, nine, and Alison Priscilla, five.

Another non-surprise had been when Mark Bennet, the

Earl of Meryton, requested Karen Jamison's hand and they married in 1824, making her the Countess of Meryton. So far, they had two children, Cyril Thomas, Viscount Netherfield, age six, and Lady Yvette Esther, who was three. Karen was with child with her third, who was expected to arrive in January or February of 1833.

"Tom, I see Lizzy and William's coaches approaching," Lady Georgiana Bennet, Duchess of Bedford called out to her husband, the ninth Duke of Bedford.

Gigi and Tom had married in 1816, also surprising no one. Their first son, the current Marquess of Birchington, was born a little over a year later. Lord Thomas Sedgewick was fifteen and at Harrow, like his father and late grandfather before him.

The eighth Duke had succumbed to heart failure some three years earlier. His death had been preceded by four years when the beloved Lady Rose joined her husband in the Kingdom of God. The dowager Duchess, who two years earlier mourned the passing of her father, had mourned her beloved Thomas for a full two years. To this day, and for the rest of her long life, she would wear the muted colours of half mourning.

The Duke and Duchess were joined by Lady Priscilla and their children. Besides Thomas there was Lord Sed Cyril, twelve; Lady Anne Esther, ten; Lady Rosanne, eight; and last but not least, Lord Wes Mark, who was all of four years old.

Darcy was the first out of the lead carriage and handed his wife and oldest daughter out of the conveyance that had transported them from the station in Bedford to the estate. Ben exited after his sister; his twin and the other four children were in the next carriage. After greeting the adults, the children disappeared into the house.

"It is so good to see you again, Lizzy," Priscilla gushed as she took her second daughter's arm, as Darcy, Georgiana, and Tom fell into step behind mother and daughter.

"It is not many weeks since you were at Pemberley Mama," Elizabeth smiled as she hugged and then kissed her mother on both cheeks.

"You will have to excuse an old lady if she forgets salient facts from time to time," Priscilla offered, winning a tinkling laugh from her daughter. Darcy grinned, for how he still loved to hear his wife's laugh.

"Mama, you look better and have a mind sharper than a woman many years your junior. I know for a fact that your mind is like a steal trap, and you forget *nothing!*" Elizabeth rebuked her mother in jest.

"You have caught me, Lizzy. I just cannot get enough of all of my sons, daughters, and grandchildren," Priscilla owned.

"As we can never have too much time with you, Mama." Elizabeth looked back at her brother and sister-in-law talking to her William. "Their Graces look well, as always."

"Have we not canvassed the subject that you are not to call us by our honorifics, Lizzy?" Georgiana asked playfully.

"Did you, I forget," Elizabeth teased the women with her into laughing.

While the other three walked towards the house, the Dowager Duchess directed her daughter to the rose garden fully in bloom, making the air smell especially fragrant. They sat on a bench. "I miss your father so very much," Priscilla told her daughter.

"We all do, Mama, but what we feel is different from your feelings, I am sure," Elizabeth soothed.

"He was so proud of all of you. Do you know how many times we discussed how our life changed because of the unknown family connections?"

"I am sure it was often, Mama." Elizabeth felt sad as she missed her father greatly.

"It was never with regret. Even when the attempt to entrap Esther was foiled, he was always positive. He loved his family above all else," Priscilla said wistfully. Some in society never learnt, compromises were attempted with both Tom and Mark, which resulted only in the destruction of the reputations for the *ladies* involved.

"Family is, and always will be, the most important value

to all of us, Mama," Elizabeth stated with certainty. While they would always miss those who were no longer with them, the lost family members would always be with them in their hearts as they together continued on as one big, extended family.

"Yes, Lizzy, family has always been more important than wealth and connections, known and unknown!" Priscilla kissed her daughter's cheek. Mother and daughter stood and walked arm in arm towards the house and their family.

The End

COMING SOON

Cinder-Liza: (Soon after this book)

No fairy godmother or magic in the story although there is some imagery we would expect to see in a Cinderella story – my apologies to those who thought there would be magic based on the title.

Mr. Thomas Bennet married the love of his life: Miss Fanny Gardiner. She gave him three children, Jane, Elizabeth and Tommy. 2 years after Tommy, Fanny was taken from her loving family birthing a second son, who was stillborn.

Another branch of the Bennet family, cousins to the Longbourn Bennets, are titled, the Earl and Countess of Holder, who live in Staffordshire with their 5 children. The two families are extremely close and after Fanny dies Bennet's cousins, at his request, keep and raise Tommy. In his grief Thomas Bennet does not think he can raise a 2-year-old at the same time as his two daughters. He also feels Tommy needs a mother figure in his life.

Martha Bingley is the widow of an honourable tradesman, Mr. Arthur Bingley, who had died of a heart attack. Bingley senior was a minor partner of Edward Gardiner in Gardiner and Associates. They had three children, Charles, Louisa, and Caroline. Unlike canon, the Bingleys are not very wealthy, and the girls have small dowries of £2,000 each.

Bennet is introduced to Martha at his brother-in-law's house. The Bingleys live in a leased house a few houses down from the Gardiners on Gracechurch street. Martha has always dreamed of climbing up the social ladder, raising her family above their roots in trade, so she compromises Bennet as he is a landed gentleman with an estate. Being an honourable man, and against advice of friends and family, he marries her.

Our '*prince*' in the story is of course none other than His Grace Fitzwilliam Darcy, Duke of Derbyshire, Earl of Lambton. Like canon his parents have already passed away. Dear old Lady Catherine de Bourgh will do anything to make her sickly daughter with a nasty disposition a Duchess. At some point the Duke purchases Netherfield to be closer to London so his sister, Lady Georgiana, will have her preferred music master close by.

Bennet never reveals the existence of his son or his relations, who are peers of the realm, to his new wife, who he dislikes intensely. The neighbours, none of whom like the new Mrs. Bennet or her children, keep the Bennet's secrets without question. Bennet allows his new wife to believe the entail on Longbourn is away from female line giving her the impression that on his death, she and her three spawn will be evicted from the estate by a distant unnamed cousin.

Sometime after sending Jane to live with his cousins, for reasons that will be revealed in the story, with Lizzy refusing to leave her father's side, Bennet has an accident which kills him. When no heir presents himself to throw her and her children, still at Longbourn, into the hedgerows, the stepmother feels more secure at the estate.

Several the usual suspects are present as well as some other characters. This is a story of hope and survival and the eventual triumph of good over evil.

The Take Charge Series:

The Take Charge series are all stand-alone books. There will be at least four books in the series and as they are not sequels or not connected one to the other, you may read them in any order you choose.

The series tells a Pride & Prejudice Variation/Vagary tale in which one of the characters we know and love from canon takes charge and assert themselves. We see how the actions of that particular character affects the others and the trajectory of each individual tale, both known from canon and some non-canon characters.

We know Elizabeth Bennet and Fitzwilliam (William) Darcy well and how they are depicted in the original, they will not have a book in their names, but will, as it should be, feature very heavily in each of the stories where someone else takes charge.

Book 1: Charlotte Lucas Takes Charge:

None of the books in this series are just about the title character, but how their taking charge affects those around them.

Fanny Bennet dies of an apoplexy two years prior to the start of this story.

As in canon, the Bingleys, Hursts, and Darcy arrive in the area residing in the leased Netherfield Park. Up until the Reverend William Collins arrival, things are not far from canon. Collins is the sycophant we all love to hate and sets his sights on Jane. Bennet tells him in no uncertain terms he will not consent to such a man marrying *ANY* of his daughters.

Charlotte Lucas overhears Collins ranting to himself about how he will evict the Bennets from Longbourn the day Bennet passes. He then tried to woo Charlotte hours later and she too rejects him. He is derisive when she rejects him out of hand, he tells her that no man would ever offer for one on the shelf, without fortune, and as homely as her.

Collins then proposes to Matilda Dudley, Lizzy's friend and Longbourn's widowed parson's daughter. Matilda accepts him much to Elizabeth and Charlotte's surprise.

Collins's words to her spur Charlotte to take charge, the story tells the tale of what she does and how it affects the lives of not a few people. The book examines how Charlotte actions change the trajectories of some of our favourite (to love and hate) characters.

BOOKS BY THIS AUTHOR

A Change Of Fortunes

What if, unlike canon, the Bennets had sons? Could it be, if both father and mother prayed to God and begged for a son that their prayers would be answered? If the prayers were granted how would the parents be different and what kind of life would the family have? What will the consequences of their decisions be?

In many Pride and Prejudice variations the Bennet parents are portrayed as borderline neglectful with Mr. Bennet caring only about making fun of others, reading and drinking his port while shutting himself away in his study. Mrs. Bennet is often shown as flighty, unintelligent and a character to make sport of. The Bennet parent's marriage is often shown as a mistake where there is no love; could there be love there that has been stifled due to circumstances?

In this book, some of those traits are present, but we see what a different set of circumstances and decisions do to the parents and the family as a whole. Most of the characters from canon are here along with some new characters to help broaden the story. The normal villains are present with one added who is not normally a villain per se and I trust that you, my dear reader, will like the way that they are all 'rewarded' in my story.

We find a much stronger and more resolute Bingley. Jane Bennet is serene, but not without a steely resolve. I feel that both need to be portrayed with more strength of character for the purposes of this book. Sit back, relax and enjoy and my hope is that you will be suitably entertained.

The Hypocrite

The Hypocrite is a low angst, sweet and clean tale about the relationship dynamics between Fitzwilliam Darcy and Elizabeth Bennet after his disastrous and insult laden proposal at Hunsford. How does our heroine react to his proposal and the behaviour that she has witnessed from Darcy up to that point in the story?

The traditional villains from Pride and Prejudice that we all love to hate make an appearance in my story BUT they are not the focus. Other than Miss Bingley, whose character provides the small amount of angst in this tale, they play a small role and are dealt with quickly. If dear reader you are looking for an angst filled tale rife with dastardly attempts to disrupt ODC then I am sorry to say, you will not find that in my book.

This story is about the consequences of the decisions made by the characters portrayed within. Along with Darcy and Elizabeth, we examine the trajectory of the supporting character's lives around them. How are they affected by decisions taken by ODC coupled with the decisions that they make themselves? How do the decisions taken by members of the Bingley/Hurst family affect them and their lives?

The Bennets are assumed to be extremely wealthy for the purposes of my tale, the source of that wealth is explained during the telling of this story. The wealth, like so much in this story is a consequence of decisions made Thomas Bennet and Edward Gardiner.

If you like a sweet and clean, low angst story, then dear reader, sit back, pour yourself a glass of your favourite drink and read, because this book is for you.

The Duke's Daughter: Omnibus Edition

All three parts of the series are available individually.

Part 1: Lady Elizbeth Bennet is the Daughter of Lord Thomas and Lady Sarah Bennet, the Duke and Duchess of Hertfordshire. She is quick to judge and anger and very slow to forgive. Fitzwilliam Darcy has learnt to rely on his own judgement above all others. Once he believes that something is a certain way, he does not allow anyone to change his mind. He ignored his mother and the result was the Ramsgate debacle, but he had not learnt his lesson yet.

He mistakes information that her heard from his Aunt about her parson's relatives and with assumptions and his failure to listen to his friends the Bingleys, he makes a huge mistake and faces a very angry Lady Elizabeth Bennet.

Part 2: At the end of Part 1, William Darcy saved Lady Elizabeth Bennet's life, but at what cost? After a short look into the future, part 2 picks up from the point that Part 1 ended. We find out very soon what William's fate is. We also follow the villains as they plot their revenge and try to find new ways to get money that they do not deserve.

Elizabeth finally admitted that she loved William the morning that he was shot, is it too late or will love find a way? As there always are in life, there are highs and lows and this second part of three gives us a window into the ups and downs that affect our couple and their extended family.

Part 3: In part 2, the Duke's Daughter became a Duchess. We follow ODC as they continue their married life as they deal with the vagaries of life. We left the villains preparing to sail from Bundoran to execute their dastardly plan. We find out if they are successful or if they fail.

In this final part of the Duke's Daughter series, we get a good idea what the future holds for the characters that we have followed through the first two books in the series.

The Discarded Daughter - Omnibus Edition

All 4 books in the Discarded Daughter series are combined into a single book. They are available individually, in both Kindle and paperback format.

The story is about the life of Elizabeth Bennet who is kidnapped and discarded at an exceedingly early age. It tells the tale of her life with the family that takes her in and loved her as a true daughter.

We follow not only Elizbeth's life, her trials and tribulations, but that of the family that lost her and all of those around her, immediate and extended family, and the effect that she has on their lives. There is love, villains, hurt, and happiness as we watch Elizabeth grow into an exceptional young woman.

If you are looking for a story that only concentrates on our heroine, then this is not for you.

Surviving Thomas Bennet

Warning: This book contains violence, although not graphically portrayed.

There are Bennet twins born to James Bennet, his heir, James Junior and second born Thomas. They boys start out as the best of friends until Thomas starts to get resentful of his older brother's status as heir.

The younger Bennet turns to gambling, drink, and carousing. In order to protect Longbourn, unbeknownst to Thomas, James Bennet senior places and entail on the estate so none of his son's creditors are able to make demands against the family estate.

Thomas Bennet was given his legacy of thirty thousand pounds when he reached his majority. He marries Fanny the daughter of a local solicitor in Oxford where Thomas is teaching. He is fired for being drunk at work. He manages to gamble away all of his legacy while going into serious debt to a dangerous man in not too many years.

When James Senior dies, Thomas and Fanny Bennet arrive at Longbourn demanding an imagined inheritance. They find out there is no more for them and leave after abusing one an all roundly swearing revenge.

James Junior, the master of Longbourn, and his wife Priscilla have a son, Jamie, and daughters Jane, Elizabeth, and Mary. Thinking he can sell Longbourn if his brother and son are out of the way, Thomas Bennet murders them and James' wife by causing a carriage accident.

The story reveals how the three surviving daughters are protected by their friends and how they survive the man who murdered their beloved parents and brother. Netherfield belongs to the Darcy's second son, William. There are many of the characters that are both loved and hated from the canon in this story, some similar to canon, a good number of them hugely different, there are also some new characters not from canon.